Rich Man's
REVENGE

REVENGE
COLLECTION

November 2015

December 2015

January 2016

February 2016

March 2016

April 2016

Rich Man's
REVENGE

Jennie
LUCAS

Katherine
GARBERA

MILLS &
BOON

Published in Great Britain 2015
by Mills & Boon, an imprint of Harlequin (UK) Limited,
Eton House, 18-24 Paradise Road, Richmond, Surrey, TW9 1SR

RICH MAN'S REVENGE © 2015 Harlequin Books S.A.

Dealing Her Final Card © 2013 Jennie Lucas
Seducing His Opposition © 2011 Katherine Garbera
A Reputation for Revenge © 2013 Jennie Lucas

ISBN: 978-0-263-91790-1

25-0316

Harlequin (UK) Limited's policy is to use papers that are natural, renewable and recyclable products and made from wood grown in sustainable forests. The logging and manufacturing processes conform to the legal environmental regulations of the country of origin.

Printed and bound in Spain
by CPI, Barcelona

DEALING HER FINAL CARD

JENNIE LUCAS

Jennie Lucas grew up dreaming about faraway lands. At fifteen, hungry for experience beyond the borders of her small Idaho city, she went to a Connecticut boarding school on scholarship. She took her first solo trip to Europe at sixteen, then put off college and travelled around the U.S., supporting herself with jobs as diverse as gas station cashier and newspaper advertising assistant.

At 22, she met the man who would be her husband. After their marriage, she graduated from Kent State with a degree in English. Seven years after she started writing, she got the magical call from London that turned her into a published author.

Since then life has been hectic, with a new writing career, a sexy husband and two small children, but she's having a wonderful (albeit sleepless) time. She loves immersing herself in dramatic, glamorous, passionate stories. Maybe she can't physically travel to Morocco or Spain right now, but for a few hours a day, while her children are sleeping, she can be there in her books.

Jennie loves to hear from her readers. You can visit her website at www.jennielucas.com, or drop her a note at jennie@jennielucas.com.

CHAPTER ONE

"BREE, wake up!"

A hand roughly shook Bree Dalton awake. Startled, she sat up with a gasp, blinking in the darkness.

Her younger sister was sitting on the edge of the bed. Tears sparkled on Josie's pale cheeks in the moonlight.

"What's happened?" Bree dropped her bare feet to the tile floor, ready to run, ready to fight anyone who had made her baby sister cry. "What's wrong?"

Josie took a deep breath.

"I really messed up this time." She wiped her eyes. "But before you freak out, I want you to know it's going to be fine. I know how to fix it."

Rather than be comforted by this statement, Bree felt deepening fear. Her twenty-two-year-old sister, six years younger than Bree, had a knack for getting into trouble. And she was wearing the short, sexy dress of a Hale Ka'nani cocktail waitress instead of their gray housekeeping smock.

"Were you working at the bar?" Bree demanded.

"Still worried about some man hitting on me?" Josie barked a bitter laugh. "I *wish* that was the problem."

"What is it, then?"

Josie ran a hand over her eyes. "I'm tired, Bree," she whispered. "You gave up everything to take care of me. When I was twelve, I needed that, but now I am so tired of being your burden—"

"I've never thought of you that way," Bree said, stung.

Josie looked at her clasped hands. "I thought this was my chance to pay off those debts, so we could go back to the Mainland. I've been practicing in secret. I thought I knew how to play. How to win."

A chill went down Bree's spine.

"You gambled?" she said numbly.

"It fell into my lap." Josie exhaled, visibly shivering in the warm Hawaiian night. "I'd finished cleaning the wedding reception in the ballroom when I ran into Mr. Hudson. He offered to pay me overtime if I'd serve drinks at his private poker game at midnight. I knew you'd say no, but I thought, just this once…"

"I told you not to trust him!"

"I'm sorry," Josie cried. "When he invited me to join them at the table, I couldn't say no!"

Bree clawed back her long blond hair. "What happened?"

"I won," Josie said defiantly. Then she swallowed. "At least I did for a while. Then I started losing. First I lost the chips I'd won, then I lost our grocery money, and then…"

Cold understanding went through Bree. She finished dully, "Then Mr. Hudson kindly offered to loan you whatever you needed."

Josie's mouth fell open. "How did you know?"

Because Bree knew bullies like Greg Hudson and how they tried to gain the upper hand. She'd met his type before, long ago, in the life she'd given up ten years ago—before she'd fallen in love, and her life had fallen apart. Before the man she loved had betrayed her, leaving her to the sheriff and the wolves—orphaned and penniless at eighteen, with a heartbroken twelve-year-old sister.

But oh, yes. Bree knew Greg Hudson's type. She closed her eyes, feeling sick as she thought of the hotel manager's hard eyes above his jovial smile, of his cheerful Hawaiian shirt that barely covered his fat belly. The resort manager had slept with many of his female employees, particularly amongst the lower-paid housekeeping staff. In the two months since the Dalton sisters had arrived in Hawaii, Bree had wondered more than once why he'd gone to such trouble to hire them from Seattle. He claimed the girls had been recommended by their employment agency, but that didn't ring true. Surely there were many people looking for jobs here in Honolulu.

Josie had laughed at her, teasing her for being "gloomy and doomy," but as Bree had scrubbed the bathrooms and floors of the lavish resort, she'd tried to solve the puzzle in her mind, and her bad feeling only grew. Especially when their boss made it clear over the past few weeks that he was interested in Josie. And made it equally clear the one he really wanted was Bree.

But of course Josie, with her innocent, trusting spirit, never noticed evil around her. She didn't fully understand why Bree had given up gambling, and insisted they work only low-wage jobs for the ten years since their father died, keeping them under the radar of unscrupulous, dangerous men. Josie didn't know how wicked the world could be.

Bree did.

"Gambling doesn't pay." She kept her voice calm. "You should know that by now."

"You're wrong. It does!" Josie said angrily. "We had plenty of money ten years ago." She turned and looked wistfully at the window, toward the moonlit Hawaiian night. "And I thought if I could just be more like you and Dad…"

"You were using *us* as role models? Have you lost your mind?" Bree exploded. "I've spent the last decade trying to give you a different life!"

"Don't you think I know that?" Josie cried. "What you've sacrificed for me?"

Bree took a deep breath. "It wasn't just for you." Her throat ached as she rose to her feet. "How much money did you lose tonight?"

For a moment, her sister didn't answer. Outside, Bree heard

the distant plaintive call of seabirds as Josie stared mutinously at the floor, arms folded. When she finally spoke, her voice was barely audible.

"A hundred."

Bree felt relief so fierce she almost cried. She'd been so afraid it would be worse. Reaching out, she gave her sister's shoulder a squeeze. "It'll be all right." She exhaled in relief. "Our budget will be tight, but we'll just eat a little more rice and beans this month." Wiping her eyes, she tried to smile. "Let this be a good lesson…"

But Josie hadn't moved from the end of the bed. She looked up, her face pale.

"A hundred *thousand,* Bree," she whispered. "I owe Mr. Hudson a hundred thousand dollars."

For a second, Bree couldn't understand the words. Lingering tears of relief burned her eyes like acid as she stared at her sister.

A hundred thousand dollars.

Turning away, Bree started to pace, compulsively twisting a long tendril of blond hair into a tight ringlet around her finger as she struggled to make sense of all her worst fears coming true. She tried to control her shaking hands. Tried desperately to think of a way out.

"But I told you, you don't have to worry!" Josie blurted out. "I have a plan."

Bree stopped abruptly. "What is it?"

"I'm going to sell the land."

Her eyes went wide as she stared at her sister.

"There's no choice now. Even you must see that," Josie argued, blinking fast as she clasped her hands tightly in her lap. "We'll sell it, pay off the debt, and then pay off those men who are after us. You'll finally be free—"

"That land is in trust." Bree's voice was hard. "You don't get possession until you're twenty-five or married. So put it out of your mind."

Josie shook her head desperately. "But I know how I could—"

"You can't," she said coldly. "And even if you could, I wouldn't let you. Dad put that land into an unbreakable trust for a reason."

"Because he thought I was helpless to take care of myself."

"Because from the day you were born, you've had a knack for trusting people and believing the best of them."

"You mean I'm stupid and naive."

Controlling herself, Bree clenched her hands at her sides.

"It's a good quality, Josie," she said quietly. "I wish I had more of it."

And it was true. Josie had always put concern for others over her own safety and well-being. As a chubby girl of five, she'd once wandered out of their Alaskan cabin into the snow, hoping to find their neighbor's cat, which had disappeared the day before. Eleven-year-old Bree had searched their rural street with their panicked father and half a dozen neighbors for hours, until they'd finally found her, lost in the forest, dazed and half-frozen.

Josie had nearly died that day, for the sake of a cat that was found later, snug and warm in a nearby barn.

Bree took a deep breath. Her little sister's heart was as big as the world. It was why she needed someone not nearly so kind or innocent to protect her. "Are they still playing?"

"Yes," Josie said in a small voice.

"Who's at the table?"

"Mr. Hudson and a few owners. Texas Big-Hat, Silicon Valley, Belgian Bob," she said, using the housekeeping staff's nicknames for the villa owners. Her eyes narrowed. "And one more man I didn't recognize. Handsome. Arrogant. He kicked me out of the game." She scowled. "The others would've let me stay longer—"

"You would have just lost more," Bree said coldly. Turning away, she went behind her closet door and yanked off her oversized sleep shirt, pulling on a bra and then a snug black T-shirt. "We'd owe a million dollars now, instead of just a hundred thousand."

"It might as well be a million, for all our chance of paying," Josie grumbled. "For all the good it will do them if I don't sell that land. They can't get blood out of a stone!"

Bree pulled on her skinny dark jeans over her slim legs. "And what do you think will happen when you don't pay?"

"Mr. Hudson will make me scrub his floors for free?" she replied weakly.

Coming around the closet door, Bree stared at her in disbelief. "Scrub his *floors?*"

"What else can he do?"

Bree turned away, muttering to herself. Josie didn't understand the situation she was dealing with. How could she? Bree had made it her mission in life to protect her from knowing.

She'd hoped they would find peace in Hawaii, three thousand miles away from the ice and snow of Alaska. She'd prayed she would find her own peace, and finally stop dreaming of the blue-eyed, dark-haired man she'd once loved. But it hadn't worked. Every night, she still felt Vladimir's arms around her, still heard his low, sensual voice. *I love you, Breanna.* She still saw the brightness of his eyes as he held up a sparkling diamond beneath the Christmas tree. *Will you marry me?*

Ugh. Furiously, Bree pushed the memory away. No wonder she still hated Christmas. Let other women go home to their turkeys and children and brightly lit trees. To Bree, yesterday had been just another workday. She never let herself remember that one magical Christmas night when she was eighteen, when she'd wanted to change her life to be worthy of Vladimir's love. The night she'd promised herself that she would never—for any reason—gamble or cheat or lie again. Even though he'd left her, she'd kept that promise.

Until now. She reached into the back of her closet, pulling out her black boots with the sharp stiletto heels.

"Bree?" Josie said anxiously.

Not answering, Bree sat down heavily on the bed. Putting her feet into her boots, she zipped up the backs. It was the first time she'd worn these stiletto boots since she was a rebellious teenager with a flexible conscience and a greedy heart. It took Bree back to the woman she'd never thought she would be again. The woman she'd have to be tonight to save her sister. She glanced at the illuminated red letters of the clock. Three in the morning. A perfect time to start.

"Please, you don't have to do this," her sister whimpered. Her voice choked as she whispered helplessly, "I have a plan."

Ignoring the guilt and anguish in her sister's voice, Bree rose to her feet. "Stay here." Squaring her shoulders, she severed the connection between her brain and her pounding heart. Emotion would only be a liability from here on out. "I'll take care of it."

"No! It's my fault, Bree, and I can fix it. Listen. On Christmas Eve, I met a man who told me how…"

But Bree didn't wait to hear whatever cockamamy sob story someone might have fed her softhearted sister this time. She grabbed her black leather motorcycle jacket and headed for the door.

"Bree, wait!"

She didn't look back. She walked out of the tiny apartment and went down the open-air hallway to the moss-covered, crumbling concrete steps of the aging building where all the Hale Ka'nani Resort's staff lived.

It's just like riding a bike, Bree told herself fiercely as she raced down the steps. Even after ten years away from the game, she could win at poker. She *could.*

Warm trade winds blew against her cold skin. Pulling on her black leather jacket, she went down the illuminated paths of the five-star resort toward the beautiful, brand-new buildings used by wealthy tourists and the even wealthier villa owners, clustered around the edge of a private, white-sand beach.

My heart is cold, she repeated to herself. *I feel nothing.*

The moon was full over the Pacific, leaving a ghostly trail across the black water. Palm trees swayed in the warmth of the Hawaiian breeze. She heard the distant call of night birds, smelled the exotic scent of fruit and spice mingling with the salt of the sea.

Above her, dark silhouettes of tall, slender palm trees swayed in a violet sky twinkling with stars. Even with the bright full moon, the night seemed black to her, wide and endless as the sea. She followed the illuminated path around the deserted pool between the beach and the main lobby. As she grew closer to the beach, she heard the sound of the surf build to a roar.

The open-air bar was nearly empty beneath its long thatched roof. Hanging lights swayed in the breeze over a few drunk tourists and cuddling honeymooners. Bree nodded at the tired-eyed bartender, then went past the bar into a connecting hall that led to the private rooms reserved for the villa owners and their guests. Where rich men brought their cheap mistresses and played private, illegal games.

Opening the door, Bree stumbled in her stiletto boots.

Clenching her hands at her sides, she took a deep breath and told her heart to be a lump of ice. Cold. Cold. Cold. She had no feelings of any kind. Poker was easy. By the time she was fourteen, she'd been fleecing tourists in Alaskan ports. And she'd learned the best way not to show emotion was not to feel it in the first place.

Never play with your heart, kiddo. Only a sucker plays with his heart. Even if you win, you lose.

Her father had said those words to her a million times growing up, but she'd still had to learn the hard way. Once, she'd played with all her heart. And lost—everything.

Don't think about it. But in spite of her best efforts, the memory brought a chill of fear. She'd been so determined to leave that life behind. What if she'd forgotten how to play? What if she'd lost her gift? What if she couldn't lure the men in, convince them to let her ante up without money, and get the cards she needed—or bluff them into believing she had?

If she failed at this, then… Bree felt a flash of sweat on her forehead. Running for the Mainland might be their only option. Or, since they had no money or credit cards and it was doubtful they'd even make it to the airport before they were caught, *swimming* for the Mainland.

She exhaled, forcing her body to calm down and her heart to slow. *It's just poker,* she told herself firmly. *Your heart is cold. You feel nothing.*

Bree went all the way down the long, air-conditioned hall. A large man weighing perhaps three hundred pounds sat at a polished oak door.

She forced a crooked smile in his direction. "Hey, Kai."

The enormous security guard nodded with a single jerk of his chins. "What you doing here, Bree? Saw your sister take off. She sick or something?"

"Something like that."

"You working in her place?" Kai frowned, looking over her dark, tight jeans, her black leather jacket and black stiletto boots. "Where's the uniform?"

"This is my outfit." Her voice was cool as she stared him down. "For poker."

"Oh." His round, friendly face looked confused. "Well. Okay. Go in, then."

"Thanks." Forcing the ice in her voice to fully infuse her heart, she pushed open the door.

The private room for the villa residents had a cavernous ceiling and no windows. The walls were soundproofed with thick red fabric that swooped from a center point on the ceiling. The effect made the room glamorous and cozy and claustrophobic all at once. To Bree, it felt like entering the tent of a sheikh's harem. But as she approached the wealthy men who were playing at the single large table, if there was a stab of fear down her spine, she didn't feel it.

She'd succeeded. She'd turned off her heart.

There were no women players. The only females in the room stood in a circle behind the men, smiling with hawkish red lips, wearing low-cut, tight silk gowns. At the table, she saw the dealer, Chris—what was his last name?—whose eyes widened with surprise when he saw her.

The four players at the table were Greg Hudson and three owners she recognized: a Belgian land developer, a long-mustached oil man from Texas and a short, bald tycoon from Silicon Valley. But where was the arrogant stranger Josie had mentioned? Had he already quit the game?

Whatever. It was time to play.

In her black leather jacket and jeans, Bree pushed through the venomous, overdressed women. Without a word, she sat down at one of the two empty seats at the table around the dealer, beside Greg Hudson.

"Deal me in," she said coolly.

The men blinked, staring at her in shock that was almost comical. One of the men snorted a laugh. Another frowned. "Another cocktail waitress?" one scoffed.

"Actually," Bree said with a grin, "I'm with the housekeeping staff, and so was my sister."

The men glanced at each other uncertainly.

"Well, well. Bree Dalton." Greg Hudson licked his lips, looking at her with beady eyes in his florid, sweaty face. "So. Did you bring the hundred thousand dollars your sister owes me?"

"You know we don't have that kind of money."

"Then I'll send my men to take it out of her hide."

Bree's knees shook beneath the table, but she did not feel fear. Her body might feel whatever it liked, but she'd disconnected it from her heart. Crossing her legs, she leaned back in her chair. "I will play for her debt."

"You!" He snorted. "What will you wager? This game has a five-thousand-dollar buy-in. You could scrub the bathrooms of the entire Hale Ka'nani Resort for years and not have that kind of money."

"I offer a trade."

"You have nothing of value."

"I have myself."

Her boss stared at her, then licked his lips. "You mean—"

"Yes. I mean you could have me in bed." She looked at him steadily, feeling nothing. Her skin felt cold, her heart as frozen as the blue iceberg that sank the *Titanic*. "You wanted me, Mr. Hudson. Here I am."

There was a low whistle, an intake of breath around the room.

Bree slowly gazed around the table. She had everyone's complete attention. Without flinching, she let her gaze taunt each man in turn, all of them larger, older and more powerful than she could ever be. "Who will take the gamble?"

"Well now." Looking her over, the Texas oil baron thoughtfully tilted back his cowboy hat. "This game just got a lot more interesting."

In the corner of her eye, she saw a dark, hulking shadow come around the table. A man sat down in the empty chair on the other side of the dealer, and Bree instantly turned to him with languid eyes. "Allow me to join your game, and I could be yours...."

Bree's voice choked off midsentence as she sucked in her breath.

She knew those cold blue eyes. The high cheekbones, sharp as a razor blade. The strong jaw that proclaimed ruthless, almost thuggish strength. So powerful, so darkly handsome, so sensual.

So impossible.

"No," she whispered. Not after ten years. Not here. "It can't be."

Vladimir Xendzov's eyes narrowed with recognition, and then she felt the rush of his sudden searing hatred like fire.

"Have you met Prince Vladimir?" Greg Hudson purred.

"Prince?" Bree choked out. She was unable to look away from Vladimir's face, the face of the man she'd dreamed about unwillingly for the past ten years.

His cruel, sensual lips curved as he leaned back in his chair.

"Miss Dalton," he drawled. "I didn't know you were in Hawaii. And gambling. What a pleasant surprise."

His low, husky voice, so close to her, so real, caused a shiver across her skin. She stared at him in shock.

Her one lost love. Not a ghost. Not a dream. But here, at the Hale Ka'nani Resort, not six feet away from her.

"So what's on offer? Your body, is it?" Vladimir's words were cold, even sardonic. "What a charming prize that would be, though hardly exclusive. Shared by thousands, I should imagine."

And just like that, the ice around her heart exploded into a million glass splinters. She sucked in her breath.

Vladimir Xendzov had made her love him with all the reckless passion of an innocent, untamed heart. He'd made her a better person—and then he'd destroyed her. Her lips parted. "Vladimir."

He stiffened. *"Your Highness* will do."

She didn't realize she'd spoken his name aloud. Glancing to the right and left, she matched his sardonic tone. "So you're using your title now."

His blue eyes burned through her. "It is mine by right."

She knew it was true. His great-grandfather had been one of the last great princes of Russia, before he'd died fighting the Red Army in Siberia, after sending his wife and baby son to safety in Alaskan exile. As a poverty-stricken child, Vladimir had been mocked with the title at school. When he was twenty-five, he'd told her that he never intended to use the title, that it still felt like a mockery, an honor he hadn't earned—and was worthless, anyway.

But apparently, now, he'd found a use for it.

"You didn't always think so," Bree said.

"I am no longer the boy you once knew," he said coldly.

She swallowed. Ten years ago, she'd thought Vladimir was the last honest man on earth. She'd loved him enough to give up the wicked skills that made her special. When he'd held her tight on a cold Alaskan night and begged her to be his bride, it had been the happiest night of her life. Then he'd ruthlessly deserted her the next morning, before she could tell him the truth. When she needed him most, he'd stabbed her in the back. Some *prince*. "What are you doing here?"

His lip curled. Without answering her, he turned away. "The table is full," he said to the other players. "We do not want her."

"Speak for yourself," one of them muttered, looking at Bree.

Looking around, she jolted in her chair. She'd forgotten the other men were there, looking at her like hungry wolves at a raw mutton chop. The beautiful, sexily dressed women standing in a circle behind them were glaring as if they would like to tear her limb from limb. Perhaps she'd taken her act a little too far.

Feel nothing, she ordered her shivering heart. *I have ice for a heart.* She looked away from the large, powerful men and sharp-taloned women. They couldn't hurt her. The only man who'd ever been able to really hurt her was Vladimir. And what more could he do, that he hadn't done already?

One thing, a cold voice whispered. Ten years ago, he'd taken her heart and soul.

But not her virginity.

And he never would, she told herself fiercely. Bree didn't know what Vladimir Xendzov was doing in Honolulu, but she didn't care. He was ancient history. All that mattered now was protecting Josie.

To save her little sister, Bree would play cards with the devil himself.

With an intake of breath, she lifted her chin, ignoring Vladimir as she looked around the table. "It is for this first game only that I offer my body. If I lose, the winner will get me, along with all the money in the pot. But if I win—" *when* I win, she amended silently "—I will only bet money. Until I possess the entire amount of my sister's debt."

As she spoke, her heart started to resume a normal beat. Bluffing, playing card games, was home to her. She'd learned poker when her father had pulled her up to their table in Anchorage and taught her at the tender age of four. By six, shortly after her mother had died two months after giving birth to Josie, Bree was a child prodigy accompanying her father to games—and, when he saw how much money she could make, his partner in crime.

Leaning forward, she looked at each man in turn, ignoring the death stares of the women behind them. "What is your answer?"

"We are here to play poker," another man complained. "Not for hookers."

Bree twirled her long blond hair slowly around one of her slender fingers and looked through her lashes at the Silicon Valley tycoon. "You don't recognize me, do you, Mr. McNamara?"

"Should I?"

She gave him a smile. "I guess not. But you knew my father, Black Jack Dalton." She paused. "Have you enjoyed the painting you paid him to steal from the archives of the Getty Museum in Los Angeles? When did you learn it was a fake?"

The Silicon Valley tycoon stiffened.

"And Mr. Vanderwald—" she turned to the gray-haired, overweight man sitting beside her boss "—twelve years ago you were nearly wiped out, weren't you? Investing in an Alaskan oil well that never existed."

The Belgian land developer scowled. "How the devil did you—"

"You thought my father conned you. But it was my idea. It was me," she whispered, lowering her eyelashes as she ran her hand down the softly worn leather of her black motorcycle jacket. "It was all me."

"You," the fat man breathed, staring at her.

She was doing well. Then, from the corner of her eye, she felt Vladimir's sardonic gaze. It hit her cheek and the side of her neck like a blast of ice. Her heart skidded with the effort it took to ignore him. He was the one man who'd ever really known her. The mark she'd stupidly let see behind her mask. She felt his hatred. Felt his scorn.

Fine. She felt the same about him. Let him hate her. His hatred bounced off the thickening ice of her scorn for *him*. She'd thought he was so perfect and noble. She'd killed herself trying to be worthy. But when he'd learned the truth about her past, he'd deserted her, without giving her a chance to explain.

So much for his honor. So much for his *love*.

Bree's lips twisted. Turning away, she gave the rest of the men a sensual smile. "Win this first hand, and you'll have me at your mercy. You'll get your revenge. Humiliate me completely. Take my body, and make your last memory of me one of your own pleasure." She gave a soft sigh, allowing her lips to part. "My skills at cards are nothing compared to what I can do to you in bed. I've learned the art of seduction. You have no idea," she whispered, "what I can do to you. A single hour with me will change your life."

Her act was one hundred percent fraud, of course. She, know the art of seduction? What a joke. She'd have no clue what she'd do with a man in bed. Since Vladimir, she'd been very careful never to let any man close to her. At twenty-eight, she was a virgin. But she did know how to bluff.

The men were riveted.

"I'm in," Greg Hudson croaked.

"And me."

"I accept."

"Yes."

As the men at the table agreed, Bree would have been fright-

ened by all the looks of lust and desire and rage, if she hadn't
frozen her heart against emotion.

But the last set of ice-blue eyes held no lust. No desire
for domination. Just pure, cold understanding. As if Vladimir
alone could see through all her tricks to the scared woman
beneath.

"As you wish," he said softly. He gave a cold smile. "Let's
play."

His low, sensual voice slid through her body. When she
looked into Vladimir's eyes, fear pierced her armor. *Pierced
her heart.* She wanted to leap up and run from his knowing
gaze, to keep running and never stop. It took every ounce of
her willpower to remain in the chair.

Clutching her jacket around her for warmth, she wrenched
her gaze away, gripping the black leather so no one could see
that her hands were shaking. "Then let's begin."

At Greg Hudson's nod, Chris the dealer dealt the cards.
Ignoring the spiteful whispers and daggered glances of the
trophy girls, Bree stared at her cards, facedown on the table.

She couldn't let herself think what would happen if she lost.
Couldn't even imagine what it would be like to let any of these
angry, fat, ugly men take their revenge on her virginal body
through rough sex.

But even more awful would be having Vladimir win. Giving her virginity to the man who'd once broken her completely?
She couldn't survive it. Not from him.

Just win, she ordered herself. All she had to do was take
this first hand, and her virginity would no longer be on offer.
It would be a long night of poker trying to win a hundred thousand dollars. But this was the most important hand.

Closing her eyes, she silently prayed. Then she picked up
the cards. Careful not to let any of the players see them, she
looked at them.

It took every ounce of her skill not to gasp.

Three kings. She had three kings, along with a four and a

queen. Three kings. She nearly wept with relief. It was as if fate had decided she was gambling for the right reasons and deserved to win.

Unless it was more than fate…

She looked up through her lashes toward the young dealer. Could he be helping her? Chris was about Josie's age, and he'd come twice to their apartment for dinner. He wasn't exactly a close friend, but he'd spoken many times with irritation about Greg Hudson's poor management skills. "You would do a better job of running this resort, Bree," he'd grumbled, and she'd agreed with a smile. "But who wouldn't?"

Now, catching her eye, the young dealer gave her a wink and a smile.

Sucking in her breath, Bree looked away before anyone noticed. Her eyes accidentally fell on Vladimir's. His eyebrows lowered, and she gulped, looking back down at her cards, hastily making her expression blank. Had he seen? Could he guess?

The dealer turned to his left. "Your Highness?"

Because of his placement at the table, Vladimir was the first one required to add a bet to the pile of chips already in the middle of the table from the ante. "Raise."

Raise? Bree looked up in surprise. He was looking straight at her as he said, "Five thousand."

Texas Big-Hat cursed and threw his cards on the table. "Fold."

"Call," Silicon Valley said, matching Vladimir's bet.

"Call," Mr. Vanderwald puffed, a bead of sweat dripping down his forehead.

"Call," Greg Hudson said.

All eyes turned to Bree.

"She's already all in," Greg Hudson said dismissively. "There's nothing more she can wager."

He was right, she thought with a pang. She couldn't match Vladimir's raise, and that meant even if she won the hand, she couldn't win anything beyond the twenty-five thousand dollars' worth of chips currently in the center. What a waste of three kings…

Bree suddenly smiled. "I call."

"Call?" Greg Hudson hooted. "You have an extra five thousand dollars hidden in the back pocket of those jeans?"

She stretched back her shoulders and felt the eyes of the men linger on the shape of her breasts beneath her black T-shirt. "I can match the bet in other ways. Instead of just an hour in bed, I'll offer an entire night." She tilted back her head, allowing her long blond hair to tumble provocatively down her shoulders. "Many chances. Multiple positions. As fast or slow or hard as you like it, all night long, and each time better than the last. Against the wall. Bent over the bed. In my mouth."

She felt like a total fool. She hoped she sounded like a woman who knew what she was talking about, not a scared virgin whose idea of lovemaking was vague at best, based only on movies and novels. But as she looked at each man at the table they seemed captivated. She exhaled. Her mask was holding. She was convincing them. Even Chris the dealer looked entranced.

Vladimir alone seemed completely unaffected. Bored, even. His lips twisted with scorn. And his eyes—

His blue eyes saw straight through her. A hot blush burned her cheeks as she said to him, "Do you agree my bet is commensurate with your five thousand dollar raise?"

"No," Vladimir said coldly. "That is not a call."

Her heart sank. "You…"

He gave her a calm smile. "That is an additional raise."

"A…a raise?" she echoed uncertainly.

"Obviously. Let us say…your added services are equivalent to an additional five thousand dollars? Yes. A full night with you would surely be worth that." He lifted a dark eyebrow. "Would you not agree?"

"Five thousand more?" Greg Hudson's voice hit a false note.

Catching himself, he shifted uncomfortably in his chair and snickered, "Fine with me. I'm half *raised* already."

"Good," Vladimir said softly, never looking away from Bree. "So we are in agreement."

Bree's brow furrowed as she tried to read his expression. What on earth was he doing?

Trying to help her? Or giving her more rope to hang herself with?

Repressing her inner tumult, she stared him down. *In for a penny...* She lifted her chin. "If it's worth five more, then why not ten more?"

The corners of Vladimir's mouth lifted. "Yes, indeed. Why not?" He looked around the table. "Miss Dalton has raised the wager by ten thousand dollars."

To her shock, one by one the men agreed to her supposed "raise," except for the Belgian, who folded with an unintelligible curse.

And just like that—oh, merciful heavens—there was suddenly a pile of chips at the center of the table worth *seventy-five thousand dollars.*

She looked at each man as they discarded cards and got new ones from the dealer.

Don't play the hand, her father had always said. *Play the man.*

She forced herself to look across the table at Vladimir. His face was inscrutable as he discarded a card and got a new one. When she'd played him ten years ago, he'd had a tight style of play. He did not bluff, he did not overbet—the exact opposite of Bree's strategy.

He lifted his eyes to hers, and against her will, her heart turned over in her chest. His handsome face revealed nothing. The poverty of his homesteading Alaskan childhood, so different from hers, had pushed him to create a billion-dollar business across the world, primarily in metals and diamonds. He was so ruthless he had cut his own younger brother out of their partnership right before a multimillion-dollar deal. It was said Vladimir Xendzov had molten gold in his veins and a flinty diamond instead of a heart. That he wasn't flesh and blood.

But if Bree closed her eyes, she could still remember their last night together, when they'd almost made love on a bear-skin rug beneath the Christmas tree. She could remember the heat and searing pleasure of his lips against her skin in the deep hush of that cold winter's night.

I love you, Breanna. As I've never loved anyone.

No one else had ever called Bree by her full name. Not like that. Now, as they looked at each other across the poker table, they were two enemies with battle lines drawn. Everything she'd ever thought him to be was a dream. All that was left was a savagely handsome man with hard blue eyes and an emotionless face.

She turned away. Greg Hudson and the Silicon Valley tycoon were far easier to read. She watched her boss get three new cards, saw the sweat on his face and the way he licked his thick, rubbery lips as he stared down at his hand. Hudson had nothing. A pair of twos, maybe.

She looked at Silicon Valley. His lips were tight, his eyes irritated as he stared down moodily at his cards. He was probably already thinking about the twenty thousand dollars he'd wagered in the pot. She hid a smile.

"Miss Dalton?" Chris the dealer said. Stone-faced, she handed in the four of spades. Waited. And got back…

A queen.

She forced herself not to react, not even to breathe. Three kings and two queens. *A full house.*

It was an almost unbeatable hand. Careful not to meet Vladimir's eyes, she placed her cards facedown on the table. How she wished she could raise again! If only she had more to offer, she could have finished off her sister's debt right now—with a single hand!

Don't be greedy, she ordered herself. Seventy-five thousand dollars was plenty. Once she had it safely in her possession, the offer of her body—and unbeknownst to the men, her virginity—would be off the table.

But still. A full house. Her heart filled with regret.

"Raise," Vladimir said.

She looked up with a frown. Why would he raise now?

His eyes met hers. "Fifteen thousand."

"Fold." With a growl, Silicon Valley tossed his cards on the table. "Damn you."

Greg Hudson nervously wiped his forehead. For several seconds, he stared at his cards. Then he said in a small voice, "Call."

They all looked at her. Bree hesitated. She wanted to match Vladimir's raise. *Yearned* to. She had an amazing hand, and the amount now in the pot was even more than her sister's debt. But without anything more to offer, she was already all in. Even if she won, she wouldn't get the additional amount.

If only she had something more to offer!

"Well?" Vladimir's eyes met hers. "Will you call? Perhaps," he said in a sardonic voice, "you wish to raise your offer to an entire *weekend* of your charms?"

Bree stared at him in shock. A weekend?

She didn't know why he was helping her—or if he thought he could hurt her. But with this hand, it didn't matter. She was going to win.

"Great idea," she said coolly. "I'll match your raise with a full weekend of my—how did you put it? My charms?"

Vladimir's lips turned up slightly at the edges, though his eyes revealed nothing.

Heart pounding, she waited for Greg Hudson to object. But he didn't even look up. He just kept staring at his own cards, chewing on his lower lip.

It was time to reveal cards. Vladimir, based on his position at the table, went first. Slowly, he turned over his cards. He had two pairs—sevens and nines.

Relief flooded through Bree, making her body almost limp. She hadn't realized until that moment how scared she'd been that even with her completely unbeatable hand, Vladimir might find a way to beat her.

Greg Hudson's cards, on the other hand, were a foregone conclusion. He muttered a curse as he revealed a pair of threes.

Blinking back tears, Bree turned over her cards to reveal her full house, the three kings and two queens. There was a smattering of applause, exclamations and cursing across the room. She nearly wept as she reached for the pile of chips at the center of the table.

She'd saved Josie.

She'd won.

Bree's legs trembled beneath her as she rose unsteadily to her feet, swaying in her high-heeled stiletto boots. She pushed the bulk of the chips toward Greg Hudson, keeping only a handful for herself. "This pays my sister's debt completely, yes? We are free of you now?"

"Free?" Greg Hudson glared at her, then his piggy eyes narrowed. "Yes, you're free. In fact, I want you and your sister off this property tonight."

"You're firing us?" Her jaw dropped. "For what cause?"

"I don't need one," he said coldly.

She stiffened. She hadn't seen that coming. She should have. A small-minded man like her boss would never stand being beaten in a card game by a female employee. He'd already resented her for weeks, for the respect she'd quickly gained from the staff, and all the notes she'd left in the suggestion box, listing possible ways to improve his management of the resort.

"Fine." She grabbed her handful of chips and glared at him. "Then I'll tell you what I should have written up in the suggestion box weeks ago. This resort is a mess. You're being overcharged by your vendors, half your employees are stealing from you and the other half are ready to quit. You couldn't manage your way out of a paper bag!"

Mr. Hudson's face went apoplectic. "You—"

She barely heard him as he cursed at her. These extra chips, worth thousands of dollars, would give both Dalton girls a new start—buy them a plane trip back to the Mainland, first and last months' rent on a new apartment, and a little something extra to save for emergencies. And she would go someplace where she'd be sure she never, ever saw Vladimir Xendzov again. "I'll just cash in these chips, collect our last paychecks, and we'll be on our way."

"Wait, Miss Dalton," Vladimir said from behind her in a low, husky voice.

Her body obeyed, without asking her brain. Slowly, she turned. She couldn't help herself.

He was sitting calmly at the table, looking up at her with heavily lidded eyes. "I wish to play one more game with you."

Nervousness rose in her belly, but she tossed her head. "So desperate to win your money back? Are times so tough for billionaires these days?"

He smiled, and it did not meet his eyes. "A game for just the two of us. Winner take all."

"Why would I do that?"

Vladimir indicated his own entire pile of chips. "For this."

The blood rushed from her head, making her dizzy. "*All* of that?" she gasped.

He gave her a single nod.

Greg Hudson made a noise like a squeak. Sweat was showing through his tropical cotton shirt as he, along with everyone in the room, stared at the pile of chips. "But Prince Vladimir—Your Highness—that's a million dollars," he stammered.

"So it is," he replied mildly, as if the amount were nothing at all—and to Vladimir, it probably wasn't.

A single bead of sweat broke out between Bree's breasts. "And what would you want from me?"

His blue eyes seared right through her. "If I win," he said quietly, "you would be mine. For as long as I want you."

As long as he wanted her? "That would make me your...
your slave."

Vladimir gave her a cold smile. "It is a wager I offer. You.
For a million dollars."

"But that's—"

"Make your choice. Play me or go."

She swallowed, hearing a roar of blood in her ears.

"You can't just buy her!" her ex-boss brayed.

"That's up to Miss Dalton," Vladimir said. He turned his
laserlike gaze on Bree. "So?"

Though there were ten other people in the room, it was so
quiet she could have heard a pin drop. All eyes were on her.

A million dollars. The choice she made in this moment
would determine the rest of her life—and Josie's. They could
pay off their father's old debts to unsavory men, the ones that
had kept them in virtual hiding for the past ten years. Josie
would be free to go to college—any college she wanted. And
Bree could start her own little B and B by the sea.

They'd no longer have to hide or be afraid.

They'd be free.

"What is the game?" she said weakly. "Poker?"

"Let's keep it easy. Leave it to fate. One card."

Her eyes widened. "One..."

His gorgeous face and chilly blue eyes revealed nothing as
his sensual lips curved. "Are you feeling lucky, Miss Dalton?"

Was she feeling lucky?

Taking a million dollars from Vladimir would be more than
sweet revenge. It would be justice for how he'd coldly abandoned her when she'd needed him most. He'd destroyed ten
years of her life. She could take this one thing from him. A
new life for her and Josie.

But risk being Vladimir's slave—forever? The thought made
her body turn to ice. It was too much to risk on a random card
from the deck.

Unless...it wasn't so random.

She looked sideways beneath her lashes at Chris, the dealer. He lowered his head, his expression serious. Was that a nod? Did she have a sympathetic ally? She closed her eyes.

How much was she willing to risk on a single card?

Are you feeling lucky, Miss Dalton?

Bree exhaled. She'd just won a hundred thousand dollars in a single game. She slowly opened her eyes. So, yes, she felt lucky. She sat back down at the table.

"I accept your terms," she stated emphatically.

Vladimir's smile widened. "So to be clear. If my card is higher, you'll belong to me, obeying my every whim, for as long as I desire."

"Yes," she said, glancing again at Chris. "And if mine is higher, you will give me every chip on that table."

"Agreed." Vladimir lifted a dark eyebrow. "Ace card high?"

"Yes."

They stared at each other, and Bree again forgot there was anyone else in the room. Until someone coughed behind her, and she jumped, realizing she'd been holding her breath.

Vladimir turned to the dealer. "Shuffle the deck."

Bree put the chips she'd won in the last game into a little pile and pushed them aside. "I will select my own card."

Her opponent looked amused. "I would expect no less."

They both turned to Chris, who visibly gulped. Shuffling carefully, with all eyes upon him, he fanned out the facedown cards. He turned them toward Bree, who made her selection, then toward Vladimir, who did the same.

Holding her breath, Bree slowly turned her card over.

The king of hearts.

She'd drawn the king of hearts! She'd won!

She gasped aloud, no longer able to control her emotions. Flipping her card onto the table to reveal the suit, she covered her face with her palms and sobbed with joy. After ten years, fate had brought the untouchable Vladimir Xendzov into her hands, to give her justice at last. Parting her hands, she lifted her gaze, waiting for the sweetness of the moment when he turned over his own losing card, and his face fell as he realized he'd lost and she'd won.

Vladimir looked down at his card. For an instant, his hard expression didn't change.

Then he looked up at her and smiled. A real smile that reached his eyes.

It was an ice pick through her heart.

"Sorry, Bree," he said casually, and tossed his card onto the table.

She stared down at the ace of diamonds.

Her mind went blank. Then a tremble went through her, starting at her toes and moving up her body as she looked at Vladimir, her eyes wide and uncomprehending. She dimly heard Greg Hudson's annoyed curse and the other men's cheers, heard the women's snide laughter—except for the woman directly behind Vladimir, who seemed to be crying.

"You—you've…" Bree couldn't speak the words.

"I've won." Vladimir looked at her, his blue eyes electric with dislike. He rose from his chair, all six feet four inches of him, and said coldly, "You have ten minutes to pack. I will collect my winnings in the lobby." As she gaped at him, he walked around the table to stand over her, so close she could feel the warmth of his body. He leaned nearer, his face inches from hers.

"I've waited a long time for this," he said softly. "But now, at last, Bree Dalton—" his lips slid into a hard, sensual smile "—you are mine."

CHAPTER TWO

BREE's heart stopped in her chest.

As Vladimir turned away, she struggled to wake up from this bad dream. She looked down at her overturned card on the table. The king of hearts looked back at her. Bree should have won. She was supposed to win. Her brain whirled in confusion.

"Wake up," she whispered to herself. But it wasn't a dream.

She'd just sold herself. Forever. To the only man she hated.

Blinking, she looked up tearfully at the young dealer, who she'd thought was her ally. Chris just shook his head. "Wow," he said in awe. "That was a really stupid bet."

Bree gripped the edge of the table with trembling hands. Staggering to her feet, she turned on Vladimir savagely. "You cheated!"

From the doorway, he whirled back to face her. *"Cheated?"*

He went straight toward her, and the crowds parted for him, falling back from his powerful presence and his expression of fury. He looked as cold as a marble statue, like an ancient tsar of perfect masculine beauty, of despotic strength and ruthless cruelty. He reached for her, and she backed away, terrified of the look in his eyes.

Vladimir dropped his hands. His posture relaxed and his voice became a sardonic drawl. "You are the one who cheats, my dear. And you'd best hurry." He glanced at his platinum watch. "You now only have—nine minutes to pack before I collect my prize."

She gasped aloud. His *prize?*

Her body—her soul!

Turning without another word, Vladimir stalked out the door with a warrior's easy, deadly grace. Everyone in the room, Bree included, remained silent until the door closed behind him. Then the crowd around her burst into noise, and Bree's knees went weak. She leaned her trembling hands against the table. Her ex-boss was yelling something in her ear: "Nine minutes is too long. I want you out of the Hale Ka'nani in five!"

Greg Hudson looked as if he were dying to slap her across the face. But she knew he couldn't touch her. Not now. Not ever.

She was Vladimir Xendzov's property now.

How could she have been so stupid? How?

Bree had never hated herself so much as she did in that moment. She rubbed her eyes, hard. She'd thought she could save her hapless baby sister from the perils of gambling. Instead, she'd proved herself more stupidly naive than Josie had ever been.

The warm, close air in the red-curtained, windowless room suddenly choked her. Pushing past the annoyed blonde who'd stood behind Vladimir's chair, Bree ran for the exit, past a startled Kai who was guarding the door. She rushed down the hall, past the deserted outdoor bar, into the dark night.

She ran up the hill, trying to focus on the feel of the path beneath her feet, on the hard rhythm of her breathing. But she was counting down her freedom in minutes. Eight. Seven and a half. Seven.

Her right foot stumbled and she slowed to a walk, her breath a rasp in her throat. The moon glowed above her as she reached the apartment building she shared with her sister.

Bree shivered as a warm breeze blew against her clammy skin. Rushing up the open-air stairs of the aged, moss-covered structure, she shook with fear. He would take everything from her. Everything.

She'd been stupid. So stupid. He'd set his trap and she'd

walked right into it. And now Josie would be left alone, with no one to watch out for her.

Bree started to reach for the doorknob, then stopped. Her body shook as she remembered the poker chips she'd been so proud to win—all of which she'd left behind. With a choked sob, she covered her face with her hands. How would she ever explain this disaster to Josie?

The door abruptly opened.

"There you are," Josie said. "I saw you come up the path. Did you manage to…?" But her sister's hopeful voice choked off when she saw Bree's face. "Oh," she whispered. "You… you lost?"

Josie spoke the words as if they were impossible. As if she'd never once thought such a thing could happen. Bree had never lost big like this before—ever. Even tonight, she would have won, if she hadn't allowed Vladimir to tempt her into one last game. Her hands clenched at her sides. She didn't know who she hated more at this moment—him or herself.

Him. Definitely him.

"What happened?" Josie breathed.

"The stranger was Vladimir," Bree said through dry lips. "The man who kicked you out of the game was Vladimir Xendzov."

Josie stared at her blankly. But of course—she'd been only twelve when their father had died, and Bree had set her sights on the twenty-five-year-old businessman with a small mining company, who'd returned to Alaska to try to buy back his family's land. She'd hoped to con him out of enough cash to pay off the dangerous men who'd tracked them down and were demanding repayment of the money Black Jack and Bree had once stolen.

She'd fallen for Vladimir instead. And Christmas night, when he'd proposed to her, she'd decided to tell him everything. But his brother told him first—and by then, it was in the newspapers. Without a word, he'd abruptly left Alaska, leaving eighteen-year-old Bree and her sister threatened by dangerous men—as well as the sheriff, who'd wanted to toss Bree into jail and Josie into foster care. So they'd thrown everything into their beat-up old car in the middle of the night, and headed south. For the past ten years, they'd never stopped running.

"You lost? At poker?" Josie repeated, dazed. Her eyes suddenly welled up with tears. "This is all my fault."

"It's not your fault," Bree said tightly.

"Of course it is!"

Josie was clearly miserable. Looking at her little sister's tearful face, Bree came to a sudden decision. She grabbed her duffel bag.

"Pack," she said tersely.

Josie didn't move. Her expression was bewildered. "Where are we going?"

Bree stuffed her passport into her bag, and any clean clothes she could reach. "Airport. You have two minutes."

"Oh, my God," Josie breathed, staring at her. "You want to run. What on earth did you lose?"

"Move!" Bree barked.

Jumping, her sister turned and grabbed her knapsack. A scant hundred seconds later, Bree was pulling on her hand and yanking her toward the door.

"Hurry." She flung open the door. "We'll get our last paychecks and—"

Vladimir stood across the open-air hallway. His broad-shouldered, powerful body leaned casually against the wall in the shadows.

"Going somewhere?" he murmured silkily.

Bree stopped short, staring up in shock. Behind her, Josie ran into her back with a surprised yelp.

He lifted a dark eyebrow and gave Bree a cold smile. "I had a feeling you would attempt to cheat me. But I admit I'm disappointed. Some part of me had hoped you might have changed over the last ten years."

Other hulking shadows appeared on the stairs. He hadn't come alone.

Desperately, Bree tossed her head and glared at him defiantly. "How do you know I wasn't just hurrying to be on time to meet you in the lobby?"

Vladimir's smile became caustic. "Hurrying to meet me? No. Ten years ago you could barely be on time for anything. You'd have been late to my funeral."

"Oh, I'd be early for your funeral, believe me! Holding flowers and red balloons!"

His blue eyes gleamed as he came toward her in the shadows. She felt Josie quivering behind her, so as he reached for her, Bree forced herself not to flinch or back away.

"People don't change," he said softly. He pulled the duffel bag from her shoulder. Unzipping it, he turned away from her, and she exhaled. Then, as he went through the bag, she glared at him.

"What do you think I have in there—a rifle or something? Didn't anyone ever tell you it's rude to go through other people's stuff?"

"A woman like you doesn't need a rifle. You have all the feminine weapons you need. Beauty. Seduction. Deceit." Vladimir gazed at her with eyes dark as a midnight sea. His handsome, chiseled face seemed made of granite. "A pity your charms don't work on me."

As she looked at him, her throat tightened. She whispered, "If you despise me so much, just let me go. Easier for you. Easier for everyone."

His lips curved. "Is that the final item on your checklist?"

"What are you talking about?"

"You've tried running, insulting me, accusing me of cheating, and now you're *reasoning* with me." Zipping up the bag, he pushed it back into her arms and looked at her coldly. "What's next—begging for mercy?"

She held the bag over her heart like a shield. "Would it

work?" she breathed. "If I begged you—on my knees—would you let me go?"

Reaching out, Vladimir cupped her cheek. He looked down at her almost tenderly. "No."

She jerked her chin away. "I hate you!"

Vladimir gave a low, bitter laugh. "So you did have a check-list. It's fascinating, really, how little you've changed."

If only that were true, Bree thought. She didn't have a plan. She was going on pure instinct. Ten years of living a scrupu-lously honest life, of scraping to get by on minimum-wage jobs, and taking care of her sister, had left Bree's old skills of sleight of hand and deception laughably out-of-date. She was rusty. She was clumsy and awkward.

And Vladimir made it worse. He brought out her weak-ness. She couldn't hide her feelings, even though she knew it would be to her advantage to cloak her hatred. But he'd long ago learned the secret ways past the guarded walls of her heart.

"You can't be serious about making me your slave forever!" she snapped.

"What?" Josie gasped, clinging to her arm.

Vladimir's eyes were hard in the moonlight. "You made the bet. Now you will honor it."

"You tricked me!"

He gave her a lazy smile. "You thought that dealer was going to stick his neck out for you, didn't you? But men don't sacrifice themselves for women anymore. Not even for pretty ones." He moved closer to her, leaning his head down to her ear. "I know all your tells, Bree," he whispered. "And soon... I will know every last secret of your body."

Bree felt the warmth of his breath on her neck, felt the brush of his lips against the tender flesh of her earlobe. Prickles raced through her, making her hair stand on end as he towered over her. She felt tiny and feminine compared to his powerful mas-culine strength, and against her will, she licked her lips as a shiver went down her body.

Vladimir straightened, and his eyes glittered like an arctic sea. "This time, you will fulfill your promises."

He made a small movement with his hand, and the three shadows on the stairs came forward, toward the bare light outside their apartment. Vladimir strode down the steps without looking back, leaving his three bodyguards to corral the two Dalton sisters and escort them down the concrete staircase.

Two luxury vehicles waited in the dimly lit parking lot. The first was a black SUV with tinted windows. The second... Bree's feet slowed.

"Bree!"

Hearing her sister's panicked voice behind her, she turned around and saw the bodyguards pushing Josie into the backseat of the SUV.

Bree clenched her hands as she went forward. "Let her go!"

Vladimir grabbed her arm. "You're coming with me."

"I won't be separated from her!"

He looked at her, his face hard and oh, so handsome in the moonlight. "My Lamborghini only has two seats." When she didn't move, he said with exaggerated patience, "They will be right behind us."

Glancing at the SUV parked behind the Lamborghini, Bree saw her sister settled in the backseat as the bodyguards climbed in beside her. Bree ground her teeth. "Why should I trust you?"

"You have no choice."

He reached for her hand, but she ripped it away. "Don't touch me!"

Vladimir narrowed his eyes. "I was merely trying to be courteous. Clearly a waste." He thrust his thumb toward the door of the bright red Lamborghini. "Get in."

Opening the door, Bree climbed inside the car and took a deep breath of the soft leather seats' scent. Fast cars had once been her father's favorite indulgence, back when they'd been conning rich criminals across the West, and Black Jack had been spending money even faster than they made it. By the time her father died of lung cancer, only debts were left. But the smell of the car reminded her of the time when her father had been her hero and their mattresses had been stuffed with money—literally. Unwillingly, Bree ran her hand over the smooth leather.

"Nice car," she said grudgingly.

With a sudden low laugh, Vladimir started the engine. "It gets me where I need to go."

At the sound of that laugh, she sucked in her breath.

His laugh...

She'd first heard it at a party in Anchorage, when Vladimir Xendzov was just a mark, half owner of a fledgling mining company, who had come to Alaska looking to buy the land her father had left in an ironclad trust for Josie, then just twelve years old. Bree had been hoping she could distract Vladimir from the legal facts long enough to disappear with his money. Instead, when their eyes met across the room, she'd been electrified. He'd grabbed an extra flute of champagne and come toward her.

"I know who you are," he'd said.

She'd hid the nervous flutter in her belly. "You do?"

He gave her a wicked smile. "The woman who's coming home with me tonight."

For an instant, she'd caught her breath. Then she'd laughed in his face. "Does that line usually work?"

He'd looked surprised, then he'd joined her laughter with his own low baritone. "Yes," he'd said almost sheepishly. "In fact, it always does." He'd held out his hand with a grin. "Let's try this again. I'm Vladimir."

Now, as his eyes met hers, his expression was like stone. He yanked hard on the wheel of the Lamborghini, pulling the car away from the curb with a squeal of tires. Bree glanced behind them, and saw her sister's SUV was indeed following them. She exhaled.

She had to think of a way to get out of this prison sentence.

She looked at the passing lights of Honolulu. The city sparkled, even in the dead of night.

Deals can always be made. Her father's words came back to her. *Just figure out what a man wants most. And find a way to give it to him—or make him think you will.*

But what could a man like Vladimir possibly want, that he didn't already have?

He was frequently in the business news—and nearly as often in the tabloids. He was the sole owner of Xendzov Mining OAO, with operations on six continents. His company was one of the leading producers of gold, platinum and diamonds around the world. He was famous for his workaholic ways, for his lavish lifestyle, and most of all for the ruthless way he crushed his competition—most spectacularly his own brother, who'd once been part-owner of the company before Vladimir had forced him out, the same day he'd abandoned Bree in Alaska. For ten years, the two brothers' brutal, internecine battles had caused them both to lose millions of dollars, tarnishing both their reputations.

Ala Moana Boulevard was deserted as they drove away from Waikiki, heading toward downtown. Along the wide dark beach across the street, palm trees stretched up into the violet sky. They passed Ala Moana Center, which was filled with shops such as Prada, Fendi and Louis Vuitton—brands that Bree had once worn as a teenage poker player, but which as a hotel housekeeper she couldn't remotely afford. Vladimir could probably buy out the entire mall without flinching, she thought. Just as he'd bought her.

Bree rolled down her window to breathe the warm night air. "So tell me," she said casually. "What brings you to Honolulu?"

He glanced at her out of the corner of his eye. "Don't."

"What?"

"Play whatever angle you're hoping to use against me."

"I wasn't…"

"I can hear the purr in your voice." His voice was sardonic.

"It's the same one you used at the poker table, whipping the male players into a frenzy by offering your body as the prize."

Anger rushed through her, but she took a deep breath. He was right—that wasn't exactly her proudest moment. She looked down at her hands, clenched in her lap. "I was desperate. I had nothing else to offer."

"You weren't desperate when you played that last card against me. Your sister's debt was already paid. You could have walked away."

Tears burned the backs of her eyes. "You don't understand. We are in debt—"

"Fascinating." His voice dripped sarcasm.

Didn't he have even the slightest bit of humanity, even a sliver of a flesh-and-blood heart? Her throat ached as she looked away. "I can't believe I ever loved you."

"Loved?" Changing gears as they sped down the boulevard, he gave a hard laugh. "It's tacky to bring that up. Even for you."

Ahead of them, she saw the towering cruise ships parked like floating hotels at the pier. She blinked fast, her heart aching. She wished both she and Josie were on one of those ships, headed to Japan—or anywhere away from Vladimir Xendzov. She swallowed against the razor blade in her throat. "You can't be serious about taking me to bed."

"The deal was made."

"What kind of man accepts a woman's body as a prize in a card game?"

"What kind of woman offers herself?"

She gritted her teeth and blinked fast, staring at the Aloha Tower and the cruise ships. Without warning, Vladimir suddenly veered the Lamborghini to the right.

Glancing behind them, Bree saw the SUV with her sister continuing straight down the Nimitz Highway, a different direction from the Lamborghini. She turned to him with a gasp.

"Where are you taking my sister?"

Vladimir pressed down more firmly on the gas, zooming

at illegal speeds through the eerily empty streets of downtown Honolulu in the hours before dawn. "You should be more concerned about where I am taking you."

"You can't separate me from Josie!"

"And yet I have," he drawled.

"Take me back!"

"Your sister has nothing to do with this," he said coldly. "*She* did not wager her body."

Bree cursed at him with the eloquence of Black Jack Dalton himself, but Vladimir only glanced at her with narrowed eyes. "You have no power over me, Bree. Not anymore."

"No!" Desperate, she looked around for a handy police car—anything! But the road was empty, desolate in the darkest part of night before dawn. "I won't let you do this!"

"You'll soon learn to obey me."

She gasped in desperate fury. Then she did the only thing she could think of to make him stop the car. Reaching between the seats, she grabbed the hand brake and yanked upwards with all her might.

Bree's neck jerked back and tires squealed as the fast-moving car spun out of control.

As if in slow motion, she looked at Vladimir. She heard his low gasp, saw him fight the steering wheel, gripping until his knuckles were white. As the car spun in a hard circle, the colored lights of the city swirled around them, then shook in chaos when they bumped up over a curb. Bree screamed, throwing her hands in front of her face as the car plummeted toward a skyscraper of glass and steel.

The red Lamborghini abruptly pulled to a stop.

With a gulp, Bree slowly opened her eyes. When she saw how close they had come to hitting the office building, she sucked in her breath. Dazed, she reached her hand through the car's open window toward the plate glass window, just inches away, literally close enough for her to touch. If Vladimir weren't such a capable driver… If the car had gone a little more to the right…

They'd have crashed through the lobby of the skyscraper in an explosion of glass.

Her reckless desperation to save her sister had very nearly killed them both. Bree was afraid to look at him. She coughed, eyes watering from the cloud of dust that rose from the car's tires. She slowly turned.

Vladimir's silhouette was framed by a Gothic cathedral of stone and stained glass on the other side of the street. A fitting background for the dark avenging angel now glaring at her in deathly fury.

"The airport." His breathing was still heavy, his blue eyes shooting daggers of rage. "My men are taking your sister to the *airport,* damn you. Do you think I would hurt her?"

Heart in her throat, Bree looked back at him. "How would I know?"

He stared at her for a long moment. "You," he said coldly, "are the only one who's put her at risk. You, Bree."

As he restarted the car and drove down the curb, back onto the deserted road, a chill went down her spine.

Was he right?

She put her hand against her hot forehead. She'd spent ten years protecting her sister with all her heart, but from the moment she'd seen Vladimir, her every instinct was wrong. Every choice she made seemed to end in disaster. Maybe Josie *was* better off without her. "Your men will take her straight to the airport? Do you promise?"

"I promise nothing. Believe me or don't."

Bree's body still shook as they drove out of downtown, eventually leaving the city behind, heading north into the green-shadowed mountains at the center of the island. As they drove through the darkly green hills of Oahu, moonlight illuminated the low-slung clouds kissing the earth. She finally looked at him.

"Josie doesn't have any money for a plane ticket," she said in a small voice.

"My men will escort her onto one of my private jets, and she'll be taken back to the Mainland. A bodyguard already procured her last paycheck from the hotel. And yours, since you no longer need money."

Bree's mouth fell open. "I don't need money? Are you crazy?"

"You are my possession now. I will provide you with everything I feel you require."

"Oh," she said in a small voice. She bit her lip. "So you mean you'll feed me and house me? Like…like your pet?"

His hands tightened on the steering wheel. "A pet would imply affection. You are more like…a serf."

"A serf?" she gasped.

"Just as my ancestors once had in Russia." He looked at her. "For the rest of your life, you will work for me, Bree. For free. You will never be paid, or allowed to leave. Your only reason for living will be to serve me and give me pleasure."

Bree swallowed.

"Oh," she whispered. Good to know where she stood. Setting her jaw, she looked out at the spectacular vista of sharp hills on either side of the Pali Highway, then closed her eyes. At least Josie was free, Bree thought. At least she'd done one thing right before she disappeared forever….

Her eyes flew open. *No.* She sat up straight in her seat. She wasn't going to give up so easily. She'd find a way to escape her fate. She *would!*

She folded her arms, glaring at him. "Where do you intend to hide me, Vladimir? Because I hardly think your shareholders would approve of slavery. Or *kidnapping.*"

"Kidnapping!" Vladimir spoke a low, guttural word in Russian that was almost certainly a curse. "After so many years of lies, do you even know how to tell the truth?"

"What else would you call it when you—"

"You had the money to pay your sister's debt. You were free to leave. But you chose to gamble out of pure greed. And now you're too much of a coward to admit you lost." He turned to her, his blue eyes like ice in the moonlight. "I let your sister go because you're the one I want to punish, Bree. Only you." He gave a slow, cold smile. "And I will."

CHAPTER THREE

VLADIMIR watched a tumult of emotions cross Bree's beautiful face. Rage. Fury. Grief. And most of all helplessness.

It was like Christmas and his birthday all at once.

Still smiling, he turned back to the deserted, moonlit road and pushed down on the gas of the Lamborghini, causing it to give a low purr as it sped through the lush mountains of Oahu's interior.

When he'd first seen young Josie Dalton at the poker game, getting lured in over her head by the hotel manager, he hadn't recognized her. How could he? He'd never met the kid before. He'd just thought some idiot girl was letting herself get played.

He hadn't liked it, so he'd tried to get her out of the game. An unusually charitable deed for a man who now prided himself on having a cold, flinty diamond instead of a heart.

Once, he'd tried to protect his younger brother. Once, he'd believed in the woman he loved. Now he despised weakness, especially in himself. But three months ago, after nearly dying in a fiery crash on the Honolulu International Raceway, he'd taken his doctor's advice and bought a beach house on a secluded stretch of the Windward Coast, to recuperate.

He'd had no clue Bree was in Hawaii. If he'd known, he'd have gotten up from his hospital bed and walked to the airport, broken bones and all. What man in his right mind would seek out Bree Dalton? That would be like yearning for a plague or other infectious disease.

She was poison, pure and simple. A poison that tasted sweet as sugar and spicy as cinnamon, but once ingested, would destroy a man's body from within, like acid. And that's just what she'd done ten years ago. Her scheming, callous heart had burned Vladimir so badly that she'd sucked all the mercy from his soul.

She'd done him a favor, really. He was better off without a working heart. Being free of sympathy or emotion had helped him build a worldwide business. Helped him get rid of a business partner he no longer wanted.

Bree had betrayed him. But so had his younger brother, in revealing that deception to a newspaper reporter while their first major deal was on the line. Burned, Vladimir had ruthlessly cut his brother out of their company, buying him out for pennies. Then he'd announced his acquisition of mining rights in a newly discovered gold field in northern Siberia. A year later, at twenty-six, Vladimir was worth five hundred million dollars, while his twenty-four-year-old brother was still broke and living in the Moroccan desert.

Though Kasimir hadn't remained penniless for long. Even living like a nomad in the Sahara, thousands of miles from the ice and snow, he'd found a way to start his own mining company, one that now rivaled Xendzov Mining OAO. Vladimir's eyes narrowed. He'd allowed Kasimir to peck away at his business for long enough. It was time for him to destroy his brother once and for all.

But first…

Vladimir's lips curled as he drove the Lamborghini through the hills toward the Windward Coast. He glanced at Bree out of the corner of his eye.

He'd told himself for years that his memory of her was wrong. No woman could possibly be that lovely, that enticing.

And it was true. She wasn't. At eighteen, she'd still been a girl.

Now, at twenty-eight, she was the most beautiful woman

he'd ever seen. Her fragility and mystery, mixed with her outward toughness, made her more seductive than ever.

And soon, he'd know her every secret. As they drove down the hills into a lush, green valley, a cold smile lifted Vladimir's lips. He would satisfy his hot memory of her—the thirst that, no matter how many cool blondes he took to his bed, still haunted him in dreams at night. He would satiate himself with her body.

He'd be disappointed by the experience, of course. His memory had amplified her into a goddess of desire. No woman could be that extraordinary. No woman could kiss that well. No woman could set such a fire in his blood. He'd built her up.

He would enjoy cutting her down.

From the moment Vladimir had heard her sultry voice at the poker table, and seen her slender, willowy body in the tight dark jeans and black leather jacket, her hazel eyes like a deep, mysterious forest and her full pink lips like the luring temptation into heaven—or hell—his every nerve ending had become electrified in a way he hadn't felt in a long, long time.

At first he'd thought it was fate. When she'd taken him up on his final bet, he'd realized the two Dalton sisters must have been working some kind of con. It was the only explanation. He could think of no other reason for Bree Dalton, the smartest, sexiest, most ruthless con artist he'd ever met, to be working as an underpaid housekeeper in a five-star Hawaiian resort.

But now he'd teach proud, wicked Bree a lesson she'd never forget. He'd have her as his slave. Scrubbing his floors. And most of all, pleasuring him in bed. He looked at her, at the way her long blond hair glowed in the moonlight, at the fullness of her breasts trembling with each angry breath. Oh, yes.

"Your girlfriend is going to hate you for this," she muttered.

In the distance, Vladimir could see the violet sky growing light pink over the vast dark Pacific. "I don't have a girlfriend."

She glared at him. "Yes, you do."

"Wouldn't I know?"

"What about the woman whose breasts were pressed against your back throughout the poker game?"

"Oh." He tilted his head. "You mean Heather."

"Right. Heather. Won't she object to this little master-slave thing with me?"

He shrugged. "I met her at the pool a few days ago. She was perhaps amusing for a moment, but…"

"But now you're done with her, so you're heartlessly casting her aside." Bree's jaw set as she turned away. "Typical."

"Do not worry. I have no intention of casting *you* aside," he assured her.

"A famous playboy like you? You'll tire of me in bed after the first night."

He found the hope in her voice insulting. Women did not wish to be cast out of his bed. They begged to get in. Hiding his irritation, he gave her a sensual smile. "Do not fear. If that happens, I'll find some other way for you to serve me. Scrubbing my floors. Cleaning my house…"

Her cheeks turned a girlish shade of pink, but her voice was steady as she said, "I'd rather clean your bathroom with my *toothbrush* than have you touch me."

"Perhaps I'll have you clean my house naked," he mused.

"Sounds like heaven," she muttered, tossing her head.

Driving along the edge of the coast, he stroked his chin with one hand. "Perhaps I'll allow my men to enjoy the show."

That finally got her. Bree's eyes went wide as her lips parted. "You…" She swallowed, looking pale. "You wouldn't."

Of course he wouldn't. Vladimir had no intention of sharing his hard-won prize—or even the image of her—with anyone. He wasn't much of a sharer, in any case. A man was stronger alone. With no gaps in his armor. With no one close enough to slow him down, or stab him in the back.

Looking away from Bree's pale, panicked face—somehow he didn't enjoy seeing that expression there as much as he'd thought he would—he turned the Lamborghini into the road to his ultraprivate, palatial Hawaii mansion. The guard nodded at him from the guardhouse and opened the ten-foot-tall electric gate.

"Relax, Bree." Vladimir ground out the words, keeping his eyes on the road. "I don't intend to share you. You're my prize and mine alone."

In the corner of his eye, he saw her tight shoulders relax infinitesimally. *This is supposed to be her punishment,* he mocked himself. *Why reassure her?*

But frightening her wasn't what he wanted, he decided. He had no interest in seeing her pitiful and terrified. He wanted to conquer the real Bree—proud and sly and gloriously beautiful. He didn't want to be tempted, even once, to feel sympathy for her.

Vladimir stopped the red car in the paved courtyard in front of his enormous beachside mansion, built on the edge of a cliff, with one story on the courtyard side, and three stories facing the ocean.

"This is yours?" she breathed.

"Yes."

"I didn't know you had a place on Oahu." She bit her lip, looking up at the house. "If I'd known you were here…"

"You wouldn't have come to Honolulu to try your con?"

"Con?" She looked genuinely shocked. "What are you talking about?"

"What do you call that poker game?"

Her big hazel eyes were wide and luminous in the moonlight.

"The worst mistake of my life," she whispered.

Her heart-shaped face was pale, her pink lips full, her expression agonized. In spite of her tough-girl clothes, the black leather jacket and stiletto boots, she looked like a young, lost princess, trapped by an ogre with no hope of escape.

A trick, he told himself angrily. *Don't fall for it.* He turned off the ignition. Grabbing her duffel bag, he got out of the car. "Come on."

Closing the door behind him, he stalked toward the front door without looking back. He'd bought this twenty-million-dollar house three months ago, sight unseen, an hour before he was released from the hospital in Honolulu. The lavish estate on the windward side of the Oahu shore was set on the best private beach near Kailua.

He went into the sprawling beach house, and heard the sound of her stiletto boots on the patterned ohia wood floor. They passed through the large, expansive rooms. Floor-to-ceiling windows on both sides of the house revealed the Ka'iwa Mountain Ridge in one direction, and in the other, the distant pink-and-lavender dawn breaking over the Pacific and the distant Mokulua Islands.

But Vladimir was used to the view. Sick of it, in fact. He'd spent weeks cooped up like a prisoner here, as he recuperated from the car race that had nearly killed him, gritting his teeth through physical therapy. No wonder, within a month of being here, he'd started seeking amusement in Honolulu, half an hour away, at a private poker game. The fact that it was illegal to gamble at any resort in Hawaii just added to the spice.

At the end of the hall, Vladimir opened double doors into the enormous master bedroom, revealing high ceilings, an elegant marble fireplace and a huge four-poster bed. Veranda doors opened to a balcony that overlooked the infinity pool and the ocean beyond it. He dropped Bree's duffel bag on the bed and abruptly turned to face her.

She ran straight into him.

Vladimir heard her intake of breath as, for one instant, he felt the softness of her body against his own. Electricity coursed through his veins and his heart twisted as all his blood coursed toward his groin. He looked down at her beautiful, shocked face, at her wide hazel eyes, at the way her pink lips parted, full and ripe for plunder.

Mouth parted, she jumped back as if he'd burned her.

"Give a girl some notice, will you," she snapped, "if you're just going to whip around like that!"

Her tone was scornful. But it was too late.

He knew.

For years, Vladimir had told himself that their passionate, innocent affair had all been one-sided—that she'd tricked him, creating a hunger and longing in him while she herself remained stone cold, focused only on the money she intended to steal from him. But just now, when he'd felt her body against his, he'd seen her face. Felt the way her body reacted. And he'd suddenly known the truth.

She felt it, too.

"You…you should…" Her voice faltered as their eyes locked. As they stood beside the four-poster bed, the brilliant sun burst over the horizon, coming through the tall east-facing windows, bathing them both in warm golden light. Everything he'd ever hungered for, everything he feared and despised, was personified in this one woman. *Breanna.*

Her long blond hair shimmered like diamonds and gold. Her eyes shone a vivid green, like emeralds. Her skin was pale and untouched, like plains of virgin white snow. Hardly aware of what he was doing, Vladimir reached out and stroked a gleaming tendril of her hair. It was impossibly soft.

He heard her soft intake of breath. "Please. Don't."

"Don't?" He looked into her eyes. "You want me," he said in a low voice. "Just as I want you."

Her luscious lips fell open. Then with a scowl, she shook her head fiercely. "You're out of your mind!"

"Don't you recognize the truth when you see it? Or have you forgotten how?"

"The only *truth* is I want you to leave me alone!"

Twining his fingers through her long blond hair, he pulled back, tilting her head to expose her throat.

"Whatever your words say," he whispered, "your lips won't lie."

And he ruthlessly lowered his mouth to hers.

His kiss was an overpowering force, savage enough to bruise. His grip was unyielding, like steel. Bree felt herself being crushed against his hard body.

Kiss? More like plunder. His lips were hard and rough. She felt his powerful hands on her back, felt their warmth through her leather jacket. The muscles of his hard chest crushed her breasts as he wrapped his arms tighter around her. He pushed her lips wider apart with his own, taking full possession of her mouth.

The tip of his tongue touched hers, and it was like two currents of electricity joining in a burst of light. Against her will, repressed desire exploded inside her, and need sizzled down her body like fire.

Her hands somehow stopped pushing against his chest, and lifted to wrap around his neck. It had been so long since she'd been touched by anyone, and he was the only man who'd ever kissed her. The only one she'd ever wanted. The man she'd loved with all her heart, the man who'd brought her to life and made her new.

Vladimir. As he kissed her, she sighed softly against his mouth. For ten long years, she'd dreamed of him every aching night. And now, at last, her dream was real. She was in his arms, he was kissing her....

But he'd never kissed her like this before. There was nothing loving about this embrace. It was scornful. Angry.

One of his legs pushed her thighs apart. His hands moved up to entwine his fingers in her hair, yanking her head back.

"No," she whimpered, feeling dizzy as she wrenched away. She put an unsteady hand to her forehead. "No."

Vladimir stared down at her. His gaze seemed almost bewildered. She heard the hard rasp of his breath, and realized that he, too, had been surprised. Then his face hardened.

"Why should I not kiss you?" He walked slowly around her, running one hand up her arm and the side of her neck. "You belong to me now, *kroshka.*"

Kroshka? She didn't know what it meant, but it didn't sound very nice.

Stopping in front of her, he cupped her chin. He handled her carelessly, possessively, as a man might handle any valuable possession—a rifle, a jewel, a horse. Insolently, he traced his hand down her bare neck. "I intend to take full possession of my prize." His hand slid over her black T-shirt to the hollow between her breasts. "Soon you will be spread across my bed. Aching for me." His hand continued to slide down her waist. Gripping her hip, he suddenly pulled her hard against his body. "Your only reason to exist now is to serve me."

Shaking, she tried to toss her head. Tried to defy him. Instead, her voice trembled as she asked, "What are you going to do to me?"

"Whatever I please." He moved his hand up her body, cupping her breast over the T-shirt, tweaking her aching nipple with his thumb. As she gasped, he smiled. "But you will please me, Bree. Have no doubt about that."

She wanted to beg him to let her go. But she knew it would do no good. Vladimir's handsome, chiseled face was hard as granite. There was no mercy in it. But she couldn't stop herself from choking out, "Please don't do this."

"My touch wasn't always so distasteful to you," he said softly. He ran his hands down her shoulders, pulling off her black leather jacket and dropping it to the marble bedroom floor. "Once, you shuddered beneath me. You wanted me so badly you wept."

Bree swallowed. She'd once been sure of only two things on earth: that Vladimir Xendzov was the last honorable man in this selfish, cynical world. And that he loved her.

"Ya tebya lyublyu," he'd whispered. *I love you, Breanna. Be my wife. Be mine forever.*

He'd been a different man then, a man who laughed easily, who held her tenderly, a fellow orphan who looked at her with worship in his eyes. Now, his handsome face was a lifetime harder. He was a different man, hard and rough as an unpolished diamond, his blue gaze as cold as the place that had been his frequent home for the past ten years—Siberia.

His grip on her tightened as he said huskily, "Do you not remember?"

Blinking fast, she whispered, "That was when I loved you."

His hands grew still.

"You must think I'm a fool." Dropping his arms, he said coldly, "I know you never loved me. You loved my money, nothing more."

"It might have started as a con," she said tearfully, "but it changed to something more. I'm telling you the truth. I loved—"

"Say those words again," he exclaimed, cutting her off in a low, dangerous voice, "and you'll regret it."

She straightened her spine and looked at him defiantly.

"I loved you," she cried. "With all my heart!"

"Be quiet!" With a low growl, he pushed her back violently against the bedpost. "Not another word!"

Bree's heart pounded as she saw the fury in his eyes. She could feel the hard wood against her back, feel his chest against hers with the quick rise and fall of her every breath.

Abruptly, he released her.

"Why did you really come to Hawaii?" he said in a low voice.

She blinked fast, able to exhale. "We got offered jobs here, and we needed them."

He shook his head, his jaw tight. "Why would you take a job as a housekeeper? With your skills?" His eyes narrowed.

"You were surprised to see me at the poker table. If you're not here to con me, who was your mark?"

"No one! I told you—I don't do that anymore!"

"Right," he said sarcastically. "Because you're honest and pure."

His nasty tone cut her to the heart, but she raised her chin. "What are *you* doing here? Because the last time I checked, there weren't many gold mines on Oahu!"

He stared at her for a long moment. "Do you truly not know?" His forehead furrowed. "It was in the news...."

"I've spent the last decade *avoiding* news about you, chief. Not looking for it!"

"Three months ago, I was in an accident," he said tightly. "Racing on the Honolulu International Speedway."

An accident? As in—hurt?

She looked him over anxiously, but saw no sign of injury. Catching his eye, she scowled. "Too bad it didn't kill you."

"Yes. Too bad." His voice was cold. "I am fine now. I was planning to return to St. Petersburg tomorrow."

Her heart leaped with sudden hope. "So you're leaving—"

"I'm not in any hurry." He gripped her wrists again. "Nice try changing the subject. Tell me why you came here. Who is your mark? If not me, then who?"

"No one!"

"You expect me to believe we met by coincidence?"

She bared her teeth. "More like bad luck!"

"Bad luck," he muttered. He moved closer to her, and his grip tightened. She felt tingles down her body, felt his closeness as he pressed her against the carved wooden post of the bed. His gaze fell to her lips.

"No," she whispered. "Please." She swallowed, then lifted her gaze. "You said...I could just clean the house...."

He stared at her. His blue eyes were wide as the infinite blue sea. Then he abruptly let her go.

"As you wish," he said coldly. "On your back in my bed, or

breaking it scrubbing my floor—it makes little difference to me. Be downstairs in five minutes."

Turning on his heel, he left the bedroom. Bree's knees nearly collapsed, and she fell back against the bed.

Vladimir didn't believe she'd ever loved him. When he'd abandoned her to the sheriff that cold December night in Alaska, he'd truly believed that her love for him had just been an act. And now he was determined to exact revenge.

His punishing, soul-destroying kiss had been just the start. An appetizer. He intended to enjoy her humiliation like a lengthy gourmet meal, taking each exquisite course at his own leisure. He would feast on her pride, her body, her soul, her memories, her youth, her heart—until nothing was left but an empty shell.

With a silent sob, Bree dropped her face in her hands.

She was in real trouble.

CHAPTER FOUR

SEVEN hours later, Bree had never felt so sweaty and filthy in her life.

And she was glad.

With a sigh, she squeezed her sponge over the bucket of soapy water. There was still almost no dirt—she guessed Vladimir's team of servants had cleaned the place top to bottom the day before. But he'd still made her scrub every inch of the enormous house's marble floor. She narrowed her eyes. Tyrannical man. Her back ached, as did her arms and legs. But—and this was the part she was happy about—she'd done it all with her clothes on. He'd thought a little cleaning could humiliate her?

Leaning back on her haunches, Bree rubbed her cheek with her shoulder and smiled at the newly shining kitchen floor.

This house was a beautiful place, she'd give him that. Glancing through the windows as she'd worked all day, surreptitiously plotting her escape, she'd seen an Olympic-sized infinity pool clinging to the edge of the ocean cliff. On the other side of the house, across the tennis courts, she'd seen a cluster of small cottages on the edge of the compound, where she guessed Vladimir's invisible army of servants lived. Yes. She'd never seen such an amazing villa estate before.

But for all its luxury, it was still a prison. Just as, for all of Vladimir's dark, brooding good looks, he was her jailer.

She scowled, recalling how he'd enjoyed watching her on all fours, scrubbing his home office that morning. Her stomach had growled with hunger as Vladimir ate a lavish breakfast, served on a tray at his desk. The delicious smells of coffee and bacon had been torture to Bree, following a night where she'd had no food and barely two hours' sleep. His housekeeper, after watching with dismay, had disappeared. But Bree was proud of herself that she hadn't given Vladimir the satisfaction of seeing her whimper.

No more whimpering, she vowed.

Bree jumped as Vladimir suddenly stalked into the kitchen, his posture angry. He stomped into the room and opened one of the doors of the big refrigerator.

Biting her lip, she looked away, scrubbing the floor harder with her sponge. But he was making so much noise, she glanced at him out of the corner of her eye.

He grabbed homemade bread from the cupboard and ripped off a hunk. Tossing it onto a plate, he chopped through it with a big knife, like a grim executioner with an ax. She gulped, watching in bewilderment as he added cheese, chicken, even mustard and tomato. He opened the fridge and added a bottle of water and then a linen napkin to the tray. His Italian leather shoes were heavy against the marble floor as he came over to her, holding out the tray with a glower.

"Your lunch," he said coldly.

Her belly rumbled in response. She'd had nothing to eat since a cheerless Christmas dinner yesterday, a bologna sandwich eaten alone at the end of her housekeeping shift. Sitting back on her haunches, Bree wiped her sweaty forehead and looked up at him.

Unlike her, Vladimir had taken a shower, and looked sleek, urbane and civilized in a freshly pressed black button-down shirt and black trousers. His tanned skin glowed with health, smelling faintly of soap and sandalwood.

While she...

She wasn't feeling so pretty. She'd peeled off her boots to work barefoot on the wet floor. Her long blond hair was twisted into a messy knot at the back of her head, to lift it off her hot neck. Her T-shirt was sweaty all the way through, and in the humidity of Hawaii, even with air-conditioning she knew she looked like a swamp creature from a 1950s horror movie.

She narrowed her eyes. If he thought she was going to lick his boots with gratitude for the simple courtesy of lunch, he had another think coming. His *serf!*

She looked at the tray. He waited.

"I don't like tomatoes," she said pleasantly.

Vladimir dropped the tray with a noisy clatter on the floor beside her. "Tough. I have no desire to cater to you, and Mrs. Kalani decided to take the rest of the day off."

Bree looked up at him, and a slow grin lifted her cheeks. "She gave you a hard time about me, didn't she?"

"Enjoy your lunch." He pointed to an immaculate section of the floor. "You missed a spot."

Vladimir had thrown the tray down as if she were the family golden retriever. Rising to her feet after he left, she washed her hands, then took the tray to the dining table like a civilized person, ready for a fight if he came back to give her one. Somewhat to her disappointment, he didn't.

Once she'd removed the tomatoes, the freshly baked bread made the rest of the sandwich delicious. Honey mustard was a nice touch, too. And the cold, sparkling water was just what she'd wanted. She wiped her mouth.

He was still a brute. Her eyes narrowed as she remembered his cold words.

For the rest of your life, you will work for me, Bree. For free. You will never be paid, or allowed to leave. Your only goal, until you die, is to serve me and give me pleasure.

He didn't know who he was dealing with. She finished off the cold water and tidied up the tray. He thought a little house-cleaning would kill her? She'd been training for this for the past ten years.

She was going to escape this captivity. As soon as she could formulate a plan.

As the afternoon wore on, Bree scrubbed her way fiercely up the stairs and then cleaned five guest bedrooms, which had already been as sparkling clean as the rest of the house. But as she reached the master bedroom, the sun was starting to lower in the western sky, and her whole body ached. She couldn't stop yawning. Looking at the four-poster bed, she was tempted to take a short power nap. Vladimir would never know, she told herself. Climbing onto the large, soft bed, she closed her eyes—just for a few minutes.

With a gasp, Bree sat up suddenly in bed. The room was now dark. She looked over at the clock. It was almost seven o'clock. Dinnertime.

She'd slept for hours.

Feeling sweaty and gross, her body aching, Bree rose stiffly from the still-made bed, stretching her arms over her head. She rubbed her eyes with her knuckles. So where was her slave driver? Why hadn't he discovered her napping? Tsar Vladimir the Terrible must be hard at work, she decided, planning a new way to humiliate her, or dreaming up some nefarious new attack on his brother. When she'd been cleaning his home office, he'd been talking rather intensely in Russian on the phone. But even then, his smoldering gaze had slowly wandered over her backside as she scrubbed the floors on all fours.

Fine. Let him look.

With a deep breath, Bree closed her eyes. As long as he didn't touch. As long as she didn't have to feel his lips, hot and hard against her own, as he held her so tightly against his body…

"You're awake."

At the sound of Vladimir's husky voice from the doorway, she jumped, whirling around. "You—you knew I was sleeping?" she stammered.

His gaze was intense as he came toward her. "Yes."

She felt suddenly very small as his tall body loomed over hers. She licked her lips. "So why didn't you wake me up and start bossing me around?"

Reaching out, he brushed a tendril of hair out of her eyes. "Because you looked like an angel."

His voice was low. Sensual. Bree's eyes widened as she looked up—no, not at his lips! His *eyes!* Trembling with awareness at how they were once again alone in his bedroom, she tightened her hands at her sides. "Um. Thanks. For letting me borrow your bed." She edged away from it. "I should probably be getting back to work...."

His eyes glimmered. "*Our* bed."

"What?"

Vladimir's large hand wrapped around the post's polished wood. "You called it my bed. It is ours."

Her lips parted. Then she folded her arms protectively against her chest. "Look. Whatever our wager was, you can't actually expect me to..."

"Expect you to what?"

"Sleep with you."

"You were serious when you offered it as a prize." He looked down at her. "'My skills at cards are nothing compared to what I can do to you in bed,' you said." His tone was mocking. "'A single hour with me will change your whole life,' you said!"

Shivering, she looked away. "I was bluffing," she said in a small voice. "I don't know how to do those things." Her cheeks colored, and shame burned through her as she looked at the marble floor. "I've never been with a man before. I've never even kissed a man—since..." She bit her lip and muttered, "Not since you."

He stared at her. "You're a *virgin?*"

His voice dripped disbelief. A lump rose to her throat, and she nodded.

"Right," he said scornfully. "You're a virgin."

She lifted her head in outrage. "You think I'm a liar?"

"I know you are." His cool blue eyes met hers. "You lie about everything. You can't help it. Lying is in your blood."

Lying is in your blood. Before Bree's mother died, her parents had been regular law-abiding citizens, childhood sweethearts married at eighteen, high school teachers who mowed the lawn in Alaska's short, bright summers and shoveled snow through eight-month winters. Her mother had taught English, her father science. Then, at thirty, Lois Dalton had contracted cancer. Newly pregnant with her second child, she'd put off chemo treatments that might risk her baby. Two months after Josie's birth, Lois had died. Jack Dalton lost his wife, his best friend and, some said, his mind....

He'd quit his job as a teacher. He left the new baby with a sitter. And every day, after he picked up Bree from first grade, he took her to backroom poker games. First in Anchorage, and then to ports where Alaskan cruises deposited new tourists each day. With each success, his plans had grown more daring. And they'd worked. At first.

Pushing the memory aside, Bree shook her head. "I'm not lying. I'm a virgin!"

"Stop it. You made the bet. You made your bed." Vladimir lightly trailed his hand above her head, along the carved wooden post. "Now you will sleep in it."

She glared at him, setting her jaw. "I only made that bet because I was desperate—because I had nothing else remotely valuable to offer! For Josie—"

"Josie was safe. You had more than enough."

A sudden thought struck Bree, and she caught her breath. "Did you...let me win?" she whispered. "Is that why you kept raising the stakes—why you egged me on during the game? So that I could cover Josie's debt?"

His jaw tightened. "I thought she was some innocent kid that Hudson had lured into the game. Not like you." His eyes flashed as he looked down at Bree. "You could have walked away. But when I offered you the one-card gamble, you accepted. There was no desperation. It was pure greed. And it told me what I needed to know."

She swallowed. "What?"

"That you hadn't changed. You were still using your body as bait."

She took a deep breath and whispered, "I never thought in a million years that I would lose that game." Exhaustion suddenly swamped her like a wave. Tears rose to her eyes. "And if you were any kind of decent man, you would never expect me to actually…"

"To what? Follow through on your promise?" He gave a hard laugh. "No, what kind of monster would expect that?"

Bree exhaled. "How stupid can I be, appealing to your better nature?"

"I won. You lost." He folded his arms, staring at her with his eyes narrowed. "You have many, many faults, Bree Dalton. Almost too many to count. In fact, your faults are like grains of sand on a beach that stretches across the whole wide world…"

"All right, I get it," she muttered. "You don't exactly admire me."

"…but I never thought," he continued, his eyes glinting, "that you'd be a sore loser."

Bree stared up at him mutinously. Then, setting her jaw, she turned away and stomped over to the bucket of cold water. She snatched up the scraggly sponge and held it up like a sword.

"Fine," she snapped. "What do you want me to scrub? The bottom of your Lamborghini? The concrete around the pool? A patch of mud by the garden? I don't even care. But we both know your house is already *clean!*"

His sensual mouth curved at the edges. Gently, he took the sponge out of her hand and dropped it with a soft splash into the bucket. "You can stop cleaning anytime you want."

She searched his eyes. "I can?"

He put his hands on her shoulders, looking down at her.

"Come to bed with me," he said quietly.

Flashes of heat went up and down her body. His hands on her shoulders were heavy, sensual, like points of light. With an intake of breath, she ripped herself away from him.

"Dream on," she said, tossing her head with every ounce of bravado she possessed.

He shrugged. "Then I'll have to find some other way to make you useful."

Bree started to reach for the bucket and sponge, but he stopped her. "No. You are right. Enough cleaning." He gave a sudden wicked grin. "You will cook for me."

Her jaw dropped. He must have forgotten the last time she'd cooked for him, taking a romantic date idea from a magazine. It had been romantic, all right—she'd nearly burned the cabin down, and then the firemen had been called. "You can't be serious."

Vladimir lifted a dark eyebrow. "Because you're still a terrible cook?"

She glared at him. "Because you know I would poison you!"

"I know you won't, because we will share the meal." He leaned forward and said softly, "Tonight I am craving…something delicious." She saw the edge of his tongue flick the corner of his sensual lips. "Something sinful."

Even though he was talking about food, his low voice caused a shiver of awareness down her spine. She swallowed.

"Well, were you thinking chicken noodle soup from a can?" she suggested weakly. "Because I know how to make that."

"Tempting. But no." He tilted his head. "A goat cheese soufflé with Provençal herbs."

Her mouth dropped. "Are you kidding?"

"Try it." His lips turned up at the corners. "You might like it."

"I might like to eat it, but I can't cook it!"

"If you cook it, I will allow you to have some."

"Generous of you."

"Of course." Innocently, he spread his arms wide. "What am I, some kind of heartless brute?"

"You really want me to answer that?"

He gave a low, wicked laugh. "It's a beautiful night. You will come out onto the lanai and cook for me."

"Fine." She looked at him dubiously. "It's your funeral."

And so half an hour later, Bree found herself on the patio beside the pool, in the sheltered outdoor kitchen, struggling to sauté garlic and flour in garlic oil.

"This recipe is ridiculous!" She sneezed violently as minced thyme sprinkled the air like snowflakes, instead of coating the melted butter in the soufflé pan. "It's meant for four cooks and a sous-chef, not one person!"

Vladimir, who sat at the large granite table with an amazing view of the sunset-swept Pacific beyond the infinity pool, sipped an extremely expensive wine as he read a Russian newspaper. "You're exaggerating. For a clever woman like you, surely arranging a few herbs and whipping up a few eggs is not so difficult. How hard can it be to chop and sauté?"

She waved her knife at him furiously. "Come a little closer and I'll show you!"

"Stop complaining," he said coldly, taking another sip of merlot.

"Oh," Bree gasped, realizing she was supposed to be whisking flour and garlic in the hot olive oil. She tried to focus, not wanting to let Vladimir break her, but cooking had never been her skill. Supervising a kitchen staff? No problem. Cracking the eggs herself? A huge mess. She suddenly smelled burning oil, and remembered she was supposed to keep stirring the milk and white wine in the pan until it boiled. As she rushed across the outdoor kitchen, her bare feet slid on an egg white she'd spilled earlier. She skidded, then slipped, and as her tailbone slammed against the tile floor, the whisked egg yolks in her bowl flew up in the air before landing, wet and sticky, in her hair.

Suddenly, Vladimir was kneeling beside her. "Are you hurt, Breanna?"

She stared at him. She felt his powerful arms around her, protective and strong, as he lifted her to her feet.

Trembling, Bree stared up at him, wide-eyed. "You called me Breanna."

He stiffened. Abruptly, he released her.

"It is your name," he said coldly.

Without his arms encircling her, she felt suddenly cold and shivery and—alone. For a moment she'd seen an emotion flicker in his eyes that had made her wonder if he…

No. She'd been wrong. He didn't care about her. Whatever feelings he'd once had for her had disappeared at the first sign of trouble.

Right?

Bree had certainly never intended to love him. The night they'd met, she'd known him only as the young CEO of a start-up mining company, whose family had once owned the land her father had bought in trust for Josie a few years before. "Promise me," Black Jack had wheezed from the hospital bed, before he died. "Promise me you'll always take care of your sister."

In her desperation to be free and keep Josie safe, Bree had known she'd do anything to get the money she needed. And the best way to make Vladimir Xendzov careless about his money was to make him care about her. To dazzle him.

But from the moment they'd met, Bree had been the one who was dazzled. She'd never met a man like Vladimir: so honest, so open, so protective. For the first time in her life, she'd seen the possibilities of a future beyond the next poker game. She'd seen she could be something more than a cheap con artist with a rusted heart. He'd called her by her full name, Breanna, and made her feel brand-new. *I love you, Breanna. Be my wife. Be mine forever.*

Now she blinked, staring up at him in the deepening twilight. Vladimir was practically scowling at her, his arms folded, his blue eyes dark.

But the way he'd said her name when he'd held her... His voice had sounded the same as ten years ago. Exactly the same.

Vladimir growled a low Russian curse. "You're a mess. Go take a shower. Wash the food out of your hair. Get clean clothes." He snatched the empty saucepan from her hand. "Just go. I will finish this."

Now, that was truly astonishing. "You—you will cook?"

"You are even more helpless in the kitchen than I remembered," he said harshly. "Go. I left new clothes for you in the bedroom upstairs. Get cleaned up. Return in a more presentable state."

Bree's lips were parted as she stared at him. He was actually being nice to her. No matter how harsh his tone, or how he couched his kindness inside insults, there could be no doubt. He was allowing her to take a shower, to change into clean clothes, like a guest. Not a slave.

Why? What could he possibly gain by kindness, when he held all the power? "Thank you." She swallowed. "I really appreciate—"

"Save it." He cut her off. Setting down the pan on the granite island of the outdoor kitchen, he looked at her. "At least until you see the dress I've left on your bed. Take a shower and put it on. Afterwards, come back here." He gave her a hard, sensual smile. "And then...then you can thank me."

Vladimir should have known not to make her cook.

He'd thought that Bree, at age twenty-eight, might have improved her skills. No. If possible, she'd grown even more hopeless in the kitchen. The attempt had been a complete disaster, even before the raw yolks had been flung all over—perhaps a merciful end before they could be added to the burned, lumpy mess in the sauté pan.

Cleaning up, he dumped it all out and started fresh. Forty

minutes later, he sat at the table on the patio and tasted his fin-ished soufflé, and gave a satisfied sigh.

He would not ask Bree to make food again.

Vladimir knew how to cook. He just preferred not to. When he was growing up, his family had had nothing. His father tried his best to keep up the six-hundred-acre homestead, but he'd had his head in the clouds—the kind of man who would be mulling over a book of Russian philosophy and not notice that their newborn calf had just wandered away from its mother to die in a snowdrift. Vladimir's mother, a former waitress from the Lower Forty-Eight, had been a little in awe of her intellec-tual husband, with his royal background. Her days were spent cleaning up the messes her absentminded spouse left behind, to make sure they had enough wood to get through the winter, and food for their two growing boys. It was because of their fa-ther's influence that Vladimir and Kasimir had both applied to one of the oldest mining schools in Europe, in St. Petersburg. It was because of their mother's influence they'd managed to pay for it, but in a way that had broken her husband's heart. And that was nothing compared to how Vladimir had found the money to start Xendzov Mining OAO twelve years ago. That had been the spark that started the brothers' war. That had caused Kasimir to turn on him so viciously.

Vladimir's eyes narrowed. His brother deserved what he'd gotten—being cut out of the company right before it would have made him insanely rich. He, Vladimir, had deserved to own the company free and clear.

Just as he owned Bree Dalton.

He had a sudden memory of her stricken hazel eyes, of her pale, beautiful face.

You called me Breanna.

Rising from his chair, Vladimir paced three steps across the patio. He stopped, staring at the moonlight sparkling across the pool and the ocean beyond.

She really must think he was a fool. She must have no respect whatsoever for his intelligence, to think that she could look at him with those beautiful luminous eyes and make him believe she'd actually loved him once. It would not work. They both knew it had always been about money for her. It still was.

I've never been with a man before. I've never even kissed a man since you.

Reaching for his wine glass, he took a long drink and then wiped his mouth. She was a fairly good liar, he'd give her that. But he was immune to her now. Absolutely immune.

Except for her body.

He'd enjoyed watching her scrub his floors, watching the sway of her slender hips, of her backside and breasts as she knelt in front of him. He'd wanted to take her, then and there.

And he would. Soon.

Their kiss had been electric. He still shuddered to remember the softness of her body as she'd clung to him. The scent of her, like orchids and honey. The sweet, erotic taste of her lips. He'd intended to punish her with that savage kiss. Instead, he'd been lost in it, in memory, in yearning, in hot ruthless need.

Gritting his teeth, he roughly tidied up the outdoor kitchen, slamming the dirty pans into the sink. No matter how he tried to deny it, Bree still had power over him. Too much. When he'd seen her slip and fall on this floor, her cry had sliced straight through his heart. And suddenly, without knowing how, he'd found himself beside her, helping her to her feet.

You called me Breanna.

Irritated, he exhaled, setting his jaw. He glanced up toward the house. It had been almost an hour. What was taking her so long?

He grabbed a plate and served her a portion of the soufflé, then took a crystal goblet from the cupboard on the lanai. He carried them both over to the tray on the granite table, beside the open bottle of merlot. He looked out at the shimmering pool, at the crashing waves of the dark ocean below the cliff. He tried to relax his shoulders, to take a deep breath.

After he'd nearly died in the car crash on the raceway, his doctor had arrived from St. Petersburg and told him he needed to find a less risky way to relax. "You're thirty-five years old, Your Highness," the doctor had said gravely. "But you have the blood pressure of a much older man. You're a heart attack waiting to happen." So Vladimir, wrapped up in bandages over his broken bones, had grimly promised to give up car racing forever, along with boxing and skydiving. He'd bought this house and started physical rehabilitation. He'd done yoga and tai chi.

Or at least he'd tried.

He hadn't made it through a single yoga class. The more he tried to calm down, the more he felt the vein in his neck throb until his forehead was covered with sweat. The pain of doing nothing, of just sitting alone with his thoughts, left him half-mad, like a tiger trapped in a cage.

He'd done extreme sports because they made him feel something. The adrenaline stirred up by thinking he might die was a reminder that he was still alive. The never ending sameness of his work, of one meaningless love affair after another, sometimes made him forget.

And *yoga* was supposed to relax him? Vladimir grumbled beneath his breath. Stupid doctors. What did they know?

He'd already had twelve weeks of twiddling his thumbs, "healing" as ordered, while knowing his brother was in Morocco, tying up various gold and diamond sources in underhanded ways. When his leg had healed enough for him to drive, Vladimir had bought the new Lamborghini to go to the weekly private poker game at the Hale Ka'nani Resort. Then he'd found Bree, who drove him absolutely insane. Even more than yoga.

But what the hell was taking her so long? The dinner he'd made was growing cold. Scowling, he looked up at the second-floor bedroom balcony. How long could it take for a woman to shower?

"Bree," he yelled. "Come down."

"No," he heard her yell back from the open French doors of the balcony.

He set his jaw. "Right now!"

"Forget it! I'm not wearing this thing!"

"Then you won't eat!"

"Fine by me!"

This dinner wasn't going at all as he'd envisioned. Growling to himself, Vladimir left the dinner tray on the table and raced inside. Taking the stairs two at a time, he went down the hall and shoved open the double doors to the master bedroom, knocking them back against the walls.

Bree whirled around with a gasp.

Vladimir took one look and his mouth went slack. His heart nearly stopped in his chest.

She stood half-naked, wearing the expensive lingerie, a pale pink teddy and silk robe he'd had a servant buy for her in Kailua. "Make it tacky," Vladimir had instructed. "The sort of thing a stripper might wear."

He'd meant to humiliate her. In spite of Bree's corrupt, hollow soul, she'd always dressed modestly. She never showed any skin—ever. Even when she'd done her best to entice the men at the poker game, she'd lured them with her words, with her electrifying voice, with her angelic face and slender body. But she'd been completely covered from head to toe, with jeans and a leather jacket.

Vladimir had never seen this much of her bare skin. Not even the night ten years ago when he'd proposed, when they would have made love if they hadn't been interrupted. The lingerie should have looked slutty. It didn't.

The pale pink color reflected the blush on her cheeks. She looked innocent and young. Like a bride on her wedding night.

Anger and frustration rushed through him. Each time he tried to humiliate Bree or teach her a lesson, she stymied him.

Furious, he crossed the bedroom. Reaching out his hand, he heard her intake of breath as he ripped off the short silken robe, dropping it to the floor. His eyes raked over the creamy skin of her bare shoulders. The slip of silk beneath barely reached the tops of her thighs, and the flimsy bodice revealed most of the curves of her breasts. He saw the thrust of her nipples through the silk, and was instantly hard.

Bree's cheeks burned red as she glared at him. "Are you happy?"

"No," he growled. He roughly pulled her into his arms. "But I will be."

Her eyes glittered. "So you won me in a poker game. Is this what you wanted, Vladimir? To make me look like your whore?"

He saw the shimmer in her eyes, the vulnerability on her beautiful face, heard the heart-stopping tremble of her voice, and felt that same strange twist in his chest. *It's nothing more than an act to manipulate me,* he told himself fiercely. Damn her!

"You sold yourself to me of your own free will," he growled. "What other word would you use to describe a woman who does such a thing?"

He heard the furious intake of her breath, saw the rapid rise and fall of her chest. But as she drew her hand back to slap him, he caught her wrist.

"Typical feminine reaction," he observed coldly. "I expected more of you."

"How about this," she hissed, ripping her arm away. Her damp blond hair slid against the bare skin of her shoulders. *"I hate you."*

His lips curled. "Good."

"I wish to God we'd never met. That any man but you had won me." Her eyes flashed fire. "I'd rather be right now in the bed of any man at the table—"

Her voice ended with a choke as he yanked her against his body. "So you admit, then, that you are exactly as I've said. A liar, a cheat and a whore."

Her beautiful hazel eyes widened beneath the dark fringe of lashes. Then she swallowed and looked down. "I was a liar, yes, and a cheat, too, but never—never the other," she said in a small voice. She shook her head. "I haven't tried to con anyone for ten years. You changed me." Her dark lashes rose. "You made me a better person," she whispered. The pain and bewilderment in her eyes made her seem suddenly young and fragile and sad. "And you left."

And he felt it again—the tight twist in the place where his heart should have been. As if he were an ogre standing over a poor peasant girl with a whip.

No! Damn it! He wouldn't feel sorry for her!

He'd show her that her overt display of a wobbly lower lip and big hazel eyes had no effect on him whatsoever!

Bree Dalton didn't have feelings, he told himself fiercely. Just masks. He glared at her. "Stop it."

"What?"

"Your ridiculous attempt to gain my sympathy. It—"

It won't work, he meant to say, but his throat closed as he was distracted by the rise and fall of her breasts in the tiny slip of blush-colored silk when she breathed. He could see the shape of her nipples and the way they trembled with every hard breath.

And he was rock hard. Their mutual dislike somehow only made him desire her more, to almost unsustainable need. What magnetic control did she have over his body? Why did he want her like this? She was a confessed liar, a con artist. She wished she'd lost her body to any man but him. How could he want her still? It was almost as if she wasn't his slave at all, but he was hers.

And that enraged him most of all.

A low growl came from the back of his throat. He was in control. Not her.

His hands tightened into fists, his jaw clenching. He wanted to push Bree against the bed, to kiss her hard, to plunge himself inside her and make her scream with pleasure. He wanted to make her explode with pure ecstasy, even while she hated him. A grim smile curved his lips. She would despise herself for that, which would be sweet indeed.

But when he took her, it would be in his own time. At his free choice. Not because she'd driven him to madness by her taunts and the seductive sway of her nubile body.

He wouldn't let her conquer him.

His shoulders ached with tension as he turned away, fighting for self-control. He looked around the master bedroom with a derisive curl on his lip. "I can see you did not finish scrubbing this floor before you took your long lazy nap. You will finish it now. While I watch."

Her expression changed. Snatching up the frayed sponge, she grabbed the bucket of cold wash water from the floor and, in a posture of clear fury, knelt down. He watched her slender, delectable body, wearing only the tiny slip of pink silk, moving back and forth on all fours as she scrubbed the floor. His mouth went dry.

Bree looked up.

"Enjoying the show?" she said coldly.

Without a word, Vladimir turned and left the bedroom. He returned a moment later with his own dinner tray and red wine. Still not speaking, he sat down in a cushioned chair near the marble fireplace. Calmly he unfolded his fine linen napkin across his lap.

"Now I am," he replied.

Sitting back comfortably in his chair, he took a sip of merlot. He had the satisfaction of seeing her eyes widen, of seeing her scowl. Then she turned back to her work, and he had the even greater satisfaction of watching Bree on all fours, her body frosted with silvery moonlight, scrubbing his floor with a sponge and a pail of water.

Outside the veranda window, the full moon lit up the shimmering dark Pacific. The large master bedroom was full of shadows, lit only by a single lamp near his massive four-poster bed. With the flick of a remote, Vladimir turned on the gas fireplace, adding soft flickering firelight to better see his dinner—and the floor show. His solid silver knife and fork slid noisily against the pure bone china, edged with 24 karat gold, as he cut the Provençal goat cheese and Gruyère soufflé. Watching her, he took a bite.

It was exquisite. He sighed in true, deep pleasure.

"Tasty?" Bree muttered, not looking at him.

"You have no idea." His homemade soufflé was indeed delicious, but he wasn't referring to the food.

"I hope you choke and die," she said sweetly.

"Don't forget the area by the bed." He watched Bree's nearly naked body shimmy as she scrubbed. His eyes ran along her slender, toned legs, the sweet curve of her backside, her plump breasts hanging down as they swayed, barely covered by the whisper-thin silk hanging from her shoulders.

Hmm. He didn't want to enjoy it *this* much. He shifted uncomfortably in his seat, moving his plate closer to his knees.

"Of course, *Your Highness*." Giving him an *I-wish-you-were-dead* glare, Bree stomped—if a woman could be said to stomp while she was crawling—over to the foot of the bed, dragging the bucket behind her. It changed her body's position, giving Vladimir an entirely different view.

He was now sitting directly behind her. All he needed to do was get down on his knees, grab her hips in his hands and pull her sweet bottom back against his groin. It was suddenly all he could think about.

You're in control, he ordered himself. *Not her.*

But his body wasn't listening. A bead of sweat formed on his forehead. His hands clenched on the silver tray in his lap. Well, why not just take her? Bree was his property. His serf. His slave. She'd sold herself to him freely, taunting him with her sexual skill. *You have no idea what I can do to you.* An untouched virgin—Bree? Impossible. She was an experienced seductress. He'd wanted her. Waited for her. For ten years. So what was stopping him?

Vladimir watched the bounce of her breasts and slow up-and-down motion of her hips as she scrubbed the floor angrily.

Not a damned thing.

He heard a loud crash of breaking china. He'd risen to his feet without even knowing it. The tray had fallen from his lap, and his dinner was now a mess of broken crockery.

At the noise, Bree leaned back on her haunches, brushing a tendril of hair out of her face with her shoulder. Turning her luscious body in the tiny, clinging silk teddy, she glared at him. "I'm not cleaning that."

Then she saw the look in his eyes. Twisting away with an intake of breath, she started to scrub the floor again. This time with enough panicked force to dig right through the marble to the house's foundation and straight through the earth to Russia.

He stepped over the broken china. He stopped behind her. He fell to his knees.

"I'm not done," she choked out.

Wrapping his body around her back, he reached in front of her. He put his larger hand over hers, forcing the sponge to be still. His hand tightened as she tried, without success, to keep scrubbing. Caught between two opposing forces, the sponge ripped apart.

Bewildered, she leaned back with half a sponge in her hand. "Look what you did," she said, blinking fast. "You destroyed it. After everything it tried to do for you…"

"Bree," he said in a low voice.

Dropping the sponge, she closed her eyes, wrapping her arms around her shivering body. "Don't…"

But he was ruthless. Grabbing her hips with both hands, he pulled her body back against his own. He felt the rapid, panicked rise and fall of her ribs beneath the chain of his arms. Felt the sweet softness of her backside pressing into his hard, aching groin.

Slowly she opened her eyes and twisted her head to glance at him. Her skin was flushed, her cheeks pink. Her lips parted. He saw the nervous flicker of her tongue against the corner of her mouth.

And he could bear it no longer.

Roughly turning her in his arms, he pulled her to face him, body to body. Twining his hands in her tangled hair, he savagely lowered his mouth to hers.

For an instant, she stiffened. Then, with a little anguished cry, her lips melted against his own. She wrapped her arms around him, and in a rush, their grip tightened as they embraced in the devouring passion of a decade's hunger.

CHAPTER FIVE

BREE had to push him away. She should. She *must*.

She couldn't.

His kiss was hard, even angry—passionate, yes, but nothing like the tender way he'd once embraced her. His chin was rough with five-o'clock shadow, and his powerful arms held her tightly against him as they knelt facing each other, bodies pressed together. Even through his black trousers, she could feel how much he wanted her. And she wanted him.

You are my serf, he'd informed her coldly. *Your only reason for living, until you die, is to serve me and give me pleasure.* She'd been enraged. She was no man's slave.

But he wasn't taking her by force, as her lord and master. No—she couldn't kid herself about that. Because no matter how badly he treated her, she still wanted him. She'd never stopped wanting him....

Vladimir's body moved as he took full, hard possession of her lips, stretching her mouth wide with his own, teasing her with his tongue. His hands moved against her back, sliding the thin, blush-colored silk teddy like a whisper against her naked skin. Her breasts felt heavy and taut, her nipples sizzling with awareness.

As he slowly kissed down her neck, her head fell backward. Breathless with need, she closed her eyes. His tongue flicked her collarbone, his hands cupping her breasts through the silk.

"Breanna," he whispered. "You feel so good. Just like I dreamed you would…"

His breath was warm against her skin as he lowered his head to suckle her through the silk.

She gasped. The sensation of his hot wet mouth against her hard, aching nipple flooded her nerve endings with pleasure. Her fingertips dug into his shoulders as her toes curled beneath her. She pulled him closer.

He sucked gently through the silk, and she felt the fabric move softly, caressing her skin. With agonizing slowness, he pulled the bodice down, and cupped her naked breasts. She felt the roughness of his palm as he rubbed her, then pinched her taut nipples, presenting first one, then the other, to the wet, welcoming warmth of his mouth. Lost in sweet pleasure, she held her breath….

She almost wept in frustration when he suddenly pulled away from her, leaving her bereft. Rising to his feet, he picked her up off the floor as if she weighed nothing at all. He carried her three steps to the bed, then tossed her on the white bedspread.

Eyes wide, Bree leaned back against the pillows and watched as Vladimir stood beside the bed, unbuttoning his shirt. His gaze locked with hers as he undid the cuffs and tossed the shirt to the floor. She had a brief vision of his tanned, muscled chest laced with dark hair before he fell on top of her, pulling her to him for a hard, hungry kiss.

It wasn't gentle or kind. It was primal, filled with fury at his unwilling need. She felt the heavy weight of his muscular body as he pushed her against the mattress. And as he kissed her, the world seemed to spin in a blinding flash of light. She kissed him back fiercely, desperately, forgetting pride and past pain beneath the overwhelming demand of desire.

Without a word, he ripped the pale pink silk teddy off her unresisting body. He looked down at her, now dressed only in the silk G-string panties he'd given her.

"I wanted you to learn your place." His voice was low, almost choked. Reaching out, he stroked her bare breasts in wonder, even as his other hand stroked up and down the length of her nearly naked body. "Instead you teach me mine." His dark blue eyes lifted to hers. "Why do you not touch me? Why do you hold back?"

She remembered her bravado at the poker table, the way she'd bragged about her skills in bed. Her cheeks flooded with heat. "I want to," she whispered. "I don't know how."

"You—don't know how?" he said in disbelief.

"I…" She swallowed. "I might have implied more than my skills actually deserve. At the poker table…"

"I don't give a damn about the game." He gripped her hand. "Just touch me. If you want to please me, touch me. If you want to punish me," he groaned, guiding her palm to stroke slowly down his chest to his belly, "touch me."

Vladimir truly had no idea that she was a virgin. Her fingers shook as she let him guide her, stroking his hard muscles, his hot, bare skin. She'd told him, but he hadn't believed her.

Suddenly, she didn't want him to know. Because how would he react if he learned the pathetic truth—that even after he'd abandoned her, she'd never wanted another man to touch her? Would his eyes fill with scorn—or pity?

She shuddered. He must never realize how much of a fool she'd been, or how thoroughly he'd destroyed her ten years ago.

She had to fake it.

Pretend to be the experienced woman he believed her to be.

So how would a sexually adventurous woman behave?

Trembling, Bree reached for his shoulders. Tossing her head with bravado, she rolled him beneath her on the bed. He did not resist, just looked up at her with smoldering eyes dark with lust. Trying to seem as if she was comfortable straddling him, with her breasts naked for a man for the first time, and wearing nothing but the tiny silk G-string, she gazed down at him. He did have an incredible body…and as long as she didn't look directly into his deep blue eyes, those eyes that always saw straight through her...

With an intake of breath, she slowly stroked down his bare chest to the waistband of his black trousers. Shaking with nerves, trying to act confident, she lowered her head.

And she kissed him.

Her lips were tentative, scared. Until she felt his mouth, hot and hard against hers, sliding like liquid silk as he kissed her back. He deepened the embrace, entwining her tongue with his. He tasted like sweet wine and spice and everything forbidden, everything she'd ever denied herself. His lips were soft and hard at once, like satin with steel. He let her set the rhythm and pace, let her lead.

And she forgot her fear. Her hands explored the warm, smooth skin of his hard chest, the edges and curves of his muscles. She stroked his flat nipples and the rough, bristly hair that stretched down his taut torso like an arrow. She heard his ragged intake of breath, and when she glanced up and saw his mesmerized expression, her confidence leaped. It was working! Growing bolder, she ran her fingertips beneath the edge of his waistband, swaying her splayed body against the thick hardness between his legs.

She'd meant it as an exploration. He took it as a taunt. With a growl, he pushed her back against the bed. Pulling off his pants and boxers, he kicked them to the floor.

She gasped when she saw him naked for the first time. He was huge. She couldn't look away. But as he pulled her back into his arms, crushing her breasts against his chest as he took possession of her mouth with a hard, hungry kiss, she forgot that fear, too.

He kissed slowly down her body, moving from her neck to the valley between her breasts to the flat plain of her belly. His hot breath enflamed her skin. Pushing her legs apart with his hands, he nuzzled her tender, untouched thighs. He kissed the edges of her G-string panties, and she felt the brief flicker of his tongue through silk.

She gasped. Need pounded through her, making her body shake as she felt his mouth move between her legs, gently suckling secret places there. She felt the heat and dampness of his tongue, teasing her on the edge of the fabric, and her back arched against the mattress. With a little cry, she stretched out her arms to grip the sheets, feeling as if she might fly off the bed and into the sky.

His fingers stroked the smooth silk, and she heard the rasp of her own frantic breathing. With tantalizing slowness, he reached beneath the fabric, stroking her wet core with a feather-like touch. He pushed a single thick fingertip an inch inside her, bending his head to suckle the top of her mound through the silk panties, and her back arched higher, her body grew tighter, and her breathing quickened, so much she started to see stars.

She heard the ripping of fabric as he destroyed the wisp of silk and tossed it to the floor.

"Look at me."

Against her will, she opened her eyes. Holding her gaze, he lowered his head between her naked thighs and fully tasted her with his wide tongue.

She cried out as she felt him tantalize, then lick, then lap her wet core. Her body twisted with the intensity of the pleasure even as her soul was torn by the intimacy of his gaze. Her heart hammered in her throat. Closing her eyes, she turned away so he could not see her tears.

His tongue changed rhythm; now he was using just the tip on her taut, sensitive nub. It was perfect. It was torture. His tongue swirled in light circles, barely touching her. She ached deep inside, wanting to be filled, wanting to have him inside her. Pleasure was building so hard and fast that her body could barely contain it. She felt an agony of need. With a whimper, she tried to pull away, but he held her firmly, not allowing her to escape from his hot, wet tongue.

Pleasure built higher and higher. "Please," she panted, nearly crying with need. "Please."

Holding her down, Vladimir thrust two thick fingertips inside her, then three. Still lapping her, he stretched her wide, his free hand pushing her back against the bed, while his tongue tormented her wet, slick core. And suddenly, she fell off a cliff. Her body exploded. She cried out as waves of ecstasy crashed around her, and she flew.

Quickly sheathing himself in a condom from the bedstand, he positioned himself between her legs. With a single rough thrust, he shoved himself all the way inside her. Gripping his shoulders, Bree cried out as sudden pain tore through her pleasure.

When Vladimir felt the barrier he hadn't expected, he froze, looking down at her in shock.

"You were—a virgin?" he breathed.

Bree's eyes squeezed shut, her beautiful face full of anguish as she turned it away, as if she didn't want him to see. He didn't move, unable to fathom the evidence he'd felt with his own body. "Why didn't you tell me?"

Trembling beneath him, she slowly opened her eyes again—limpid hazel eyes that glimmered like an autumn lake dark with rain. "I did," she whispered. She took a ragged breath. "You didn't believe me."

Vladimir stared at her beautiful face. Around him, the whole world suddenly seemed to shake and rattle. But the earthquake was in his own heart. He felt something crack inside his soul.

Everything he'd thought about Bree was wrong.

Everything he'd believed her to be—*wrong.*

With a ragged intake of breath, he pulled away. Sitting back on the bed, he choked out, "I don't understand."

"Don't you?" She sat up against the headboard, and her eyes shimmered in the silver-gold moonlight dappling the high-ceilinged bedroom. She licked her lips. "When you didn't believe me, I started hoping I could keep my virginity a secret. So you wouldn't…"

She stopped.

"So I wouldn't what?"

Her lips trembled as she tried to smile. "Well, it's pathetic, isn't it?" She didn't try to cover her nakedness, as another woman might have done. She just looked straight into his eyes, without artifice, without defenses. "There was no other man for me. Not before you. And not after."

Staring at her, Vladimir felt as if he'd just been sucker punched.

She'd told him the truth. All these years he'd thought of Bree Dalton as a liar, or worse. But even when she'd looked him in the eyes and told him she was a virgin, he hadn't believed her.

Who was the one who didn't recognize the truth when he saw it?

Who was the one who'd forgotten how?

Setting his jaw, he looked at her grimly. "And Alaska?"

She looked down, her eyelashes a dark sweep against her pale skin. "Everything your brother tried to tell you, that Christmas night he burst in on us, was true," she said softly. "I never had the rights to sell Josie's land. I was trying to distract you, so you'd put down earnest money in cash before you realized it, and my sister and I could disappear into a new life."

"To con people somewhere else."

"It was all I knew how to do." Bree lifted her gaze. "It never occurred to me that I could change. Not until…"

Her voice trailed off.

Yes, Vladimir, I'll marry you. He could almost hear her joyful, choked voice that Christmas night, see the tears in her beautiful eyes as she'd thrown her arms around him and whispered, "I'm not good enough for you, not by half. But I'll spend the rest of my life trying to be."

Now, his hands tightened into fists. "You had plenty of chances to tell me the truth. Instead, you let me find out about your con from Kasimir. You let me shout at him and throw him out of your cabin as a damned liar. You let me leave that night, still not knowing the truth. Until I started getting phone calls the next morning, and discovered from reporters that everything he'd told me about you was true."

"I wanted to tell you. But I was afraid."

"Afraid," he sneered.

"Yes," she cried. "Afraid you wouldn't listen to my side. That you'd abandon me, and I'd be left with no money and no defenses against the wolves circling us. I was afraid," she whispered, "you'd stop loving me."

That was exactly what had happened.

"If that is true, and you were truly intending to change purely because of this *love* for me," he said, his voice dripping scorn, "why didn't you go back to your old life of cheating and lying the instant I left?"

Her eyes widened, then fell. "It wasn't just for you," she muttered. "It was for me, too." She looked up. "And Josie. I wanted to be a good example. I wanted us to live a safe, boring, respectable life." Hugging her knees to her chest, she blinked fast, her eyes suspiciously wet. "But we couldn't."

"You couldn't be respectable?"

"We never felt safe." She licked her lips. "Back in Alaska, some men had threatened to hurt us if I didn't replace money we'd stolen. But my father had already spent it all and more. It was a million dollars, impossible to repay. So for the last ten years, I made sure we stayed off the radar. No job promotions. No college for Josie. Never staying too long anywhere." Bree's lips twisted. "Not much of a life, but at least no legs got broken."

His hands clenched as he remembered the angry looks of the players at the poker game, when she'd told them how she'd cheated them. "Why didn't you tell me about this?"

"I did," she said, bewildered at his reaction. "A few times."

"You told me you had debts," he said tightly. "Everyone

has debts. You didn't tell me some men were threatening to break your legs."

She took a deep breath, her face filled with pain.

"Not mine," she whispered. "Josie's."

Vladimir rose to his feet. Still naked, he paced three steps, clenching his hands. His shoulders felt so tense they burned. He was having a physical reaction.

If he'd been wrong about Bree, what else had he been wrong about?

He stopped as he remembered his brother's face, contorted beneath the lights of the Christmas tree. *You're taking her word over mine? You just met this girl two months ago. I've looked up to you my whole life. Why can't you believe I might know more than you—just once?*

But Vladimir, two years older, had always been the leader, the protector. He could still remember six-year-old Kasimir panting as he struggled through the snowy two miles to school. *Wait for me, Volodya! Wait for me!*

But he'd never waited. *If you want to follow me, keep up, Kasimir. Stop being slow.*

Now, as Vladimir remembered that long-lost adoration in his brother's eyes, his heart gave a strange, sickening jump in his chest. Tightening his jaw, he pushed the memory away. He looked at Bree.

"No one will ever threaten you or yours again."

Her lips parted. "What will you do?"

He narrowed his eyes. "They threatened to break a child's legs," he said roughly. "So I'll break every bone in their bodies. First their legs. Then their arms. Then—"

"Who are you?" she cried.

He stopped, surprised at the horror on her face. "What?"

"You're so ruthless." She swallowed. "There is no mercy in you. It's true what they say."

"You expect me to, what—give them a cookie and tuck them into bed?"

"No, but—" she spread her arms helplessly "—break every single bone? You don't just want to win, you want to crush them. Torture them. You've become the kind of man who..." Her eyes seared his. "Who'd destroy his own brother."

For a moment, Vladimir was speechless. Then he glared at her. "Kasimir made his own choice. When I wouldn't listen to his words about you, he told the story to a reporter. He betrayed me, and when I suggested we split up our partnership, it was his choice to agree—"

"You deliberately cheated your own brother," she interrupted, "out of millions of dollars. And you've spent ten years trying to destroy him. You don't just get revenge, Vladimir. You deal a double dose of pain—breaking not just their legs, but their arms!"

Pacing two steps, he clawed back his dark hair angrily. "What would you have me do, Breanna? Let them threaten you? Pay them off? Let them win? Let my brother take over my company? Not defend myself?"

"But you don't just defend yourself," she said. "You're ruthless. And you revel in it." Her eyes lifted to his. "Has it made you happy, Vladimir? Has destroying other people's lives made yours better?"

He flashed hot, then cold. As they faced each other, naked without touching, in a bedroom deep with shadows and frosted with moonlight, a mixture of emotions raced through his bloodstream that he hadn't felt in a long, long time—emotions he could barely recognize.

Bree took a deep, ragged breath.

"I loved you. I loved the honest, openhearted man you were." Tears glistened like icicles against her pale skin. "The truth is, I love him still."

Vladimir sucked in his breath. *What was she saying?*

"But the man you are now..." She looked at him. "I hate the man you've become, Vladimir," she whispered. "I hate you now. With all my heart."

He took a single staggering step. He held out his hand and heard his own hoarse, shaking voice. "Bree…"

"No!" She nearly fell off the bed to avoid his touch. Snatching the crumpled, pink silk robe off the floor, she covered her naked body. "I should never have let you touch me. Ever!"

She fled from the bedroom, racing down the hall.

For an instant, Vladimir stood frozen, paralyzed with shock.

Then, narrowing his eyes, he yanked on a pair of jeans and followed her grimly. Downstairs, he heard the door that led to the pool bang. He followed the sound outside. From the corner of his eye, beneath dark silhouettes of palm trees against the sapphire sky, he saw a pale flash going down the cliff toward the beach.

He followed. Striding around the pool, he pushed through the gate and went down steps chiseled into the rock, leading to the private, white-sand beach. At the bottom, surrounded by the noisy roar of the surf lapping the sand at his feet, he looked right and left.

Where was she?

The large Hawaiian moon glowed like an opalescent pearl across the dark blue velvet ocean, its light sparkling like diamonds.

I loved the honest, openhearted man you were. Her poignant words echoed in his mind. *I hate the man you've become.*

Closing his eyes, he thought of how he'd spent the past ten years, constantly proving to himself how hard and heartless he could be. Betraying others before they could even *think* of turning on him.

Half the world called him ruthless; the other half called him corrupt. Vladimir had worn their hatred like a badge of honor. He'd told himself that it was the fate of every powerful man to be despised. It only proved he'd succeeded. He'd conquered the world. He'd just never thought it would be so…

Meaningless. Bleakly, he looked out toward the dark waves of the Pacific.

Has it made you happy? Has destroying other people's lives made yours better?

The warm breeze felt cool against his bare skin. He'd loved her so recklessly. The night he'd proposed to her, in front of the crackling fire that dark, cold Christmas, had been the happiest of his life.

Until Kasimir had burst into her cabin and called Vladimir a fool for falling into a con woman's trap. The fighting had woken up her kid sister upstairs, so after tossing his brother out, he'd gone back to his hotel alone. He'd been woken by the ringing of his cell phone—and questions from a *Wall Street Journal* reporter.

Vladimir put a hand to his forehead.

For the past ten years, this woman he'd called a liar and a whore had been quietly working minimum-wage jobs, in a desperate attempt to provide an honest life for her young sister. While he…

Vladimir exhaled. He'd done exactly what she said. He'd cut all mercy from his heart, to make damn sure no one ever made a fool of him again. He'd closed himself off completely from every human feeling, and he'd tried to eradicate the memory of the woman who'd once broken him.

The moon retreated behind a cloud, and he saw a shadow move. He stumbled down the beach, and as the moon burst out of the darkness, he saw her.

Silvery light frosted the dark silhouette of her body as she rose like Venus from the waves. His heart twisted in his chest.

Breanna.

CHAPTER SIX

BREE stood alone in the surf, staring bleakly out at the moon-lit ocean, wishing she was far, far away from Hawaii. She felt the waves against her bare thighs, felt the sand squish beneath her toes. She shivered in the warm night, wishing she was a million miles away.

How could she have given him her virginity?

How could she have let him kiss her, touch her, make her explode with pleasure? *How?*

Allowing Vladimir to make love to her had brought back all the memories of the way she'd once loved him. How could she have allowed herself to be so vulnerable? Why hadn't she been able to protect herself, to keep her heart cold?

Because he'd always known how to get past all her defenses. Always. He hadn't forced her. He hadn't needed to. All he'd done was kiss her, and she'd surrendered, melting into his arms. And she'd been able to hold nothing back. Her feelings had come pouring out of her lips. How she'd loved him.

How she hated him.

When Vladimir had said that no one would ever threaten her or Josie again, she'd been relieved. Grateful, even. Then he'd spoken with such relish about breaking all their bones.

Bree had no love for the men who'd made their lives a misery over the past ten years. But she would have paid back every penny if she could. And seeing Vladimir, the prince she'd loved at eighteen, turned into this…this *monster*…was unbearable.

She'd thought the man she'd loved had betrayed her. But it was far worse than that.

The charming, tender-hearted man she'd loved was dead. Dead and gone forever. And left in his place was nothing but a selfish, coldhearted tycoon.

She missed the man she'd loved. She missed him as she hadn't allowed herself to do for a full ten years. The way he'd held her, respected her, the way he'd made her laugh. He'd still been strong, but he'd looked out for those weaker than himself.

But that man was gone—gone forever.

Tears streamed unchecked down her cheeks as she bowed her head and cried in the moonlight. Even the cool water of the ocean couldn't wash away her grief and regret.

For all these years, she'd pompously lectured Josie that she must be strong as a woman—must never give a man power over her. Bree wiped her eyes.

She was a fraud. She wasn't strong. She never had been.

"Breanna."

She heard his low, deep voice behind her. Whirling around with a gasp, she saw him walking at the edge of the surf, coming toward her.

"Vladimir," she whispered, taking an involuntary step back into the ocean. "You followed me?"

"I couldn't let you go." He walked straight into the waves, never looking away from her. Moonlight traced the strong muscles of his naked chest, and the dark hairline leading to the low-slung waistband of his jeans.

She folded her trembling arms over her wet, flimsy robe. "What more could you possibly do to hurt me?"

His eyes were dark and hot, his voice low. "I don't want to hurt you. Not anymore. Never again."

"Then what do you want?" Then suddenly, Bree knew, and her body shook all over. Backing away, she held up her hand. "Don't—don't come any closer!"

But he didn't stop. He waded nearer, until the water rose

higher than his thighs, to his lean, sexy hips, where the wet jeans clung.

Vladimir's gaze fell to her body. Looking down, she realized her robe was completely soaked and sticking to her skin. Even in the moonlight, the color of her nipples was visible through the translucent, diaphanous pink silk.

They stood inches apart, waist-deep in the ocean. Their eyes locked. A current of electricity flashed through her.

"I won't be your possession, Vladimir," she whispered. "I won't be your slave."

His lips curved. "How could a woman like you," he said, "ever be any man's slave?"

A large wave pushed her forward, and the palm she'd held out against him fell upon the hot, bare skin of his solid chest. Without moving her hand, Bree looked up at him. Her heart was beating wildly.

"But you're mine." His dark eyes gleamed as, grabbing her wrists, he pulled her tightly against his body. Twining his hands through her wet hair, he cupped her face and tilted her mouth upwards. "You've always been mine."

"I'm not—"

"Your own body proved it. You belong to me, Breanna. Admit it."

She shook her head wildly. "I despise you."

"Perhaps I deserve your hatred." His words were low, barely audible over the surf and the plaintive cry of faraway seagulls. "But you belong to me, just the same. And I'm going to take you."

As the surf thundered against the beach, Vladimir lowered his mouth to hers.

His kiss was searing, passionate. But she realized something had changed. As he held her against his body like a newly discovered treasure, his lips were exploratory, even tender. His kiss was full of yearning and heartbreak—of vulnerability.

It was the kiss she remembered. The exact way Vladimir had kissed her when Bree's world had been reborn.

A choked sob came from the back of her throat. Wrapping her arms around his shoulders, she kissed him back with all the aching passion of lost time. Standing on the edge of the moon-drenched ocean, they clung to each other as the waves tried, but failed, to pull them apart.

Without a word, he lifted her against his naked chest. Their wet bodies dripped water as he carried her out of the ocean, back to the white-sand beach. And as he carried her up the moonlit cliff path that led to the villa, she closed her eyes, clinging to him.

You're mine. You've always been mine. Your own body proved it.

It was true. Even though she hated him, it had always been true.

Bree was his. And whether she wished it or not, she always would be.

Vladimir left a trail of sand and water as he crossed the floor of their bedroom, then gently lowered Bree to her feet beside the bed.

Neither of them spoke. Almost holding his breath, he slowly stroked down her soft arms to her slender waist. He undid the silken tie of her robe. Never taking his eyes from hers, he peeled the wet, translucent silk off her shoulders and dropped it to the floor.

She now stood before him naked and beautiful, her eyes luminous in the moonlight. Looking at her, this sensual angel, Vladimir trembled, racked with desires both sacred and profane.

He'd taken her virginity. He couldn't undo that.

But he could change her memory of it.

Pulling her naked body into his arms, against his bare chest, he cupped the back of her head, tangling his hands in her long wet hair, and lowered his mouth to hers.

This time, without so much anger and prejudice in his heart, he finally felt her inexperience, the way she held her breath as she hesitated, her lips shy, then tried to follow his lead. He noticed everything he hadn't wanted to see.

This time, he did not plunder. He kissed her softly. Slowly. His lips suggested, rather than forced; they taught, rather than demanded. He let her set the pace. He felt her small body tremble in his arms, and then, with a deep sigh from the back of her throat, she relaxed. Her arms reached around his neck, and he felt her mouth part for him, offering freely what he'd earlier taken like a brute.

As Vladimir held her naked, soft form, still wet from the ocean, waves of desire pummeled his own body with need. But he controlled himself. He would not take her roughly. This time, he would give her the perfect pleasure she deserved. The night he'd wanted to give her long ago…

Standing beside the four-poster bed, he kissed her for a long time, holding her tight. The two of them swayed in the shadows of the bedroom. Her soft breasts felt like silk, brushing against his bare chest. His ran his hands over the smooth, warm skin of her back, beneath her wet hair.

Their kiss deepened. He did not force it, and neither did she. It just happened, like magic, as the hunger grew like fire between them. He felt the tip of her tongue brush his, and his whole body suddenly felt electric. He could almost see colors in bursts of light behind his closed eyes, like an illumination in the darkness. She was his guiding light and North Star. His one true point.

He held on to her as if, by kissing her, he could go back in time and be the openhearted young man he'd once been. The fearless one…

Bree's hands moved slowly down the sides of his body, pausing at the recent scars. She drew back to look at his skin. "The racing accident did this?"

He didn't trust himself to speak, so he gave a single unsteady nod.

Her fingers traced the other scars she saw. "And this?"

"Boxing."

"And this?"

"Skydiving."

"So reckless," she sighed. "Don't you know you could die?"

"We're all going to die," he said roughly. "I was trying to feel alive."

Her fingertips explored, accepted fully. As she touched his scars, he held his breath, feeling his soul laid bare.

"Still sorry the car accident didn't kill me?" he said in a low voice.

She stopped at the waistband of his jeans and looked up at him with troubled eyes. For a moment, she didn't answer. Then she shook her head, moving her hand over his heart.

"No," she whispered. "Because I think the man I loved is still inside you."

He grabbed her wrist. "He's dead and gone."

She raised her eyes.

"Are you sure?" she said softly.

The look in her hazel eyes made Vladimir's heart twist in his chest. It was as if she knew exactly who he was, scars and all. As if she saw right through him. Straight to his broken soul.

Turning away without a word, he unzipped the fly of his jeans. He wrestled the wet denim to the floor. Grabbing her wrists, he pulled her to the bed, with her naked body on top of his. The feeling of having her like this—Breanna, the woman he'd hated for ten years, the first and last woman he'd let himself love—left him dizzy.

"I'm not that man," he said aloud, to both of them.

Pulling her wrists from his grip, she put her hands on either side of his face.

"Let me see," she whispered. Lowering her head, she kissed him.

As her sweet mouth moved against his lips, the weight of her naked body pressed against him, and it felt like heaven. Her hands moved slowly across his skin, down his arms, to his hips. Lowering her head, she followed the same path, kissing down his chest to his flat belly.

When he felt the heat of her breath against his thighs, he squeezed his eyes shut, suddenly afraid to move. She paused. Then, tentatively, she reached out her hand and stroked him, exploring the length of his shaft. He gasped softly. Then he felt her weight move on the bed, and suddenly her lips and breath were on him. He felt her mouth against him, her tongue stroke his shaft to the tip.

He gasped again.

She moved slowly, and he suddenly realized this was new to her; she'd never explored any man so intimately before. The thought of this—that she'd waited all this time for him, only for him—was too much for him to endure. He felt her soft warm mouth enfold him, and he sucked in his breath. One more flicker of her tongue—

Sitting up, he grabbed her, rolling her over. Lying on top of her, he looked straight into her eyes and breathed hoarsely, "No, Breanna. No."

Putting his hand on her cheek, he lowered his head to hers. As he kissed her lips, his hands stroked her satin-soft skin, cupping her breasts. Moving down her body, he kissed first one breast, then the other, with hot need, suckling her until she gasped. His fingertips caressed down her belly. When he reached the mound between her legs, he stopped. His body was shaking, screaming for him to push inside her.

But he did not. He moved abruptly to the bottom of the bed. Taking one of her feet in his hands, he slowly kissed it, suckling her toes, tasting salt from the Pacific on her sweet, warm skin. He felt her tremble as he kissed the hollow of her foot, then moved up her leg to her calf, and the tender spot behind her knee. When he reached her thighs, he pressed them apart, spreading her.

He risked a glance upward. Her face was rapt, her eyes tightly closed. He heard the rasp of her breath and felt the tremble of her legs as she nervously tried to close them. Smiling to himself—he could hardly wait to give her this pleasure— he held her legs splayed and kissed slowly up the soft skin of her thighs. He moved higher and higher, teasing her with his breath, until he finally spread her wide. Lowering his head, he took a long, deep taste.

He had the satisfaction of hearing her cry out as her body shook with need. Slowly, deliberately, he moved his tongue, widening it to lap at her, then pointing the tip to penetrate a half inch inside her. He felt her body get tighter and tighter, saw her back start to arch off the mattress, as before. But this time, he wanted to give her more.

Flicking his tongue against her swollen nub, he pushed a thick knuckle of his folded finger just barely inside her. She felt wet, so wet for him. One of her hands rested on his head, clutching his hair, no longer trying to pull him away, embarrassment and fear forgotten beneath the waves of pleasure. Her other hand gripped the tousled white sheets of the bed. Her body grew tense and tenser beneath him, until she started to lift off the mattress, as if gravity itself were losing power over her. She held her breath, and then with a loud cry, she exploded. He felt her body contract hard around his knuckle.

Sheathing himself in another condom—except this time, his hands shook so badly he nearly dropped it—he positioned himself as she was still gasping in kittenish cries of pleasure. He wanted to plunge himself inside her.

But *he did not*.

Even now, he forced himself to stay in control. He entered her body inch by inch, stretching her wide to fully accept him, doing it slowly, so that she could feel him inside her, and he could feel every inch of her. Her eyes opened with wonder, locking with his own. They never looked away as he slowly filled her, so slowly that the exquisite pleasure almost felt like pain. He finally pushed himself inside her, all the way to the hilt.

And he forgot to breathe. She felt so good. This was ecstasy he'd never felt before. *Faster,* his body screamed. *Harder, faster, deeper, now!*

But with a will of iron, he gritted his teeth and ignored his body's demand. He forced himself to go slow for her, in a way he'd never done before for any woman. He wanted this to be what she would remember from her first night of making love. Not the ruthless, rough, crude way of before.

Gripping her hips to steady his pace, he started to slowly ride her. Her hands held his backside, pulling him more tightly inside her, deeper, and deeper still.

He felt her body tighten again, and as he lowered his head to suckle her breasts—first one, then the other—his hardened body moved in a circular motion against hers as he thrust inside her.

Closing her eyes, she clutched his shoulders, digging her nails into his flesh. Vladimir's heart was pounding in his throat with the need to explode inside her, but he forced himself to relax, to wait. He just needed to see her face light up, to hear her gasp. He just needed to feel her tighten around him one more time....

He pounded inside her, harder and deeper, and her hips lifted to meet the force of his thrust. Lowering his head once more, he kissed her. As their lips met, he heard her suck in her breath, felt her body tighten....

And then she screamed, even louder than she had before. In that same instant, he finally let himself go. It felt so good.... So good...

Stars exploded behind his eyes, and his own ecstatic shout

rang in his ears. Their joined cries of pleasure echoed in the quiet moonlit night, louder than the distant roar of the sea.

Afterwards, they collapsed into each other's arms. Exhausted, he held her close, kissing her temple, whispering her name like a prayer. "Breanna…"

Vladimir woke abruptly when he heard his cell phone ringing. Blinking in surprise, he saw gray dawn breaking over the clouds. He'd slept all night in Bree's arms.

He looked down. She was still sleeping, cradled naked against his chest.

He'd lowered his guard and slept with a woman in his arms—something he'd never been able to do with anyone but her. The tension in his shoulders was gone. His head didn't hurt. His heartbeat was soft and slow. It was the best sleep he'd had since the accident.

Was this what peace felt like?

His phone buzzed again. Getting up quietly from bed, he picked it up from the nightstand and left the bedroom. Closing the door silently behind him, not wanting to wake her, he put the phone to his ear. "Yes?"

"Your Highness." It was John Anderson, his chief of operations. "The Arctic Oil merger is now urgent. Your brother just had a huge oil find in Alaska. On the land he bought last spring from that Spaniard, Eduardo Cruz."

"Wait," Vladimir growled. His hands were shaking as he went down the hall to his office. So much for peace. He could feel his heartbeat thrumming in his neck, hear his own blood rushing in his ears. His brother had that effect on him. He closed the office door. "Go."

"Sir, if the find is as substantial as it seems, oil might soon flood the market, causing the price to drop…."

Vladimir paced as he listened, clawing back his hair. Usually business calmed him, because he relished a fight. But not when the news involved his brother.

Volodya, Volodya, please wait for me! Closing his eyes,

Vladimir could still see his baby brother's chubby face as he'd toddled after him through the snow those long-ago, hungry winters. Sometimes supplies at the homestead grew lean, and Vladimir had gone out with their father to hunt rabbits. *I want to hunt, too.* Once, Kasimir had idolized his big brother. Now, he enjoyed taunting and hurting Vladimir any chance he could get. Kasimir would probably be the death of him.

As his COO droned on, Vladimir barely listened. He felt weary. For ten years now, he'd fought this fight. There was no longer any joy in it. He'd taken up hobbies like car racing, risking death for the sake of cutting a few seconds off his time. He'd taken women, in endless, meaningless one-night stands. He'd been starving to feel something. Anything. But lately, even the thrill of cheating death had brought only a tiny blip.

There were no new worlds to conquer. He'd been going through the motions for a long time. He felt nothing.

Not until last night.

Not until Breanna returned to him.

He exhaled. *Breanna.*

She made him *feel,* after years of deadness. She'd brought pleasure. Yearning. Anger. Guilt. Desire. All wrapped up in a chaotic ball. He felt as if he'd just woken out of a coma, after years of dull gray sleep.

Perhaps he was incapable of love, with a soul twisted and gnarled like a tree split by lightning. He'd told her the truth: he'd never be the man he'd once been—naive and trusting enough to give away the shirt off his back. Not even for a woman like her.

Barely hearing his COO's voice, Vladimir looked through the window of his villa's home office. The bright Hawaiian dawn was burning through the low-swept morning clouds still kissing the green earth. The sky was turning blue, as blue as the sparkling ocean below.

He had the sudden memory of Breanna rising from the waves in the moonlight last night, her short silk robe stuck to her like a second skin as rivulets of water streamed down her breasts to her thighs. Vladimir shuddered, turning instantly hard. Instead of satiating him, making love to her had only increased his hunger.

"...So what should we do, Your Highness?" his COO finished anxiously.

Vladimir blinked, realizing he hadn't been listening to the man for the past ten minutes. But he suddenly felt bored by business matters—completely bored. Even though it involved his brother. "What is your opinion?"

"We'll have someone at our Alaska site infiltrate your brother's mining operation to see if the data is accurate. If it is, we can try to influence the political process to delay their building. We could even consider some kind of sabotage at the mine. Although of course it would in no way be traceable back to you, sir...."

You're ruthless. And you revel in it. The realization of how low he'd sunk caused Vladimir to flinch. "No."

"But, Your Highness..."

"I said no." Clawing back his hair, he paced across his office with his phone at his ear, prowling in circles around his desk.

"So what are your orders, Your Highness? How shall we make sure your brother does not succeed?"

Vladimir abruptly stopped. He'd been wrong about Breanna.

Could he have similarly been wrong about Kasimir, over-reacting to his brother's betrayal?

It was an accident. His brother's voice had been muffled, humble, on the phone the next day from St. Petersburg. *When you wouldn't believe me, I was angry and drunk at the airport bar. I didn't realize the man sitting next to me was a reporter for the* Anchorage Herald. *Forgive me, Volodya.*

Vladimir's hands tightened into fists. But he hadn't accepted the apology. He'd been angry, humiliated, haunted. And he feared his stupidity might jeopardize the Siberian mining rights that were about to come through, rights that could make or break the fledgling company. "If you can't trust my leadership, we should end this partnership."

"Leadership? I thought we were supposed to be equals," his brother had retorted. When Vladimir maintained a frosty silence, Kasimir had said harshly, "Fine. I'll keep the rights in Africa and South America. And you can go to hell."

Vladimir had been angry enough to let his brother go without telling him about the Siberian rights worth potentially half a billion dollars. He'd effectively cheated Kasimir out of his half.

Perhaps... He took a deep breath. Perhaps Kasimir had some cause to seek revenge against him.

"You will do nothing." Now, Vladimir stared out the window toward the palm trees and blue sky. "My brother's operation in Alaska does not affect us. Leave him alone. May the best company win."

"But, sir!"

"Xendzov Mining can win in a fair fight."

"Of course we can!" the man replied indignantly. He continued in a bewildered voice, "It's just that we've never tried."

"No more dirty tricks," Vladimir said harshly.

"It will be harder—"

"Deal with it."

The man cleared his throat. "You were expected in St. Petersburg today for the signing of the Arctic Oil merger. How long do you wish us to delay...?"

Vladimir gritted his teeth. "I will be at the office tomorrow."

"Good." He audibly exhaled. "With ten billion dollars on the line, we don't want anything to—"

"Tomorrow." Vladimir hung up. Tossing his phone on his desk, he left the study, with its computers and piles of paperwork. Walking outside to the courtyard, he stopped by the pool. Closing his eyes, he turned his face toward the bright morning sun. He felt the warmth of the golden light, and took a breath of the exotic, flower-scented air.

I think the man I love is still inside you.

He's dead and gone.

Are you sure?

Slowly, Vladimir opened his eyes. He looked up at the twenty-million-dollar mansion that he'd bought as a refuge, but which had felt like a prison.

Bree Dalton had brought it to life. As she'd done to him.

But what right did he have to keep her prisoner?

He'd told himself she deserved it. She was the one who'd betrayed him ten years ago, then foolishly wagered her body in a card game. Let her finally face the consequences of her actions.

He paced around the edge of the pool, then stopped, clawing back his hair. But she'd offered her body in desperation. He'd abandoned her without a penny in Alaska, with men threatening them for money. And yet, even under that pressure, Bree had managed to come through the fire with a soul as pure as steel.

He still wanted to find those men and break their legs, their arms. Every bone in their bodies. But there was something he wanted even more.

He wanted Breanna.

His long-dormant conscience stirred, telling him he had no right to keep her. If he truly believed that she'd never meant to betray him, that she'd wagered herself only to protect her little sister, then he should let her go. If he kept her as his slave, it would make him no better than the criminals who'd imprisoned her with debts. He was selfish, but not a monster.

Wasn't he?

Pushing the thought away, he pulled out his cell phone and made a few calls. One to an investigator. The other to his secretary, to arrange a Russian visa. Then he picked a wild orchid from the garden and went back inside the house. He'd given his household staff the day off, after Mrs. Kalani's reaction to his treatment of Bree yesterday. So the enormous kitchen was quiet as he made her a breakfast tray. Putting the orchid in a vase, he walked up the stairs to their bedroom.

Breanna was still drowsing in bed. But as he pushed open the door, she sat up, tucking the sheet modestly over her naked breasts.

"Good morning," she said shyly.

Vladimir went to the bed. She looked so innocent and fresh and pretty, the epitome of everything good. He put the breakfast tray into her lap. "I thought you might be hungry."

"I am." Her cheeks blushed a soft pink as she looked down at the tray, with its toast and fresh fruit and fragrant flower. "Thank you." Looking up, she gave him a sudden wicked smile. "Last night left me really, really hungry."

The bright, teasing look on her face took his breath away. He said abruptly, "I have to go to St. Petersburg today."

Her face fell. "Oh." Looking away, she said stiffly, "Well. Good. I'll be glad to be free of you."

"Too bad." Turning her face roughly, he cupped her cheek. "You're coming with me."

Her eyes lit up. Then she scowled, glaring at him. "Because I'm your property and slave, right? Because you get to boss me around and take me wherever you want, right?"

He kissed her bare shoulder. "You got it."

She shivered as his lips touched her. "You are such a jerk—"

Leaning over the tray, he kissed her lips, long and thoroughly, just to remind her who was in charge. Her lips parted so sweetly, it took all his strength to stop. He needed to order his private jet to leave within the hour. He had no time to make love to her.

But as he drew away, he saw that the white cotton sheet had fallen from her heedless hands, revealing the glory of her naked, trembling breasts. Against his will, he leaned forward to kiss her again, and they both jumped as they heard the breakfast tray crash to the floor.

Bree gave an impish laugh. "Maybe you should consider paper plates. I know you're rich and all, but honestly, I can't clean up all your broken china."

With a growl, Vladimir pushed her back against the bed.

"Don't worry. You'll never clean for me again," he whispered. "From now on…there's only one thing I want you to do for me."

Forcing his conscience to be silent, he lowered his mouth to hers. As he tasted the sweetness of her lips, he knew he wouldn't give her up. She was his. He'd won her—she belonged to him, for as long as he desired her. If that meant he was a monster, so be it.

I think the man I love is still inside you.

He's dead and gone.

Are you sure?

As Vladimir felt her naked body move like silk beneath him, she gave a trembling sigh. She wrapped her arms around his neck and pulled him down to heaven.

Yes. He was sure.

CHAPTER SEVEN

Russia.

AS A child, Bree had traveled down the rocky, forest-covered Alaskan coast with her father, seeking gullible tourists off cruise ships for poker games. Her favorite village had been Sitka, once the capital of Russian America. At twelve, she'd looked across the gray, frozen Bering Sea and dreamed of the distant, ancient, mysterious land of the tsars.

When wooden Orthodox churches were being hacked out of the wilderness in Alaska, St. Petersburg was already a century old, built on the orders of a tsar. She'd dreamed of someday seeing the palatial Russian city, the onion domes of its cathedrals shining with silver and gold.

But Bree never dreamed she'd come here as the cosseted mistress of a prince. For two days now, she'd been living in his three-story palace outside the city, built like a fortress on a hill, overlooking the Gulf of Finland on the Baltic Sea. She'd spent her days shopping in the most exclusive boutiques of the city, accompanied by his bodyguards and his chauffeur.

She spent her nights in Vladimir's bed. He came to her in the middle of the night, waking her, making love to her in darkness, setting her body ablaze from the inside out. He burned her with the fire of their mutual need. Each night, she fell asleep in his arms, satiated with pleasure.

But each day, she woke up in the cold gray winter dawn, bereft and alone.

Vladimir was extremely busy, working on the Arctic Oil merger. Even if he was using her only for sex, she shouldn't take it personally. Right? That was what she'd expected. Wasn't it? She should be grateful for this life he'd given her, one of luxury, pleasure and comfort. Most women would envy her. She should make the best of things.

So she tried.

Left alone all day, she went shopping, as Vladimir had ordered. Four bodyguards took her out in a black limousine with bulletproof glass. Expensive designer shops closed their doors to all other customers so Bree could shop alone, quite alone, with only sycophantic store clerks for company.

Maybe it would have been fun if Vladimir had been with her. Or Josie. Bree missed her sister like a physical ache in her heart. She'd tried multiple times over the past few days to call her, but Josie never answered. Bree tried to squelch her worries. Surely Josie was fine. It was just her own loneliness, playing tricks on her mood, that made Bree anxious.

But after two exhausting days of shopping, shocked at the outrageous prices, she was desperate to find something, anything, else to do. "Buy a wardrobe of winter clothes," Vladimir had said, shoving his credit card into her hand. "And lingerie." Wanting to be done, she'd randomly grabbed two items the clerks were pushing on her—a long, puffy black coat and an expensive lingerie set with a white lace bustier, G-string and garter belt—and practically ran from the store. The bodyguards formed a tunnel to her waiting black limo, and she fled past the annoyed faces of Russian women waiting outside.

But now, on her third day in St. Petersburg, as she sat alone at a very long table in the empty palace, eating an elegant lunch prepared by the Russian-speaking housekeeper, Bree felt a rush of pure relief when her cell phone rang. She snatched it up. "Hello?"

"What are you wearing?"

At the sound of Vladimir's low, sensual voice, her shoulders relaxed. "I thought you might be Josie."

"Sorry to disappoint you."

"I'm glad to hear your voice." Her hand tightened on her phone. "I'm, um, wearing my old flannel pajamas and big bootie slippers from home."

"Sounds sexy. Want to come over?"

"Come where?"

"To my office."

She blinked. "Why?"

"I have a fifteen-minute break coming up. I thought I'd have you for lunch."

A shiver of sensual delight went through her at his words. Straightening in her antique chair, she retorted, "Forget it. I'm not going to rush over to your office like some kind of booty-call delivery service. I might be your sex slave, but I do have some standards."

"I think you'll change your mind when you hear what I want to do to you…."

She listened to his low growl of a voice describing his intentions in graphic detail, and her hand went limp until the phone fell from her grasp and clattered to the floor. She snatched it up.

"I'll be right there," she said breathlessly. Clicking off, she pulled her new lingerie from the designer bag and tugged it on. Covering herself with the black puffy coat, that trailed to her ankles, she replaced her slippers with black stiletto boots and went outside, where a bodyguard held open her limousine door.

Bree's heart pounded as the chauffeur drove into the heart of St. Petersburg. She barely saw the elegant buildings lining the snowy streets and icy Neva River. All she could think about was what waited for her. *Who* waited for her.

The limo arrived at a sprawling eighteenth-century building. A bodyguard opened her door and said in heavily accented English, "This is office, miss."

She looked up and down the block. The structure seemed to stretch endlessly along the avenue. "Which one?"

The bodyguard looked at her. "All. Is Xendzov building."

"All of it?" Bree looked at the classically columned building in shock. It was one thing to theoretically know that Vladimir was rich. It was another to see this enormous building, an entire city block, and know it represented a mere fragment of his worldwide empire.

Swallowing nervously, she went into the foyer and took an elevator to the top floor. Down the hall, through a wall of glass, she saw men in suits packed around a conference table, some of them pounding the tabletop as they argued, while secretaries refilled their coffee cups and took notes.

Vladimir looked devastatingly powerful and ruthless, in a shirt and tie. And clearly, she wasn't the only woman to think so. She noticed how the secretaries walked a little more slowly and swayed their hips a little more around him. The beauty of Russian women was justly famous. Their skirts were short, their hair long, their stiletto heels high. They clearly knew their feminine power and were willing to sacrifice comfort in order to hold a man's attention.

Bree's confidence tumbled. If Vladimir was surrounded by women like this, why on earth had he sent for her? The sexy playfulness of her errand disappeared. What a laugh. It was like dialing out for a hamburger, when he was surrounded by steak!

He would laugh in her face when he got a good look at her in this stupid lingerie. Her cheeks burned and she started to turn around.

Their eyes met through the glass.

Spinning on her heel, Bree practically ran down the hallway. If she could just reach the elevator…

His hand gripped her upper arm, whirling her to face him. "Where are you going?"

She licked her lips, looking up at this broad-shouldered, powerful man standing in his own building, surrounded by his paid employees. Vladimir had rolled up his shirtsleeves, revealing sleekly muscled forearms laced with dark hair. His tie had been loosened around his thick neck, as if he'd been fighting corporate war all day.

She tried to pull away, but his grip was like iron. "I never should have come here," she said. "Haven't you humiliated me enough?"

Vladimir frowned, drawing closer. "What are you…?" People passed them in the hall, two men in suits and three women in tiny skirts, all looking at them with intense interest. Narrowing his eyes, he growled, "Come with me."

He pulled her into the nearest private office, closing the door behind them. She wrenched her arm away, blinking fast. Her eyes were stinging with unshed tears as she tossed her head. "You're out of your mind if you think…"

She gasped as, without a word, he roughly yanked open her oversized coat. He saw the lingerie, the white lace bustier, G-string panties and garter belt, and drew in a breath. He looked at her darkly.

"And *you* are out of your mind," he said in a low voice, "if you think I'm going to let you leave."

He ripped off her long coat, dropping it to the floor. Pushing her against the wall of the private office, he kissed her hard. Bree's body stiffened as his mouth plundered hers. She felt the soft, demanding steel of his lips against her own. Against her will, a moan came from the back of her throat, and her arms lifted to wrap around his neck.

His hands roamed over her body. He cupped her breasts, then undid her bustier in a single motion, dropping the white lace from her skin. Still kissing her passionately, he pushed her toward the desk, which he cleared with a sweep of his arm, knocking papers and computer topsy-turvy to the floor.

She could not resist. As he pressed her back against the desk, she relished the feeling of his weight. He kissed down her neck to her bare breasts, ravishing her body, and she panted, suddenly breathless with need. Her hands reached beneath his shirt to stroke his taut, hard chest.

Then she heard a noise at the door.

Dazed, Bree looked over and saw a man staring at them from the doorway. He said something in Russian, before Vladimir turned his head. The man's mouth snapped shut, his face red with the apparent effort of choking back his words. Turning, he left instantly, closing the door behind him.

But the damage was done. The man had seen her draped nearly naked across Vladimir's desk. Horrified, Bree said angrily, "That man's got some nerve, bursting into your office without warning!"

"This is his office—" Vladimir leaned back on the desk, tilting his head "—not mine."

"What?" she squeaked, sitting up.

"My office is on the other side of the building. Would have taken too long."

He leaned forward to kiss her, but she jerked back, nearly falling off the desk. "Are you crazy? I'm not going to fool around with you in someone else's office!"

"Why not?" he said lazily. "What does it matter? This building is mine. This office is mine. Just as you…"

She folded her arms over her naked breasts, glaring at him. "Just as I am?"

"Yes." Standing up, he tucked a tendril of hair behind her ear and said huskily, "Just as you are."

A pain went through her chest. His words were playful, but he was speaking a truth she'd been trying to conveniently forget: that Vladimir owned her. She was his property.

Bree's cheeks flooded with shame as she remembered the expression on the man's face when he'd seen Vladimir lying on top of her on the desk. He'd looked at her as if she were a prostitute. And glancing down at herself in only a G-string and garter belt, a sex-time delivery service, Bree felt a lump rise in her throat. Leaning down, she picked up the discarded bustier off the floor.

The smug masculine smile dropped from Vladimir's face. "What are you doing?"

She put on the long black coat, stuffing the bustier into the pocket. "Returning to my prison."

"Prison?" he repeated. "I have given you a palace. I've given you everything a woman could possibly desire."

"Right." She zipped the puffy coat all the way to her throat. As she turned away, she felt like crying.

Vladimir stopped her at the door. "Why are you so sad?"

The ache in her throat made it impossible to talk. She shook her head, unable to meet his eyes.

"You were—embarrassed?"

"Yes," she choked out.

"But why?" he demanded. "He is nothing. No one. Why do you care?"

Bree lifted her eyes. "Because I, too, am nothing," she whispered. "And no one."

He shook his head in exasperation. "I don't understand what you're talking about."

To you. I am nothing and no one to you. She turned her head. "I don't expect you to understand."

"Fine," he said coldly. "If you don't want to be here, go home."

She lifted her gaze hopefully. "Home to my sister?"

"Our home! Together!"

Her shoulders slumped. She stared down at her feet.

"There is no *together* at the palace," she said in a small voice. "There's just me. Alone."

"You know I am dealing with a complex merger, Breanna," he said tightly. "I have no time to—"

"I know." Her lips twisted. "I should just be grateful you show up in my bed in the middle of the night, right? Grateful you're so very, very good to me."

He ground his teeth, his eyes dark.

"I gave you my credit card. You should have bought out half the city by now. You should be enjoying yourself. You can buy whatever you wish—clothes, furs, shoes. And a ball gown. It is supposed to be fun."

"Fun," she muttered.

He scowled. "Is it not?"

"Shopping all by myself in a foreign city, as your bodyguards keep other people out of the store, and six different salesgirls try to convince me that a puce-colored burlap sack with ostrich feathers looks good on me…?" Bree shuddered. "No. It's not fun." She indicated the long black coat. "This is the sum total of my purchases."

He blinked. "The coat?"

"And the lingerie."

"Damn it, Bree, you aren't in Hawaii anymore. I told you to buy warm clothes."

"Who cares if I feel warm?" She glared at him. "I'm just your possession. My feelings don't matter."

He stared at her, and the air around them suddenly became electrified. "Of course they matter." He took a single step toward her. "Breanna—"

A knock sounded at the door. An older man poked his head in, an American with wire-rimmed glasses and anxious eyes. "Your Highness. Excuse me."

"What is it, Anderson?" Vladimir demanded.

The man looked at Bree and then cleared his throat. "We've reached an impasse, sir. Svenssen is demanding we retain every member of his company's staff."

"So?"

"Arctic Oil has a thousand employees we don't need. Drillers. Cafeteria workers in Siberia. Accountants and secretaries. Dead weight."

Dead weight. Bree's spine snapped straight. He would no doubt consider her and Josie *dead weight,* too, with their ten years of backbreaking, low-paying cleaning jobs. Every month, they'd experienced the painful uncertainty of never knowing if their jobs would last, or if they'd be able to pay their bills. Biting her lip, she glanced up and saw Vladimir watching her. His eyes narrowed.

"Tell Svenssen," he said slowly, "we'll find places for all his current employees. At their current pay level or better."

His employee gaped, aghast. "But, sir! Why?"

"Yes, why?" Bree echoed. She took a deep breath and gave him a trembling smile. "Don't tell me you've actually got a heart."

His lips abruptly twisted. "To the contrary." He turned back to Anderson. "I merely want to ensure that we're well staffed for future expansion."

"Expansion?" The man visibly exhaled in relief.

Vladimir lifted a dark eyebrow. "That should simplify your negotiations." Turning to Bree, he took her hand. "I will be unavailable for the rest of the day," he said softly.

"You will?" she breathed.

"But Prince Vladimir—"

He ignored the man. Pulling Bree from the office, he led her down the hall to the elevator. As he pushed the button, she looked at him, her heart in her throat.

"Where are we going?"

He tilted his head, giving her a boyish grin that took her breath away. "I'm going to show you my beautiful city."

His voice was casual. So why did she feel as if something had just changed between them, changed forever? She tried not to feel his strong, protective hand over her own, tried not to feel her own heart beating wildly. "But your merger is important. You said—"

"My people will manage. Let them earn their overpriced salaries."

"But why are you doing this?"

"I've realized something." Vladimir's eyes were ten shades of blue. "You belong to me."

She exhaled. "I know," she said dully. "You already said—"

"You belong to me." He cupped her cheek. "That means it's my job."

"What is?"

He looked intently into her eyes, and then smiled. "To take care of you."

Vladimir's mouth fell open as he stared at the beautiful angel who stood on a pedestal before him. Literally.

"Do you like it?" the angel said anxiously. "Do you approve?"

Bree was trying on her fourth designer ball gown, a strapless concoction in pale blue that revealed her elegant bare shoulders, the curve of her breasts and her slender waist above wide skirts of shot silk. She looked like a princess. Ethereal. Magical.

Intoxicating.

"I can't possibly let you buy this," the enchanted beauty said fretfully. "You won't let them tell me how much it costs, but I'm sure it's very expensive."

Vladimir lifted his hand, signaling to the five saleswomen who were hovering around them in the luxury designer atelier. "We will take it."

With a happy gasp, the salesgirls descended on Bree with sewing pins and measuring tape, to shape the couture gown perfectly to her body. Bree looked at them in dismay. But it was nothing compared to the sick expression he'd seen on her face when his COO had wanted to fire all the workers he called "dead weight."

Vladimir had lied. He wasn't planning an expansion. He'd just been unable to bear the emotions he'd seen on Bree's face: the anger, the powerlessness, the desperation. It reminded him how she'd spent ten years wasting her talents in minimum-wage jobs, because the man she'd trusted to protect her had left her to face all her enemies alone.

Now, she bit her pink, full lower lip. "I shouldn't let you do this."

"It's already decided." Rising to his feet, he felt glad once more that he'd decided to take the day off and spend it with her, leaving even the bodyguards behind. He put his hand on her shoulder. "You need a dress. I'm taking you to a very elegant ball for New Year's Eve."

Bree's dark-fringed hazel eyes went wide. "You are?"

"You will be," he said huskily, "the most beautiful woman there."

"I—I will?"

Her cheeks blushed in girlish confusion. Her charming innocence, at such odds with the wickedly seductive vixen she'd been when she'd shown up at his office building in lingerie hours before, made Vladimir want to kiss her.

So leaning forward, he did.

Her lips felt hot and velvety-soft. Her mouth parted for him, and he deepened the kiss. With a gasp, Bree started to wrap her arms around him.

Then she winced, pulling away. Rubbing her arm, she looked down at her skin. She'd been pricked by the needle of the salesgirl attempting to pin the waist of Bree's bodice.

Vladimir saw a small red dot of blood on Bree's skin, and was blinded by instant, brutal rage. He turned on the hapless girl and spoke harsh words in Russian.

The salesgirl choked back a sob and answered him with a flurry of begging and excuses. He stared at her, implacable as stone.

The salesgirl fell to her knees in front of Bree, holding the hem of the blue silk ball gown as she gazed up with imploring eyes.

Bree looked up at him uneasily. "What's she saying?"

"She's begging for mercy," Vladimir said coldly. "She's

saying she's the sole support of an aging mother and two-year-old son, and she's begging you to intervene with me, so I don't have her fired."

"You wouldn't do that!"

"I have just told her I will."

"What?" Bree gasped, staring at him. "No!"

"She hurt you," he said tightly.

"It wasn't her fault!" Bree tugged on the young woman's arms, forcing her to rise. "I'm the one who moved. And you're the one who kissed me! She never meant to stick me with her needle!"

"What does her intention matter? The pain for you was the same."

Bree was staring at him as if he were crazy. "Of course it matters! Why would I punish her for something that she didn't even mean to do? It was an accident!"

It was an accident. The memory of his brother's miserable, humbled voice on the phone ten years ago floated unbidden through Vladimir's mind. *Forgive me, Volodya. I'm sorry.*

"Don't have her fired. Don't!"

Bree's beautiful face came into focus. "Josie and I have been fired like this before." Her eyes were pleading as she clutched his arm. "You don't know what it's like, to always know that your boss or a single customer can just snap his fingers and take away your livelihood and your pride and your ability to feed your family." She swallowed, her heart-shaped face stricken. "Please don't do this."

Vladimir's lips parted. He didn't even realize he'd agreed to her request until he saw Bree's beautiful face light up with happiness. He dimly heard the grateful sobs of the Russian girl, but as Bree threw her arms around him, he felt only her. Saw only her.

"Thank you," she whispered. She drew back, tears sparkling in her eyes. "And thank you for that huge tip you gave her as an apology. I never expected that." A smile lifted Bree's trembling lips. "I'm starting to think you might have a heart, after all."

Huge tip? Looking down, Vladimir saw that his wallet was indeed open in his hand, and was now considerably lighter. The salesgirl was holding a wad of rubles, weeping with joy as she shared the unexpected largesse with the others.

"It was kind of you, to care for her."

His cheeks burned as he turned back to Bree. "I don't give a damn about her."

"But—"

He cut in. "I did it for you."

She took a deep breath.

"That's why I know you have a heart," she whispered.

And Vladimir knew she was right. Because in this moment, his heart was beating erratically, misfiring, racing.

Taking her hand in his own, he pulled her down from the pedestal. "I just want you to be happy," he said roughly. He didn't know how to manage this reckless, restless yearning he felt every time he looked into her beautiful face, every time he touched her. He looked down at her hand, nestled so trustingly in his. "I want to give you a gift."

"You already did."

"Tipping a salesgirl doesn't count."

She looked down at the exquisite blue ball gown. "You're buying me this dress."

"I want to do something for you," he growled. "Something you actually care about. Anything."

Her eyes went wide with dawning, desperate hope.

"Set me free," she choked out.

Let Bree go? He couldn't. *Wouldn't.* After ten years, he'd found her again. What were the chances of them walking into the same poker game in Hawaii? Surely fate had placed her there for a reason?

She'd brought sunlight and warmth into his life. But if he

let her go, she might leave. He couldn't take that risk. Not now. She meant too much.

Folding his arms, he scowled. "You lost fair and square."

"But this is what I want, more than anything—"

"*No,* Breanna." He set his jaw. "Something else."

Crushing disappointment filled her eyes. She looked down. "My birthday is in a few days. Let me fly back to the States and spend it with my sister. I'm worried about her...."

"Josie is fine. My men left her in Seattle, as she requested. She has money. She is fine."

"So why haven't I been able to reach her phone?" She swallowed. "I've always taken care of her...."

"She's a grown woman," he said, irritated. "And you coddle her like a child."

Her eyes flashed. "Coddle!"

"Yes, *coddle.* She will never grow up until you allow her to make her own choices, and live with the consequences!"

Bree stiffened. "Like you did, you mean—cheating your brother out of the company?"

He glared at her. "He chose to leave, rather than accept my leadership. It made him strong. Strong enough to be my rival!"

"Your enemy, you mean!"

Controlling himself, Vladimir exhaled. "Breanna, I don't want to fight."

She licked her lips, then shook her head. "I don't, either. But I have a reason to protect Josie. I told you, there are men who want to hurt us...."

With a harsh word and a clap of his hands, Vladimir scattered the salesgirls, leaving him alone with Bree in the dressing room. Coming closer, he put his hands on her shoulders and said in a low voice, "Those men won't be bothering you."

She blinked. "They won't?"

"My people tracked them down. One of the men was already dead, unfortunately." Vladimir gave a grim smile. "But the other two will never bother you or Josie again."

Her eyes were huge. "What did you do?" she whispered. "Tell me you didn't…break anything."

Vladimir narrowed his eyes. "I wanted to. But I respected your request. I paid them off. Also, my investigator gathered enough evidence to have them both thrown in prison for the rest of their lives. If they ever cross your path again, even accidentally, that information will go to the local police. And they will die in jail." He looked at her blank face, suddenly uncertain. "Is that satisfactory?"

"Satisfactory?" She took a deep breath, then with a sob, threw her arms around him. "Thank you," she whispered. "We're free!"

He looked down at her, wiping the tears off her cheek gently with his thumb. "I'll never let anyone hurt you or your sister, Breanna. Ever again."

Her lower lip wobbled. "Thank you."

Seeing her reaction, he wanted to do more. He heard himself say, "And I'll have my men look around Seattle. See if they can track Josie down."

"Okay," she sniffled.

"Do you have any idea where she might be?"

She shook her head. "We used to say that when we got back to the Mainland, if we had money, we'd start our own bed-and-breakfast, or a small hotel." Her cheeks flushed. "But the truth is, that's my dream, not hers. She wants to go to college."

"Don't worry. I'll find her." Pulling his phone out of his pocket, he turned away. He was stopped by Bree's small voice.

"People call you ruthless. But it's not true."

Slowly, he turned to face her.

Bree's hazel eyes were luminous, piercing his soul. "When we met, I thought you'd changed completely from the man I loved. But you're still the same, aren't you?" she whispered. "The other man—he's just the mask you wear."

Vladimir's forehead broke out in a cold sweat. He felt bare

beneath the spotlight. "You're wrong," he said roughly. "I *am* ruthless. Selfish, even cruel. Don't believe otherwise."

She shook her head. "You're afraid people will take advantage, so you hide your good heart—"

"Good heart?" He grabbed her shoulders, looking down at her fiercely. "I am selfish to the bone. I will never put someone else's interests ahead of my own. I cannot *love,* Bree. That ability is no longer in me. It died a long time ago."

"But—"

"Would a good man keep you prisoner against your will?"

She lifted her gaze. Her hazel eyes were suddenly troubled, opaque, full of shadows.

"No," she whispered.

No. That one word caused an unexpected wrench inside him. As the two of them stood in the huge private dressing room of the designer atelier, her expression became impassive—her poker face. He wondered what she was thinking. In this moment, when he felt so strangely vulnerable, his insight into her soul suddenly disappeared.

"I'm not a good man, Bree," he said in a low voice. To prove it further—to both of them—he lowered his mouth to hers, kissed her hard enough to bruise. She kissed him back with fierce passion, but he felt her withholding something he wanted. Something he needed.

Unzipping her blue ball gown, Vladimir kissed the bare skin of her neck. Her hair smelled like sunlight and passion fruit, like vanilla and the ocean, like endless summer.

Her strapless silk bodice fell, revealing her white bustier. They were surrounded by mirrors on three sides, and as he saw endless reflections of him touching her, he felt so hard he wanted to take her roughly, against the wall. So he did. As the dress fell to the hardwood floors, he unzipped his pants and lifted her, shoving her roughly against the mirrored wall. Barely pausing to sheath himself in a condom, he thrust inside her. Wrapping her legs around his hips tightly, she clutched his shoulders as he filled her, slamming her against the wall. Five thrusts and she was moaning. Ten thrusts and she clutched her fingertips into his shoulders as her body tightened, her back arching. Fifteen thrusts and she screamed with pleasure in cries that matched his own.

Afterwards, for an instant, panting and sweaty, he just held her, his eyes closed. Then slowly he released her legs, letting her body slide down his. The passion had been hotter than ever.

But he knew something had changed between them. An unbridgeable gap.

"Get dressed," he said. "We have dinner reservations."

"Fine," she said dully, not meeting his eyes.

He zipped up his pants, and she put on her new clothes, the slim-fitting black pants, sheer black top over a black camisole, and black leather motorcycle jacket he'd bought for her earlier at a department store on Nevsky Prospekt. All afternoon, he'd insisted on buying everything he saw in her size, anything she could possibly want to wear for the rest of her life, for any season and any event.

Compensating, he thought. Though he knew she couldn't be bought.

Even if he'd bought her.

"Before dinner," he said brightly, despising the false cheer in his voice, "I wish to buy you something truly special. A fur coat. White mink, perhaps, or Barguzin sable—"

Bree shook her head. "No, thanks."

"Russian furs are the best in the world."

Her eyes were cold. "I don't want a fur."

He set his jaw. "You're pouting."

"No." She looked away. "I just used to have a dog when I was a kid," she mumbled. "I loved that dog. We used to explore the forest all summer long. He had a soul. He was my friend."

She was talking about her dog? Vladimir exhaled. He'd been bracing for her anger, since the only thing she really wanted was the one thing he wouldn't, couldn't, give her. Relieved, he lifted his hand and lightly traced the bare skin of her collarbone. "I still don't understand the connection."

"I'll put it in simple terms." Pulling away from him, she folded her arms. "No fur."

"As you wish," he whispered, taking her hand in his own. He felt her shiver. He looked at her. Her expression was completely unreadable. He sighed. "Come."

Leaving the dressing room, he went out to meet with the salesgirl and finish the details of the order, arranging for the hand-stitched ball gown to be delivered the next day. Vladimir took Bree outside, where his bodyguard awaited them beside his bulletproof limo.

"Where are we going?"

"You'll see."

"I'm tired of shopping."

"You'll like this."

Twenty minutes later the limo pulled to a stop. Helping her out himself, Vladimir led her past two security guards into a tiny, high-ceilinged shop in the belle epoque style, with gilded walls and colors like a cloisonné Easter egg. Everything about the jewelry store bespoke elegance, taste and most of all money.

"What are we doing here?" Bree scowled. "I thought we had dinner reservations!"

He gave her a teasing smile. "This won't take long."

A short, plump man with wire-rimmed glasses and a short white beard, wearing an old-fashioned pin-striped suit with a vest, came eagerly from behind one of the glass cases. "Welcome, welcome, Your Highness," he said in Russian.

"Speak in English so she'll understand."

"Of course, Prince Vladimir." Tenting his hands, the jeweler turned to Bree and switched to accented English. "My lady. You are here for a necklace, yes? For the New Year's Eve ball at the ancient palace of the Romanov tsarina?"

Bree glanced up at Vladimir. "Um. Yes?"

He smiled back at her, feeling a warm glow at the thought

of spoiling her. "I wish to buy you a little something to wear with the ball gown."

"I don't need it."

"*Need* has nothing to do with it." He lifted a dark eyebrow. "Surely you won't deny me the small pleasure?"

Her scowl deepened. "No. How could I?"

He ignored her insinuation. "Surely," he said teasingly, "you will not tell me that diamonds remind you of a former pet? That they possibly have a *soul?*"

She looked down at the floor.

"No," she whispered. "A diamond is just a cold, heartless stone." Vladimir frowned. She suddenly seemed to recall she was speaking to the CEO of Xendzov Mining, one of the largest diamond producers in the world. Flashing him a wry smile, she amended, "But they are pretty. I'll give you that."

"So you'll let me buy you something."

"Don't you have a closetful of diamonds back home? I'm surprised you don't use them like rocks to decorate your garden."

"My company produces raw diamonds. We sell them wholesale. The fine art of polishing them into exquisite jewelry is not our specialty." He lifted his hands to indicate the little jewel box of a shop. "This is the best jewelry store in the world."

"Really? In the world?"

He gave her a sly smile. "Well, the best in St. Petersburg. Which means it is the best in Russia. Which means, naturally, that it is the best in the world."

Staring at him for a moment, she shook her head with a sigh. "All right." Her tone was resigned. "Since it seems I have no choice."

Vladimir had truly expected this to be a quick stop en route to dinner at the best restaurant in the city. He'd assumed Bree would quickly select one of the most expensive necklaces in the store: the looped rope of diamonds, the diadem of sapphires, the emerald choker that cost the equivalent of nine hundred thousand dollars. But an hour later, she still hadn't found a necklace she wanted.

"Six million rubles?" she said now, staring down incredulously at the ropes of diamonds patiently displayed by the portly jeweler. "How much is that in dollars?"

He told her, and her jaw dropped. Then she burst into laughter. "What a waste!" She glanced at Vladimir. "I won't let you spend your money that way. Might as well set it on fire."

He didn't have nearly the same patience as the jeweler. "Money isn't a problem," he said tightly. "I have more than I could spend in a lifetime."

"Lucky you."

"I mean it. After you make a certain amount, money is just a way to keep score."

"You could always donate the money to a charity, you know. If you hate it so much," she said tartly.

He gave a low laugh. "I didn't say I hate it. If nothing else, it gives me the opportunity to drape you in diamonds."

"Against my will."

"I know you will love them. All women do."

"*All* women?"

That hadn't come out right. "It's a gift, Bree. From me to you."

"It's a chain." She reached out a hand and touched the glittering diamond rope resting on the glass case, then said bitterly, "Diamond shackles for an honored slave." She looked up at the jeweler. "No offense."

"None taken, my lady."

She looked at Vladimir. "Thanks for wanting to buy me a gift. But I don't need a chain to remind me of my position."

Vladimir felt irritated. He'd wanted to buy something that would please her, to distract her from the one thing he would not give: her freedom. "I am trying to make you happy."

"I can't be bought!"

"You already were," he said coldly.

Bree gave an intake of breath, and her eyes dropped. "Fine. Buy it for me, then. Because you're right. You can do whatever you want."

Her voice dripped with icy, repressed fury.

This was turning into a disaster. Vladimir's intention in bringing her here had been to make her cry out in delight, clapping her hands as she threw her arms around him in joy. But it seemed no cries of joy would be forthcoming.

He forced his clenched hands to relax. "I think we're done." Turning away from the jewelry case empty-handed, leaving the disappointed jeweler behind them, Vladimir put his hand on her back. It was an olive branch, an attempt to salvage the evening. "Fine. No diamonds. But you will enjoy dinner."

"Yes," she said. "Since you are telling me to enjoy it, I must."

They were very late for their reservation. But when they finally arrived at the restaurant, adjacent to an exclusive hotel on the Nevsky Prospekt, he had the satisfaction of seeing Bree's mouth fall open.

Art-nouveau-style stained glass gleamed in a wall of windows. Shadowy balconies and discreet curtained booths overlooked the center parquet floor, filled with tables covered with crisp white linen. White lights edged the second-floor balustrade, and tapering candles graced the tables with flickering light as uniformed waiters glided among the planted palm trees, serving rich, powerful guests.

The maître d' immediately recognized Vladimir. "Your Highness!" Clapping his hands, he bowed with a flourish and escorted them to the best table.

"Everyone is looking at us," Bree muttered as they walked across the gleaming parquet.

Relieved she was finally talking to him again, Vladimir reached over to take her hand in his. "They're looking at you."

As they were seated, Bree's cheeks were pink, her eyes glowing in the flickering light of the candles and warmth of the high-ceilinged restaurant. Soaring above them on the ceiling were nineteenth-century frescoes, country scenes of the aristocracy at play.

When the waiter came, Vladimir ordered a short glass of vodka, then turned to Bree. "What would you like to drink?"

She tilted her head. "The same."

"It's vodka."

"I'm not scared."

"Are you sure?" He lifted a dark eyebrow. "You don't strike me as much of a drinker."

She shrugged. "I can handle myself."

Her bravado was provocative. He looked at her beautiful, impassive face, at the way her dark eyelashes brushed her pale skin, at the way her stubborn chin lifted from her long, graceful neck. He wondered what she would say if she knew what he was thinking.

"Your Highness?" the waiter said in Russian.

Vladimir turned back to him and gave the order. After the man left, Bree said abruptly, "Where did you learn Russian? It wasn't at school."

"How do you know?"

"I don't," she admitted. "But I know you and your brother grew up on the same land that now belongs to Josie—or will, in three years." She tilted her head. "It's funny we never met. Both of us growing up in the same state."

"That land was in our family for four generations. A thousand miles from anything. You know." He drummed his fingertips on the table, looking for the waiter with the vodka. "So we kept to ourselves. My father spoke Russian with us. He was proud of our history. He homeschooled us. In the long winters, we read Pushkin, Tolstoy." Vladimir's lips twisted. "It was my mother who made sure our home had food and wood. The land is our legacy. In our blood."

"Why did your mother sell it to my father?"

His body tightened. "I was desperate for money to start

our business. Kasimir absolutely refused to sell. He'd made some deathbed promise to our father. But I knew this was the only way."

"You had nothing else to sell? You couldn't take a loan?"

"Mining equipment is expensive. There is no guarantee of success. Banks offered to loan us a pitiful amount—not nearly enough to have the outfit I wanted. We'd already sold the last item of value our family possessed—a necklace that belonged to my great-grandmother—to help fund college in St. Petersburg. *Spasiba,*" he said to the waiter, who'd just placed their drinks on the table. Reaching for his vodka, he continued, "So I talked to my mother. Alone. And convinced her to sell."

"Behind your brother's back?" Bree's eyes widened. "No wonder he hates you."

Knocking back his head, Vladimir took a deep drink and felt the welcoming burn down his throat. "I knew what I was doing."

"Really." Bree's cheeks were pink, but her troubled gaze danced in the flickering candlelight. "Do you know what you're doing now?"

"Now?" He set his glass back on the table with a clunk. "I am trying to make you happy."

Her eyes were impassive. "Without letting me go."

Reaching across the table, he took her hand in his larger one. "I have no intention of letting you go. Ever."

"Why?" She swallowed, then glanced right and left at all the well-dressed people around them. "You could have any woman you want. Even the gorgeous secretaries at your office…"

"But I want only the best." His hand tightened over hers. "And the best is you."

She stared at him, then shook her head. "I can see how you twist women's hearts around your little finger."

"There's only one woman I want." He looked at her beautiful, stricken face over the flickering candle. "I've never forgotten you, Breanna. Or stopped wanting you."

He felt her hand tremble before she wrenched it from his grasp. She reached wildly for her untouched glass of vodka and, tilting back her head, drank the whole thing down in a single gulp.

That gulp ended with a coughing fit. Reaching around her, he patted her on the back. Her face was red when she finally managed a deep breath, wheezing as she quipped, "See? I know how to handle vodka. No problem."

Somewhat relieved by her deliberate change of subject, Vladimir laughed, his eyes lingering on her beautiful face. He'd said too much. And yet it was oddly exhilarating. The adrenaline rush of emotional honesty put skydiving to shame, he thought. About time he tried it.

The waiter returned to take their order, and Vladimir requested a dinner that included Astrakhan beluga caviar and oysters, vodka-marinated salmon and black risotto, steak in a cream sauce and a selection of salads, breads and cheeses. Bree shook her head in disbelief when the exotic food started arriving at the table, but ninety minutes later, as she gracefully dropped the linen napkin across her mostly empty plate, she was sighing with satisfied pleasure.

"You," she proclaimed, "are a genius."

He gave her a crooked grin, ridiculously pleased by her praise. "I've come here a few times, so I knew what to order."

"That was perfect." She rose to her feet. "If you'll excuse me."

"Of course." Vladimir watched her disappear down the hall toward the ladies' room, and realized he was sitting alone at the best table in the most famous restaurant in St. Petersburg, grinning to himself like a fool. Feeling sheepish, he looked around him.

His gaze fell on a face he recognized, of a man sitting alone in a booth on the other side of the restaurant. This particular man in this particular place was so unexpected that it took him thirty seconds to even place him, though they'd spent many hours across the same poker table over the past two months. The Hale Ka'nani hotel manager, Greg Hudson. What was he doing in St. Petersburg?

Perhaps the man was on vacation. In Russia. In winter. Telling himself he didn't care, Vladimir turned his chair away, so the man was out of his sight.

Today was the best day Vladimir had had in a long time. Even though leaving subordinates to handle the merger so he could spend time with his mistress was reckless, irresponsible, foolish. Even though he'd likely lose a fortune retaining all the employees of Arctic Oil. Even so.

Instead of feeling guilty, he kept smiling to himself as he recalled how Bree's eyes sparkled when she was angry at him. The way her body had felt, pressed against his in the mirrored dressing room of the boutique. She was fire and ice. She was life itself.

"Hawaii has changed you completely." His doctor had been shocked by the test results that morning, when Vladimir stopped on the way to the office. "You've recuperated from your injury better than I ever dreamed. Even your blood pressure is improved. What have you been doing? Yoga? Eating bean sprouts? Whatever it is, clean living is making you healthy. Keep it up!"

With a laugh, Vladimir glanced down at his empty vodka glass and half-eaten plate of beef rib eye drenched in sauce. Clean living? No. *Good* living. It wasn't yoga and bean sprouts. It was laughter, good company and lots of sex.

It was Breanna.

Vladimir shifted impatiently in his chair, craning his head to look past the waiters and candlelit tables toward the wood-paneled hallway. His lips rose in unconscious pleasure when he saw Bree coming back down the hall.

Then a dark figure came out of the shadows to accost her. Seeing Greg Hudson, Vladimir rose to his feet. Bree looked surprised, then angry, as the man spoke to her. Vladimir clenched his jaw as he strode rapidly toward them. Hudson's eyes went wide when he saw him coming. Turning, he ran out of the restaurant.

"What did he say to you?" Vladimir demanded.

Bree turned with a carefully blank look on her face. Her poker face, he thought, but he could see her lips trembling. Her gaze dropped. "Nothing."

"Tell me."

"He…" She licked her lips. "He told me he's in St. Petersburg to collect a debt, and happened to see me." Her eyes carefully remained on the gleaming parquet floor. "He said he's going to be very rich in a few days, and he would pay a lot of money to be my next lover. He wondered if there was some kind of waiting list."

Anger made Vladimir's vision red. He started to turn, his hands clenched. "I will kill him."

"No. Please," Bree whispered. She put her hand on his arm. "Just take me home."

People in the restaurant were staring at them, whispering behind their hands. "But we already ordered dessert," he said tightly. "Chocolate cake. Your favorite."

"I just want to go." Her cheeks were red. "And forget this day ever happened."

Forget this day ever happened? The wonderful day he'd spent with her—the hours he'd spent watching her laugh, telling her the truth, buying her things, trying so hard to please her—as he'd never tried to please any woman? "I don't want to forget."

She looked away. "I do."

Shoulders stiff, Vladimir went across the restaurant and tossed thirty thousand rubles on their table. Getting her leather coat, he wrapped it around her shivering shoulders and led her out into the cold, dark night. As his chauffeur drove their limousine home, Vladimir looked out at the snowy streets of

St. Petersburg. It had been the best day of his life, but it had ended with Bree in tears.

He wanted to blame the fat little hotel manager. But he knew there was one person at fault for the way she'd been so crudely insulted as a woman who could be bought and sold at any man's will.

Vladimir himself.

CHAPTER EIGHT

THE next night, Bree paused as she got ready for the New Year's Eve ball. She looked wanly out the tall curved window of their bedroom.

The wintry Gulf of Finland on the Baltic Sea looked nothing like Hawaii's warm turquoise waters. It was even worse than Alaska's frigid sea. Even in the weak, short hours of daylight, the Russian waves were choppy and gray. But the sun had set long ago, and the world was dark. The black, icy water here could suck the life out of you within seconds if you were dumb enough to fall into it.

Kind of like falling in love with a man who would neither love you back nor set you free.

Bree closed her eyes. Yesterday, the workaholic tyrant had been neither workaholic nor a tyrant, playing hooky from work to entertain her. Letting people keep their jobs in his merger. Tipping that saleswoman at the boutique. Getting rid of the men who'd threatened Bree and her little sister. And more.

I've never forgotten you, Breanna. She would never forget the stark vulnerability in his blue eyes. *Or stopped wanting you.*

Bree trembled with emotion, remembering. Thank heaven she'd been able to cover her reaction by gulping that nasty-tasting vodka. She should probably be grateful for Greg Hudson, too. His words had brought her back to reality with a snap.

Bleakly, she opened her eyes. She was alone in their bedroom, with one leg propped up on the bed, pulling on sheer black stockings as she got ready for the New Year's Eve ball. Her beautiful haute-couture princess gown was on the bed, waiting to go over her new black lace bra, panties and garter belt. Vladimir had bought out every expensive store in the city. "I am trying to make you happy," he'd said. But she couldn't be bought that way. Only two things could make her happy, and they were the very things he would not or could not give her. Freedom. Love.

I am selfish to the bone. I will never put someone else's interests ahead of my own.

She couldn't let herself fall for him. She'd loved him once, and it had nearly killed her. She'd lost everything.

Never again. Unless they were equals, loving him was only a different kind of bondage. Especially since, in the eyes of the world, Bree was nothing more than his whore.

Hadn't meeting with her ex-boss proved that?

"Well, well, what a pleasant surprise," Greg Hudson had drawled, stepping into her path in the hallway last night. "If it isn't the poker-playing maid herself."

She'd been shocked to see her former boss's beady eyes and sweaty face. Instead of a tropical shirt, he was dressed in the required jacket and tie, probably borrowed from the restaurant, since they didn't fit his lumpy body.

"Mr. H-Hudson," she'd stammered. "What are you doing in St. Petersburg?"

"Call me Greg." He came closer, crowding her space in the darkened hallway. "I'm here to collect a big debt. Thought I'd celebrate at the best restaurant in town."

"You left the Hale Ka'nani?"

His expression darkened. "I got fired. The hotel's owner found out I took a bribe." He tilted his head, his eyes sly. "Didn't you ever wonder why I hired you and that sister of yours?"

Bree sucked in her breath as all her old worries came back. "Someone bribed you to hire us? Who?"

Leaning forward, he wheezed, "Even he didn't think I'd be as successful as I was. In a few days, I'll be paid, and given a huge bonus. I'll be rich enough to pay you directly, for services rendered. I want to be on your waiting list. Name your price." He'd stroked her upper arm, and she'd caught the scent of whiskey, heavy and sour, on his breath before he saw Vladimir and turned away. "Come to me when Xendzov is done with you."

Bree's face burned as she remembered the humiliation of that moment. She'd been completely unprepared for it. And even more unprepared for the suspicion that had slithered into her soul ever since.

Who would have paid Greg Hudson to hire the Dalton sisters at the Honolulu resort?

All night Bree had stared up at the bedroom ceiling in the dark gray light, going through countless scenarios in her mind. It could have been one of her father's old enemies. Or…it could have been Vladimir himself. To make her his prisoner forever, to enjoy at his will.

I've never forgotten you, Breanna. Or stopped wanting you.

She sighed. But that didn't make sense, either. He'd been surprised to see her. She'd seen it in his face, in his body. He'd had no idea she was in Hawaii.

So who?

Vladimir had been an extraordinarily tender lover last night, but even as he'd made her body shake and gasp with pleasure, her soul had been haunted by the question. Finally, at breakfast that morning, before he'd left for work, he'd stated, "I'm sorry you were insulted last night. It will never happen again."

"Thank you," she'd murmured, though they both knew it was a lie. There was no way he could prevent that. If she wasn't insulted to her face, she'd still be able to see it in people's eyes.

She was his possession. Nothing more, nothing less.

Now, staring out at the dark, wintry night, Bree felt an ache in her throat. She finished pulling on her stockings, attaching them to her garter belt. If only she had someone to talk to about this. If only she could talk to Josie...

Vladimir's voice was husky behind her. "Are you ready?"

With an intake of breath, Bree turned to face him. He stood in the doorway, half in silhouette. He looked broad-shouldered and impossibly handsome in a dark, exquisitely cut tuxedo. She tried not to notice. "Have you found Josie?"

"Josie?" he repeated absently. He came toward her, his blue eyes gleaming as they traced slowly down her nearly naked body in the black lace. "Forget the ball. Let's stay home for New Year's Eve."

She felt his gaze against her skin the same as if he'd stroked her with his fingers. Her breath caught in her throat, and she trembled with desire and something more—something that went straight to her heart. She wrapped her arms around herself. "My sister. Have you found her yet?"

He blinked, then his eyes lifted to hers. "Not yet. My investigator did trace her back to Hawaii."

"Hawaii!" Something was wrong. Bree could feel it. "Why would she go back?"

He shrugged. "Perhaps she forgot something at your old apartment."

"Spending every penny she owns, just to go back for some old sweater or something?"

Vladimir pressed his lips together. Bree saw him hesitate, then reluctantly say, "Apparently she was trying to get the police to take an interest in your case. But they laughed at her, both in Seattle and Honolulu." He looked at Bree sideways. "They thought our wager sounded like a lovers' game between consenting adults."

"Right." She had a sick feeling in the pit of her stomach. "So where is she now?"

He shook his head. "The trail went cold."

Josie was missing? Bree opened her mouth, then stopped.

Telling him her fears would do no good. She feared it would only set off another tirade from him about how Josie was a grown woman and that Bree should allow her sister to face her own consequences.

And for all she knew, he was right. For ten years, her fears had been on overdrive where Josie was concerned. How was Bree supposed to know when it was rational to worry and when it was not?

"We'll find her." Vladimir was watching her. "Don't worry."

"I'm not," she lied.

"Good." Reaching into his pocket, he held out a flat, black velvet box. "This is for you."

She flinched when she saw the jewelry box. He'd known she hated the diamond necklace, but *he'd bought it anyway.* The chain of her captivity.

"You went back and bought it," she said dully.

He glanced at the blue silk ball gown draped across their bed. "It goes with your dress."

Ice filled her heart, rushing through her like a frozen sea. In spite of all appearances to the contrary yesterday, he didn't care about her feelings. He wanted to dress her to appear well. Like a show dog on display. "You are too kind."

A smile curved his sensual mouth, as if he knew exactly what she was thinking. "Open it."

"You."

"Don't you want to see it?"

"No." Closing her eyes, she lifted her hair. "Just do it," she choked out.

Bree heard the box snap open. She felt the warmth of his body as he moved to stand behind her. She felt a heavy weight against the bare skin beneath her collarbone. It was surprisingly heavy. Frowning, she opened her eyes.

A simple gold chain hung around her neck, with an enormous green pendant wrapped in gold wire. Shocked, she touched the olive-green jewel, the size of a robin's egg. "What's this?"

"It's a peridot," he said quietly. "Carved from a meteorite that fell to Siberia in 1749. It once belonged to my great-grandmother."

Bree's mouth fell open. "Your—"

"The pendant was a wedding gift from my great-grandfather, before he sent her and their baby son into exile. To Alaska."

Bree felt the roughness of the peridot beneath her fingertips. The sharp crystalline edges had been worn smooth by time.

"We sold this necklace to a collector, to help pay for college." He ran a finger along the chain. "It took me years, and a large fortune, to get it back." He put his hand over the stone, near her heart, and lifted his gaze. "And now it is yours."

Bree gasped. Feeling the weight of the necklace and the warmth of his hand, she looked down at the stone. In the shadowy bedroom, the facets flashed fire, green like the heart's blood of a dragon. "I…I can't possibly keep this."

"Too late." Vladimir's handsome face was expressionless.

"But it's too valuable." She swallowed as her fingers stroked the gold chain against her skin. Their hands touched, and she breathed, "Not just the worth of the stone, but the value to your family…"

Drawing back, he said harshly, "It is yours." He turned away. "Finish getting ready. I will wait for you downstairs."

She suddenly felt like crying. "Wait!"

He stopped, his back stiff, his hands clenched into fists.

"This should belong to someone you care about," she whispered. "Someone…someone special."

He didn't turn around.

"You are special to me, Breanna," he said in a low voice. "You always have been."

She couldn't just let him leave. Not when he'd proven to her, once and for all, that she was more than a paid concubine. As he headed for the door, she rushed across the room, catching him from behind. Wrapping her arms around his body, she pressed her cheek against his back. "Thank you."

Slowly he turned around in her arms.

"I need you to know. You are more than just my possession." His darkly handsome face was stark. Vulnerable. "You are…"

"What?" Her throat ached.

"My lover."

Unable to speak, she nodded.

Wiping her cheek with his thumb, he said in a low voice, "Come. Get dressed. We don't want to be late." He gave her a crooked smile. "I don't want to miss kissing you at midnight."

Seeing that boyish, vulnerable smile, her heart twisted. "No. We don't want to miss that."

He picked up her silk ball gown from the bed, and she stepped into it. As he pulled it up around her, she felt his fingers brush against her spine. She looked back at him with an intake of breath. His gaze was hungry, his eyes dark as the midnight sea. She should expect more than just a kiss to celebrate the New Year.

She wasn't his girlfriend. She wasn't his wife. But perhaps…

Her fingertips ran softly over the necklace that had once belonged to a Russian princess, and a green stone that two hundred and fifty years ago had landed in Siberia from the farthest reaches of space. Perhaps he did care for her, after all.

Could that caring ever turn to something more? To love?

I cannot love. She heard the echo of his hard voice. *That ability is no longer in me. It died a long time ago.*

As Vladimir finished zipping up the ball gown, he turned her to face him. Brushing tendrils of hair from her face, he looked down at her with electric blue eyes. "Are you ready?"

Looking up at his handsome face, Bree tried not to feel anything. But her heart slammed against her ribs.

His forehead furrowed. "Bree?"

She turned away with a lump in her throat. "I, um, need some lipstick." Going to the mirror, she made her lips bright

Chanel red. Lifting the silk hem of her gown, she stepped into her expensive shoes with sparkling crystals decorating the four-inch heels, and took a deep breath. "Ready."

Downstairs in the foyer, Vladimir took a sharply tailored black coat from the closet, wearing it over his tuxedo. Then he removed a black hanging bag from the closet. He unzipped it. In dismay, Bree saw white fur.

He noted her expression. "Don't worry. It's fake."

Dubiously, she reached out and stroked the soft white fur. "It seems real."

"Well." His lips curved in amusement. "It's *very* expensive. Twice the price of the real thing." Lifting the white fur coat from the bag, he wrapped it around her bare shoulders. "I can't have you getting cold, *angel moy,*" he said softly.

"What does that mean?"

"My angel."

She bit her lip, faltering. "I'm nobody's angel."

He smiled. Pulling her close by the lapels of the white faux fur, he looked down at her. His blue eyes crinkled. "Wrong."

Bree's heart squeezed so hard and tight she couldn't breathe. Still smiling, he held out his arm and led her outside into the cold, frosty night.

The limousine whisked them to a small town on the edge of St. Petersburg, to a palace that had once belonged to a Romanov tsarina three hundred years before. Bree's eyes widened as the road curved and she got her first view of it. With a gasp, she rolled down the window for a better look.

Beneath the frosted winter moon, she saw the palace that had once been a summer getaway for the Russian royal family. The elegant structure, wide and sprawling, looked like a wedding cake, decked with snow. The limo drove up the avenue, past a wide white lawn lit up by flickering torches.

The limo stopped, and a valet in breeches and an eighteenth-century wig opened Bree's door and helped her out. Feeling the shock of cold, bracing air on her face, she looked around in awe. She touched the green peridot against her skin, beneath her white fur. Standing in this courtyard, she could almost imagine herself as the princess of an ancient, magical land of eternal winter.

She could almost imagine she was a Russian prince's bride.

His bride. As Vladimir took her hand in his own, smiling at her with so much warmth she barely even needed a coat, she could not stop herself from wondering, just for an instant, what it would be like to be his wife. To be the woman he loved, the mother of his children.

"Are you still cold?" he murmured as they passed the bowing doormen.

She shook her head.

"But you're shivering."

"I'm just happy," she whispered.

Stopping inside the palace doors, he pulled her into his arms. Kissing the top of her hair, he looked down at her with a smile.

"At last," he said softly. "I have what I wanted."

Searching his gaze, Bree sucked in her breath. That smile. She couldn't look away. It was so open. So…young. He looked exactly like the young man she'd first fallen in love with, so long ago.

The man she'd never stopped loving.

As he took her hand to lead her down the elegant hallway, Bree nearly stumbled in her sparkling high-heeled shoes.

She was in love with him.

She could no longer deny it, even to herself.

Vladimir took her into the ballroom, and Bree barely noticed the exquisite, lavishly decorated space, the gilded walls or the crystal chandeliers high above. She barely spoke when he introduced her to acquaintances. As he led her out onto the dance floor, she didn't see all the gorgeous people all around them.

She saw only him. She felt only his arms around her, and the rapid thrum of her own heart.

She loved him. It was foolish. It was wrong. But she could no more stop herself than she could stop breathing. She loved him.

For hours, they danced together. They drank champagne. They ate. They danced some more. For Bree, it all flashed by in a moment. In his arms, she lived a lifetime in every precious minute. The regular laws of time were suspended. Hours sped by in seconds.

Suddenly, as they were dancing, the music stopped. Lifting her cheek from his chest in surprise, Bree saw it was nearly midnight.

Vladimir looked down at her as they stood unmoving on the dance floor, and as the last seconds of the year counted down, for Bree it was as if time not only became suspended, but was reversed. His gaze locked with hers, and ten years disappeared.

She was eighteen and he was twenty-five. They were in each other's arms. The world was new. Brand-new.

He cupped her face. "Breanna…"

Cheers went up around them in the ballroom as she heard the last seconds of the year counted down in a jumble of languages, German, French, Chinese, Spanish, English, and Russian loudest of all.

"Pyat…"

"Cheteeri…"

"Tree…"

Lowering his head, Vladimir said huskily, "Let's start the New Year right…"

"Dva…"

"Ahdeen…"

His lips pressed against hers, smooth and rough, hard and sweet. He kissed her, and fire flashed not just through her body, but her soul.

"S'novem godem!" Raucous cheers and the sound of horns and singing revels exploded across the ballroom. "Happy New Year!"

When Vladimir finally pulled away from their embrace,

Bree stared up at him, her heart in her throat. She swayed, nearly falling over without his arms around her.

"S'novem godem," he murmured, cupping her cheek tenderly. "Happy New Year, *angel moy.*"

She looked up at him.

"I love you," she choked out.

He stared at her, his eyes wide.

All around them, people were dancing to the music of the orchestra, laughing, drinking champagne, kissing each other. But Vladimir was completely still.

Tears filled Bree's eyes as she gave him a trembling smile. "Even when I hated you, I loved you," she whispered. "When I made the wager in Hawaii to be yours forever, part of me must have been willing to lose that bet, or I never would have made it." She licked her lips. "You have always been the only man for me. Always."

He did not answer. His face was pale, his blue eyes as frozen as a glacier.

A chill of fear sneaked into her soul.

"And what I need to know is…" She bit her lip, then lifted her gaze to his. "Can you ever love me?"

Vladimir's eyes suddenly narrowed. He cleared his throat.

"Excuse me," he said shortly. He walked past her, leaving her alone on the dance floor.

Mouth agape, Bree turned and stared after him in amazement. Her cheeks went hot as she noticed exquisitely dressed Russians and other wealthy, beautiful people staring at her with open curiosity. Embarrassed, she walked off the dance floor.

She'd never felt so alone. Or so stupid.

She lifted her hand to the necklace, to the heavy weight of the peridot against her bare skin.

He cares for me, she repeated to herself silently. *He cares.*

But even that beautiful jewel seemed small consolation, considering that she'd just confessed her love for him, and he'd left her without a word.

Maybe he was called away on urgent business. At midnight. On New Year's Eve. She clawed back tendrils of her long blond hair. Why had she told him she loved him, and worse, asked if he could ever love her back? She knew he couldn't! He'd told her that straight-out, from the start!

Oh, God. She covered her face with her hands. She was an idiot.

Maybe when he came back, she could give a hearty laugh, as if it had all been a joke. She could tell him she'd been pretending to have Stockholm syndrome or something. She could be persuasive with her lies, as she'd been long ago. She could turn off her soul and disconnect from her heart. She knew how.

But…

She pulled her hand away. *She didn't want to.* She was tired of bluffing. She didn't want to be that con artist anymore. Ever again.

And sometimes telling the truth, showing her cards, would mean she lost the game.

She gave a ragged laugh. She'd never expected the cost to be this high. Snatching a flute of champagne from a passing waiter, she tried to sip it nonchalantly, as if it was quite enjoyable to be standing on the edge of the dance floor in a blue Cinderella gown, alone in a crowd of strangers. But as minutes passed, she suddenly wondered if Vladimir was even coming back. For all she knew, he'd already jumped into the limo and was heading for the airport.

Why not? He'd abandoned her before. Without a single word.

She squeezed her eyes shut. *Please don't leave.*

A prickle went up her spine as she felt someone come up behind her. Vladimir, at last! In a rush of relief, she turned.

But it wasn't Vladimir. A different man stood before her, slightly younger, slightly thinner, but with the same hard blue eyes—only filled with cold, malevolent ruthlessness.

"Kasimir?" Bree whispered. "Kasimir Xendzov?"

"Having a good time?" he replied coldly. Before she could

answer, he grabbed her arm and pulled her away from the crowd, into a private alcove. She stared at him. She'd met him only once before, in Alaska, the Christmas night he'd burst in upon them, desperate to tell his brother the truth about Bree's con. He'd been twenty-three then, barely more than a boy. Now...

Bree shivered. Now he was a man—the type of man you would never want to meet in a dark alley. She yanked her arm away from his grasp. "What do you want? If you've come to find your brother—"

"I haven't come to see my brother." Kasimir gave her a cold smile. "I came for you."

"Me?" she breathed.

"It's about...your sister."

"Josie?" An icy chill went down her spine. "What about her?"

He came closer, invading her personal space. She instinctively backed away. He straightened, and his eyes glittered. "I've married her."

"What?" Bree gasped.

He gave her a cold, ruthless smile. "Your little sister has become my dear, dear wife."

"I don't believe you!"

For answer, he pulled something from his pocket and held it out to her on his palm. Josie's cell phone. Bree snatched it up. There could be no doubt. She saw the colorful rhinestones that her sister had glued to the back in the shape of a rainbow.

"I asked her to marry me some time ago," Kasimir said, "and she refused. Until you disappeared. Then she came back. She offered to do anything, *anything,* if I would only save you from my evil brother. Marriage was my price."

"But why would you want to marry her?" Then suddenly Bree knew, and her heart dropped to the floor. "The trust," she said dully. "You want her land."

"It's not *hers,*" he said tightly. "It's been in my family for a hundred years. It never should have been sold. We've fought for it, died for it—" Catching himself, he relaxed his clenched hands. "So. The land will be mine in three days, when the banks reopen. After that, I can either divorce her quickly with a nice settlement, or…"

"Or?"

His eyes met hers coldly. "Or I can seduce her, make her fall in love with me and destroy her pitiful little heart. I can force her to be my wife forever, and you will never see her again. It is your choice."

Bree flinched, even as her heart pounded with fear. "How do I know this isn't all some lie? It might just be some sick joke, some game in the battle between you and your brother—"

Taking the cell phone away from her, he dialed a number, then pressed the phone back against Bree's ear. She heard her little sister's voice.

"Hello?"

Bree gripped the phone. "Josie," she gasped. "Where are you?"

"I'm so sorry, Bree," her sister whispered. "The poker game was all my fault. I was trying to save you. That's why I married him…."

"But where are you?" Bree cried.

Kasimir yanked the phone away. As he disconnected the call, Bree went for him, her hands outstretched. He pushed her away easily, tucking the phone in his tuxedo jacket pocket.

"Tell me where she is," she cried. "Or—or I'll kill you!"

"You're scaring me," he drawled.

"Then…" Bree had already threatened to kill him. What could be more frightening than that? She lifted her chin furiously. "I'll tell Vladimir!"

Kasimir's expression was cold. "Go. Tell him."

She was flabbergasted at his casual tone. "But he will destroy you!"

"He's tried to destroy me for years," he said scornfully, "and

I only grow stronger." He moved closer. "And you are wrong, Miss Dalton," he said softly, "if you think his desire for you will make him sacrifice anything for you or your family. He cares for you because you please him in bed, and he values that pleasure. But given the choice between helping you or himself, he will not hesitate."

Was Kasimir right? She licked her lips, barely hearing the music from the nearby ballroom. With a deep breath, she lifted her hand to her necklace. She felt its rough weight around her throat.

"Vladimir cares for me," she whispered.

"Because he gave you my great-grandmother's necklace?" His brother lifted a dark eyebrow. "He sold that once, you know. And he will sell you, if it ever gives him any advantage."

"You're wrong."

"Try him and see," Kasimir suggested silkily. "Go to him. Explain how Josie agreed to marry me and give me every acre of the land. He will say her predicament is her own fault, for being foolish enough to seek me as her ally. Vladimir is not a man who excuses mistakes. He punishes them." His brother narrowed his eyes. "He will not lift a finger to save her."

Bree trembled in her blue silk ball gown. Was it true?

Vladimir had cut Kasimir out of his life completely, cheating him out of hundreds of millions of dollars, just because of a few angry, drunken words to a reporter. He'd forced Bree to live as his mistress even when she'd begged him for her freedom—all because of a one-card wager. "You made the bet," he'd said. "Now you will honor it." Thinking of how he'd just abandoned her on the dance floor when she'd told him something he apparently didn't want to hear—that she loved him—Bree's heart lifted to her throat.

Would he treat Josie any more mercifully?

"She will never grow up," she remembered his hard voice saying. "She will always be helpless and weak, unless you allow her to face the consequences of her own actions."

"What do you want me to do?" she whispered.

Kasimir's eyes glittered. "You will help take back what should have been mine." Pulling an envelope from his pocket, he handed it to her. "Make him sign this."

"What is it?"

"A deed that transfers control of his company to me."

Bree stared down at the paper. "I hereby renounce all shares in Xendzov Mining OAO," it read, "giving them freely and in perpetuity to my brother...."

She looked up, openmouthed. "He will never sign it."

"You are a clever girl, with a flair for trickery and deceit." Kasimir tilted his head. "For your sister's sake, you will make him sign. Even if it causes you a small twinge of grief." He walked slowly around her. "Your lies caused *me* a great deal of grief ten years ago. I am glad to finally see you and my brother suffer—together. I could not have it planned better."

Bree's heart gave a sickening thud.

"It was you," she breathed. "You're the one who arranged for us to be taken to Hawaii. You're the one who bribed Greg Hudson to hire us."

Kasimir smiled. "My brother was stuck there, bored out of his mind, attending the same poker game each week. I knew he had a weakness for you. I hoped seeing you would cause him pain." Kasimir snorted. "Instead, you created an opportunity for justice I never could have imagined. You insinuated yourself into his life. Like a disease."

"Even if his signature is obtained through trickery," she said desperately, "it will never stand up in court."

"Then you have nothing to worry about, do you?" he said coolly. "Bring the signed document to my house in Marrakech within three days."

"And if I fail?"

He looked straight into her eyes, like an enemy looking over the barrel of a gun. "Then you'll never see your sister again. She'll disappear into the Sahara. And be mine. Forever."

Bree shook her head with a weak laugh. "You're joking."

"I am a madman. Ask my brother. He knows." Kasimir looked at her blue silk ball gown. "Your sister was frantic about you. She came to me, begging for help. She was willing to do anything to save you, even sacrifice her own soul." His lips twisted into a sneer. "And for the last two hours I've watched you, drinking champagne, dancing in his arms, giggling like a whore." She flinched as he growled, "So much for Josie's *sacrifice*."

Bree sucked in her breath, lifting her gaze. "You like her, don't you?" she said slowly. "I can see it in your eyes. I can hear it in your voice. You don't want to hurt her."

Kasimir glared at her, gritting his teeth. "What I *want* is revenge. And I will have it." Turning away, he said over his shoulder coldly, "You have three days."

CHAPTER NINE

WITH a low curse, Vladimir shoved the short fat man out of the palace, into the dark, deserted garden.

"What the hell are you doing in St. Petersburg?" he demanded.

"I'm allowed to visit here, if I want. You don't own this city, Xendzov," Greg Hudson brayed in response, shivering in his badly fitting tuxedo. "It doesn't *belong* to you!"

"Wrong," Vladimir replied coldly, shoving him again. Moments before, in the middle of Bree's innocent, tearful declaration, he'd seen Greg Hudson skulking near the buffet table. Vladimir had been overwhelmed by Bree's three simple words. He hadn't known how to react to them.

Seeing Greg Hudson, he'd known exactly what to do.

Fury had filled him at the sight of the man who'd insulted her, offering money to be *on her list*. He'd dragged him out of the ballroom, wanting to knock him to the ground and kick him repeatedly in his soft belly until he learned to respect women. Especially Vladimir's woman. "You will leave this city and never come back."

Hudson quivered like a rabbit. "Think you're something big, do you, Mr. Hoity-Toity Prince? You have no idea how you've been played!"

Ignoring him, Vladimir lifted his fist. "Were you following her?"

The man flinched. "No! I swear! I just happened to be in

town—" he looked up slyly "—to see your brother. The other prince."

Vladimir slowly lowered his fist. "You know Kasimir?"

"He owes me money."

"For what?"

The man looked smug.

Grabbing him with one hand, Vladimir lifted his other fist and thundered, "For what?"

"He offered me a lot of money to hire those Dalton girls. And a bonus if I could arrange for you to meet the older one. By accident."

Vladimir's body turned hot, then cold. His hand tightened on the man's lapel.

"If you ever disrespect Miss Dalton again," he said evenly, "if you so much as mention her name or look at her picture in the newspaper, you will regret it for the rest of your short life." He gave him a hard stare. "Do we understand each other?"

"Y-yes," the man stammered. "I never meant any harm."

Vladimir let him go, and Hudson fell back into the snow. Leaping up again with a gasp, he fled into the night, slipping on ice in his haste, leaping over a snowdrift as he called wildly for his driver.

Relaxing his clenched fists, Vladimir exhaled.

Slowly, he turned back toward the palace. But he felt numb, as frozen as if he'd fallen asleep in the white snow. He looked out at the fields in the moonlight. So soft. So beautiful. So mysterious.

So treacherous.

Breanna's beautiful face appeared in his mind. Was it possible…could it be that meeting her had been more than a coincidence? That it had been a plan cooked up by Bree and Kasimir, to finally get their revenge for his treatment of them ten years ago?

Was he a gullible fool falling for the same woman's lies—twice?

If Kasimir hired Hudson, Vladimir told himself harshly, *Bree didn't know.*

Or did she? Against his will, a gray shadow of suspicion filled his soul.

As he entered the ballroom and walked through the crowds, his feet dragged. He had no idea what to do. What to say to her.

"I love you," Bree had said. His heart beat with the rhythm of her words. "And what I need to know is, can you ever love me?"

How could she love him? Bree was too smart for that. He'd warned her that he would never love her. Told her it was impossible. He wanted to make her happy, yes. He'd bought her clothes, spent time with her, gotten rid of the men who'd threatened her and Josie. But what had that cost him, really? Nothing.

No matter what she seemed to think, there was no shred of goodness in Vladimir's soul. He would never risk or sacrifice anything that truly mattered.

All he had to offer was sex and money—and though Bree seemed to very much enjoy the sex, she didn't care about money. So what could she possibly see to love in his black soul?

He'd kept her against her will. Stolen her freedom for his own selfish pleasure. She should hate him. Instead, she'd offered him everything. Not just her body, but her soul. Her warmth, her tenderness and adoration, her honest heart.

If it really was honest.

No. He wouldn't think that. It was Kasimir who'd arranged their meeting, not Bree. But why? What could possibly be his goal?

Vladimir pushed through the crowd, his pulse throbbing in his throat. He had to find Breanna. He hungered to feel her in his arms, to know she was real. To look into her eyes and see that she wasn't—couldn't be—allied with his brother against him. Vladimir needed her. That was as good as love, wasn't it?

She deserves a man who can love her back with a whole, trusting heart. The thought whispered unbidden in his mind.

Not the careless, shallow affection you can give her, the shadowy half love of a scarred, selfish soul.

She's mine, he told the voice angrily.

So you'll keep her as your prisoner forever, taking her body every night without ever returning her love? Until you see the adoration in her eyes fade to anger, then bewildered hurt, and finally dull, numb despair?

Vladimir closed his eyes. He couldn't let that happen. Not to Breanna. He couldn't feed on her youth and energy, like a vampire draining love and life from her body.

If he couldn't love her, he had to let her go.

But damn it. *How could he?*

He sucked in his breath when he saw her across the ballroom, like a modern-day Grace Kelly, willowy, blonde, impossibly beautiful in her strapless, pale blue ball gown. But her shoulders drooped. She stood alone by the dance floor. Shame shot through him. He could only imagine what she was thinking, after the way he'd left her.

Grabbing two flutes of champagne, he came up behind her, then touched her on the shoulder. "Breanna…"

She jumped, turning to face him. Her eyes were wide, her cheeks pale. "Oh. It's you."

"Who were you expecting?"

She tried to smile, but her expression looked all wrong. "A handsome prince."

He wondered if she'd seen that little weasel Greg Hudson, in spite of his effort to get the man out of the ballroom quickly. "Did someone…bother you?"

"Bother me?" She tossed her head with forced bravado. "You know I can take care of myself."

"Tell me what's wrong," he said quietly.

She took a deep breath, then lifted stricken eyes to his. "You just…ran away so fast from me on the dance floor, I thought you'd be halfway to Berlin by now."

Ah. He suddenly knew why she was upset. "Um. Right."

The collar of his shirt felt tight. "Sorry I left like that. I was... thirsty." That sounded ridiculous. He pushed a champagne flute into her hand. "I got you something to drink."

Vladimir waited for her forehead to crease in disbelief, for her to demand why he'd really run off the instant she'd told him she loved him. For her to challenge and goad him into telling her the truth.

But she didn't. Her fingers closed around the stem of the crystal flute, but her thoughts seemed a million miles away.

"Hey." He touched her cheek lightly, and she lifted startled eyes. "Are you angry with me?"

Her lips parted, then she shook her head.

"No," she whispered. "Why would I be?"

Putting the flute to her lips, she tilted back her head and gulped down the expensive champagne like water.

For a long, awkward moment, Vladimir just stood there, pretending nothing was wrong. They didn't speak or touch or even look at each other as, all around them, people drunkenly, joyously celebrated the New Year. Finally, Vladimir could bear it no longer.

"I don't blame you for being angry." Taking the empty glass from her hand, he deposited it on the tray of a passing waiter, along with his own untouched champagne. He took her hand in his. "But Bree," he said slowly. "You have to know how I feel...."

With a sudden intake of breath, she looked up, her hazel eyes luminous. "It's my sister. She needs my help."

Her *sister?* He'd been raking himself over the coals, hating himself for hurting her, and all this time she'd been thinking about that hapless sister of hers?

He exhaled. "You need to stop worrying about her. My men will soon track her down. In the meantime, she's a full-grown woman. Treating her like a child, following her around to fix her slightest problem, you'll make her believe she's useless and incompetent. And she will be."

"But what if, this time, she really needs my help?" Bree's beautiful face grew paler. She searched his gaze with an intensity he didn't understand. "What if she's done something—something that might destroy her life forever—and I'm the only one who can save her?"

Irritated, he set his jaw. "Like you saved her from the hundred thousand dollars she lost at the poker game? When you risked yourself, offering your body to strangers, to save her from the consequences of her actions?"

Her voice was very small. "Yes."

Narrowing his eyes, Vladimir shook his head. "If she didn't learn from that, she never will."

"But—"

"There is no *but*," he said harshly. "She is twenty-two years old. She must learn to make her own choices, and live with them."

Bree's shoulders were rigid. She fell silent, turning away as she wiped her eyes. On the dance floor, people were still swaying to the music, toasting the New Year with champagne and kisses. But somehow, he wasn't quite sure how, the mood between him and Bree had utterly changed. And not for the better.

"I'm sorry," she said in a low voice, not looking at him. "I can't just abandon the people I love the instant they make a mistake. I'm not *you*," she said tightly.

Feeling the sting she no doubt intended, he said in a low voice, "My brother made his own choice to get out of the company."

"Because you made him feel worthless for a single mistake. When all he did was tell you the truth about yours."

"Falling in love with a woman who was deceiving me," he said, watching her.

"Yes," she whispered. She shook her head. "No wonder he hates you."

"He intends to destroy me," Vladimir said shortly. "But not if I ruin him first."

Her expression became bleak. "Neither of you will ever give up, will you? No matter who gets hurt."

There was no way she was working with Kasimir, Vladimir thought. *No way.* He exhaled. "Forget it." He gave her a crooked smile. "Sibling relationships should be my last topic of advice to anyone, clearly. Or relationships of any kind. What do I know about loving anyone?"

But his attempt at an olive branch failed miserably. Her eyes looked sadder still. She glanced down. "I'm tired."

"All right," he said in a low voice. "Let's go home."

As soon as we get back to the palace, I'll seduce her, he told himself. They would get everything sorted out in bed.

But once they arrived there, Bree was even more distant, colder than he'd ever seen her. Colder than he'd ever imagined she could be.

She didn't fight with him. She just withdrew. She moved away when he tried to pull her in his arms. "I want to go to bed."

"Great," he murmured. "I'll come with you."

"No." She practically ran up the stairs, then looked down from the top landing, a vision in a blue gown, like a princess. Like a queen. "Tonight, I sleep alone."

Her voice wasn't defiant. It wasn't even angry. It was inexpressibly weary.

He frowned, suddenly puzzled. None of this made sense, but he knew one thing: somehow, some way, he had screwed up. "Bree," he murmured, "what you said to me, back on the dance floor—"

"Forget about it." She cut him off and drew a deep breath, her hands tightening at her sides. "It doesn't matter. Not anymore."

But it did matter. He knew that from the way his heart seemed about to explode in his chest. But he couldn't let himself feel this. He couldn't...

Anger rushed through him, and he grabbed at it with both

hands. Climbing the stairs, he faced her. "You can't keep me out of our bed, Bree. Not tonight. Not ever."

She looked at him coldly.

"Try it, then, and see what happens, Your *Highness*."

Turning on her heel, she left him. And if Vladimir had had any hope that he might be able to warm her up, as he climbed naked into bed beside her ten minutes later, those hopes were soon dashed. Bree lay on the other side of the large bed, pretending to be asleep, creating a distance between them so clear that the space between them on the mattress might have been filled with rabid guard dogs and rusty barbed wire.

Their romantic, magical night hadn't exactly gone as planned. Lying in bed, Vladimir tucked his hands behind his head and stared at the shadows on the ceiling. The reason for her coldness was all too clear. She'd said she loved him, and he hadn't said it back.

But he couldn't say it. He didn't feel it. He didn't *want* to feel it.

There. There it was.

He didn't want to love her.

He'd done it once. He'd given her everything, believed in her, defied his brother and all the world for her sake. And he'd only proved himself a fool. He would never let himself feel that way again. He would never give his whole heart to anyone.

Especially not Breanna. No matter how much he admired her, or how much he cared. He wouldn't let her have the power to crush his heart ever again.

But as a gray dawn broke over the first day of the New Year, Vladimir looked down at Breanna beside him in bed, listening to her steady, even breathing as she slept. He saw trails of dried tears on her skin.

Tomorrow was her birthday, he remembered. She would be twenty-nine years old. She'd saved herself for him for ten years. She'd been brave enough to give herself to him completely, holding nothing back.

I love you. Her words haunted him. *Even when I hated you, I loved you. You have always been the only man for me. And what I need to know is—can you ever love me?*

Instinctively, his hands pulled her sleeping body closer. He breathed in the vanilla-and-lavender scent of her hair.

Could he continue to use her beautiful body in bed, keeping her prisoner to his pleasure, watching as her love for him soon turned to hatred, then numb despair?

He had no choice.

Sitting up, Vladimir leaned his head against the headboard, feeling bleak.

If he couldn't love her, he had to let her go.

Bree woke up with a gasp of panic and fear.

Seeing she was alone in bed, she fell back against the pillow with a sob. Within three days, she would have to betray someone she loved. Who would it be?

Josie?

Vladimir?

She felt sick with grief and guilt and fury. Numbly showering and getting dressed, she went down downstairs, where she spoke in terse monosyllables when Vladimir greeted her, wishing her a cheery Happy New Year. She kept her distance from the man she loved, sitting as far as possible from him at the long table as they ate the elaborate holiday breakfast prepared by the chef. She stopped all of Vladimir's attempts at conversation and just generally made herself unpleasant. But having him close, looking into his handsome, trusting face, was like poison to her.

For some reason, he was bending over backward to try to be nice to her, which made her feel even worse. But by late afternoon, her rudeness had managed to push him to the limit. With a muttered, inaudible curse, he stomped off to work in his home office.

And Bree exhaled, her heart pounding and blood roaring through her ears.

What should she do?

She had to save her little sister. There was no question. Whatever it took to save Josie, she would do. Immediately.

Except...

Betray the man she loved? Could she really steal Vladimir's company, his life's work, the only thing he truly cared about—and give it to his brother?

Bree's mind whirled back and forth in such panic that her body trembled and her knees were weak beneath the strain.

The clock was ticking.

"You have three days," Kasimir Xendzov had told her. Less than that now. She looked at the clock. Her hands shook, desperate to take action. But what action?

She could contact the police. True, they were in Russia and Josie was...anywhere in the world. But they could contact Interpol, the American Embassy, something!

But while Bree was trawling through layers of international bureaucracy and jurisdictional red tape, Josie would be gone, never to resurface.

I can seduce her, make her fall in love with me and destroy her pitiful little heart, Prince Kasimir had said. *I can force her to be my wife forever, and you will never see her again.*

Bree paced across the morning room, stopping to claw her hand through her tangled hair. She felt like crying. She didn't know what to do.

Tell Vladimir everything, her heart begged. *Throw yourself on his mercy and ask for help.*

Right, she thought with a lump in her throat. Since Vladimir was such a merciful man.

But still, three times that afternoon, she went down the hallway of the palace to the door of his study. Three times she raised her hand to knock, wanting to confess everything. But each time, something stopped her.

His own words.

She is twenty-two years old, he'd said harshly. *She must learn to make her own choices, and live with them.*

And each time, Bree put her hand down without knocking. What if Vladimir said Josie had brought this on herself, by seeking Kasimir's help?

If Bree told him everything, and he refused to help her, she would lose her chance to get him to sign Kasimir's document. And all hope for Josie would be gone. Her baby sister would be left terrified and alone, somewhere in the Sahara. Bree would never see her again.

Vladimir doesn't even love you, a voice argued.

But I love him. She swallowed. *He deserves my loyalty.*

And what about your little sister, whom you've always protected? What does she deserve?

Bree covered her face with her hands. She was stuck, frozen, equally unable to betray either of them. And time was running out.

If only fate could make the decision for her…

"Breanna." She jumped when she heard Vladimir's voice behind her. "I'm sorry if I've neglected you today." He put his arms around her, nuzzling her neck. His voice was humble, as if he thought he was to blame for their estrangement. "I should work tonight. Paperwork for the new merger has piled up, and it all needs my signature by tomorrow."

Twisting her head, Bree looked back at him, her heart breaking. He'd just told her exactly how to get Kasimir's document signed. Was it fate?

"But let it wait until tomorrow." Smiling down at her, he kissed the top of her head. "Shall we have dinner?"

But by the end of the night, Vladimir's smile had turned to bewilderment. They slept in the same bed, a million miles apart. When Bree woke up alone the next morning, January 2, she realized two things.

Today was her birthday. She was twenty-nine years old.

And the whole meaning of her life came down to this one choice. Which of the people she loved would she betray?

Sitting up in bed, she looked at the gilded clock over the marble fireplace. Over half the time since Kasimir's ultimatum was gone, and she'd done nothing. She'd neither tried to trick Vladimir into signing the dreadful contract, nor confessed the truth and begged him for help. For the past day and a half, since midnight on New Year's Eve, she'd always felt one breath away from crying. So she'd pushed him away, to keep him from seeing into her soul. In response to Vladimir's innocent question yesterday, asking what she wanted for her birthday, she had answered so rudely that she blushed to remember it now.

She couldn't tell him what she really wanted for her birthday.

Freedom from this terrible choice.

Bree's knees trembled as she slowly climbed out of bed and fell blearily into the shower. She got dressed in a black button-down shirt and dark jeans. She combed out her long, wet hair. She pulled it back in a severe ponytail.

Cold, she told herself as she slowly pulled on her black stiletto boots. *My heart is cold. I am an iceberg. I feel nothing.*

Tucking the document Kasimir had given her beneath her black shirt, she went down the wide, sweeping stairs in Vladimir's eighteenth-century palace, as if she were going to her death.

After so many gray, snowy days, brilliant sunshine was pouring in through the tall windows, leaving patterns of golden light on the marble floor. She'd been happy here, she realized. In spite of everything. She'd loved him.

Looking back now, Bree saw it had been enough. They'd been happy. Why hadn't she appreciated that happiness? Why had she fretted, worried, groused about Vladimir's one major flaw—that he didn't want her to ever leave him? What kind of stupid flaw was that? Why hadn't she just fallen to her knees in gratitude for all the blessings she'd had—so unappreciated then, and now so swiftly gone?

Creeping softly to the open door of his study, she peeked inside. Empty. Holding her breath, keeping her mind absolutely blank, she swiftly walked inside and stuck the page in the middle of the pile of papers she'd seen him working through yesterday. She would distract him today, and if luck was on her side, he would sign it without reading it. She felt confident he wouldn't suspect her.

He trusted her now.

As Bree left the study on shaking legs, she hated herself with every beat of her heart.

Perhaps having his company stolen wouldn't hurt him too badly, she tried to tell herself. Hadn't Vladimir insinuated that it had become a burden? "Money is just a way to keep score," he'd said. Perhaps he would someday understand, and forgive her.

But even now, Bree knew she was lying to herself. Even if he was able to accept losing Xendzov Mining—even if he started over and built a successful new company, as Kasimir had—she was making herself his enemy for the rest of his life. The fact that she'd done it to once again save her sister would not gain her any points, either. He would despise her. Forever. Everything between them, every good memory, would be lost.

Bree walked heavily down the gilded hall, past the arched windows. She heard the sharp tap of her stiletto boots against the marble floor. Brilliant January sunlight reflected off the white snow and sparkling Gulf of Finland. She looked out the windows, and saw sun as warm as his touch. Sky as blue as his eyes.

Suddenly even walking felt like too much of an effort. She stopped, staring at the floor, her heart in her throat.

"Breanna. You're awake."

Blinking fast, she looked up. Vladimir was coming down the hall toward her, looking impossibly handsome in a white button-down shirt and black slacks. An ache filled her throat as she looked into the perfect face of the only man she'd ever loved. The man she was about to lose forever.

"I have something for you. A birthday present."

Her voice was hoarse. "You shouldn't have."

He gave her a crooked grin. "You can't already hate it. You don't even know what it is yet."

The warmth of Vladimir's grin lit up his whole face, making his soul shine through his eyes, making him look like the boy she'd known. Like everything she'd ever wanted.

Swallowing, she looked down at her stiletto boots. "I'm just not in much of a party mood."

He took her hand. She felt his palm against hers, felt his fingers brush against her own as he pulled her gently down the hall. "Come see."

He led her into a high-ceilinged room centered around a glossy black grand piano. The conservatory had a wall of windows overlooking the sea. Antique Louis XIV chairs flanked the marble fireplace, and expensive paintings covered the walls, along with shelves of first-edition books.

"I know you said you didn't want a fur coat," Vladimir said. "But if you're going to live in St. Petersburg, you need some Russian fur to keep you warm...."

Bree saw a lumpy white fur stole on the pale blue couch beside the window. With an intake of breath, she cried, "Vladimir, I told you—"

He gave her a crooked half grin. "Just go look."

Hesitantly, Bree walked toward the blue couch. She got closer, and the lump of white fur suddenly moved, causing her to jump back with a surprised little squeak. From the pile of fur, a shaggy white head lifted.

She saw black eyes, a pink tongue and a wagging tail. Vladimir lifted the puppy into her arms.

"She's an Ovcharka. A Russian sheepdog." Lowering his head, he kissed her softly. "Happy birthday, Breanna."

With a little bark, the white puppy wiggled her tiny furry

body with joy, warm and soft in Bree's arms. Cuddling the dog close, she looked up at Vladimir's smiling face, and felt a bullet pierce her throat.

She burst into tears.

"Bree, what is it?" He bent over her, his handsome face astonished and worried. "You seemed sad about the dog you'd lost long ago, so I thought… But I see I've made a mistake." He clawed back his dark hair. "It was a stupid idea."

"No," she choked out. She tried to wipe her tears off her cheek with her shoulder. "It was a wonderful idea," she whispered. "The best in the world."

"Then why are you crying?" he said, bewildered.

Trying to choke back her tears, she buried her face in the dog's soft, warm fur. "Because I love her." Looking up, she whispered, with her heart in her throat, "And I love you."

He grinned, clearly relieved. "What will you name her?"

Heartbreak. She stared at him for a long moment, then looked at the windows. "Snowy."

"Snowy, huh? Did you put a lot of thought into that?" But the teasing grin slid from his face when she gave him no answering smile. He cleared his throat. "Well, I have one more surprise for you. But you'll have to wait until dinner to get it."

As the day wore on, Bree's heart broke a little more with each hour. They played with the puppy, then had a delicious late lunch with champagne. Afterward, the palace staff rolled in a giant, lilac-frosted cake on a cart.

"Chocolate cake," Vladimir said happily. "With lavender frosting."

"Is this my big surprise?" she asked, dreading further kindness.

"No. And don't ask me about it. You won't get it out of me. Even if you use your feminine wiles."

He said it as if he were rather hoping she would try. It had been two nights since they'd made love. It felt like a lifetime.

The heat in his eyes made her cheeks go hot, along with the rest of her body. Trembling, she pretended not to notice.

The servants sang Happy Birthday to her in cheerful, slightly off-key English, led by Vladimir's low, smooth baritone. He lit the two wax candles on the cake—one shaped like a 2, the other a 9.

He nudged her with his shoulder. "Make a wish."

Leaning toward the flickering candles, Bree closed her eyes, wondering what she'd done to deserve this fresh hell. And knowing it wasn't what she'd done, but what she was about to do.

She took a deep breath, her wish a silent prayer: *I wish I didn't have to hurt you.*

She blew out the candles, and everyone applauded.

As the staff departed, after giving Bree their well wishes in a mixture of English and Russian, Vladimir took her in his arms.

"Do you want to know about your other gift?" he said softly.

She gulped. "I thought you weren't going to tell me."

"If you kiss me, I might change my mind."

But she backed away. "I'm not really in a kissing mood, either," she mumbled.

From the corner of her eye, she saw the stiffness of his posture, and felt his hurt. "Very well," he said finally. "It is your special day. You don't have to do anything you don't want to do."

He paused. She didn't move. His hands tightened at his sides.

"So I'll just tell you what the big surprise is, shall I?" he said. "I've bought you a hotel. The Hale Ka'nani Resort."

She looked up with a gasp. "What?"

"You dreamed of someday running a small hotel." He gave her a crooked smile. "I bought you one."

"But the Hale Ka'nani isn't *small!* It must have cost millions of dollars!"

"Two hundred million, actually."

"What?"

"Don't worry." His lips lifted in a smile. "I got a good deal."

"Are you out of your mind?"

"It's an investment. In you."

Tears filled her eyes. "Why would you do something so stupid?"

"Because…" he said softly, reaching a hand toward her cheek "…with your brilliant strategic mind, Bree, I've always known you were born to rule an empire."

Trembling, fighting tears, she stumbled back from his touch.

"I need to take Snowy for a walk," she blurted out, and, picking up the puppy, she fled to the white, snow-covered lawn outside. Once there, Bree dawdled, taking as long as she could, until her cheeks and nose felt numb from the cold and even the puppy was whimpering to go back to the warmth inside. It was past dusk when she finally returned to the conservatory, her feet heavy, her heart full of dread.

To her surprise, the room was empty. The puppy flopped down on a rug near the warm fire, and Bree frowned. "Where is he?" she said aloud.

The puppy answered with a stretch and a yawn, clearly intending to have a long winter's nap.

Bree went down the hall, passing various rooms. Then she saw Vladimir. In the study. At his desk. Signing papers.

Shock and horror went through her like lightning.

"What are you doing?" she breathed.

"There you are." His voice was cold, and he didn't bother to look up. He seemed distant—and how could she blame him? "I will join you for a late dinner after I finish this."

He was signing the papers by rote, with rapid speed, as if his mind was on something else. She saw Kasimir's contract peeking out beneath the next paper. "Stop!"

"I got your message loud and clear, Bree." He pushed the

top paper aside. "You don't want anything from me. You can't even bear to look at me—"

As he reached, unseeing, for Kasimir's contract, Bree suddenly knew.

She couldn't let him sign it. She couldn't betray him.

She *couldn't*.

With a choked gasp, Bree flung herself across his study and blocked him the only way she knew how. Shoving his chair back, she threw her leg over him, straddling him, separating him physically from his desk. Tangling her hands in his hair, pressing her body against his, she leaned forward and kissed him.

At first he froze. For one dreadful instant she thought he would push her away. Then a sound like a low sigh came from the back of his throat, and his powerful arms wrapped around her. His lips melted roughly against hers.

The pen in his hand dropped to the floor. The pile of papers on his desk was forgotten.

Holding her against his chest, Vladimir rose and, in a savage movement, swept the papers off his desk. Pressing her back against the polished oak, he looked down at her with eyes so full of emotion that her heart caught in her throat.

"Now, Bree," he said hoarsely, as he lowered his mouth to hers. "I need you now."

CHAPTER TEN

VLADIMIR had never felt such fire.

Bree had never initiated lovemaking before. The heat of her passion, in contrast to her earlier ice, burned through his body, incinerating his soul. Moments before, he'd felt dark and angry, rebuffed in all his efforts to show he cared, to make her birthday special, and to compensate for those three little words he could not say.

But now, as they desperately ripped off each other's clothes on his desk, as they kissed and suckled and licked, he felt her soft body move and sway beneath him, pulling him deeper, deeper. And suddenly those same unthinkable, forbidden three words rose in his heart, like sunlight bursting through a dark cloud.

Could he…? Did he…?

Bree moved, rolling him beneath her on the desk. Her silken thighs wrapped around his hips. He looked up at her expressive face, at her breasts swaying like music. A glowing sunset through the study's window washed her pale shoulders red, the color of a ruby.

The color of his heart.

With a gasp, she impaled herself upon him, pulling him deep inside her. As he filled her completely, for the first time in ten years everything was clear.

He loved her.

He'd been afraid to see it. He'd tried to deny it, to ignore it.

He'd buried himself in work, in sex, in dangerous sports. But he could not deny it any longer.

He loved her. The truth was he'd given her his heart long ago. When he thought she'd betrayed him, his heart had simply frozen, like an arctic sea. But from the moment he'd seen her again, across the poker table at the Hale Ka'nani, his heart had begun to thaw. Feeling the sting of her cold rejection today had taught him that he still felt pain. He still had a beating heart.

A heart that loved her.

Whatever the cost. Whatever the risk.

His love for her was absolute. He could not change it.

He wanted to go back in time and be the generous, trusting man he'd once been. He wanted to be the man who deserved Breanna Dalton.

When she gasped with pleasure, he tilted back his head and the first hoarse cry escaped his throat. Their joy built together, until he could no longer tell where his voice ended and hers began.

With a final cry, she collapsed in his arms. He held her tightly, both of them still sprawled on his desk. As he stroked her naked back, his heart pounded in his chest. He wanted to blurt out the words. But words were cheap. He would show her, the only way he knew how. He would do what terrified him most.

"I'm letting you go, Breanna," he said quietly. "I'm setting you free."

For a moment, he thought she hadn't heard. Then she lifted her head to look into his eyes. He'd thought she would be happy. Instead, she looked stricken, almost gutted.

Vladimir frowned.

"Don't you understand?" Reaching up, he caressed her cheek, tucking wild tendrils of sweaty blond hair behind her ear. "You're no longer my property. You're free."

"Why?" she choked out. "Why now?"

He smiled despite the lump in his throat. "Because…" Cupping her face with both his hands, he looked straight into her eyes. "I'm in love with you, Breanna."

Pulling back, she gasped, as if his words had caused her mortal injury.

He sat up on the desk beside her. "It took me ten years to realize what I should have admitted to myself long ago. I never stopped loving you. And I never will."

Blinking fast, she looked away.

"But what if I don't deserve your love?" she whispered. "What if I've done things that…"

"It doesn't matter." Gently, he turned her to face him. "Somehow, in spite of all my flaws, you decided to love me. I was too much of a coward to do the same." Lifting her hand to his lips, he kissed her skin fervently, then looked at her with tears in his eyes. "Until now."

She sucked in her breath.

"Whatever you do," he said quietly, searching her gaze, "for the rest of your life, I will love you. For the rest of mine."

Bree started to speak, then shook her head as silent tears spilled down her cheeks.

Was she so amazed, then, that he could return her love? The thought of that shamed him, reminding him how selfish he'd been. Pulling her back into his arms, he held her. When she claimed she was too tired to eat dinner, he took her to bed. He held her through the night as she cried herself to sleep. He didn't understand her tears. But as Vladimir stroked her hair and naked back, he vowed that he would never give her any reason to cry again. Ever.

His heart was irrevocably hers. But she was free.

Would she choose to stay with him? Or would she go?

Shortly before midnight, when Breanna finally slept, Vladimir realized he had to prepare for the worst. Pulling on a robe, he quietly left their bedroom and went downstairs to his office. Turning on his computer by habit, he looked for his cell phone. He'd order the jet to be available in the morning, to take her wherever she wanted to go. Then he prayed he could convince her to stay....

His foot slid on the mess of papers scattered across the floor. In the dim glow of light from the computer screen, the first words on the page of a contract he'd never noticed before caught his eye. Bending over, he picked it up.

I hereby renounce all shares in Xendzov Mining OAO...

His heart stopped in his chest. Hand shaking, he turned on a lamp, thrusting the paper beneath the light.

...giving them freely and in perpetuity to my brother, Kasimir.

He read it again. Then again.

This contract had been slyly slipped into the pile of papers on his desk. And with sickening certainty Vladimir knew how it had gotten there. Only one person could have done it.

He closed his eyes. When he'd first seen Bree in Hawaii, he'd assumed she was there to con someone. Later he'd convinced himself that meeting her at that poker game had been wild, pure coincidence. Even when he'd discovered from Greg Hudson that Kasimir had deliberately tried to plot that meeting, he'd convinced himself that Breanna, at least, was innocent.

Exhaling, he crushed the paper against his chest.

But his first instincts had been right all along. She'd been in Honolulu for a con. And just like ten years ago, Vladimir had been her mark.

As he opened his eyes, the dark shadows of his study were bleak. All color had been drained from the world, leaving only gray.

Bree and his brother had to be working together. After Vladimir had started attending private poker games in Honolulu, while recuperating from his racing accident, Kasimir had arranged for Bree to get a job there. His brother must have known all along that she was the poison Vladimir could not resist. The poker game, the wager, the whole affair had been a setup from start to finish.

All so that Bree could infiltrate his house and infiltrate his soul.

All so that Vladimir would sign this document.

His hands shook as he looked down at the contract.

His brother had baited his hook well. And so had she.

Bree had tricked him, the same way she'd done ten years ago. And Vladimir was so stupid that instead of being on his guard, he'd been fooled even worse than before. He thought of how he'd tried to please her, giving her his great-grandmother's peridot, buying her a puppy, buying her a hotel, and worst of all, declaring his love—when all the time, all he was to her...was a job.

He leaned back wearily in his desk chair. Just hours before, the purpose and meaning of his life had seemed so clear. So bright and full of promise. He'd felt young again, young and fearless. For that one shining moment, he'd been exactly the man he'd always wanted to be.

Rising to his feet, Vladimir poured himself a glass of vodka over ice. Going to the window, he swirled the tumbler, watching the prisms of the ice gleam in the scattered moonlight.

He could still destroy her.

Destroy Breanna? The thought made him choke out a low sob and claw back his hair.

Was there any way he could be wrong? Any way she could be innocent?

All the evidence pointed against her. It was obvious she was guilty. He looked down at the contract on his desk.

But should he believe the proof of his eyes?

Or the proof of his heart?

Standing alone in the shadows of his study, Vladimir drank the vodka in one gulp and put the glass down softly on a table.

Loving her had brought him to life again. Going back to the window, he opened it and leaned against the sill. He took a deep breath of the cold air, smelling the frozen sea, hearing the plaintive cry of distant, unseen birds. Midnight in Russia, in January, was frozen and white, gray and dead.

But still, he knew spring would come.

He took another deep breath. Everything had changed for him. And yet nothing had.

He loved her. And he always would.

Vladimir looked back down at the unsigned contract. In a sudden movement, he leaned over the polished wood of his desk where, hours ago, he'd made love to her, the woman he loved. Where he'd looked into her beautiful face and told her his love for her would last forever.

Slowly he reached for an expensive ballpoint pen. He looked down, reading for the tenth time the contract that would forever give his billion-dollar company to his brother.

And then, with a jagged scrawl, Vladimir signed his name.

The warm sunlight on Bree's face woke her from a vivid dream. She'd been standing with Vladimir on a beach in Hawaii, the surf rushing against their bare feet, the warm wind filled with the scent of flowers as they spoke their wedding vows.

Vladimir's eyes looked blue as the sea. *I, Vladimir, take you, Breanna, to be my wife....*

Smiling to herself, still drowsing, Bree reached out her arm. But his side of the bed was empty.

With a gasp, she sat up.

Last night, she'd thrown herself at Vladimir because she'd been physically unable to let him sign away his company to his brother. But she still didn't know what to do. She couldn't betray him. Or her sister.

I'm in love with you, Breanna. I never stopped loving you. And I never will.

She trembled, blinking back tears.

He loved her.

But even before he'd spoken the words, she should have known. He'd shown her his love a hundred times over, with each gift more precious than the last. Bree looked down at Snowy, curled up in a ball at the foot of her bed. Vladimir dreamed bigger things for her than she dared dream for herself, buying her a Hawaiian resort to support her dream of running a small bed-and-breakfast. And last night, he'd set her free. He'd sacrificed his own needs for hers.

Bree took a deep breath, setting her jaw.

She was going to tell him everything.

Pulling on a T-shirt and jeans, she went downstairs, her whole body shaking with fear. She tried not to think of Josie, or the risk she was taking. When Bree told him her sister was in danger, he wouldn't coldly reply that Josie should face the consequences of her own actions. Would he? He would help Bree save her.

But if he didn't…

Oh, God. She couldn't even think of it.

Going down the hallway, she looked in his office. It was empty. Her cheeks grew hot as she saw the desk where they'd made love so passionately last night. Then she stiffened. With an intake of breath, she rushed into the room and rifled quickly through the documents now stacked neatly on his desk, intending to destroy the contract before Vladimir ever saw it.

Then she gasped. Lifting the page, she stared at his scrawled signature.

He'd done it.

He must have had no idea what he was signing. But he'd transferred his company to his younger brother.

Bree closed her eyes, holding the paper to her chest. Why had he finally decided to love her now, of all times? It had taken Vladimir ten years to trust her again. It would take a single act for her to wipe that trust off the earth forever.

But what if this was a sign? What if this was the universe telling her what to do?

Midnight tonight was the deadline to save her sister, and Bree held in her hands the golden ticket. And unlike Vladimir's mercy, it was guaranteed. She could exchange it for Josie, then return to Russia and beg for Vladimir's forgiveness. After all, if anyone was going to be thrown on his mercy, shouldn't it be Bree herself, not her helpless younger sister?

Even if I give Kasimir this contract, it'll never stand in any court, she told herself. Vladimir was powerful, well connected. He would be fine.

Even if he had enemies aplenty who would rejoice to see his downfall....

I'm in love with you, Breanna. She whimpered as she remembered the dark midnight of Vladimir's eyes, the hoarse rasp of his voice. *I never stopped loving you.*

With a choked sob, she ran upstairs. Not letting herself look at the mussed-up sheets of the bed where he'd held her last night as she wept, she packed up her duffel bag, tucking the paper beneath her passport.

"Are you leaving?"

Looking up with an intake of breath, she saw Vladimir in the doorway, wearing a black button-down shirt and black trousers. His face was half-hidden in the shadow.

She swallowed. "Yes." She turned away. "You set me free. So I'm going." *Forgive me. I can't take the chance.*

He exhaled, and came closer. When she clearly saw his face, she nearly staggered back, shocked at the luminous pain in his eyes. Then she blinked, and it was gone.

"I have a plane waiting to take you wherever you want to go," he said.

"Just like that?"

"Just like that."

"You knew I would leave?"

"Yes." Lifting his gaze to hers, he whispered, "But I hoped you wouldn't. I hoped you could—love me—enough."

Her heart was slamming against her chest. She wanted to sob, to throw her arms around him, to pull out the contract and rip it up in front of his eyes. "Perhaps I'll come back."

"Perhaps," he said, but his lips twisted. "And Snowy? Are you leaving her behind?"

"Of course not," Bree said, shocked. "I wouldn't abandon her!"

"No," he replied quietly. "I know that. You wouldn't abandon anyone you truly loved."

Bree swallowed. "Vladimir, I told you the truth. I do love you. But I—"

"You don't have to explain." His eyes met hers. "Just be happy, Bree. That's all I want. All I've ever wanted."

"Your great-grandmother's necklace is on the nightstand," she said in a small voice.

"That was a gift." Picking up the necklace, he held it out to her. "Take it."

She shook her head. "That belongs to…to your future wife."

Coming up behind her, he said softly, "It belongs to you."

He put the necklace around her neck. She felt the cool, hard stone against her skin, and grief crashed over her like a wave. Closing her eyes, she sagged back against him. He wrapped his arms around her, cradling her against his chest for a single moment.

Then he let her go.

"I will always love you, Breanna," he said in a low voice. He turned away. "Goodbye."

Vladimir left their bedroom without looking back. She wanted to chase after him. She wanted to fall at his knees, weeping and begging for his forgiveness.

But she couldn't. She had the signed contract. Fate had made the decision for her.

It won't stand up in court, she told herself again, her teeth chattering. *After Josie's safe, I'll come back. I will somehow make him forgive me….*

Bree had no memory of collecting Snowy and her duffel bag. But somehow, twenty minutes later, they were in the back of the limo, driving away from the palace. Her puppy sat in her lap, whining as she looked through the window at Vladimir's palace, then plaintively up at her mistress.

As Bree looked back at the fairy-tale palace, snow sparkled on Vladimir's wide fields and on the forest of bare, black trees around the palace of blue and gold. And she realized she was weeping, pressing her hand against the necklace at her throat.

Bree felt something prick her finger. Looking down, she saw the peridot's sharp edge had pricked her skin. A Russian prince had once sent his beloved wife and child into the safety of exile, with this necklace as their only memento of him, before he'd died alone in Siberia, in ultimate sacrifice.

A sob rose to Bree's lips. As Vladimir had sacrificed…

Her eyes widened. With an intake of breath, she looked back at the palace.

You knew I would leave?

Yes. His eyes had seared hers, straight through her soul. *But I hoped you wouldn't. I hoped you could—love me—enough.*

What had Vladimir sacrificed for her?

Was it possible…that he *knew?*

"Stop," she cried to the driver. "Turn around! Go back!"

The puppy barked madly, turning circles in her lap as the limo stopped, struggling to turn around on the long, slender road surrounded by snow.

Bree didn't care if the signed contract had miraculously fallen into her lap. She didn't care what the universe might be trying to tell her. *The choice was still hers.*

All this time, she'd thought she had to choose between the two people she loved. She didn't.

She just had to choose herself.

Ten years ago, loving Vladimir had changed her. He'd given her a second chance at life. He'd shown her she could be something besides a poker-playing con artist with a flexible conscience. He'd made her want to be *more.* To be honest and true, not just when it was convenient, but always.

This was the woman she was born to be.

And she would never be anything else ever again. Not for any price.

Before the limo stopped in the courtyard, Bree had thrown open the door, leaving her duffel bag and valuables behind as she leaped headlong into the snow. Her puppy bounded beside her, barking frantically as Bree ran straight back to the only answer her heart had ever wanted.

She found him in his study, standing by the window that overlooked the sea.

"Vladimir," she cried.

Slowly he turned, his handsome face like granite. It was only when she came closer that she saw the tears sparkling in his eyes.

He wasn't made of ice. He was flesh and blood. And letting her go had ripped him to the bone.

Choking back a sob, she threw herself into his arms. She jumped up, hugging him even with her legs. Startled, he caught her, holding her against him.

"Are you really here?" he breathed, stroking her hair, as if he thought she was a dream. "You were free. You had the signed contract. Why did you return?"

Bree slowly slid down his body, her eyes wide. "You knew."

Blinking fast, Vladimir nodded.

"Why did you do it?" she said. "Why would you set me free, when you knew you'd lose everything?"

His phone rang from his pocket, but he ignored it. He cupped her face, tracing his thumbs against her trembling mouth. "Because I knew I'd already lost everything, if you walked out my door." He shook his head. "I had to know. If you really loved me. Or if you…didn't."

"And what did you decide?" she whispered through numb lips.

"I decided it didn't matter." He looked straight into her eyes. "I meant what I said. Whatever you do, I will love you, Breanna. For the rest of my life."

She burst into tears, pressing her face against his chest. "I'm sorry," she sobbed as her tears soaked his shirt. "I was wrong to think I could ever betray you."

He stroked her hair gently. "Did my brother promise you money to pay off your old debts? Is that why you agreed to help him?"

"*Help* him?" Drawing back, Bree looked at Vladimir. "I had no idea he was behind us getting jobs in Hawaii. Not until he threatened me!"

Vladimir's hand grew still. "He threatened you?"

"At the New Year's Eve ball."

He sucked in his breath. "Kasimir was there?"

"He found me on the dance floor when I was alone. Right after I told you I loved you—when you took off…."

"*That* was why you've been acting so distant?" Vladimir looked at her, his expression fierce. "What did he say to you?"

A lump rose in her throat.

"He's married Josie," she whispered. "He's holding her hostage."

"What?" Vladimir cried.

"He wanted to get back your family's land, and it was the only way to break the trust. Josie agreed to marry him, because she thought it was the only way to save me."

"From what?" he demanded.

"From you." With a bitter laugh, Bree wiped her eyes. "Funny, isn't it?"

His face filled with cold rage. His phone started ringing again. He didn't move a muscle to answer. "Hilarious."

"He said if I ever wanted to see her again, I had to bring the signed contract to his house in Marrakech before midnight tonight."

Vladimir looked ready to commit murder. "Why didn't you tell me?"

"I'm sorry," Bree said miserably. "I was afraid you'd say it was Josie's own fault, and that she should face the consequences."

He scowled. "She's just a kid. I never meant she should—"
He broke off with a curse as, for the third time in five min-
utes, his phone started ringing again. He snatched it up angrily.
"What the hell do you want?"

Then Vladimir froze.

"Kasimir," he said quietly. "About time."

Stricken, Bree held her breath, staring up at him.

His eyes narrowed. "She already told me. Your plan to turn
us against each other didn't work." He listened, then paced
three steps. "I am willing to make the trade."

Bree covered her mouth with her hands, realizing that Vladimir was offering to give up his billion-dollar company to save
her baby sister. Then he scowled.

"Kasimir, don't be a fool! You can still—"

Vladimir stopped, then pulled the phone from his ear, staring at it in shock.

"What happened?" Bree said anxiously. "What did he say?
Is he willing to make the trade?"

"No," Vladimir said, sounding dazed. "He said he no longer has any intention of divorcing her. He told me I could keep
my stupid company."

Her mouth dropped open. "He said that?"

"His exact words." Vladimir's lips twisted. "It seems he
cares about keeping her more than hurting me."

Bree took a deep breath. She could still hear Kasimir's cold
words. *What I want is revenge. And I will have it.* "I'm not so
sure…."

Then she remembered the anger in his blue eyes.

So much for Josie's sacrifice, he'd accused her bitterly.

Bree had wondered about that then. It seemed even more
certain now. She licked her lips. "Is it possible…he *could* care
for her?"

"I don't know about that. But he won't hurt her. My brother
had—has—a good heart."

"How can you say that, after how he's tried to destroy you?"

Vladimir's jaw tightened.

"Perhaps he had a good cause," he admitted in a low voice. Shaking his head, he continued, "But your sister is in no danger. Kasimir hates me, and perhaps you. But he has no quarrel with her."

"If I could only be absolutely sure—"

"She is safe," Vladimir said simply. "I would stake my life on it. And the fact that he actually wants to stay married to her…" He slowly smiled. "It's interesting. Very interesting."

His phone rang abruptly in his hand, and he put it to his ear. "Hello?"

Kasimir? Bree mouthed.

He shook his head at her, his hand tightening on the phone. "Lefèvre, at last. Give me some good news." He listened. And then a smile lifted his handsome face. Seeing that smile, Bree's heart soared. She suddenly knew everything was going to be all right.

He hung up. "My investigator has found her."

Bree gave a joyful sob. "Where is she?"

"Safe." His smile widened. "And very close."

Bree started to turn. "We should go to her—"

Vladimir grabbed her by the wrist. "First things first," he growled. "I want to do this before anything else comes between us." And before her amazed eyes, he fell to one knee.

"I don't have a ring," he said quietly, "because I didn't let myself hope this could happen." Quirking a dark eyebrow, he gave her a cheeky grin. "And I think I'd better let you pick out your own ring, in any case."

She held her breath.

His darkly handsome face grew serious. Vulnerable.

"Will you marry me?" he whispered.

Marry him? Bree's heart galloped. Vladimir wanted her to be his wife, the mother of his children—just like she'd dreamed?

He swallowed, and his stark blue eyes became uncertain.

"Will you have me, Breanna?" Reaching up, he gripped her hands in his own. "Will you be mine?"

Tears rose to her eyes.

"I am yours already. Don't you remember?" The corners of her trembling lips tugged upwards. "You own me, heart and soul."

He exhaled in a rush. "Does that mean you'll be my wife?"

"Yes." Tears streamed unchecked down her cheeks as she pulled on his hands, lifting him to his feet. "With all my heart."

Vladimir cupped her cheek. "I belong to you," he vowed. "Now and forever."

As their white Russian puppy leaped and barked in happy circles around their feet, he wrapped Bree in his arms. Lowering his head, he kissed her with the passion and adoration that promised a lifetime. And she knew, come what may, that he would always love her, because she'd been brave enough to love herself.

"Never play with your heart, kiddo," her father had once told her. "Only a sucker plays with his heart. Even if you win, you lose."

But as Bree looked up into the face of the man she loved, the man she would soon wed, the man who would bring Josie safely home—she suddenly knew her father was wrong. Because when the chips were down, love was the only thing worth a risk. The only thing worth gambling for.

Playing with all your heart…was the *only* way to win.

* * * * *

SEDUCING HIS OPPOSITION

KATHERINE GARBERA

Katherine Garbera is the *USA TODAY* bestselling author of more than forty books. She's always believed in happy endings and lives in Southern California with her husband, children and their pampered pet, Godiva. Visit Katherine on the web at www.katherinegarbera.com, or catch up with her on Facebook and Twitter.

This book is dedicated to my son, Lucas,
who continues to make me laugh with his insight
and wit.

One

Justin Stern pulled his Porsche 911 to a stop in the parking lot of the Miami-Dade County Zoning Offices. As the corporate attorney and co-owner of Luna Azul he was always busy and he liked that. Unlike his younger brother Nate, who was out partying every night and keeping the nightclub in the public eye, Justin preferred the quiet comfort of his office. He had worked hard to make sure that Luna Azul was where it was today from a financial perspective and he was determined to see it continue to grow.

That's what he was doing here today—ensuring that the future of the club didn't just rely on the nightclub crowd. He had negotiated the purchase of a strip mall that was run-down and in desperate need of repair. He'd researched the deed and found that it had changed hands about ten years ago and that had been the start of the disrepair of the buildings.

He envisioned an outdoor plaza with restaurants and shops that would help revitalize the area and bring a new revenue stream into the Luna Azul Company.

All he needed to do was file the final paperwork here today, and they could proceed with the expansion plans.

It was a beautiful spring morning, but he took no notice of it as he walked to the building. He took the stairs to the eleventh floor instead of the elevator because elevators really weren't an efficient use of time. He was happy to see there were only two other people in the waiting room. He took a number from the reception desk and then took a seat next to a very pretty Latina woman.

She had thick hair that curled around her face and shoulders in soft waves. Her skin was flawless, her olive complexion making her brown eyes seem even bigger. Her lips were full and pouty; he found he couldn't tear his eyes from her face until she raised one eyebrow at him.

"I'm not a creep," he said with a self-effacing grin. "You're just breathtaking."

She flushed and rolled her eyes. "As if I'd believe that line."

"Why wouldn't you?" he asked, turning to face her.

"I'm used to smooth-talking men," she said. "I can spot one a mile away."

"Just because I'm complimenting you doesn't mean that I'm BSing you," he said. She was really lovely and he liked the soft sound of her voice. She was well put together. He had no idea of designers or fashion but her clothes looked nice—feminine. For the first time in a very long time he didn't mind having to wait.

"I suspect you can be very charming when you put your mind to it," she said.

"Perhaps," he said. "Not really. I'm usually straight to the point."

"You don't strike me as blunt," she said.

"I am," he said. He wasn't giving her a line—she really was gorgeous. She had caught his eye and distracted him. And he didn't mind at all. That was the surprising part for him. "Your eyes…are so big, I could get lost in them."

"Your eyes are so blue that they look like the waters in Fiji."

He laughed out loud. "Is that what I sound like to you?"

"Yes," she said with a smile. "Honestly, I'm not all that."

She was all that and a lot more, but he wasn't the best when it came to talking to women. In a corporate boardroom or at a negotiating table he was the best but one-on-one when he was interested in a girl…well that was when he got caught up.

"What brings you here?" he asked, then shook his head. "Zoning."

"Zoning," she said at the same time. "I'm here to file an injunction.

"Is it for your own company or a client?" he asked, wanting to know more.

"My grandparents think that an outside company is trying to buy their property and turn it into some big commercial club. So I'm checking it out for them."

"Do you live here in Miami then? Or just your grandparents?"

"My entire family lives here," she said. "But I live in New York."

"Oh. So ours will have to be a long-distance relationship," he said.

She raised her eyebrow at him. "This relationship might not make it out of the waiting room."

"I'm not giving up on us so easily," he said.

"Good. One of us should fight for this," she said, deadpan.

"I guess it will be me," he said with a grin. He couldn't help it. Something about this woman just made him smile.

A nattily dressed man came to the counter. "Number fifteen."

She glanced at the paper in her hand. "That's me."

"Just my luck. Any chance you'll give me your number?"

She tucked a thick strand of her hair behind her ear and reached into her handbag. "Here's my card. My cell number is on the bottom."

"I will call you," he said.

"I hope so...what's your name?"

"Justin," he said standing up and taking the card from her, but he didn't look at it. "Justin Stern. And what should I call you other than beautiful?"

She was quiet a moment as she looked him over, a light going on in her eyes. "Selena," she said. "Selena Gonzalez."

She walked away and he watched every sway of her hips. Then her name registered. Gonzalez was the last name of Tomas's big-gun lawyer and granddaughter. Selena Gonzalez...wait a minute; he was lusting after the corporate lawyer Tomas Gonzalez had called in from New York to stop his plans for the strip mall.

That wasn't cool.

Dammit, he wanted to call her. It wasn't very often

he met a woman who got his rather odd sense of humor and could banter with him. But now…

Then again, she didn't live here. She was in town for a few weeks at most, he thought. That made her the perfect woman for him.

Was he out of his mind? She was gumming up the plans he'd worked hard for. And if she was anything like her grandfather, she'd be stubborn and unwilling to realize that change was necessary if they were going to keep their section of Calle Ocho alive and kicking.

Selena Gonzalez left the zoning board with the information she needed and an injunction in hand. The emergency call from her grandfather three days ago made it sound like there was going to be a big bad company trying to take away her grandparents' market. From the information she just received…well, she still wasn't sure.

Justin Stern had intrigued her and made her wish that he was a stranger. But she'd heard enough about the smooth-talking rich boy who was trying to muscle out her grandparents to know that Justin wasn't the Mr. Congenial he had portrayed in the waiting room.

If the Luna Azul Company did succeed in developing the old strip mall that housed her grandparents' business now she had a feeling their neighborhood would change. She'd seen the plans that had been submitted by the company—they showed an upscale shopping area designed to bring tourists into the neighborhood. That wasn't what her grandparents' Latin American grocery store was about, but it wasn't the nightclub they feared would be built, either.

As she drove home, she took in the lush, tropical sights of Miami. Her family had wanted her home for a long time. She acknowledged to herself that if it hadn't been for this legal emergency she'd still be ignoring their pleas.

This area made her…it made her all the things that she didn't like about herself. When she was home she was impulsive and passionate. And made stupid decisions—like giving her number to a handsome stranger in a waiting room.

And after all that had happened with Raul ten years ago, she'd been afraid to come back home. She hadn't wanted to face her past or the memories that lingered everywhere she went in her old home and her old neighborhood. As she parked in front of her grandparents' house, she drew a deep breath.

"Did you get the injunction?" her grandfather asked, the minute she stepped through the door.

He wasn't an overly tall man—probably no more than five-eleven. Life had been good to Tomas Gonzalez and he wore his success with a gently rounded stomach. He could be tough as nails in business but he always had a smile for his family and a hug and kiss for her. One of fifteen grandchildren that lived in a three-block radius of his house, Selena had always felt well loved in this home. Especially after her parents' death eleven years ago. A drunk driver had taken both of her parents from her in one accident, leaving her little brother and her alone to face the world. Her grandparents had stepped in but it hadn't been the same.

"I did, *abuelito,*" she said. "And tomorrow I will go down to the Luna Azul Company offices and talk to them about our terms if they still want to go ahead with their plans."

She sat down at the large butcher-block table in the kitchen. The kitchen was the one room where they spent most of their time at her grandparents' house. Her grandmother was in the other room watching her shows.

"Very good, *tata*. I told you we needed you," he said. *Tata* was his nickname for her—just a sweet little endearment that made her feel loved every time he used it. "Those Stern brothers think they can come in and buy up all our property but they aren't part of our community."

"*Abuelito,* the Luna Azul Company has been a part of the community for ten years. From what they told me in the zoning office, they've done a lot for our community."

Her grandfather threw his hands up in the air. "Nothing, *tata,* that's what they have done for our community."

She laughed at him. She was used to his being passionate, even melodramatic about Little Havana. Her grandfather was part of the pre-communist Cuba—an energetic and creative environment—and he'd brought that with him to Miami when he'd become an exile. He still talked about Cuba with fond memories. It was a Cuba that no longer existed, but his stories were always enjoyable.

"What are you two laughing at?" her grandmother asked, coming in to refill her espresso cup with sugar and coffee.

"Those Stern brothers," her grandfather said. "I think Selena is just what we need to keep them in their place."

Her grandmother sat down beside her. She smelled of coffee and the gardenia perfume she'd always worn. She wrapped her arm around Selena's shoulder. "You promised to stay until summer, *tata*. Will you be able to take care of all this by then?"

She hugged her grandmother back. "Definitely. I want to make sure that you get the most out of this new development."

"Good. We want to own our market…the way we used to," Grandfather said.

Selena felt a pang around her heart as she realized that the reason they didn't own their own market was because of her. They were mere renters in the market the Sterns planned to develop, but once they had owned the place. Until Selena messed everything up. She had to make this right for them. "I met Justin Stern at the zoning office. So I will set up a meeting with him," Selena assured her grandparents.

"Good," her grandmother said. "I am going back to my shows. Are you staying at your house?"

"I haven't decided yet," she said. She still owned a house here. She didn't know if she wanted to go back and stay in it all alone. But staying here wasn't a solution; after living alone for so long, she needed her space.

She shrugged. "What's the use of owning a house if you never use it."

"I will send Maria over to make sure it's clean and ready for you," her grandmother said.

"That's not necessary," Selena said. Her grandparents were the caretakers of the old Florida house while she was in New York. It was the house she'd lived in with Raul while they'd both been in school at the University of Miami. There were a lot of memories in that place.

"I can clean it out if I need to," Selena said.

"No. We will make it ready for you. You concentrate on Luna Azul and Justin Stern," Grandfather said.

She shook her head. "He's a very charming man, *abuelita*. Have you met him?"

"No, but *abuelito* has, several times. You find him shrewd, right?" her grandmother said, turning to her husband.

"*Si*. Very shrewd and very…he watches people and then he makes an offer that is exactly right for you. He's like the devil."

Selena laughed, thinking that her grandfather's observation was spot on. "He is silver-tongued."

"*Si*. Watch yourself, *tata*. You don't want to fall for another man like that," her grandfather said.

She wrapped an arm around her own waist as her grandmother got to her feet and yelled at her grandfather in Spanish, telling him to let sleeping dogs lie. Selena quietly left the kitchen, going into the backyard and finding a seat on the bench nestled between blooming hibiscus plants underneath a large tree covered with orchids.

She'd stayed away for so long because of Raul and everything that had happened between them. But now that she was back she was going to have to face her past and really move on from it. Not run away as she'd done before. And she liked the thought of focusing on Justin Stern. He was just the man she needed to forget the past and start to live again here.

Justin signed a few papers that were waiting for his signature and then sent his administrative assistant out for lunch. *An injunction*. Selena Gonzalez with her sexy body and big eyes had filed an injunction against the company to keep them from beginning with their construction work until they proved that they were using local vendors. Now their plans for a ground-breaking in conjunction with the tenth anniversary gala was going to be slowed down if not halted.

"Got a minute?"

Justin glanced up to see his older brother Cameron standing in the doorway. Cam was dressed in business casual, as was his way. He was the one who ran the club and made sure the business there was on track. Unlike Justin, who always wore a suit and spent the majority of his time at his office here in the downtown high-rise complex.

"Sure. What's up?"

"How'd things go at the zoning office?" Cam asked, coming inside and sitting down in one of the leather armchairs in front of his desk.

"Not so good. The Gonzalez family filed an injunction against the building. I'm going to spend the afternoon working on the paperwork we need to file in response. I'm hoping to speak with their lawyer later and see if we can negotiate some kind of deal."

"Damn. I wanted to have the ground-breaking at the tenth anniversary celebration. I was also hoping we could maybe sign up some new, high-profile tenants, but this could put a damper on things."

"I will do what I can to make it happen. Don't get your hopes up, the neighbors and existing tenants in that market don't like us."

"Use your charm to convince them otherwise," Cam said.

"I'm not charming."

"Hell, I know that. You should send Myra."

"My assistant?"

"Yes, she's friendly and everyone likes her."

She was nice, but she didn't have the right kind of

experience to talk to the current occupants of the strip mall and make them understand what was needed.

"I'll head over there after I talk to Selena."

"Who is Selena?"

"Tomas Gonzalez's lawyer."

"Sounds like all the opening you need to get them on our team."

"Stop trying to manipulate me into doing what you want," he warned his brother.

"Why? I'm good at it."

Justin threw a mock punch at Cam who pretended to take the hit.

"Go. I have real work to do," Justin said.

"I will."

Cam left and Justin leaned back in his chair. He had plenty of business to keep him occupied but instead he was thinking of Selena Gonzalez—the lawyer and the woman.

His intercom buzzed. "There's a Ms. Gonzalez on line one."

Speak of the devil. He clicked over to the correct line. "This is Justin," he said.

"Hello, there."

"Hi. I must be remembering our conversation wrong," he said.

"I know I said I'd let you call but I've never been one of those women who waits for a man." Her voice was just as lovely over the phone as it had been in person. He closed his eyes and let the sound of it wash over him. She was distracting. And he needed to keep her from shaking him from his target.

"I'm glad to hear that. I thought you might be difficult given that you filed an injunction against me."

"That wasn't personal, Justin," she said. And he liked the way his name sounded on her lips.

"Yes, it was, Selena. What can I do for you?"

"I didn't realize we had mutual interests," she said. "When we met, I mean."

"I know what you meant…by mutual interests do you mean we both want to ensure that the Latin market is a vibrant part of the community?

"I want to make sure that some big-deal club owner doesn't take the community heritage and bastardize it for his own good."

"I guess you're not coming in here with any pre-conceived notions," he said wryly.

"No, I'm not, I know exactly what kind of man I'm up against. My *abuelito* said you are a silver-tongued devil and I should watch myself around you."

"Selena, you have nothing to fear from me," he said. "I'm a very fair businessman. In fact, I think your *abuelito* will be very happy with my latest offer."

"Send it to me and I will let you know."

"Come down to my office so we can talk in person. I prefer that to emails and faxes."

He leaned back in his chair. He knew how to negotiate, and having Selena here on his own turf was the way for him to get what he wanted. No one could turn him down once he started talking. To be honest, he'd never had a deal go south once he got the other party in the same room with him.

"Okay, when?"

"Today if you have time."

"Can you hold on?"

"Sure," he said. The line went silent and he turned to look out his plate-glass windows. The skyline of downtown Miami was gorgeous and he appreciated how lucky he was to live in paradise.

"Okay, we can do it today."

"We?"

"My *abuelito* and I."

"Great. I look forward to seeing Tomas again."

"And what about me?" she asked.

"I've thought of little else but seeing you again."

She laughed. "I'm tempted to believe you, but I know you are a businessman and business must always come first."

She was right. He wanted her to be different but the truth of the matter was that he was almost thirty-five and set in his ways. There was little doubt that someday he might want to settle down but it wasn't today.

And it wouldn't be with Selena.

"Good girl," he said.

"Girl?"

"I didn't mean that in a condescending way."

"How did you mean it?" she asked.

He had no idea if he'd offended her or not. "Just teasingly. Maybe I should stick to business. I'm much better at knowing what not to say."

She laughed again and he realized how much he liked the sound of that. He thought it prudent to get off the phone with her before he said something else that could put the entire outdoor plaza project at risk.

"I'll see you then. How does two o'clock sound?" he said.

"We'll be there," she agreed and hung up.

Two

As Selena and her grandfather left for their meeting, her other relatives were arriving to start cooking the dinner. Since she hadn't been home in almost ten years, the entire Gonzalez clan was getting together for a big feast.

To some people coming home might mean revisiting the place they had grown up, for her coming home meant a barbeque in the backyard of her grandparents' house and enough relatives to maybe require an occupancy permit.

Being a Gonzalez was overwhelming. She had forgotten how much she enjoyed the quiet of her life in Manhattan until this moment. This was part of what she'd run from. In Miami everyone knew her, in Manhattan she was just another person on the street.

She had the top down on her rental Audi convertible and the Florida sunshine warmed her head and the breeze stirred her hair as they drove to Justin Stern's office.

Having the top down did something else. It made conversation with her *abuelito* nearly impossible and right now she needed some quiet time to think. Though Justin Stern had flirted with her, she knew he was one sharp attorney and she'd need to have her wits about her when they talked.

"Selena?"

"Si?"

"You missed the turnoff," her grandfather said.

"I…dang it, I wasn't paying attention."

"What's on your mind?"

"This meeting. I want to make sure you and *abuelita* are treated fairly."

"You will, *tata*."

She made a U-turn at the next intersection and soon they were in the parking lot of Luna Azul Company's corporate headquarters. The building was large and modern but fit the neighborhood, and as she walked closer, Selena noticed that it wasn't new construction but had been a remodel. She made a mental note to check on this building and to investigate if having the Stern brothers here had enhanced this area.

"You ready, *abuelito?*"

"For what?"

"To take on Justin."

"Hell, yes. I've been doing it the best I can, but…we needed you," her grandfather said.

They entered the air-conditioned building. The receptionist greeted them and directed them to the fifth floor executive offices.

"Hello, Mr. Gonzalez."

"Hello, Myra. How are you today?" her grandfather

asked the pretty young woman who greeted them there.

"Not bad. Hear you've brought a big-gun lawyer to town," she said.

"I brought our attorney. Figured it was about time I had someone who could argue on Mr. Stern's level."

Myra laughed and even Selena smiled. She could tell that her grandfather had been doing okay negotiating for himself. Why had he called her?

"I'm Selena Gonzalez," Selena said stepping forward and holding out her hand.

"Myra Temple," the other woman said. "It's nice to meet you. You will be meeting in the conference room at the end of the hall. Can I get either of you something to drink?"

"I'll have a sparkling water," her grandfather said.

"Me, too," Selena said and followed her grandfather down the hall to the conference room.

The walls were richly paneled and there was a portrait of Justin and two other men who had to be his brothers. There was a strong resemblance in the stubborn jawline of all the men. She recognized Nate Stern, Justin's younger brother and a former New York Yankees baseball player.

Her *abuelito* sat down but she walked around the room, and checked out the view from the fifth floor and then the model for the Calle Ocho market center.

"Have you seen this, *abuelito*?"

He shook his head and came over to stand next to her. The Cuban American market that her grandparents owned was now replaced with a chain grocery store. She was outraged and angry.

"I can't believe this," Selena said.

"You can't believe what?" Justin asked as he entered

the conference room. Myra was right behind him with a tray of Perrier and glasses filled with ice cubes.

"That you think replacing the Cuban American market with a chain grocery store would be acceptable."

"To be honest we haven't got an agreement with them yet," Justin said. "This is just an artist's concept of how the Market will look."

"Well the injunction I filed today is going to hamper your agreement with them."

"It will indeed. That's why I invited you here to talk."

She was disgusted that she had fallen for his sexy smile and self-deprecating charm at the zoning office because she saw now that he was a smooth operator. And she'd had her fill of them when she was younger. It made her angry to think that in ten years she hadn't learned not to fall for that kind of guy.

"Then let's get to work," she said. "I've drawn up a list of concerns."

"I look forward to seeing them," Justin said. "And Tomas, it's nice to see you again," he said, shaking the older man's hand.

"I'd prefer it if we could stop meeting," Tomas said.

"To be fair I'd like that, too. I want to move this project forward," Justin said.

She bet he did, he was probably losing money with each day that they waited to break ground on their new market. But she was here to make sure that he realized that he couldn't come in and replace traditional markets with a shiny upscale shopping area with no ties to the community.

"What is your largest concern?" he asked. "This was a Publix supermarket strip mall before you first came to it, Tomas. So you have had chain grocers in the neighborhood before. We can invite another retailer if you'd prefer that."

Selena realized that Justin didn't necessarily understand what their objection to his building in the community truly was.

"Justin, this strip mall is part of the Cuban American community. Our family's store isn't just a place for people to pick up groceries, it's where the old men come in the morning for their coffee and then sit around and discuss the business of the day. It's a place where young mothers bring their kids to play in the back and have great Cuban food.

"This is the heart of the neighborhood. You can't just rip it out."

Justin knew this meeting wasn't going to be easy. He'd figured that out the moment he met Selena. She was the kind of woman that made a man work for it. And he knew that she was looking out for the interests of her community and to be fair he needed that community to want to shop there. Even though they'd do a good crossover business from the club and he had an arrangement with some local tour companies to add the new Luna Azul Market to their tourist stops once it opened, it would be the neighborhood residents that would make or break this endeavor.

"I'm open to your suggestions. So far Tomas has only demanded that we leave the strip mall the way it is and I think that we both know that isn't a solution."

"We both don't know that," she said.

"Have you been down to the property lately?" he asked her. "The mall is old and run-down. The families that you speak of are dwindling, isn't that right, Tomas?"

Tomas shrugged but then glanced over at Selena.

"The buildings need repairs and the landlord...you, Justin, should be making them."

"I want to make more than repairs. I'm not even sure if they meet the new hurricane wind resistance standards."

Selena pulled out a notebook and started writing on it. "We will check into it. Have you considered forming a committee with the community leaders and your company?"

"We've had a few informal discussions."

"You need to do a lot more than that. Because if you want the neighborhood support you are going to have to open a dialogue with them."

"Okay," Justin said. "But only if you serve on the committee."

She blinked up and then tipped her head to the side. "I don't think that I need to be on there."

"I do," Justin said. "You grew up there, and are also familiar with the legal and zoning issues. You will be able to see the bigger picture."

"I don't think—"

"I agree with him, *tata,* you should be on there," Tomas said.

"Tata?" Justin asked, smiling.

She glared at her grandfather. "It's a nickname."

She blushed, and it was the first crack he'd seen in her all-business, tough-as-nails shell.

The business deal was going to go through whether Tomas and his allies wanted it to or not. Justin had already scheduled a round of golf with the zoning commissioner, Maxwell Strong, at the exclusive club he belonged to to get him to change his mind. And over the next week he'd work on finding a way out of the legal hole that Selena had dug for him. But he wanted to see more of her.

And this committee thing would be perfect. Plus, he did actually want the community behind the project. "Myra, will you set up a meeting time for us...I think we should use Luna Azul. Tomas and Selena will send you a list of people to invite."

"I'd like to take a closer look at the plans for the market," Selena said.

"I'll leave you two to discuss that," Tomas said. "I need to call around and see when everyone will be available to meet."

"Myra will show you to an office you can use," Justin said.

After Tomas and Myra left the room, Justin studied Selena for a minute. Her head was bent and she was making notes on her legal pad. He noticed that her handwriting was very neat and very feminine.

"Why are you staring at me?"

"I thought I already told you that I like the way you look."

"That wasn't just you trying to...I don't know what you were up to. Did you know who I was in that lobby of the zoning office?"

He shook his head. "No. I wish I had known."

"Why?"

"Maybe I could have talked you out of filing that injunction," he said with a laugh.

She chuckled at that. "Wow, that's putting a lot of pressure on your supposed charm."

He grabbed his side pretending she'd wounded him. "Good thing I'm tough-skinned."

"You'd have to be in order to work in the neighborhood you do. How did you and your brothers manage to make

Luna Azul a success without getting the community behind you?" she asked him.

"Some locals do frequent the club but we rely on the celebs for business. They bring in their own crowd of followers. We book first-rate bands and we have salsa lessons in the rooftop club...so we do okay. Have you ever been there?"

She shook her head. "I left Miami before you opened your doors."

"Why did you leave?" he asked.

"None of your business," she replied with a tight look that told him he'd somehow gone too far.

"My apologies. I expected you to say you needed some freedom...would you have dinner with me tonight?"

"Why?"

"I believe in keeping my enemies close."

"Me, too," she said.

"I'll take that as a yes."

"It is a yes. But I'll pick the place." She wrote an address at the bottom of her legal pad and then tore the paper off and handed it to him. "Be there at seven. Dress casual."

"Do I need to bring anything?"

"Just your appetite."

She gathered her things and then stood up and walked out of the conference room. He watched her leave.

Inviting Justin to her family get-together was inspired. He wanted to do business in this community but he didn't understand it. This would be his lesson.

On her way home, she'd driven down to the strip mall to see her grandfather's store, and it had been run-down more than she expected.

Something was needed, but an outlet mall or a high-

end shopping plaza wasn't it. The Calle Ocho neighborhood leaders wouldn't stand for. Plus, she wanted
to ensure that her grandparents got the best deal possible.

They had always been at the center of things in Little
Havana and she wasn't about to let Justin Stern take that
away from them.

She also stopped by her house. When she entered,
she was swamped with memories but managed to brush
them aside as she freshened up and got ready to walk
back over to her grandparents'. The last thing she wanted
was to be here, she realized. She packed a bag with
some clothes she found in the closet, locked the house
and pointed her rented convertible toward the beach.

Her New York law practice had made her a wealthy
woman. And considering this was the first real break
she'd taken from work in the last eight years she thought
she deserved a treat. All she did was work and save her
money. Well that wasn't completely true—she did have
an addiction to La Perla lingerie that wouldn't stop. But
for the most part all she did was work.

So as she pulled up at the Ritz and asked for a suite
for the next month, Selena knew she was doing the
right thing. She was in luck and was soon ensconced in
memory-free luxury. Just what she needed.

As she was settling in, her cell phone rang and she
glanced at the number. It was a local number but not
one she recognized. She answered it anyway. "This is
Selena."

"This is Justin. How about if we have drinks at Luna
Azul first so you can see the club?"

"No."

"Just a flat-out no, you aren't going to even pretend
to think it over," he said.

"That's right. I am not staying near there, anyway. I'm at the Ritz," she said. She was kicked back on the love seat in her living room reading up on Justin on her laptop.

"How about a drink in the lobby bar?" he suggested. His voice was deep over the phone—very sexy.

"Why?" she asked. She wasn't sure spending any time alone with him was the right thing. She wanted to keep it all business between them. That was the only way she was going to keep herself from acting on the attraction she felt for him.

"I want a chance to talk to you alone. No business—just personal stuff."

"No business? Justin, all we have between us is business." She hoped that making that statement out loud would somehow make it true. She didn't want to admit to herself or Justin that there was a spark.

"But we could have so much more."

"Ha! You don't even know me," she said.

"That's exactly what I'm hoping to change. What harm could one drink do?"

"One drink," she repeated. Hell, who was she kidding? She was going to meet him. She'd invited him to her welcome-home party so he could get to know her family and not only because of business. She wanted to see how he was with them to get the measure of the man he was.

"Just one," he said. "I'll do my best to be charming and try to convince you to stay for more."

"I'm a tough cookie," she said.

"I think that's what you want the world to believe but I bet there's a softer woman underneath all that."

She hoped he never found out. She had tried so hard to bury the woman—*girl*—she'd been when she'd graduated from the University of Miami and left her hometown behind. Were there still any vestiges of that passionate side of her left after Raul had broken her heart?

Sure she dated, but she was careful that it was just casual, never letting her emotions get involved. Raul had taught her that the price to be paid for loving foolishly wasn't one that only she paid. Her grandparents had almost lost their business because of her poor judgment in men, and Selena had vowed to never be that weak again.

"Pretty much what you see is what you get with me," she said, uncomfortable talking about herself. "What about you? Are you all awkward charm and sleek business acumen?"

He laughed. "I guess so. It's hard when you grow up with a charismatic brother—everyone just expects you to be the same."

"How many brothers do you have?" she asked. Though she'd spent the afternoon reading about them on the internet she wanted to hear how he described his family. She had no idea what it had been like to grow up the son of a wealthy, semi-famous pro golfer or to have a brother who played for the Yankees. "I know your dad played pro golf."

"Yes, he did. I have two brothers…"

"That's right. And you're the middle one?"

"Yes, ma'am. The quiet one."

"I haven't seen you quiet yet."

He laughed again and she liked the sound of it—a little too much. No matter how charming he was she wasn't going to let him past her guard. She had to take control and remind him that they were doing things on her terms. "Okay, so one drink. Why don't you come by around—"

"Five. We can have hors d'oeuvres, too."

"Five? That's two hours before our date. How are you going to make one drink last that long?" she asked, but she was already getting up and starting to ready herself to meet him. It was only forty minutes until five.

"If things go well I don't want to cheat you out of spending time alone with me."

"You are so thoughtful," she said.

"I am. It's one of my many gifts."

"I'll remember that when we are doing our negotiations for the marketplace," she said with a laugh. "Five o'clock in the Ritz lobby bar."

"See you there," he said and hung up.

She went into the bedroom and looked at herself in the mirror. She looked like she'd just come from work. She opened her closet and realized she had a closet full of casual and work clothes. Not exactly the sexiest clothing in the world.

Did she want to look sexy for her date with Justin?

"Yes," she said, looking at herself in the mirror. If she was going to get the upper hand on Justin she was going to need to pull out all the stops.

It sure was going to be fun to go head-to-head with Mr. Know-Your-Enemies.

Three

Justin valet-parked his car and walked into the lobby of the Ritz on South Beach. The view from the restaurant here was breathtaking and easily one of the best in this area. He glanced at his watch. He was a few minutes early and as he scanned the lobby he didn't see Selena.

He walked to the lobby bar and found seating for two in a relatively quiet area. He knew that he had to get to know Selena better for business reasons. He had to know how she thought so he could make sure he made the right offer—one she'd accept so that he could get the market back on track. He hadn't gotten the Luna Azul Company to where it was today by not knowing how to read people.

But he wasn't going to deny that he wanted Selena. There had been a moment in the conference room this afternoon when he'd wished they were alone so he could pull her into his arms and see if he could crack her reserve with passion.

"Justin?"

He glanced over his shoulder and felt like he'd been sucker punched. The prim, reserved woman he'd flirted with was gone and in her place was a bombshell. Maybe it was just her thick ebony hair hanging in waves around her shoulders, or the red lipstick that drew his eyes to her full mouth. But his gut insisted that it was the curve-hugging black dress she wore that ended midthigh. He skimmed his gaze down to her dainty-looking ankles and those high-heeled strappy sandals that made him almost groan out loud.

"Selena," he said, but his voice sounded husky and almost choked to him.

She arched one eyebrow and smiled. "Happy to see me?"

"That is an understatement. Let me get us a drink. What's your poison?"

"Mojito, I think. I need something to cool me down."

He signaled the cocktail waitress and placed their drink order before diving right in. "Tell me about yourself, Selena. Why are you living in New York when your family is still here?"

"No small talk?" she asked, turning her attention away from him and skimming the room.

"Why bother with that?" he asked. "We both want to know as much about each other as we can, right?"

"Definitely. I just didn't plan on going first," she said with a smile as she turned back to face him again.

Every time she talked he tried to concentrate on her words but he couldn't take his eyes from her lips. He wanted to know how they would feel under his own.

What kind of kisser would she be? Would she taste as good as he imagined?

"I'm a gentleman," he said. And he didn't want to show her any weakness.

"So it's ladies first?" she asked.

"In all things, especially pleasure," he said.

She blushed as their waitress arrived with the drinks. She started to take a sip but he stopped her.

"A toast to new relationships."

"And a quick resolution to our business problems," she said.

He clinked his glass to hers and watched as she took a swallow of her cocktail. When she took the glass from her mouth she licked her lips and he felt his blood begin to flow a little heavier in his veins as his groin stirred.

He wanted her.

That wasn't news. But sitting here with her in the bar was starting to seem like a really dumb idea. He needed all his wits about him because it was apparent that Selena was playing with her A-game and he needed to as well.

"You were going to tell me all your secrets," he said.

She laughed. "I was going to tell you the official version of my life."

"I'll take whatever you offer," he said.

"I bet you will. Okay, where to start?"

"The beginning," he suggested, shifting his legs to make room in his pants for his growing erection.

"Birth?"

"Nah, skip to college. I did a little internet research on you and saw that you graduated from the University of Miami. What made you choose to go to Fordham Law

School instead of choosing something closer to home?" he asked.

"I needed a change of scene. I was pretty sure that I wanted to practice corporate law and I had done an internship for one summer with the firm that I work for now. So it made sense to go there."

"That's about the same time your grandparents sold the marketplace and switched over to being renters in the space. Did they do that to pay for your education?" he asked.

Her face got very tight and she shook her head. "I had a scholarship."

"I did a deed search to see who had owned the property before the previous owner and it was your grandfather. I can't understand why he sold," Justin continued. He really wanted to know why ten years ago, Tomas had made the decision to sell the marketplace property and become a rental tenant instead. That made no sense to Justin as a businessman. But it also made no sense based on what he knew of Tomas. Tomas liked being his own boss.

"What about you? Harvard law graduates can usually write their own ticket to any law firm but you came back home and worked with your brothers instead, why?"

Justin stretched back and looked at her for a minute. That was complicated. He couldn't tell her that coming back was the hardest decision he'd ever made because even his brothers didn't know that.

"They needed me," he said. It was close to the truth. He didn't hold with outright lies.

He took another sip of his drink and then leaned forward. "Why are you here now?"

"My grandfather said you were too slick and he couldn't trust you."

"That's hardly true. Tomas is very shrewd. And don't change the subject. Why did he sell the marketplace if not for your education?"

She flushed and her hand trembled for a minute and then she took a sip of her drink.

He waited for her to answer but she didn't say anything.

"Selena?"

"That is a private matter and I won't discuss it with you."

Selena was surprised that he'd dug back on the deed. But she shouldn't have been. She may have momentarily distracted Justin with her clothing and changed appearance but he'd adjusted quickly by pulling the rug out from under her with that question.

"Okay. I can respect that. I was just thinking that if they hadn't sold the property perhaps it wouldn't be so derelict now," Justin said.

He was right. Selling that property had been a mistake and that was why she was here. To right the wrong she'd caused when she'd allowed herself to get suckered by a smooth-talking con man ten years ago.

She'd never seen him coming, Raul had swept her off her feet, and then once she'd fallen for his sweet talk, he'd used that love she had for him against her. The con he'd run on her had been simple enough. He was starting his own company, a luxury yacht business, and needed some initial investors. She'd put all of the inheritance she'd gotten from her parents into it, and in a calculated move on Raul's part she'd convinced her grandparents to mortgage the market and invest, as well. Raul took all the money and disappeared overnight.

The ensuing investigation into Raul's disappearance

had been an upheaval in their lives. It had taken almost two years to get it sorted out and at the end with lawyers' fees and private investigator charges her grandparents had no money left. They were forced to sell the marketplace and become renters. Raul was eventually caught and brought to justice, but their money was never repaid.

It had been one of the most humiliating times of her life and she'd been very glad to escape Miami to Fordham where she knew no one. She'd started over and been very careful since then not to let her emotions get the better of her.

"You are very right," she said. She took another sip of her mojito. The smooth rum and mint drink was soothing. Justin watched her each time she swallowed and she knew she'd been distracting him all evening.

She liked the feeling of power it gave her to know that she could manipulate him. She wondered if that was what Raul had felt as he'd slowly drawn her into his web. Had it been the power? She hadn't thought of that in years, but her experiences with men had taught her that in all relationships—personal and business—it all came down to who had something the other wanted. And right now, she had something that Justin wanted a lot.

"I know," he said. He was cocky and she had to admit that it was a trait she was beginning to enjoy in him.

He seemed so in control. She'd been told she gave that impression, as well, but she knew underneath her professional persona she was usually a mess. Was it the same for him? But she couldn't detect any chinks in his armor. She was starting to realize that even distracted he was going to be a tough opponent.

She leaned forward to place her drink on the table

and noticed his eyes tracked down toward her breasts. She shifted her shoulders so the fabric of her dress drew the material taut over her curves and then sat back.

"Have you thought of selling the property back to my grandparents? I think that would be the easiest solution." Then she could conclude this business in Miami and take the first flight back to New York and her nice, safe, regular life. A place where the businessmen she encountered looked dull and gray like a Manhattan winter instead of like Justin, who was tan, vibrant and hot...just like Miami.

"I don't think so," he said, looking back up at her eyes. "Your grandparents don't..."

"What?"

"They don't have the resources to make the property profitable the way that the Luna Azul Company does. I mean, they would probably fix up their market but it is going to take a lot of capital to revamp the entire area. And that is the only way you are going to keep your current clientele and get new customers."

He had a point but she didn't like the thought of an outsider owning the market. It also irked her that this situation was entirely her fault. If she hadn't fallen for Raul so many years ago, her beloved *abuelito* wouldn't have to deal with the Stern brothers on their terms.

"Granted but if you take away the local feel of the marketplace, you will lose money."

"That's where you come in. I liked your idea of forming a committee. I wish I'd thought of it sooner," Justin said. "But enough business. I want to know the woman behind the suit. I like your dress by the way."

She tossed her hair and made herself let go of the work part of being with Justin. There was nothing to be accomplished tonight. He'd either come around to her way of thinking or he'd find out how many complications she could put in the way of his business deals.

"I noticed you liking it."

"Good. Are you finished with your drink?"

"Why?"

"I want to take you for a walk along the beach."

"I'd like that," she said, getting to her feet. "I miss the beach."

"I live right on it. That was one thing that motivated me to come back home after Harvard. I like living somewhere so temperate."

"What else?" she asked. She suspected that family must be important to him. That was at odds with what she usually encountered in type-A, driven business executives, but then Justin didn't exactly fit the mold of what she expected from guys to begin with.

"Why are you really here?" she asked as they stepped out into the warm early-evening.

"I told you I like to know my opponents," he said.

"I can see that," she said. She did as well. Normally when she was negotiating something for her company she spent a lot of time researching the players involved in the deal. Winning almost always came down to who had the most information. "You were trying to throw me off my game a little, right?"

"In part," he admitted. "But honestly, you aren't what I was expecting from the Gonzalezes' lawyer."

"Because I'm a girl?" she asked using his term. "You know that calling me a girl wasn't exactly flattering?"

"I didn't mean it that way," he said. "It's because you're so sexy. I can handle going up against a girl but when she is making me think of long, hot nights instead of business—well I figured turnabout was fair play and I should do something unexpected like ask you out."

She bit her lower lip. He was a very frank man, which shouldn't surprise her. From the moment they'd met he'd been that way. He was the kind of man who shot from the hip and didn't worry about the consequences.

And she was a woman who'd been damned by the consequences of her reckless heart before. She had to remember that her grandparents were in this situation with the Luna Azul Company specifically because she'd followed her heart and they had paid the price.

"I'm not looking for a relationship," she said. "I am focused on my career."

"I can see that," he said. "But unless you're into lying to yourself, you'll admit that there is something between us."

She could admit that. There was a powerful attraction between them. Something that was more intense than anything she'd ever experienced before. She wanted to blame it on Miami and her old self, but she knew that it was Justin. If she'd been here with any other man she wouldn't have felt like this.

That was enough to make her pause. Justin was different and that very difference was enough to make him dangerous.

"Lust," she said. "And that is nothing more than a chimera."

"An illusion? I don't think so. Lust is our primal instincts telling us to pay attention. You could be a potential mate for me," he said.

She stopped walking on the wooden boardwalk and turned to face him. He'd put on a pair of aviator-style sunglasses and with his jacket slung over his shoulder he looked like he'd stepped off a yacht. He seemed like a man who was used to getting everything he wanted.

"What?" she asked. "There is no way you and I could

ever be mates. I just don't know if I should believe you or not. You're not really looking for a mate for more than one night, right?"

"Usually, I'd say so, but the way I am reacting to you throws my normal playbook out the window."

She shook her head. "Your playbook? Any guy who has one of those isn't someone I'm interested in."

"That sounded worse than I meant it to. I was trying to say that this attraction I feel for you is making me forget every rule I have about mixing business and pleasure."

"I can't afford to take a chance like that with you, Justin."

"Because of Tomas?"

She wished it were that simple. "If it didn't involve my grandparents…"

"What do you mean?" he asked.

She had no idea. She wished she had some answers. "Say I met you on vacation, I'd jump into a fling with you. But this is my home and my family and I can't afford to compromise anything."

"There is no need to compromise anything," Justin said, putting his hand in the center of her back and urging her to start walking again.

She shook her head and the scent of gardenias surrounded him. He closed his eyes and breathed deeply. Why was it that everything about Selena was a turn-on for him? "I'm not going to take no for an answer. We are both good at negotiating."

"This isn't easy for me. My grandparents deserve my undivided attention, I owe them," she said.

"Why do you owe them?" he asked. He wanted to know more about what had happened ten years ago and he was determined to get some answers, but not right now.

"I just do."

He nodded. "Well, I owe my brothers, and my company deserves my undivided attention, but I can't think of business when I'm with you. Right now all I can think of is your mouth and how it will feel under mine."

"Saying things like that is not helping me," she said, closing her eyes and wrapping her arms around her own waist.

If he pushed a little bit harder he could have her. He knew that. But he didn't want to crumble her defenses. He pulled her closer to him and moved them off the path out of the way of other walkers. "Have you thought about it?"

She nibbled on her full lower lip as she looked up at him. "I have, but I'm not about to play into your hands so easily."

He lowered his head, wanting to kiss her but at the same time wanting—no needing—her to want it too. He wanted her to be so attracted to him that she forgot her rules and her fears and everything else just faded away.

"Justin, stop manipulating me."

"I'm not," he said. "I want to see what it will take for you to forget about business and just see me as a man."

"Stop trying to play me," she said. "Just be yourself."

"I don't think you'd trust me," he said.

"I don't trust you now," she said. "And that feeling that you are toying with me is never going to help your case. I do want you but I don't want to be your pawn."

Her honesty cut straight through him. He really didn't

want her to be his pawn. He wanted her to be his woman. That was it.

He needed Selena no matter what the circumstances. And he was going to do whatever he had to to make that happen. He couldn't just walk away.

"I'm sorry. I was trying—"

"I know what you were trying to do," she said, lifting one hand and tracing the line of his lips. "I can understand it because I don't want to end up the weak one either."

He could hardly think when she touched him. He slid his hands together at her waist and pulled her more closely into his body.

He rubbed his lips against hers briefly and then stepped back before he gave in to temptation and ravished her mouth.

"We need...to walk," he said.

He took her hand with his and led her down the path. She laughed softly and he knew she was very aware of his desire. That didn't bother him at all. He wanted her to be very aware of him as a man and he knew that he'd accomplished that.

"We can't walk away from this," he said.

"I know," she admitted. "But I won't let this kind of attraction take control of my life."

He understood that. As a man, part of him was glad to hear that she wanted him that powerfully. The other part, the businessman who never took a day off, was glad to hear it, too, because it meant that he had the potential to use that attraction to get what he wanted.

Walking took the edge off her and allowed him to start thinking of something other than lifting her skirt and finding the sweetness between her legs. "What if we pretend you are on vacation?"

"Why?"

"Then it's like you said, we're just two people who are attracted to each other."

"Like a vacation fling?" she asked.

"Exactly like that. No talking about our families and their business interests. Just two people who've met and started an affair," he said.

"So it ends when I go back home?" she asked.

His gut said no. He didn't want to think about Selena leaving but he put that down to the fact that she was new to him. "If that is what we both decide, then yes."

She pulled her hand from his, stopped walking and turned to look out at the ocean. She wrapped one arm around her waist and he wondered if he'd ever know her well enough to know what she was thinking.

"I wish it could be that simple," she said, "But we both know there is no way we're going to be able—"

"I'm not someone who takes no for an answer," he said.

She glanced over her shoulder at him and he saw that fiery spark was back in her eyes. This couldn't be more than a fling and he wanted to keep it light. But the only way he was going to be able to deal with her in the boardroom was if he had her in his bedroom.

"I'm not going to let you bully me into making a decision like this."

"Is that what I'm doing or is that what you are telling yourself?"

She turned to face him full-on and walked over to him, hips swaying with each step. His mind went blank and suddenly he didn't care why she agreed but only that she did. He needed her to be one hundred percent his. And nothing was going to stand in the way of that. Not business and not even the lady herself. He knew that Selena Gonzalez wanted him and now he just had to find the right button to push, to convince her that she was willing to take a chance on him.

"I know my own mind, Justin Stern," she said as she closed the gap between them. She put her hands on his shoulders and tipped her head back to look up at him. "And I know exactly what I want."

She went up on her tiptoes, tunneled her fingers into his hair and planted a kiss on him that made him forget everything else. All he did was feel.

Her breasts cushioned against his chest. Her supple hips under his hands as he rested them there. Her soft hair brushing his cheek as she turned her head to angle her mouth better over his.

And then the thrust of her warm tongue into his mouth. How she slowly rubbed hers over his and then lifted her hands to his face to hold him right above the jaw. She kept his head steady as she tasted him and he let her.

Hell, there was no stopping this woman. She had turned his own game back on him and left him standing still. He drew his own hands up to her tiny waist and pulled her off balance into his body.

He sucked on her tongue when she would have pulled it back. Her hands slid down his neck to his shoulders and she moved her head again and a tiny moan escaped her.

His erection nudged the top of her thighs and he shifted his hips against hers and heard her moan again. This was more like it, he thought. This was the kind of negotiation he wanted. Both of them alone together.

Just man versus woman and let the winner take all.

Four

Selena had forgotten what it was like to turn the tables on a man sexually. She did it all the time at work but this was personal and she liked it. A heady mix of passion and power consumed her and she knew that it was well past time she got back in touch with this side of herself.

She'd given in to Justin not just because of the lust that was flowing between them but also because she needed to reclaim her femininity.

She took Justin's hand and led him back to the hotel. "Why are we wasting our time out here when we could be up in my room?"

"Your room? I thought you weren't sure about my proposition."

"I guess you think too much." Turning the tables on Justin had knocked him off balance and she knew he would be easier to deal with now. "I like the idea of a vacation fling. It's been too long for me and being with you…well let's just say you are the perfect distraction."

He frowned at her, but she didn't care. She wasn't stupid. She knew that even though Justin wanted her—she knew he wasn't faking his attraction to her—a part of him was focused on how to use the lust they both felt to his own advantage.

And she wasn't going to let him do that. She wanted him. She needed a distraction from being back here in Miami. She was thinking too much about the girl she had been and Justin was the distraction she needed.

"Come back to my room," she said, leaning closer and kissing his neck right under his ear. "That's what we'd do if we were on vacation."

Justin nodded. "But we aren't on vacation."

"Have you changed your mind?" she asked.

"No. But I don't like the way you changed yours. What's going on behind those beautiful brown eyes?" he asked.

She pulled back. She couldn't do this. It wasn't like her to just impulsively invite a man back to her room. He was right, what was she thinking?

"Nothing. Nothing is going on," she said. "I think I had a momentary fever but it is passing now."

She felt small and a bit rejected. She'd actually never been that bold with a man before. The dress and the way that Justin treated her had made her feel like she was sexy, an enchantress, and now she was realizing she was still just Selena.

"I think we should head back to the hotel. I need to freshen up before heading to dinner. I will meet you there."

She turned to walk away needing to get back to her

room. She needed to find someplace private to sit down and regroup.

"No."

She glanced over her shoulder at him.

"No?"

"That's what I said. I am not letting you run away," he said, taking her hand in his. "What's going on with you?"

She shook her head and swallowed hard. "I'm sorry. You are making me a little...crazy."

"That's good. That's what I was going for...trying to distract you," he admitted.

"Well, you did a good job tonight. But that won't affect me in the boardroom when we are meeting with your group and the community leaders."

"I didn't think it would. To be honest I'm trying to even the scales. You have me thinking about your curvy body and kissing you instead of business and I wanted you to think of me."

"Does that mean you don't really want a vacation fling with me?"

"Hell, no. I want you more than I want my next breath. But I want you to want it for the right reasons—not because you think it will help you in the boardroom. I do believe we can keep this attraction between us private and explore it."

She thought about what he was saying. She wanted him and she wasn't going to deny it. "I'm not—Miami is more than just my home. It's the place that shaped me into the woman I am today and coming back here is stirring up all kinds of things in me I didn't expect."

"Like what?" he asked.

Justin was dangerous, she thought. He made her feel

so comfortable and safe that she would tell him almost anything. "This dress for one thing. I bought this for you."

"I like it."

"That was my intention, but at home…in Manhattan I'd never wear this."

"Good," he said, leading them back toward the hotel. "Be yourself with me, Selena. I want to see that woman you keep tucked away from the rest of the world. I don't want to be like every other guy to you."

"There is no way you could be. My family told me you're the devil."

He laughed. It was a strong masculine sound and it made her smile. "I haven't been called the devil before."

"To your face," she said.

"Touché," he said as they reached the hotel and stepped into the air-conditioned lobby.

Chills spread down her arms and she shivered just a bit. "Are we okay now?" he asked.

"I think so," she said. "I will meet you—"

"Get whatever you need. I want to take you to Luna Azul."

"Why?"

"I want to show you my family," he said.

"After," she said. "I need some time to myself before we go to dinner at my grandparents."

"Really? I was hoping you'd go with me. I don't want to walk in there by myself."

"Since when does the devil show fear?" she asked.

"I have no idea, since I'm not the devil," he said.

"What are you?" she asked.

"Just a man who likes a pretty girl and doesn't want to screw up again."

Selena watched him walk away, wondering if she'd underestimated him and if that would be at her own peril.

Justin sat quietly in his car parked on the street in front of the Gonzalez home. Selena had withdrawn into herself and there had been no drawing her out. He had a feeling that Selena's attitude was the least of his problems as he got out and walked up the driveway to the house.

There was music coming from the backyard and the delicious smells of charcoal and roasting meat wafted around him. This was a cozy neighborhood, the kind of place where he could buy two or three houses and not feel the sting in his checkbook, but a place where he'd never fit in.

Was this what Selena had been talking about when she said Luna Azul didn't belong in Little Havana?

"*Amigo,* you coming?"

The guy who walked by him was in his early twenties with close-cut dark hair and warm olive-colored skin. He wasn't as tall as Justin and his face was friendly.

"I am indeed," Justin said. He had a six-pack of Landshark beer in one hand and some flowers for Selena's grandmother.

"How do you know Tomas?" the young man asked.

"We're in business together." Justin wasn't about to pretend he had any other reason to be here. In fact, in light of his drinks with Selena he thought wooing her was going about as smoothly as the entire buying-the-marketplace deal. What was it with the Gonzalez family? Was it impossible to find a common path with them?

"Truly? My *abuelito* usually doesn't do business with...wait a minute, are you Justin Stern?"

"That's me," he said. Great, nice to know that he already had a reputation here and he hadn't even arrived yet.

"Oh, ho, you have some guts showing up here," the kid said.

"I was invited, and I'm not a bad guy," Justin told him. "I am trying to find a way to make that market viable, not to run your grandparents out."

The kid tipped his head to the side, studying him. "I'm watching you."

"I'm glad. Family should look out for one another. And I'm not going to take advantage of your grandparents or your family. My main concern is making money from the property we bought."

"Is money all you care about?"

Justin shook his head. He saw Selena walking up toward the house from where they stood in the shade of a large palm tree. She'd changed from the sexy dress she had worn earlier into a pair of khaki walking shorts and a sleeveless wraparound top. She was enchanting, he thought.

He forgot about how unwelcome this guy was making him feel and focused on Selena.

"Leave him alone, Enrique. He's not a bad guy," Selena said as she came up to them.

"He told me the same thing," Enrique said. "Are you sure about him?"

Selena shrugged. "Not one hundred percent but I'm getting there."

"If we do business with your family," Enrique said, turning to Justin, "I want to talk to you about deejaying at Luna Azul. Why do you only hire New York and LA deejays?"

Justin had very little to do with the everyday running

of the nightclub he owned with his brothers. "I don't have an answer for that but I can find out. If you send me a demo tape—"

"I don't think Enrique wants to work for you," Selena said.

"I'll make my own decisions, *tata*," Enrique said. He reached around Justin and hugged her. She hugged him back.

"Enrique is my little brother," she said.

"I'm taller than you now, sis. I think that makes me your 'big' little brother," Enrique said with a grin that was familiar to Justin. He'd seen it on Selena's face a few times.

"You'll always be my baby brother," she said, looping her arm through Enrique's and Justin was relegated to following the two siblings up the walk to the house.

Justin had the feeling he'd always be an outsider. Too bad his little brother wasn't here tonight. This was exactly the type of party that Nate was better at than he was.

But he was here to achieve two things: first, to have Tomas lift the injunction against Luna Azul and second, to get Selena to be that warm, seductive woman she'd been on the beach again.

He'd pulled back for her sake, had instinctively known that she wasn't the kind of woman who could start an affair, even a short-term one, with a man she barely knew.

But tonight he'd change all of that. He slipped his arm through Selena's free one and she hesitated and lost her footing, glancing up at him.

"What are you doing?"

"Just making sure everyone knows who invited me to the party."

Enrique laughed. "No one's going to doubt that, bro. This is Selena's welcome-home party. Did you know she hasn't been back here since my tenth birthday?"

Why not? "No, I didn't know that. I'm honored to have been invited to this party then."

"Don't forget that," Enrique said. He dropped Selena's arm to open the front door of the house. The air-conditioned coolness rushed out and the sounds of the party filled the lanai.

"Enrique's in the house," Enrique yelled and there was a round of applause.

Selena took a deep breath. "I am not sure this was my best idea."

"I am. I want to get to know your family."

She paused there on the step so that they were almost eye level. "Why? So you can use it to your advantage?"

"No, so I can start to understand you."

He put his hand on the small of her back and directed her into the living room. Everyone surrounded her and welcomed her home. But standing to the side, Justin realized that Selena hesitated to be a part of them. She held a part of herself back and he wanted to know why.

Selena was amazed to see Justin actually fitting in with her family. He was standing by the grill talking to the men about baseball of all things. But then she guessed he would know a little bit about the sport thanks to his brother, the former ball player.

"What's the matter, *tata?* Aren't you enjoying your party?"

Her grandmother sat down beside her and put her arm around Selena's shoulders. For just a minute she felt like she was twelve again and a hug from this woman could solve all of her problems. She put her head on her grandmother's shoulder and just sat there enjoying the scent of gardenia perfume and how safe she felt at this moment.

"No, I'm not. I feel like everyone is watching me," Selena said.

"They are. We have missed you so much since you left."

"I don't want everyone to remember what happened. I'm sorry, *abuelita*. Did I ever tell you how sorry I was?"

Her grandmother tucked a strand of Selena's hair behind her ear and kissed her lightly on the cheek. "You did. Stop living in the past, that's all done and we are better for it."

"Better? If it wasn't for me you wouldn't be in this position with Justin Stern."

"And you wouldn't have met him. I've noticed you watching Mr. Stern."

Selena blushed. "Given my track record with men, that should alarm you, *abuelita,* not make you smile."

Her grandmother laughed. "The heart doesn't care about the same things as the brain. My own sister Dona was in love with a gringo and our papa forbid her from seeing him and do you know what she did?"

"She ran away and married him and they lived happily ever after. Even reconciling with the family eventually," Selena said. She'd heard this story many times but for the first time she understood what her grandmother had been trying to say to her. "Why would Aunt Dona do that? I mean living away from the family is hard."

"She wasn't on her own, *tata,* not like you in New York. That's why I think everything has happened for a reason. A man drove you away from your family and this man," she said, gesturing to Justin, "has brought you back to us regardless of his intention."

"I'm not sure I'm ready to see Justin as a white knight."

"He is cute, though."

"*Abuelita,* I'm not sure you should be noticing that."

"Why not? It's not like I said he has a nice butt," she added with a wink.

"But he does have one, doesn't he?" Selena agreed and then blushed, remembering the way the rest of his body had felt pressed to hers.

"He sure does."

"*Abuelita,* what would *abuelito* say if he heard you talking like that?"

"He knows where my heart lies," she said. "Can I say something to you, *tata?*"

"Of course."

"You have never known where your heart lies," she said. "You were always fixated on getting out of here and doing bigger and better things, but I don't think you understood the true cost."

There was truth there. Truth that Selena had never wanted to acknowledge before and she knew that it was time to. Maybe it was because she was thirty now and had made enough mistakes in her life to have really experienced the ups and downs in life. "I think you are right."

"I know I am," her grandmother said with a laugh. "Are you thirsty? I need another mojito."

"Did I hear my lady ask for a mojito?" Tomas asked coming over to them.

Her grandmother stood up and kissed her grandfather. "Yes, you did."

Selena watched them together and felt a pang in her heart. Her own parents had married young and filled their house with love and laughter and a few tears when it took so long for her mother to have a second child. She wanted what those couples had. That was her destiny. Though she loved her job and her apartment in Manhattan.

"Come and dance with your grandfather," Tomas said, drawing her to her feet.

"Wouldn't you rather dance with *abuelita?*"

"I will dance with her later. Right now I want to dance with my beautiful granddaughter. I'm so happy you've come home, *tata.*"

Enrique was playing music with a strong Latin beat, mixing the contemporary artists with the old ones her grandfather and his brothers liked. The song playing was a samba and she danced with her grandfather, forgetting all of her troubles and her worries. Laughing with her cousins and aunts and uncles over missteps and bumping hips.

She closed her eyes and for a second allowed herself some self-forgiveness and enjoyed being back in the best home she'd ever found. She enjoyed the smile on her grandfather's face and the way her little brother looked as he spun the music and watched their family.

Her family.

Her eyes met Justin's and she felt a pulsing start in the very core of her body and move up and over her. She wanted that man. But she could never have Justin and have her family, too. Because no matter what he might say, his objective was always going to be money and hers had to be the heart of this family and the community they lived in.

She turned away from him. She wished she were the big-city woman she'd thought she was. Someone who could have a short-term affair that was about nothing but sex. But a big part of her wasn't sure that she could. She was still the sheltered Latina she'd always been. And being back here she felt more that woman than ever before.

She wanted more from Justin Stern than just sex. And he could never give her that.

Five

Justin liked Selena's cousins, Paulo and Jorge. They made him laugh and he understood them because they were both successful businessmen who were used to doing what they had to to get the job done. If only Tomas were a little more like his grandsons, then Justin had the feeling he wouldn't be facing an injunction.

"I'd love to have you on a committee I'm putting together to make sure that the renovation of the Cuban American marketplace is both profitable and a benefit to Little Havana."

"I'll think about it. But my plate is pretty full," Jorge said.

"I'll do it," Paulo said. "We need new investors to come here and I really like what you've done with Luna Azul. That's the kind of club we need down here. And it drives business to my restaurant."

"That's the kind of synergy I think we can have at the marketplace."

"You should call it a Mercado instead of marketplace," Selena said coming over to join them.

"She's right," Jorge said. "I think you should have a Latin music store there. My boys have to drive across town to find the music and instruments they need. And you could tie it to the bands that play at Luna Azul... have them stop in there for a release party or a little concert."

"I like that idea," Justin said. But discussing business while Selena was standing so close that she was pressed against his arm wasn't conducive. He could barely think since all of the blood in his body was racing to his groin and not his brain.

"Did you invite them to be on the community committee?"

"I did," he said.

"Good, so you are done talking business?"

"No," Justin said.

"He's like us, *tata,* he'll be dead and buried before he stops trying to make a deal," Paulo said.

Justin laughed and Selena smiled but he could tell that her cousin's words disturbed her. A few minutes later the food was ready and the other men moved to prepare the platters for everyone to eat. He took Selena's arm and drew her away from the crowd.

"Why does what Paulo said bother you?" he asked her.

"It just reaffirmed my fears that you are attracted to me because it might make dealing with my family easier," she said.

That was blunt and honest and he shouldn't have been

surprised, since Selena wasn't the kind of woman who was tentative about anything.

"I want you," he said. "That's it, end of story. If you said to me right now that you were going to keep that injunction in place against my company until we both died, it wouldn't change a thing. I still want you naked and writhing against me."

"Lust."

"We discussed that."

"I know. And I thought I'd found a solution."

"Vacation fling," he said.

"It's the only way to keep this in perspective," she said.

He understood where she was coming from. He'd watched his own father love a woman who didn't want him. Not the way he wanted her. It had always been Justin's fear in relationships. He knew that if he ever fell in love it would dull his razor-sharp edge when it came to business. And he'd been careful to make lust his criterion for a relationship. Never really getting to know the family or friends of the women he slept with.

"I'm not going to lie to you, Selena. I will use whatever means necessary to make that marketplace successful, but that will not change how I feel about you. And I always go after what I want."

"I bet you get it, too," she said.

"Yes, I do. Today has been eye-opening for me."

"Because of that dress I wore earlier?" she asked.

"Partly. I don't think I've recovered full brain function since then."

She laughed. "It's nice to know I have a little power over you."

"You have more than you know. Inviting me here was

a very well-played move on your part. Talking to your cousins made me realize that we should be reaching out here more than we do. Luna Azul is successful in this location without community support. Imagine what we could do with support."

"I have imagined it. That's why it is important that my grandparents are in on the ground level."

"I see that. I can't wait to have the first committee meeting."

"Me, too," she said.

"Now about us," he said after a few minutes of silence had fallen between them.

"There isn't any *us*."

"Not yet," he said. "But we both want it, so it's silly to pretend that we don't."

"Vacation fling, right?"

"I'm open to suggestions," he said. "I don't want to forget that you have a life in another part of the country and that you will be going back there."

"That was a surprisingly honest thing for you to admit," she said.

"There is no reason for me to pretend that you don't have the potential to be a heartbreaker. I've never met another woman like you, Selena."

He was a shoot-from-the-hip kind of guy and he wasn't going to change at this late date. Especially where Selena was concerned. She needed to know that even though he was suggesting a vacation fling, he wanted it as badly as she did. He couldn't get her out of his mind and until he did he had the feeling he was going to be operating on backup power instead of at full strength.

Everyone filled their plates and sat down to eat, and though he knew these people thought he was their enemy, he felt like he could be part of this family. He wanted to be here not as a business rival, but as Selena's date.

After dinner was over, Selena mingled for the rest of the evening trying to stay as far from Justin as she could.

He'd waved at her earlier and said goodbye, but that was it. She tried not to be disappointed. After all that had been her one desire, right? She'd been tired of trying to avoid him and the attraction she felt for him. Now she could just be a granddaughter and a niece and a cousin and not have to answer uncomfortable questions about a man who was too good-looking and a point of conflict with her family.

"Why are you hiding out over here?" Enrique asked as he sat down next to her on the wrought-iron bench nestled between the hibiscus trees.

"I'm not hiding out," she said. "I'm just taking a break."

"From the family?" he asked. "I guess when you aren't used to it our kin can be a little overwhelming."

She had to agree. It had been so long since she'd been to a family gathering that she found it tiring and loud. And she wasn't sure she fit in here anymore.

"Are you used to it?" she asked him.

He shrugged. "It's all I know."

"Have you thought any more about coming to New York and living with me for a while?"

She wanted her baby brother to see more of the world than just this slice of it but so far he'd resisted her efforts to bring him up north to the city.

"I have, *tata,* but I don't think I will do it. I like Miami and the family and everything. And I don't want to move away from here."

She nodded. She understood where Enrique was coming from. When she'd left home, she'd felt she had to and those first few years had been terrifying. She'd hated being away from everything familiar. That first October had felt so cold and she'd almost come back home; only shame had kept her in New York. Only slowly had she shed the girl she'd once been and become the woman she was today.

"It's an open invitation."

"I know it is, sis. How'd you like my music?"

"I loved it. You are a talented deejay."

"I know," he said with an arrogant grin. "I'm going to use Justin Stern to get a gig at Luna Azul."

"How is that going to work? He's not an easy man to use," she said. She didn't want her brother and Justin spending too much time together.

"He wants something from us and I will offer to help him get it if he helps me."

Her brother was always working an angle. "Be careful. Justin isn't the kind of guy who gives up things easily."

"I can tell that. But I think with the right manipulation it could work."

"Let me know if I can help. He's putting together a committee to discuss his marketplace. Perhaps you can get a gig at the ground-breaking if we reach an arrangement with his company."

"Great! I like that idea, *tata*."

She hugged him close. "I knew you would."

She missed Enrique probably the most of all the people she'd left behind. He'd only been ten when she'd left. It had been just a year after their parents had died and she knew she should have stayed to help in raising him but she'd been too young to do that. And after Raul and the con he'd run on her family, she'd had to get away and prove herself.

"I wish you'd move back here, *tata*."

"I can't."

He nodded. "A group of us are going clubbing, you want to join?"

"Who?"

"The cousins. Some of them are older than you."

"Geez, thanks."

"You know what I mean," Enrique said. "It will be fun. And it's not like you have to be at work tomorrow."

"That's true. I'm on vacation—sort of," she said, thinking back to earlier when Justin had offered to be her vacation fling. Was she overthinking this?

"You are on vacation. Come on, live a little."

She nodded. "I'd like that. Am I dressed okay?"

"You're perfect," Enrique said. "Hey, guys, Selena is coming with us."

"Great, let's go."

She followed Enrique over to Jorge and Paulo and a group of her other cousins. The tiki torches that had been placed around the edge of the yard still burned and there were plates and cups littering every surface.

"I have to help clean up first," she said. Her grandparents didn't need to be doing all this work by themselves.

"No, you don't," her grandmother said as she came up behind her and wrapped an arm around her waist. "Go and have some fun with your cousins. Remember what it's like to have family around you."

"*Abuelita,* I always remember that."

"Then I hope you also know that we love you. I will call you in the morning," her grandmother said.

"I'm not staying at my house, *abuelita*."

"Where are you staying then?"

"At the Ritz. Call me on my cell phone, okay?"

"*Tata*..."

"I just couldn't stay there. I hope you aren't upset."

"I'm not upset, but I worry about you."

"The hotel is nice and I can relax there," Selena said.

Her grandmother hugged her. "Then that is all that matters."

"Whatever you do, don't call too early, *abuelita*," Jorge said. "We are going to be partying all night. It's not too often the prodigal daughter returns home."

Selena shook her head. "I'm not the prodigal anything."

Jorge put his arm around her as they walked through the house. He and she had been so close growing up. Their mothers were twins and the two of them had been born only eight days apart. Jorge was more than a cousin to her. He was her big brother and her childhood twin.

"That's the sad part, *tata,* you don't even realize how important you are to us all and how much we've all missed you."

"But I am responsible for ruining—"

"You aren't responsible for anything but the actions you took to make things right. And you did make up for everything that happened long ago. Stop punishing yourself for it," Jorge said.

"I'm not punishing myself."

"Yes, you are. And it's time you stopped."

* * *

Nate and Cam weren't pleased with the news that they'd have to wait on the ground-breaking. Actually, Nate didn't seem to care too much but Cam was ready to use every contact he had to make the Gonzalez family suffer.

"We can't do that," Justin said as he sipped his Land-shark beer and relaxed in the VIP area of the rooftop club at Luna Azul.

"I know but it would make me feel good. Tell me what you have planned."

"I'm taking the zoning commissioner out for some golf, which should help to speed up the review process. We haven't broken any laws and I've reviewed the injunction they filed against us."

"Are we in the right?"

"We haven't done anything yet so technically we're fine. There is a zoning provision to keep the marketplace as part of the community. I think this committee will satisfy that."

"Good. Then there's no problem?"

"Cam, bureaucracy runs slowly. And you want everything finished yesterday. We are going to be lucky to have a ground-breaking at the tenth anniversary party."

Nate shook his head. "Cam, are you going to stand for that defeatist attitude?"

"Shut up, little bro," Justin said. "We have to be realistic."

"I don't have to be," Cam said. "I have you to do that. I think I will be on the committee with you and we will get as many local business owners involved with the anniversary celebration as we can. Once they have a vested interest in the celebration they will help make things happen."

"I agree," Justin said. "I have a young deejay who I can get to play at the marketplace ground-breaking—he is Tomas Gonzalez's grandson."

Cam nodded over at him. "You're already taking steps to make this happen. Keep us updated on your progress."

"I will. How's everything else going at the club? Do you need anything from me?" Justin asked.

"Just get the approvals for that ground-breaking taken care of, we can handle the rest," Nate said.

"I will. I'm going to take a few days for a staycation," Justin said.

"What? You can't take any time off," Cam said. "Not now."

"I guess I'm explaining this wrong. I'll be working every day but at night I'm going to be staying at the Ritz," Justin said.

"Why?" Nate asked. "I mean the Ritz is nice but why not stay at your home?"

There was no way he was going to tell his brothers that this move involved a woman. "I just haven't had a break lately and staying at the Ritz will give me one."

"As long as you are still working, it doesn't matter to me," Cam said.

"I might have you check in on some friends who are staying down there," Nate said.

"I don't want to have to check in on your celebs."

Nate ran with the celebrity crowd—all friends he'd made back when he'd been a major league baseball player. And Nate still used these connections for the club, even though he was recently engaged to Jen Miller, a dance instructor at Luna Azul. They were a cute couple and very happy together. Justin was surprised that his playboy brother had fallen for the pretty dancer and her quiet lifestyle.

While Justin was glad his younger brother had kept in contact with the glitter set, the last thing he wanted was to have to socialize with them.

For the most part he had nothing in common with people who traded on their looks or talent to get by in the world. He'd always used hard work and determination.

"Fine. We can have drinks tomorrow night when I'm down there."

"Why do we have to?" Justin asked just to needle his brother.

"Because you are making me drive down there. And you're buying!" Nate said as his cell phone rang. He glanced at the screen and then excused himself.

Warm breezes blew across the rooftop patio. "I like this place," Justin said.

Cam arched one eyebrow at him. "I'm glad to hear it, considering you helped me build it."

Justin nodded. "I know. I wonder how different it could have been if we had real community support?"

Cam took a sip of his whiskey and then rubbed the back of his neck. "In the early days it would have made a big difference. I hate to think of what it was like before Nate got injured and came home...do you remember that first summer when he just sat in the back of the club and his baseball playing friends visited?"

"Yes. You wanted to turn the club that we'd invested every last penny in, into a sports bar."

"Hey, it seemed like a good idea at the time," Cam said.

"It was a good idea, I'm just glad we didn't have to do

it. By the way, Selena suggested calling the marketplace the Mercado. I like it."

"Yes, I like it, too. Who is Selena?"

Justin took a deep breath. It didn't matter that he and Cam held equal positions of authority in the company; Cam was always going to be Justin's big brother. "She's the lawyer the Gonzalezes hired. She's also their granddaughter."

"Pretty?"

"Breathtakingly beautiful," Justin admitted.

"Can you still be objective? If not, we can use one of your junior managers to take the lead on this."

"No," Justin said. "I've got this under control."

"Is she staying at the Ritz?"

Justin just nodded.

"I'm not sure how under control you have this," Cam said.

"I'm not going to let you down or do anything to hurt the Luna Azul."

"I know that," Cam said. "What about yourself? Are you going to do anything to harm *you?*"

Justin finished his drink with a long, hard swallow and then got to his feet. "I'm the Tin Man, Cam. No heart. So nothing to be hurt by Selena."

Justin walked away from his brother and wished that it wasn't true. But he had learned a long time ago that women and love never really touched him on a deep level. True, this attraction to Selena was intense but it would burn out like all things did.

Six

Justin walked through his house, pausing beneath the portrait of his family that had been done when Cam graduated high school. They looked like the perfect family. Picture-perfect, he thought. On the outside they'd always made sure to present a front that others would envy.

And what a front it was. His father, the pro golfer, who traveled to tournaments in his private jet, and their socialite mother, who moved in all the right circles and made sure that her sons were successful and dated the right kind of girls.

He glanced up at his mother, really staring at the blonde woman with her perfectly coiffed hair, and wondered why she'd never been happy with their family. No matter how well he did in school or how well Nate had played baseball, she'd never been pleased with them.

She'd never smiled or shown them any real signs of love or affection.

He'd often thought that all women were that way but he'd seen his brother fall in love with Jen and therefore got to see a different side to women. Jen had cracked through Nate's doubts. Justin was still a bit cynical but seeing how Jen and Nate had worked together to make their relationship successful…well, it made him wonder why his mom hadn't tried just a little bit harder to make it work with his dad.

"Mr. Stern?"

He glanced over his shoulder and saw his butler standing there. "Yes, Frank?"

"I have your bags ready. Do you want me to drive you to the Ritz?"

"No. I'm going to take the Porsche."

"I will park it in the circle drive. Do you need anything from me?"

"No. You can take the next two weeks off."

"Thank you, sir, but I don't have anywhere to go," Frank said.

Justin knew that Frank was always at work and he appreciated it. "Don't you have any family?"

"Not really. I left them behind a long time ago. I could go to Vegas but I really don't like to go more than once a year."

Justin smiled at his butler. Frank was a very carefully measured man. He didn't want to give in to his enjoyment of gambling and let it become an addiction. Frank would only go to Vegas and only once a year.

"I get that."

"Can I ask you a question, sir?"

"Go ahead."

"Why are you going to the Ritz? You have a better place here."

Frank was making perfect sense, logically speaking. "I am…let's just say there is a woman at the Ritz."

"And you want to be closer to her? I think you should invite her here," Frank said.

"That would make things a lot more complicated."

"I guess it would," Frank said.

It probably still didn't make sense, but Frank was his employee and was never going to tell him he was barking mad, even if that was what he thought. Frank was good at holding his tongue. "Frank, sometimes I think I don't pay you enough!"

"I agree, sir," Frank said. "I'll bring the car and get your bags in it."

"Thank you, Frank."

"Just doing my job, sir."

"I appreciate it," Justin said. Frank left and Justin moved away from the portrait.

Was he making the right decision or was he just going to come off as a stalker? If he and Selena were going to have a vacation fling it would make sense for them to both be at the hotel. That's how vacation flings happened.

He knew from experience. He liked the anonymity that being at the hotel would afford them. If he brought her to his home, she'd see his family and his neighbors and it would make their fling seem more real.

And when she left to go back to New York he'd have memories of her in his space. He didn't want that. He wanted their relationship to be uncomplicated. To be a true fling. One where neither of them got hurt.

He wasn't going to pretend that she didn't have the potential to hurt him. He had no idea what the outcome would be of an affair with her but he couldn't resist the thought of having her in his arms.

He wanted her.

That was the bottom line and he was going to do whatever he had to in order to get her. He didn't care if he had to pay the cost later.

All around him were the trappings of success and that made him even more determined to ensure that this thing with Selena worked out. He wasn't used to failing and he wouldn't this time. Selena was the first thing he wanted just for himself.

Selena was buzzed and hot and had forgotten the last time she'd had this much fun. Clubbing wasn't her thing. To be honest it never had been. She'd always been a very studious girl and when she'd met Raul he'd kept her isolated from others. Part of the reason his con had worked so well.

But tonight she didn't want to think about any of that. Jorge came out of the club and sat down next to her on the bench. "Are you hiding out?"

"No. Cooling down. I haven't danced that much in years," she admitted.

"What do you do for fun in New York?" he asked.

"Nothing. I don't have fun. I just work and go home."

"All work and no play makes for one big boring life, *tata*."

"It didn't seem so bad until tonight," she admitted. "It's a quiet life but also an uncomplicated one."

Jorge put his arm along the back of the bench and hugged her to his side. "You need to relax."

"I think you are right. Tonight was a lot of fun. I

never guessed that just dancing would be so liberating. I forgot about everything when I was out there."

Jorge smiled at her. His grin reminded her of her father's and she felt a pang in her heart. She missed her parents so much.

"That's the point of clubbing. I think we will have to take you out again."

"I might let you," she said. "But I'm worn out now. I am going to call a cab to take me back to my hotel."

"Hotel? Why aren't you staying at your old house?" Jorge asked.

"Too many memories," she said.

He nodded. "Why haven't you sold that place?"

She shrugged. "I sometimes get income from renting it and I give that money to *abuelito*. It's the least I can do."

"*Tata,* you have to let go of the past or you are always going to be stuck in it," Jorge said.

"I did let go, remember? I live in New York," she said.

"That wasn't letting go, that was running away," Jorge said. "You are punishing yourself by staying away. No one in the family blames you for what happened. You need to forgive yourself."

"That is easier said than done," she said.

"Don't I know it," he said.

"How do you know that?" she asked.

"I had an affair last year. Carina took me back and she says she's forgiven me, but I don't think I will ever feel worthy of her again."

"Carina is a nicer person than I am," Selena said. "I would never…"

"I thought so, too. But what I have with her is worth

fighting for. I had no idea how much I loved that woman until I thought I'd lost her forever."

"Love is so complicated," Selena said. Raul had been able to manipulate her because she'd been totally in love with him. Other people had told her he wasn't the perfect angel she'd believed him to be but that hadn't mattered. In her mind and in her heart she'd made excuses for him. She didn't want to do the same with Justin.

"Yes it is," Jorge said. "But there is nothing else like it on earth. I wouldn't trade my feelings for Carina for anything."

"Did I hear my name?" Carina asked, coming out to join them. "I wondered where you got to."

"Just visiting with Selena. I don't think she knows how much we all miss her."

"We do all miss you," Carina said. She looked over at Jorge, and Selena had the impression that Carina still wasn't sure of her man. She might have forgiven her husband, but it was clear that she hadn't relearned how to trust him.

"I'm calling a cab," Selena said.

"No, don't," Jorge said. "We will take you home. I'm ready to be alone with my woman."

Carina closed her eyes as Jorge hugged her close and it was almost painful to watch them together now that Selena knew their secret. She wondered if all couples had a secret. Something that bound them together and made them stronger. And she did believe her cousin and his wife would be stronger once Carina knew that Jorge was sincere. But that would take some time.

Jorge went in to tell the rest of her cousins that they were leaving.

"Tonight was fun," Selena said.

"Yes, it was. It's not really my scene—I like to stay

at home, but Jorge likes to hit the clubs and we have worked out a compromise where we will do it once a month," Carina said.

"Does that work?" Selena asked.

"It does. I actually like going out with him. It's not the way I thought it would be. And Jorge has agreed to take ballroom dancing classes with me."

Selena couldn't see her cousin doing ballroom dancing, but if it made Carina happy, she guessed that he would do it. "Where do you take lessons?"

"At Luna Azul. Jen Miller, who teaches their Latin dance classes, also knows ballroom and she is showing us a few moves."

"Do you think Luna Azul has been good for the neighborhood?" Selena asked her, her head clearing from the mojitos she'd been drinking all night.

"I do. They have captured the feel of old Havana in the club. My papa won't admit it to his friends but he likes going there because it reminds him of the stories his *abuelito* used to tell of pre-Castro Havana."

"I need to check it out and learn a bit about the enemy."

"I think you will be surprised by how much it fits given that they are outsiders."

Jorge came out of the club and they left. During the ride, Selena sat quietly in the backseat of the Dodge Charger. She thought about Justin Stern and dancing with him. She had a feeling that he'd claim to be an awkward dancer, but prove to be very efficient at it.

She closed her eyes and thought about the night and what she'd learned. She'd almost made a costly emotional mistake when she'd asked Justin up to her room. But living at the hotel was giving her the distance she needed from her family and tomorrow she'd figure out how to start a fling with Justin. Flirting with him earlier and dancing tonight had stirred her blood. She wanted Justin Stern and she wasn't going to deny herself.

Justin checked in and got settled in his hotel room. He'd left a voice mail for Selena. He was surprised she was out so late. It was almost midnight. Where was she?

He didn't like the tight feeling in his chest or the anger he felt at not knowing where she was. They were nothing but business rivals to each other. Nothing more than that. He'd have to remember that fact.

He paced around his room like a caged tiger. She was probably with another man. Why shouldn't she be? There wasn't another man in this city who was bringing as many complications to the table as he was. Not one. And he knew it.

She was the last woman he should be this obsessed with but the truth was he did want her. And he should never have let her go when he'd had her in his arms earlier.

The only time they were going to be this unaware of the complications of hooking up was right now. Before they got to know each other better. That was how things like this worked.

He didn't think about it anymore but just walked out of his room. He needed a walk to clear his head.

The elevator opened as he was standing there and Selena got off the car.

"What are you doing here?" they said at the same time.

"I'm staying here," she said.

"So am I."

"Why?" she asked. "And how did you get on my floor. That is almost stalkerish."

"I'm not stalking you. I had no idea this was the floor you were on. I asked for a suite."

"Okay, fine. But why are you here?"

"If we are going to have a vacation affair, we both should be on vacation."

She tipped her head to the side. "I guess that makes a little sense. But…I liked staying here where no one knew me."

"We just met," he pointed out.

"That's true but you are already trying to worm your way under my defenses."

"Worm? That isn't exactly flattering."

She smiled. "Good, it wasn't meant to be."

"Where have you been tonight?" he asked.

"Clubbing with my cousins. I've never been clubbing before," she said. "Have you ever gone?"

"Yes. I'm co-owner of a nightclub, remember?"

"That's right. You probably write it off on your taxes as research."

He did, but he didn't say so. "Did you dance with a lot of men?"

"Jealous?"

"Incredibly," he said, moving closer to her. She was leaning against the wall next to the elevator and he put his hands on either side of her head.

He leaned in closer until his lips brushed against hers. "Who did you dance with?"

"My cousins, my brother, but I dreamed it was you," she said with her eyes half-closed. "I don't think I should have told you that."

He felt that tight ball in his stomach relax. "You definitely should have told me."

He kissed her softly on the lips and she wrapped her arms around his neck.

"Are you a good dancer?" she asked as he broke the kiss.

"I don't know. No one has ever complained," he said.

"I knew you'd say something like that. Do you like holding me?" she asked.

He realized she was a little tipsy and saying things that she probably wouldn't have otherwise.

"I do. Do you like being in my arms?"

"Definitely. But you are just my vacation stud, remember that," she said to him.

"I won't forget it. Which room is yours?"

"Number 3106," she said. "Why?"

"I think we should get you to your room and out of the hallway."

"Good idea. I'm tired, Justin."

"I know, sweetie."

"Sweetie? Did you call me sweetie?"

"I did. Any objections?"

"No. I think I like it, but we're really not close enough for you to call me that."

"I wish we were," he said.

"Do you?"

"I wouldn't have said it if it weren't true."

"Are you a straight talker?" she asked.

"Sometimes. With you I am more than I want to be. You seem to bring out the awkward truth in me."

She giggled, and the sound enchanted him. She was such a sweet girl when her defenses were down. He helped her open her door and saw that her suite was laid out the reverse of his.

"I wanted you in my room earlier," she said.

"Not really," he said. "I think you were trying to throw me."

"I was," she admitted. "But a part of me did want you here. It's so much easier to start an affair before you have time to think of the risks involved."

"Yes, it is. But we aren't going to start one tonight," he said.

"We aren't? Why not?" she asked.

He leaned down and kissed her because he was human and a man who wanted her very much. The kiss was passionate and intense, all the things he'd known it would be, but at the same time the taste of those minty mojitos she'd been drinking all night lingered on her tongue. She wasn't herself tonight. And he wanted her to be fully aware of what she was doing when they did become lovers.

She wrapped her arms around his neck and tipped her head back to look up at him. "I like the way you feel in my arms."

"I do, too. I've never had a woman fit so well in my arms before. Your head nestles just right on my shoulder, your breasts are cushioned perfectly on my chest," he said, and he slid his hands down her back to her hips, "and your hips feel just right against mine."

She swiveled her hips against his. "Yes, they do. Are you sure you don't want to stay with me tonight?"

"No, I'm not sure," he said, but he wasn't going to. He wanted Selena but he wanted her on his terms. And that meant having her respect. She was going to be a vacation fling, not a one-night stand. So he slowly drew her arms down from his shoulders and gave her a kiss that almost killed him when he pulled away.

"Good night, Selena," he said and then walked out of her suite and went down the hall to his.

Vacation affair be damned, he already cared about her more than he wanted to admit.

Seven

Two days later, Selena wasn't too sure how she found herself on Justin's yacht sailing around Biscayne Bay.

True, he hadn't given up his pursuit of her at all. She'd been surprised when he'd taken a suite on the same floor as her at the Ritz but she shouldn't have been. He was a very thorough man.

"I forgot how much I like Miami," she said.

"And the nights here?" he asked. She stood next to him in the cockpit while he piloted the boat. He'd told her when they arrived that he had a staff of three, but most of the time preferred to do short trips by himself.

"Definitely. I love the nights," she said, putting her hand on his shoulder and rubbing it. She liked the way his hard muscles felt under the cloth of his dress shirt.

"I thought the committee meeting went well today," he said.

She shook her head. "We're on vacation, so we can't talk business."

He arched one eyebrow at her. "Are you sure?"

She nodded. She'd had fevered dreams of Justin for the last two nights. Since she'd met him he was someone she just couldn't turn her back on, and tonight with the sea breeze in her hair and the smell of the ocean surrounding her, she realized she wasn't going to just walk away from Justin Stern. It might not be the smartest thing she ever did but she knew she was going to have an affair with this man.

She wanted to know the man beneath the clothes. The one that few others had seen and that would belong to only her.

Belong to her? she wondered. Did she really want him to be hers? She wanted him in her bed taking care of her sexual needs, but for anything else?

"Very sure. But it's a fling, Justin, it can't be more than that."

"I agree. Do you mind helping me out with dinner?"

"Uh, I guess not. I should tell you my culinary skills are limited," she said. "I live on takeout and microwave dinners."

"They must agree with you," he said, skimming his gaze over her body, lingering at her curves.

"They do. What do you need from me?" she asked.

"I have a picnic basket on the table in the galley and a bottle of pinot grigio chilling in the wine refrigerator. Will you bring them up?"

"Yes, are we dining on the deck?"

"Yes, aft…you'll see where the cushions are set up. I'm going to find a safe place to drop anchor and then I'll meet you down there," he said.

She moved to go past him down the short flight of stairs but he stopped her with a hand on her waist.

"Yes?"

"I'm very glad we have this time together," he said. It was one of those awkward things that he sometimes said that made her heart skip a beat. He was sweet when he wasn't so arrogant and cocky.

"Me, too," she said.

He leaned down and rubbed his lips over hers. His breath was minty but when he opened his mouth and his tongue swept into hers she tasted *him*. She held on to his shoulders; he deepened the kiss and she realized this was what she'd been craving. This was what she needed.

She'd been alone too long. Working to forget the pain she'd run from and afraid to take a chance on being with another man. Now Justin seemed like he was the remedy.

They hit a wave and it jarred them off balance. She fell into Justin, who was careful to keep them both on their feet.

"I better pay attention to where we are going," he said.

"Yes, you better. I have plans for you," she said.

He wriggled his eyebrows at her. "You do?"

"Indeed…you mentioned a bottle of wine and I might need a big strong man to open it for me."

He threw his head back and laughed. She smiled at him. This was what she needed. A nice break from a long day of negotiating. And it didn't matter that she was with the man who'd been arguing with her all day.

She climbed down the steps and went into the galley. She'd been on yachts before and though there was luxury in every inch of the boat it didn't make her feel uncomfortable. Justin had made this place homey. Selena's favorite touch was a picture on the galley wall of Justin and his brothers, all shirtless and looking yummy, playing a beach volleyball game.

She leaned in closer for a better look at the photo and realized that Justin had a scar on his sternum. Reaching out she traced the line and wondered how he got it. There was so much more to him than what she knew from the boardroom, but she knew she had to be cautious with him on their personal time.

If this was going to be a fling, then she shouldn't know too much about him. How was that going to work? She wanted to know everything about Justin. She needed to figure out what made him tick so she could make sure he didn't get the upper hand on her.

Could she do it?

Hell, she knew she was going to try. She wasn't about to walk away from him whether that was wise or not.

She heard the engine stop and the whir as he dropped anchor and realized she was staring at his photo instead of doing what he'd asked of her.

She opened the wine refrigerator and grabbed a bottle of Coppola Pinot Grigio and then picked up the picnic basket, which was heavy.

She emerged from the galley just as he came down from the pilot deck.

"Let me get the basket," he said.

She handed it over to him and followed him to the back of the boat where he'd already arranged some cushions. With a flick of a button, music started playing. She shivered a little as she realized that this evening was part of a fantasy she'd always harbored. Not one she'd ever told another soul about but somehow Justin had gleaned enough from her to know that this was what she'd always wanted.

Justin had always loved the water. It was the one place where he and his brothers had been alone with their father. Since his mother got seasick she never came out on the boat with them.

His dad had taught all three of the boys everything they needed to know about sailing—and navigating the waters around *her.* But that was it. He didn't have any useful lessons when it came to women. As Justin and his brothers had gotten older, their father merely warned them not to fall in love.

Love is a sweet trap, my boys, Justin remembered his father saying.

Sitting on the deck in the moonlight, listening to the soft voice of Selena, Justin couldn't see what his father had meant. Not with this woman.

"Dinner was very nice," she said. "Though I don't know that your culinary skills are any better than mine."

"Just because I had a little help from Publix?" he asked.

"Yes. And I am going to treat you to dinner tomorrow night."

"You are?" he asked. Perfect, he already planned for the two of them to spend every night together. It would be difficult later in the month as he started to have commitments with the tenth anniversary celebration. He knew he needed to make every minute with her count.

"Definitely. I will even cook for you. The one dish I know how to make."

"What is it?" he asked, suspecting that she must be

able to cook even though she said she mostly had others cooking for her. He did the same thing because when you only cooked for one it wasn't that much fun.

"A traditional Cuban one. I'm not going to say any more. I want you to be surprised."

"I already am. I thought you were never going to ask me out," he said with a mock frown.

"I haven't had a chance. You've been hitting on me since we met. I couldn't get a word in edgewise."

"It's your fault."

"How do you figure?" she asked.

"You are one hot mama! I knew I couldn't let the chance to get to know you pass me by."

She put her wineglass down and moved over so she was sitting next to him. She had her legs curved under her body and as she leaned forward her blouse shifted, and he glimpsed the curve of her breasts encased in a pretty pink bra.

"I am so glad you didn't," she said in a soft, seductive voice.

Everything masculine in him went on point and he knew that he was tired of waiting. Tired of playing it safe with her. Life seldom offered him a chance like Selena represented. She was everything he wanted in a woman.

He reached out and touched her, tracing the line of her shirt and the soft skin underneath. She shifted her shoulders as she reached for him.

"Unbutton your shirt," she said. "I want to see your chest."

"You do?" he asked.

She nibbled on her lower lip as she nodded at him.

"You do it," he said.

She arched one eyebrow at him. "I should have guessed you'd want to be in charge here."

"I am always in charge," he said, bringing her hands to his mouth and placing a wet, hot kiss in the center of her palms before putting her hands on his chest.

She took her time toying with the buttons, caressing his chest as she undid each one. She paused at the scar on his sternum; she traced the edges of it with her forefinger.

"How did you get this?"

"I wish I had some glamorous tale to tell you but it happened when I was in college—young and a little bit reckless, I'm afraid."

"How?"

"It's not sexy, let's not talk about it," he said.

"I want to know. I have a long scar on my thigh which I might show you if you tell me how you got this," she said, running the edge of her nail over the line of the scar.

He shuddered in reaction, loving her hands on his body. He was intrigued, too, wanted to see her thighs and what she was talking about.

He took her hand in his and rubbed it on his chest where she'd been stroking him. "Frat party plus pretty girls plus impulsive need to show off equaled this scar."

She started laughing. "I wouldn't have pegged you for the show-off type."

"I guess I'm not trying hard enough if you can't see me strutting my stuff to get your attention."

She leaned in close, coming up on her knees and putting both hands on his shoulders. "You have my attention, Mr. Stern. What are you going to do with it?"

He put his hands on her waist and drew her even

closer to him until she was straddling his hips and her skirt fell over his lap. When she shifted, he felt the core of her body brush over his erection.

"I guess I have your attention," she said.

"You do. Now about that scar on your thigh," he said.

"I haven't decided if you've told me enough to get to see it."

"I am going to see it," he said, sliding his hands up under her skirt and caressing every inch of her thigh. He couldn't feel anything on her left thigh but on her right one there was a slight abrasion. "I think I've found it."

"You have," she confirmed. Then she leaned down to kiss him and he let her take control of this moment.

Justin's hands slid up and down her back and she forgot everything but the sensations he evoked in her. She put her mind on hold and just reveled in the sensation of being on the sea on this beautiful warm night with this man who wanted nothing but her body.

There was a freedom in this that she had never experienced before. A freedom to be here with him. It didn't matter that later she might regret this. Right now it was exactly what she needed.

"Why did you stop kissing me?" he asked.

"I'm trying not to think," she said. "It's not working."

"Then I'm not doing my job," he said. "I should be sweeping you away from your worries."

"You should be…I think talking isn't going to help. Why don't you put your mouth on me and make me forget."

He arched one eyebrow at her. "Do I have that power over you?"

"You have no idea," she admitted.

She had tried to justify this attraction, to blame it on the fact that she was back in Miami. But that wasn't it—she knew it was Justin, pure and simple.

She wanted his mouth on hers. She needed his hands sliding over her body, and she had to touch him. She was tired of being good and living an honest life. Not that there was anything dishonest about this, but she just needed a chance to let loose and Justin had offered her that.

"Kiss me."

"Yes," he said. His mouth found hers. He sucked her lower lip between his teeth and held it gently there while he suckled.

She swept her hands under his shirt enjoying the warmth of his skin and the strength of his muscles under her fingers. She liked the light dusting of hair on his chest and how it felt as she ran her hands over him. She lingered at his scar, tracing the outside edges of it and then followed the trail of hair as it narrowed on his chest and dipped into his waistband.

She pulled back so she could see him. He lounged back against the pillows and cushions with his shirt open. He looked like a pasha of old and she felt like a willing sex slave sent to please him.

She shifted back so her thighs rested on her heels. She pushed his shirt off his shoulders and he pulled his arms out of it.

He reached for the sash on the left side of her blouse and undid it. As the fabric fell open he put his hands on her waist and drew her up and back over his thighs. He reached under her shirt, his large hands rubbing over her bare midriff and then spanning her waist.

"You are so tiny," he said.

"I'm not," she said. She was an average-size girl; it was just that Justin was a big man with big hands.

He pushed her blouse off her shoulders and it fell off her arms behind her. He brought his hand up and slowly traced the pattern of her bra. Traced it from her clavicle down her chest to the curve of her breast.

He ran his finger down the edge where the cup met the other and then back up. She had goose bumps on her chest and her nipples stirred inside the cups of her bra. Wanting to feel that firm finger of his on them.

He reached behind her and undid the clasp and then carefully peeled the cups away until her breasts were revealed to him. He dropped the bra on the deck where her blouse was.

He cupped both breasts in his hands, letting his big palms rub both of her nipples in a circular motion. The sensation started a chain reaction in her. She loved the feeling and shifted her hips against his erection to satisfy the ache that started at the apex of her thighs.

He spread his fingers out, caressing the full globes of her breasts, and then slowly drew his right hand up to the tip of her nipple. But he didn't linger there.

He circled her areola with his forefinger and then bent forward, holding her back with one hand. She felt the brush of his breath against her nipple as it tightened and then a tiny lick of his tongue.

"More," she said. She was desperate to feel his entire mouth on her nipple. "Suckle me."

He shook his head and she felt his silky hair against her breast as he continued to trace over her breast and nipple with his tongue.

The crotch of her panties was moist and she felt almost desperate to feel more of his mouth against her.

She tried to shift her shoulders and force him to take more of her nipple but he just pulled his head back.

"Not until I'm ready," he said.

"Be ready," she ordered him.

He gave her a purely sexual smile. "Not yet."

He treated her other breast to the same delicate teasing and she was squirming on his lap when he lifted his head. But when she put her hands on his chest and saw him shiver, she knew she had her own power over him.

And it was intoxicating. Leaning forward she tunneled her fingers through his hair and let the tips of her breasts brush against this chest.

He moaned, the sound low and husky.

"Do you like that?" she asked, whispering into his ear.

"Very much," he said. Using his grip on her waist he pushed her back into the cushions and came over her.

His hips were cradled between her thighs and his arms braced his weight above her. He rotated his hips and his erection pressed against the very center of her.

She moaned softly and he leaned down over her.

"Do you like that?"

"Yesss."

He smiled down at her and lowered his head to her body. He used his mouth at her neck and nibbled his way down to her breasts.

He cupped them in his hands as she undulated under him, trying to get closer to what she needed. And what she needed was this man. She needed to feel him naked above her and hot and hard inside her.

She shifted her legs, curving her thigh up around his hips. The position shifted him against her and he said her name in a low, feral tone of voice.

He didn't stop in his slow seduction but his hands swept down her body and she felt her skirt slowly lifted until the juncture of their bodies wouldn't allow it to come any farther up. She lifted her hips and moaned as the tip of his shaft rubbed her.

He pushed her skirt higher and then she felt his hands on her butt. He rubbed his palm over her and then pulled her skimpy bikini panties down. He leaned up over her, kneeling between her legs as he stripped them off.

He tossed them aside and looked down at her. His chest rose and fell with each breath he took and his skin was flushed.

His erection was visible behind the zipper of his pants and she felt another surge of power that she affected him so visibly.

She lifted her arms behind her head and twined her fingers together, the movement forcing her breasts forward.

He watched each move she made. She brought her left leg up and then slowly let it fall wide, exposing her very center to him. He put his hand on her ankles and drew her legs open even farther and then leaned forward.

"You are truly the most beautiful woman I've ever seen," he said. "I want to take my time and explore every inch of you, but my body wants something else."

"What do you want, Justin?"

"To hear you moaning my name while I'm buried inside of your silky hot body."

"Me, too," she said. This wasn't about power but about pleasure. And it had been too long since she'd enjoyed a man just for the pure thrill of it.

"Come to me," she said.

He shook his head. "No. I want to make this last. I

want to make you come so much that you forget every other man but me."

She tipped her head to the side studying him. He'd already wiped every man from her mind. She only saw him. She'd dreamed of him before this…was this a mistake?

She shook her head as she felt his hands on her again. She didn't care if this wasn't smart. She wanted Justin and she was going to have him. Tomorrow she'd sort out the problems this brought to her. This night was hers.

She felt the warmth of his breath on her stomach and his finger caressing the outer edge of her belly button. He drew his hands down her hips, then down farther until he found that scar on her thigh. He traced it with his finger, then lightly with his tongue.

His mouth on her sent pulses of warmth through her core and she knew she was close to orgasm. Every pleasure point she had was pulsing.

He parted her thighs and dropped nibbling kisses up their length. His fingers skimmed over her feminine secrets and then came back. He rubbed his palm over her center and her hips jerked upward.

She felt the cool night air on her most private flesh before his breath bathed her. His tongue danced over her flesh and she clenched her thighs around his head. He put one of his hands on her stomach and shifted between her legs, lying down there.

He lifted his head and looked up the length of her body. Their eyes met and something passed between them. She didn't know what but she felt like he'd found a secret she'd kept hidden even from herself.

He lowered his head again and when he sucked on her intimate flesh everything inside of her clenched. Her breasts felt too full, her nipples were tight little points and she was wet and dripping. She wanted him inside of her and she grabbed at his shoulders hoping to hurry him. To make him come up over her. But he stayed where he was.

His tongue and teeth were driving her toward a climax, which felt too intense. She lifted her thighs and held his head to her body with her hands in his thick silky hair. She arched her hips as she came in a blinding rush.

"Justin, yes, keep doing that," she cried out. She couldn't stop the sensations rushing through her. They were intense and almost scary in the pleasure they created.

He kept his mouth on her until she stopped trembling in his arms. She tugged at his shoulders, wanting him to come up over her. But he sat back on his heels between her legs and watched her.

She wanted to give him the same pleasure he'd given her. She sat up and pushed him back against the pillows and reached for his zipper, carefully lowering it and freeing his erection from his boxers. There was a tip of moisture at the tip and he shuddered when she wiped it off with her finger and brought it to her mouth to lick it.

He tasted salty and vaguely like his kisses. She stroked his shaft from the root to the tip, swiping her finger over the tip each time. With her other hand she cupped him and squeezed gently.

His breath sawed from his body as he grew even harder in her hand. She leaned forward and let her hair brush over his erection. He shuddered again and his hands burrowed into her hair as his hips came forward and the tip of his erection touched her lips.

She licked the tip and then took him into her mouth.

He moaned that deep guttural sound of his again. She loved the feeling of him in her mouth. He was too big for her to take his entire length but she stroked her hand on him and drew her mouth up and over him, sweeping her tongue over the tip.

His hands tightened in her hair and he drew her off his body. "No more. I need to be inside you."

"Now?" she asked. It was what she was craving, too.

"Now," he said, pushing her onto her back and coming down between her legs. He found her opening with the tip of his erection and it was the naked flesh-on-flesh moment that jarred her.

"You feel so good," he said. "Should I get a condom?"

"I'm on the Pill," she said.

"Good," he said and thrust into her.

She came in that instant, just a tiny fluttering of a climax as he filled her all the way to her womb. His abdomen hit her in the right spot and he drew back and entered her again. Slow, long thrusts that made her moan and writhe beneath him.

His chest and shoulders were above her and she held him tight, lifted herself closer to him. "You feel so good."

"So do you," he said. His hips moved with surety between her legs until she was overwhelmed with the feel of him.

The hair on his chest abraded her aroused nipples and she shuddered again as she felt everything inside of her building to another climax. And this one felt even more intense than the other two he'd given her.

He put his hands under her, cupping her buttocks in his hands and lifting her hips higher so that he could get deeper on each thrust. He leaned over her, whispering dark sex words into her ear and she felt the first fingers of her orgasm teasing her. Making her shiver under him. Then he drew back and thrust heavily into her, his hips moving faster and faster until she screamed with her climax.

She felt his hips continue to jerk forward and the warmth of his seed spilling inside of her. He thrust two more times before collapsing on her. He breathed heavily and his body was bathed in sweat. She wrapped her arms and legs around him and held him to her like she'd never have to let go.

She looked up at the night sky and realized that she really didn't want to have to let him go.

Eight

The last thing that Justin wanted to do was get up and move away from Selena. Holding her in his arms was the most addicting thing he'd ever done. But the sea breezes were getting stronger and he knew they couldn't stay on the deck all night. He slipped out of her and rolled to his side, coming up on his elbow.

Her lips were swollen from his kisses and her eyes sleepy as she looked up at him. He drew one finger over her lips and then realized that he was never going to get enough of her. He was spent from making love but he still wanted to lie next to her and hold her in his arms.

That was dangerous stuff.

Tomas Gonzalez may have found the one weakness that Justin had. One he himself hadn't realized until this very second.

"I guess we have to get up," she said.

"I was thinking about carrying you down to the bedroom."

"What are you waiting for?"

He scooped her up in his arms and then stood up. He liked the feel of her there. She wrapped one arm around his shoulders and her long, silky hair rubbed against his arm as he carried her down the stairs.

The stairs were narrow but he turned to enable them both to fit. She felt right here—in his arms and on his yacht.

He glanced down, noticing she stared up at him. "What are you thinking?"

"That this was exactly what I needed," she said.

He felt the same way but he'd never admit that out loud. Already he knew that if he was going to continue to keep control over this affair he needed to play his cards close to his chest. Make love to her—he knew he had to keep doing that. There was no way this one time had satiated him. He was satisfied but he still craved more.

He laid her on the center of his bed with the navy blue comforter and stood next to her. He wanted this to be more than he knew it could be. More than she wanted from him. But it wasn't.

"I have to wash up," he said. It wasn't romantic but then sex technically wasn't supposed to be about romance. It was dirty, hot and sweaty and it made him feel very primitive and possessive. Especially with her.

He padded in his bare feet to the head and washed up quickly, bringing a warm washcloth back to the bed to gently wash between her legs. She was still where he'd left her and when he pulled the covers back and laid down, she curled onto her side and put her arm around his waist.

He put his arm around her and drew her closer to him. The soft exhalation of her breath stirred the hair on his chest. And it was only as the moonlight trickled through the porthole window that he realized she hadn't said anything since he'd carried her downstairs.

"Are you okay?" he asked, rubbing his arm up and down hers.

She shrugged.

"Selena?"

"Yes?"

"Talk to me," he said. He wanted to know her secrets and this moment was as close as they were going to get to really seeing the truth in each other. They were both vulnerable.

Yes, he realized, she was vulnerable. That wasn't what he intended to make her feel but he was very glad that what they'd shared had affected her.

"I'm not sure what to say. I thought that I'd have an affair with you and still be able to keep you off your toes in the boardroom but now I'm second-guessing that. I'm not sure that this was wise," she said.

He tipped her head up to him so that their eyes met. "I'm not sure it was, either, but I don't think we could have waited much longer for this."

"Why?"

He needed her but he wasn't going to admit it. "The attraction between us is very strong."

"Yes, it is."

"I for one was distracted all day today by the small glimpses I got of your cleavage each time you leaned forward to gesture to something on the map."

She laughed, and it was a sweet sound. "I will have to remember that."

"I have no doubt that you will. Let's not overthink this," he said. "We are two people out of time here. Our ordinary worlds are far away and for now there is only the two of us."

"You make it sound so simple and so appealing. But I know that every action has a reaction."

"And every reaction is bad?" he asked.

"Not at all. But every reaction causes ripples and I don't want to hurt my grandparents...not again."

He shifted them on the bed so she was lying on her back and he was next to her propped up on his elbow.

"Tell me about it," he invited. "Whatever it is that you did to hurt them before."

She brought her arms up to her waist and hugged herself and he didn't like that. He was here with her now; she should turn to him for comfort.

He stroked her arm and she patted his hand.

"I don't think it's the right story for tonight but I will tell you about it sometime."

"Tomorrow?" he asked. "After you cook me dinner."

"Stop being so bossy," she said, but she smiled when she said that, so he suspected she didn't really mind.

"It's part of my charm."

"You always put such a heavy burden on your charm."

"And it doesn't measure up?"

"You measure up just fine," she said, sweeping her hands down his chest and cupping him in her hand.

He was no longer interested in talking and instead made love to her in his bed, then held her quietly in his arms afterward as they both drifted to sleep.

* * *

The next morning, Justin showered in the guest room while Selena used the master bathroom. He gathered her clothing first and left it lying on the bed so she'd find it when she came out.

He hadn't planned on making love to her last night, but then he hadn't planned on much when it came to Selena Gonzalez.

She totally knocked him for a loop. Since the first time he'd laid eyes on her he'd been lost. That wasn't right, he was a very successful businessman and he didn't get lost. He always had a motivation for everything he did. He had to remember that Selena wasn't only an attractive woman, she was also a powerful adversary.

That's right, he was doing what he had to in order to ensure that Luna Azul continued to prosper. And no matter that he was determined to keep the personal and business parts of their lives separate, he knew something had changed between them last night.

His BlackBerry pinged and he glanced at the screen to see the reminder of his 10:00 a.m. tee time with Maxwell Strong. He still had an hour but getting the boat back to the marina and then dropping Selena at the Ritz was going to eat into his time.

He got dressed and checked the master bedroom. Selena's clothes were gone. When he got upstairs, he found her sitting on the bench at the stern of the boat. She had on a pair of huge sunglasses that covered not only her eyes but also most of her face.

She might be wearing yesterday's clothing but she didn't seem unkempt. In fact she looked cool and remote—untouchable.

He paused and studied her, realizing that just because he'd had her body last night didn't mean he'd come close to unraveling all the secrets that made Selena who she was.

"Ready to head back to the real world?" he asked.

She tipped her head to the side and studied him. "I guess we have to. I have a meeting this morning that I'm going to be late for unless we get moving."

"I have one as well," he said. "I have a Keurig machine in the galley if you want some coffee."

"No thanks. I'm a tea drinker," she said.

"I wouldn't have pegged you for one," he said, climbing the stairs to the pilot house.

He glanced over his shoulder and saw that she'd followed him.

"Why not?"

"You just don't look the type."

"There's a tea type?" she asked.

A part of him knew it was time to let this conversation drop but another part was just dying to see how she'd react. "Yes, I'm thinking white-haired old ladies sitting around in homemade sweaters, having little cakes and drinking tea out of pots covered in quilted cozies."

She punched him in the arm. "Not only old ladies drink tea. And those cozies can be very nicely made."

"I told you I didn't see you as a tea drinker."

"You aren't winning any points for that," she said.

He pushed the button to turn on the engines and the boat roared to life. But he didn't really want to head back to the port. He wanted to stay out here on the sea with just Selena. If he were a different man he'd ask her to run away with him or maybe just kidnap her and sail off for some exotic port of call, but he wasn't.

And they both had family to think of. The Gonzalez family would probably crucify him if he tried to abduct their prodigal daughter.

"Why are you looking at me like that?"

"I'm contemplating kidnapping you and keeping you naked in my bed."

She shook her head. "You'd never do it. You'd never let your brothers down like that."

"You wouldn't go for it either. I bet you'd jump overboard and swim back to Miami if I tried it."

She shrugged. "Maybe."

He steered them to the harbor, the engines and the sea wind whipping around them. "No maybe about it. You feel guilty where your grandparents are concerned and you'll do whatever you have to in order to make them proud this time."

She wrapped an arm around her waist and turned away from him, staring out over the horizon. He wondered if she'd really be happy running away with him. Lord knew he was tempted, but she had been right. He would never do that until he had everything settled for Luna Azul. It wasn't just a company he worked for, it was his family legacy, and he wasn't about to lose it.

"When are you going to trust me with your past?" he asked her.

"Tonight," she said. "I want you to come to my house. It will be easier to talk about the past if you are there. But if we do this…we won't be a vacation fling anymore."

"Are you sure you want to chance it?"

She studied him for a long minute and he had the feeling that she was searching for answers in his face. He wanted her to find what she was looking for but this morning he didn't have any notion of what she needed from him. After making love to her last night he'd thought he'd know her better but instead he found she was still a mystery to him.

"Yes. I think that we have to keep moving forward. I don't want to walk away...not yet."

He knew that the end was possible—even probable given the way they'd come together—and he was bracing himself for it. Still, starting a relationship and expecting it to end wasn't the best idea.

"We're like a short-term partnership," he said.

"Trust you to put it in terms that would be better suited to the boardroom, but yes, that's exactly what we are. It will be mutually advantageous to both of us while it lasts."

"And pleasurable," he added. He slowed the boat as they reached the marina and he maneuvered his yacht into its slip before turning off the engine.

"What time tonight?" he asked her.

"Seven? Is that too early?"

He took her hand and led her down the gangway to the deck. "No, it sounds just right. Do you want me to drop you at the Ritz?"

"Yes, please," she said.

He drove her to the hotel and let her off, then watched her walk away. He pulled back out into traffic before she was inside the hotel because he didn't want to sit there and think about how hard it was to let her go.

Nine

Selena drove through Miami like the devil himself was chasing her. She wanted to escape her thoughts. It wasn't that she was afraid of Justin; it was simply that he represented a part of her that she wanted to pretend didn't exist anymore. She wanted to drive away from the area and never look back. But running away wasn't her style any more, either.

She pulled into the parking lot of Luna Azul. At a little after ten on Tuesday morning there wasn't much action here. She had an appointment with Justin's older brother, Cam. Through the grapevine she'd heard that he had been the one to raise his younger brothers after both parents were killed. Cam had been twenty at the time.

She pushed her sunglasses up on her head as she entered the cool dark interior of Luna Azul. The club was gorgeous with a huge Chihuly installation in the foyer. The building had once been a cigar factory back in the early 1900s. It was inspired by the success of Ybor Haya's factories in Key West and Ybor City near Tampa Bay.

The Miami factory had been started by the Jimenez brothers and prospered for several years until cigarettes became more popular and eventually the company went out of business. When Selena had been growing up this factory was a derelict building that was a breeding ground for gang-related trouble.

Seeing it today, she had to admit that the Stern brothers had improved this corner of their neighborhood.

"You must be Selena."

She glanced up as Cam Stern walked toward her. He was the same height as Justin and they both had the same stubborn-looking jaw, but there the resemblance ended. Justin was simply a better-looking man. Where Justin's eyes were blue, Cam's were dark obsidian, and Cam wore his hair long enough to brush his shoulders.

"I am indeed. You must be Cam," she said, holding out her hand.

He shook her hand firmly and then let it drop. "I'm glad you could come down here. I wanted you to see what we've been doing here in the last ten years and why it's important that we get the Mercado project going so we can revitalize the area the way we did with the club."

"No one doubts you can pour money into a project and make it successful. I've said as much to Justin. The Gonzalez family is concerned that you are going to take away a vital community shopping center and make it an upscale shopping area of no use to the local residents. We aren't interested in having more of the celebrities you bring down here socializing while families are trying to buy their groceries."

Cam tilted his head to the side. "I can see that you have inherited your grandfather's fire."

"I'm flattered you think so, but I'm not half as obstinate as he is."

Cam laughed as she'd hoped he would. And she realized that Cam was a nice guy. Not because of the laughter but because he'd asked for this meeting. She suspected that he was trying to help her and the rest of the committee understand and see the human face of Luna Azul.

"I grew up here on Fisher Island, Selena—is it okay to call you by your first name?" he asked.

"Of course, I'm planning to call you Cam."

He smiled at her. "Let's go up to the rooftop. I want to show you our club up there."

"I want to see it. My younger brother has told me that he is interested in deejaying here and he has heard that the rooftop club is all Latin music."

"That's right. We start each evening with a couple of professional dancers teaching our guests how to salsa. Then we have a conga line to get them out there onto the dance floor."

"Sounds fun. One thing that Enrique also mentioned is that most of the staff isn't from our neighborhood."

"That's true. We had so much resistance from the local leaders when we bought the club that I didn't get any local talent auditioning for the roles we had. I had to look beyond Little Havana to find the people I needed," he said. "But that's beginning to change."

For the first time she truly understood how hard it must have been for the Sterns to come in here and try to open this place up. And when they got off the elevator at the rooftop club she was astounded by the feel and look of it. To be honest she felt like she was stepping into one of her grandfather's pictures of old Havana.

"This is perfect," she said. "My *abuelito* would love this. It looks like the patio where he and my grandmother met."

"Thank you," Cam said. "We spent a lot of time trying to capture the feeling of Cuba pre-Castro."

"You did it. But why did you choose to build here? You could have chosen downtown Miami or South Beach and not encountered any resistance."

He glanced out in the distance where the skyline of Miami was visible. "I wanted to be a part of this community. When I was a boy we had a nanny from Little Havana and Maria used to tell me stories of Cuba when she'd put us to bed each night."

"That's sweet. So you did it for her?"

He arched one eyebrow at her in a way that reminded her of his brother. Justin was in her mind today. No matter what she tried, he wasn't going to be easy to relegate out of her head.

"I did it because this building came on the market—it had been foreclosed on. It was a bargain. Justin was still in college and it was before Nate made it big in baseball. I had Maria's stories and a building I could afford and I thought I might have a chance at making this work—about as much a chance as a blue moon."

"A slim one," she said.

He nodded and despite the fact that he was supposed to be the big bad corporate enemy of her grandparents she understood that he and his family had come to this neighborhood the same way her family had. Looking for a chance to put down roots and make their fortune.

* * *

The Florida sun was bright and hot as Justin drove his golf cart over the course. Next to him Maxwell talked about his daughter's impending high school graduation and the fact that she was making him nuts.

"I thought kids were easier once they were no longer toddlers," Justin said.

"That's a lie parents try to spread around to convince other adults to join their club of misery," Maxwell said with a laugh.

"I know you'd do it again," Justin said.

"I would. She's a great kid. It's just since January she's been like a crazy person. Her moods swing and she goes from being so mature I can see the woman she's become to being more irrational that she was when she was six. It's crazy. But I know you don't want to hear about that."

"Nah, I don't mind hearing about your family. You give me a little insight into how the other half lives."

"Ever think of joining the married ranks?" Maxwell asked.

"Haven't found the right girl yet," Justin said, but that was his standard line. The truth was that he was married to his work. But he wouldn't mind making a little more time for Selena. That thought slipped through without him realizing it.

He wondered what their children would look like—what?! Hell, no he didn't wonder about that. He was focused on the Mercado and making that successful. "It'd be hard to have a wife when I have to spend all my hours at the office trying to figure out things like this zoning hiccup."

Maxwell laughed. "I knew that was the real reason you invited me out here today."

"Hey, I listened to your kid's stories," Justin said with a grin. He and Maxwell were friends; they'd played together on the same beach volleyball team a few summers ago.

Maxwell had also been very helpful when Cam had wanted to add the rooftop club to Luna Azul. There had been an issue with the noise and it had taken some careful negotiating with Maxwell and the zoning office to get that taken care of.

"That you did. Well near as I can tell you aren't in any direct violation of zoning laws with your proposed marketplace. There is an ordinance in that area that specifies we have to bid the work out to local craftsmen before giving you the go ahead. So if you told me you were getting bids from all Little Havana companies I'd see no reason to deny you the building permits you need."

Justin nodded. That made sense. He pulled to a stop at the seventh hole and Maxwell got out and set up his shot. He had the committee to think about and knowing them as he was coming to, he thought he could get them to recommend the construction companies he used for bids.

"What about the vendors?"

"You have to use a local vendor to replace an existing local vendor. So in your plaza, you have a Cuban American grocery store. If you want to get rid of the one there you have to go with a local chain. You might be able to get a Publix in there but nothing national. I think I saw Whole Foods on your specs, that won't be possible."

Justin wasn't surprised. "Is that legal?"

"Pretty much. You can file a lawsuit if you want but it will take you years to get it through the court system.

It's easier to just work with the local business owners and get them on your team."

"That's what you think," Justin said.

Maxwell laughed. "Your problem is that you are used to being the boss. You might have to compromise."

"No way," Justin said with a pretend frown. "Seriously, I have a committee that has local business owners on it so I think we should be able to get some movement on this soon. What do you need from me?"

"Some quiet so I can take my stroke," Maxwell said.

Justin was quiet as Maxwell took his shot and got close to the hole. Justin had played this course a million times since he was a boy. His father had taught him to play here at the country club and he was normally able to make a hole-in-one on this green.

He lined up and took his shot landing it in the hole. Maxwell whistled but they had played together before and pretending he couldn't do something when he could went against Justin's grain.

"I need to see three bids from the construction companies you are using, making sure at least one is local to Little Havana and then you are good to go. Don't forget what I said about the tenants because they won't."

"I hear that. You know when Cam first bought the club they wanted nothing to do with him so we never considered that they'd want to be part of the marketplace," Justin said.

"You are in a different place than you were then. I'm just guessing here but seeing the success you guys have made of Luna Azul probably has a lot of business owners at that strip mall hoping that you can do the same thing to their businesses, which is why they don't want you to use outside vendors this time."

"It's nice to see how much ten years has changed things," Justin said.

"It is. Sitting in my office it's hard to remember ten years ago, I mean I'm looking at changes in some areas that we thought we'd never see. Swampy area that is now being zoned commercial. That's crazy, man."

"It is," Justin said. The conversation turned to the Miami Heat's chances of making the finals this year and they finished their round of golf. Justin knew that he'd learned nothing that he couldn't have found out from talking to Maxwell on the phone but this had been nicer and for a few hours he'd been able to stop thinking of Selena and how she'd felt in his arms last night.

The committee meeting was scheduled for five o'clock that evening and Selena arrived ten minutes late because her grandmother had found out she wasn't staying in her house and had wanted to talk. Luckily Selena's brother had stepped in and gotten their grandmother off her back so that she didn't have to delve into why she owned a home and didn't want to stay there.

Selena thought a woman as superstitious as her *abuelita* would just understand about ghosts from the past and memories that lingered in a place.

She also thought her reasons would be obvious to anyone who'd known what she'd been through with Raul. She thought a bit more about how she'd let him steal so much from her. Not just her grandparents' money but also the home she'd inherited from her great aunt. It wasn't full of childhood memories but it had been a place that Selena had made into a home and Raul had stolen the safety of that home from her.

Tonight she realized was her chance to return and maybe reclaim it. It wasn't lost on her that she was inviting a man she wasn't sure she could trust to help her do that.

She walked into the downtown offices of the Luna Azul Company fully expecting to see Justin in the conference room but instead Cam was there. She frowned but then told herself that didn't matter. This was the business side of their relationship.

Did they have a personal side? She felt like they were lovers and that was it. She had to remember there was no relationship. It didn't matter that she had slept in his arms, there wasn't anything permanent between them.

The room was filled with her friends and cousins. The community leaders were her family. Everyone with a stake in the Mercado was here.

"Justin is running late today. And now that Selena is here we can get started. I'm happy to say that after meeting with Selena and talking to Justin, I think we can come up with a solution that will work for all of us."

"We will see," her grandfather said.

"I think you'll be pleased, Tomas," Cam said. "I feel like I should apologize for not coming to the community leaders before you went to the zoning commission. It is just that ten years ago when we opened the club no one wanted us to be a part of the community."

"Times have changed," Selena said. "Now what is it you have to offer us?"

"First off we would like to hire a local construction company to do the renovations and Justin is going to bring the solicitation for bids. Can you recommend some companies to us?"

Selena liked the sound of this. She wondered if last night was the reason why Justin had changed his mind. "We can forward you a list. Pedro, you have just added on to your bookstore."

"Yes, I did and I'm very pleased with the work I had done. That is great for the construction companies, Cam, but what about the business owners who are already in the marketplace?" Pedro asked.

"We will be using the existing vendors for the most part but we will be redesigning the stores," Justin said entering the room.

He had been outside today—his tan was deeper. He was dressed the same way he'd been when he left her this morning and it felt like it had been longer than eight hours since she'd seen him.

"We don't want slick-looking new stores," Tomas said.

"I will be consulting with each of you individually. I'd like to schedule meetings over the next few days to figure out what you think will work and for us to consult with you. Then hopefully you will lift your protest and we can get to work."

"We'll see," Selena said. "Justin, do you have the requests for bid?"

"I do," he said, handing them to her.

She glanced down at the forms and skimmed them. "Can I have a few minutes to meet with the committee without you guys?"

"Sure," Cam said.

The two men left the boardroom and Selena stood up and looked at her grandfather and the other men and women she'd grown up with. "I think we are in a position to get what we want if we handle this carefully. No one can be thrown out of their business due to the constraint that another local must be brought in if they don't renew your lease."

"That's good news. Now how do we keep the Cuban American feel in this new development?" Tomas asked.

"How many of you have been to Luna Azul?"

A few hands were raised but not enough. "Tonight's assignment, folks, is to go check out your enemy. I want you to visit the downstairs club to see the kind of effort they have put into redoing the building, but I think you will all be impressed by what they've created on their rooftop club. That's the kind of ambiance and feeling I want to see them bring to the Mercado."

"What do you mean by that? I can't take your *abuelita* to a night club."

"It's not a night club like you are thinking, *abuelito*. And you have to do it. Then we will all meet tomorrow... can we use your bookstore again, Pedro?"

"*Si*, that sounds good to me."

"They are going to build their marketplace no matter how many obstacles we put up. We just have to ensure they build it the way we want it," Selena said.

There were a chorus of murmurs around the table but everyone agreed to go to Luna Azul that night. "Will you be there?" Tomas asked.

"I checked out the club earlier. And I have plans tonight," she said.

"With who?" her grandfather asked.

"None of your business," she said.

"It must be a man," Pedro said.

"Never you mind," Pedro's wife Luz said. "She told you to keep your nose out of it."

"I am. It's just not like our Selena to have a date."

And this was why she lived several states away from these people. She knew they loved her and cared about her but she didn't like having her entire life discussed in a committee meeting.

"Okay, that's it. I'm going to go and get the Stern

brothers and tell them we should be ready to meet with them again early next week."

"That works for me," Pedro said and soon everyone else agreed. The other business owners left and Selena's grandfather kissed her before following them out.

He paused on the threshold of the conference room. "Come for breakfast tomorrow so we can talk."

"*Abuelito*—"

"No arguments, *tata*. I want to know about this man you are seeing."

"You don't have to worry about him being like Raul."

"I'm not, *tata*. The fact that you are being so secretive tells me that you're worried, though."

"Fine, but I'm coming for lunch, not breakfast."

"Agreed."

She stood there watching him walk away. Realizing that he was entirely correct—she was afraid of letting Justin in because she knew deep down that love was a losing game, at least where she was concerned.

Ten

It had been a long day, Justin thought as he drove through the quiet tree-lined neighborhood to Selena's house. The buildings around here were relatively new since this area had been hit hard by Hurricane Andrew back in '92 and completely rebuilt.

He felt good about all he'd accomplished today. Normally at this point in a negotiation he'd be chomping at the bit to close the deal, but this time he knew as soon as everyone was happy, Selena was out of here and that was the last thing he wanted.

Her suggestion that the Luna Azul Mercado committee go to the club tonight was genius. Nate and Cam were going to ensure they all had a good time; Nate had even invited his good friend, the rapper and movie star Hutch Damien, to join them. Nate's fiancée Jen Miller was going to teach them all a few salsa steps and use them for the opening conga line.

He pulled to a stop in the driveway of the address that Selena had given him. She was going to cook him a traditional Cuban meal.

He rubbed the back of his neck and sighed. As far as business decisions went, his being here wasn't his best. That was it. He could tell himself that he was doing this to blow off steam or to learn his enemy a little better but at the end of the day he knew he was here for one reason and one reason only.

He wanted to be.

Selena was changing him. And he knew that she didn't want to and was probably not even aware she was doing it. She had her own agenda and her own secrets. Secrets he was determined to find out tonight.

The front door opened and she stepped out onto the small porch. She was barefoot and wore a pair of khaki Bermuda shorts and a patterned wraparound shirt.

"Are you going to come in or just sit out here all night?" she asked.

"Oh, I'm coming in," he said, pushing the button to put the top up on his car and gathering the flowers and wine he'd brought for her.

Though his parents' relationship wasn't the best, his father had always said that you don't go to visit a woman empty-handed.

He came up her walkway noticing that the lawn was well kept but rather plain. There were no flowers in the beds at the front of the house and compared to her neighbors, this house seemed a little…lonely.

As did Selena as she stood there on her porch with one arm wrapped around her waist. She stepped inside as he came toward her and he followed her into the tiled foyer, which was done in deep, rich earth tones in a Spanish design.

As they headed farther into the sparsely furnished house, the walls were painted a muted yellow. There was a family portrait hanging in a position of prominence in her formal living room and the dining room was to the right.

"Whose house is this?" he asked.

"Mine," she said.

"Where you grew up?" he asked.

"No. I…I inherited it from my great-aunt. I usually rent it out and give my grandparents the income from it. But since I was back in town, my *abuelita* didn't book anyone for this summer."

"So why are you staying at the Ritz instead of here?" he asked. This home was warm and welcoming, though he could tell that she didn't live in it. There was a formal feeling that didn't fit with the Selena he'd come to know.

"I just…there are ghosts of the past here and I really want to focus on doing my job and going back to New York. Besides I can't pretend to be on vacation if I'm staying here."

"Fair enough," he said. "I brought these for you."

He handed her the flowers, which she raised to her nose to sniff. The bouquet held roses and white daisies.

"Lovely," she said without looking up from the flowers. "I'm going to put them in water. Want to come in the kitchen with me? Or you can wait outside back by the pool."

"I'll stay with you," he said, following her through the living room into the eat-in kitchen, which was made for entertaining. There was a breakfast bar with two stools and place settings. She walked around and opened a cabinet to find a vase and put the flowers in water. Then she leaned on the counter and looked at him.

"Thank you. I think my dad was the last man to give me flowers."

He knew her parents were dead so that meant it had been too long since a man had treated Selena right.

"You are very welcome," he said, putting the bottle of red wine on the counter.

"Dinner's almost ready. I thought we could have a drink and sit outside by the pool," she said.

"Sounds perfect to me," he said. She mixed them both mojitos and then led the way out to the pool deck. There was a fountain in the center of the traditional rectangular pool. She sat down on one of the large padded loungers and he took a seat next to her.

"So…how did things go today with my brother?" he asked. "Why didn't you mention your meeting was with him?"

"Probably the same reason you didn't tell me you were golfing with Maxwell this morning."

He laughed at that. "I guess we both are doing what we have to in order to win."

"Indeed. One thing I observed at the club today was a true love and appreciation of Cuban American society and history."

"We are definitely indebted to the community, which is why we want to make the marketplace the best it can be."

"I can see that. Your brother told me about your nanny."

"Maria? She was a great storyteller. She had a gift for making everything she said seem real."

"My papa was like that. He'd tell me grand stories before bed every night about a tiny girl who would fly to the moon and the adventures she'd have there." Selena smiled to herself. "He made me feel invincible."

Justin sat on the edge of his chair facing her. "What or who made you realize you weren't?"

Selena didn't want to talk about her past but with Justin she knew she would. Normally, she didn't date. That was pretty much how she'd avoided talking about her family and Raul for the last ten years. She'd had some casual boyfriends but those relationships had been brief, defined by their jobs and busy schedules.

Being back in Miami had awakened something long dead inside of her and she knew that she wasn't going to be able to just shrug this off.

"It's a long story and not very flattering," she said.

"I'm listening," he said. "Not judging."

She was glad to hear that but it didn't make finding the right words any easier. In her head were all the details, she knew the facts about what happened but she realized that she'd never had to really talk about them out loud.

"You are the first person I've attempted to tell this to," she said.

"I'm flattered."

She shrugged. "I'm not really sure I can talk about it now."

"This is the reason that your grandparents sold the marketplace?" he asked. He'd respected her privacy and stayed away from digging into her past on his own. He trusted her to tell him. Selena was nothing if not a woman of her word and he'd come to really respect her during the time they'd spent together.

"Yes, it is. I guess I'm making this into something more than it really is...I fell in love with a con man and it took a lot of money to make him go away. My *abuelito* went to the cops and they set up a sting to capture Raul—that's the man I was conned by—and he eventually was arrested and convicted. I made sure my grandparents got their money back but it took too long for them to buy back the marketplace."

He took a deep breath as anger exploded inside at the way she'd been treated. He was glad that Tomas had had the foresight to make sure that the man who'd hurt her had been caught and prosecuted.

He didn't want to say the wrong thing but he was so angry that a man had betrayed her love that way. He could scarcely sit still. He stood up and paced around, wanting to do something to make it right.

"I don't know what to say. This isn't what I expected to hear from you about your past."

"I'm not the girl I used to be. I don't…I don't get involved with men on such a deep level anymore. It happened right after my parents died."

"That bastard took advantage of you when you were vulnerable," he said.

He got out of his lounger and scooped her up into his arms before sitting back down on her chair and cradling her. "You are a very strong woman, Selena. I think you should take great pride in the fact that an event that could have made you bitter and resentful instead made you stronger."

She tipped her head up to look him in the eyes and he realized it would be so easy to get lost in her big brown orbs. "Do you mean that?"

"You know I don't say things I don't mean."

"That is true," she said. "You shoot straight from the hip, don't you?" She smiled and gently stroked his cheek.

He smiled at her because he knew she wanted to lighten this moment but it didn't change the fact that he was still angry on her behalf and he wanted answers. He wanted to make sure the person who hurt her never came near her again. Make sure that she was never hurt again. Make sure that she was protected.

The intensity of his feelings surprised him. But a few minutes later when she told him she had to go check on dinner, he finally let her go. He sat there by her pool realizing that no matter how much he'd been trying to tell himself that she wasn't going to matter to him, she did. Selena wasn't just his vacation fling; she meant more.

He should have acknowledged that from the beginning. He didn't flirt in waiting rooms or go out of his way to date women he had business dealings with. She was different.

She called him to dinner a few minutes later and they ate at her patio table with soft music coming from the intercom. He tried to keep the conversation light but it was harder than he'd thought it would be.

"I guess you are looking at me differently now," she said as they finished their meal.

He nodded. "Yes, I am. I'm sorry but I wish that I had five minutes alone with that bastard Raul."

"I shouldn't have told you," she said.

"You needed to," he said. "If you have never talked about it until now, then it was past time. Have you been back to Miami since everything happened?"

"For Enrique's high school graduation. But I flew in on a Friday night and out on Sunday morning. I didn't really have time to do anything but marvel over the fact that my baby brother had grown up."

"So how does it feel being in Miami this time

around?" Justin asked. "I guess that you're ready to deal with it."

She shrugged delicately and looked away from him. "I thought so…actually that's a lie. I figured what happened ten years ago wouldn't bother me anymore. But being here…dealing with you and knowing that if I hadn't fallen for Raul's sweet lies my grandparents wouldn't have to be negotiating with your company for their livelihood, well that forced me to face the fact that this is all my doing."

"I don't think it's that bad. Your grandparents don't blame you for anything and I know you are smart enough to realize now that Luna Azul isn't the devil."

She tipped her head to the side studying him. "I'm not sure. I fell for a smooth-talking man once and I don't want to make the same mistake again. Especially since it will be my grandparents who pay the price once again."

He didn't like the fact that she'd put him in the same category as a con man. "I've never lied to you and I'm not trying to cheat you or your grandparents out of anything. I resent the fact that you said that."

Selena rubbed the back of her neck. The last thing she'd intended to do was to offend him, but he had to understand that she was trying to protect herself.

"I didn't mean to say that you were swindling me or my grandparents," she said.

"Yes, you did. You wanted to make sure that I understood that you don't trust me."

"You? It has nothing to do with you," she said. She wasn't thinking, just reacting, and she realized she was being truer with Justin than she'd been with any man before. "I don't trust men. That's it, period, end of story.

I want to believe you when you say you are dealing honestly with me, but then I find out you are meeting with the zoning commissioner behind my back."

"Maxwell and I are friends. And you did the same thing to me. Going to meet my brother. What did you think that Cam would do, offer you better terms?" he asked.

An argument was brewing and she knew she was responsible for it. She'd simply wanted to tell him that trusting him wasn't easy for her and now she'd somehow gotten them into a mess that she had no idea how to get out of.

"I thought he'd give me some insight into whether he was the same kind of man you are. The kind of man I can trust. Because you aren't the only Stern brother that my grandparents and the other business owners are going to have to deal with."

He leaned back in his chair. "Damn, I'm sorry I got a little hot under the collar."

"A little? That's an understatement."

He shook his head. "You make me passionate, so of course I'm upset that you'd lump me in the same category as a guy who'd bilk your grandparents out of their fortune."

"I'm sorry about that. I didn't mean it that way," she said, then paused. "Do I really make you passionate?" she asked.

"Hell, yes. I know we just broke our number one rule about not talking about business when we are alone—"

"That was a stupid idea. I can't keep up two lives. I mean it would be nice to think that I could do it but to be honest I feel too much when I'm here. And it's clear to me you do, too."

"Yes, I do. In the spirit of open communication, I knew I wouldn't be able to think clearly unless I got the passion I felt for you out of my system."

"Oh, really?" she asked, getting up and coming around to his side of the table. He scooted his chair out and pulled her down on his lap.

"Yes, really."

She toyed with his collar, caressing the exposed skin of his neck. "Is it working?"

"Not yet. The more I get to know about you, Selena, the more I need to know. I feel like I will never be able to know enough about you and that's not acceptable. I never let anyone have that much control over me."

"So I can control you?" she asked, trying to keep things flirty and light because otherwise she was going to have to face the fact that Justin was more of a man than any other guy she'd ever let into her life.

For one thing, he was willing to admit that this was confusing him as much as it was confusing her. That shouldn't turn her on, but it did. It made her want to wrap her entire body around his and make love to him here on her patio. But she wasn't going to do that. She couldn't.

Already he was starting to become more important to her than she'd expected him to be. She had to remember that she was leaving in a few weeks.

"About as much as I can control you," he said. His hands settled on her waist and she looked down into his eyes.

There was something so pure about the color of his eyes and she felt like she could get lost in them. Get lost in the life that she once had and the life that she'd always dreamed of having. Dreams that had been swept away by Raul's actions.

"I'm afraid," she admitted in a soft whisper and put her head down on his shoulder.

"Afraid of what?" he asked, his hands moving smoothly over her back.

She didn't know if she could put it into words but then the simple truth was there. "You…me. I guess I'm scared of the way you make me feel. I've been so focused on my career and I've found a way to live with the past and with my mistakes. But now you are making me want again."

"Wanting is good," he said.

She turned her head on his shoulder and kissed his neck. "Wanting is very good. But I'm afraid that it is changing me. I thought I knew who I was. I thought that the woman I'd once been was completely gone but being back here has made me realize I'm not sure who I am."

He tipped her head back so that he could look down in her eyes. "You know who you are, you just didn't want to admit that there was still a part of you that could be passionate about a man and about this place."

She leaned up and kissed him hard on the lips. "Why do you think that?"

"Because it's in your eyes. I don't see a woman who doubts herself at all."

"I'm not talking about confidence," she said.

"What are you talking about then?"

"I'm talking about dreams," she said. "I thought that I was the kind of woman who would be happy with a career and a life in the big city…not the city of my childhood but a new place. A place where I'd carved out my own life. But I think I just realized that I haven't been living."

"You haven't?" he asked.

She shook her head, letting her hair brush over his hands as she leaned forward and kissed him gently. No matter what else came from her time with Justin she'd always be grateful to him for making her realize what had been missing in her life.

"No, I've been hiding and I'm just now realizing that I let Raul steal something from me. And you, Justin Stern, my *abuelito*'s silver-tongued devil, are slowly giving it back to me."

Eleven

Justin carried Selena back over to the lounger where he'd held her earlier. He'd had enough of talking. What he needed was something that made sense to him. Something he didn't have to dissect and analyze. He needed to have her body, naked and writhing, under him.

He needed them both to get out of their heads and he needed that right now. He lowered her onto the lounger and sat next to her hip.

"What are you doing?"

"If you can't figure it out then I'm not doing it correctly."

She shook her head. "It feels like lovemaking."

"Then that's what it is," he said. "I was hoping you'd say it felt like an erotic dream come true."

"It's more than that. Last night was so much more than I thought I'd find with a man…"

"That's what I wanted to hear," he said.

"I'm glad. I didn't expect to like you."

"Same here. But I knew from the moment I sat down next to you in the zoning office that you were different."

She smiled up at him. "Really. I thought you were just this crazy guy who thought with his libido instead of his head."

She made him feel good and happy, he thought. It didn't matter what the future held at this moment—he was more relaxed and turned on than he'd ever been.

He reached for the tie that seemed to hold her blouse together and undid it. He pulled the fabric open and found there was a little button on the inside that still had to be unfastened. But he was distracted from getting her completely naked by the one breast he had already uncovered.

She wore a nude colored mesh bra that was almost like a second skin. He growled low in his throat and caressed the full globe of that revealed breast, moving his fingers up to her nipple. "I love this bra."

"I'm glad. I wore it for you."

"What else did you wear for me?"

"Why don't you make yourself comfortable and I'll show you?" She stood up and he moved so he was lying back on the lounger. Selena was innately sensual and despite what she'd said about not knowing who she was, he knew she was one of the most confident women he'd ever met. There was something very sure about her, as she slowly removed her blouse and dropped it on the other chair.

"So you like this?" she asked cupping her breasts and leaning forward.

"Very much." Not touching her was torture but he

was determined to let her have this moment. And to let
her seduce him.

She put her hands to her waistband and slowly lowered the zipper. Through the opening in her shorts he
saw her smooth stomach and belly button before she
slowly parted the cloth.

"I'm not sure you really want to see this," she said.

"Trust me, I do."

"Then take off your shirt."

"Show me a little something and I'll consider it."

She turned around and swiveled her hips at him. She
lowered the fabric of her shorts the tiniest bit so that he
saw the indentation at the small of her back and the thin
nude colored elastic at the waist of her panties.

"Whatcha got for me, Justin?"

He stood up; being passive wasn't in his nature. He
toed off his loafers and started unbuttoning his shirt. He
let it hang open as he came up behind her. He wrapped
his arms around her waist and bent to taste the side of
her neck.

"This is what I have for you," he said. Taking her hips
in his hands and drawing her back until her buttocks
was nestled against his erection. He rubbed up and down
against her.

She shivered delicately and tossed her hair as she
turned her head to look back at him. "That's exactly
what I need."

"I'm glad," he said, nibbling against her skin as he
talked. He moved his hands over her stomach, feeling
the bare skin. He dipped his finger in her belly button
and her hips swiveled against his.

He pushed hands lower into the opening of her shorts
and cupped her feminine mound in his hand. She was
humid and hot and she shifted herself against his palm.

He pressed against her and she swiveled her hips again, this time caressing him.

He loved the feel of her against his erection. He pushed her pants down her legs and then reached between them to open his own pants and free himself.

He groaned when he felt the naked globes of her ass against his erection. She had on a thong.

"God, woman, you are killing me," he rasped in her ear.

"Good. I have thought of nothing else but you and me like this since you dropped me off this morning."

"Me, too," he admitted. He kept caressing her between her legs and used his other hand to push the thin piece of fabric that guarded her secrets out of the way.

She moaned his name and parted her legs, shifting forward so that he could enter her more smoothly. He held her hips with both of his hands as he pushed up inside her. He started moving, listening to the sounds she made.

He loved her sex noises and had a feeling he'd never tire of hearing them. Her velvety smooth walls contracted around him with each thrust he made. He felt his orgasm getting closer with each thrust into her body.

Everything started tingling, and then he erupted with a deep pulse. He heard her cry out as he emptied himself into her. She slumped forward in his arms and it took all of his strength to keep them on their feet. As soon as he was able to, he pulled out and lifted her in his arms, carrying her into the house.

"Where's your bathroom?" he asked. She liked the way that sex roughened his voice and made it low and raspy. At this moment she felt like the other things she spent all day worrying about didn't really matter.

"Down the hall, first door on the left."

He carried her down the hall, but she hardly paid attention to any of it. Just kept her head on his shoulder and thought about how nice it was to have a big strong man to carry her. It wasn't that she couldn't take care of herself because she could; it was that she didn't have to do anything right now.

She felt safe and…cherished. That was it. She'd never experienced it before. He made her feel like she was the most important person in his world at this moment. And she wasn't going to allow herself to analyze it and dissect it and figure out why she shouldn't just enjoy it.

He set her on the counter. Her bathroom had a large garden tub with spa jets. He turned the tap and adjusted the temperature.

He was a very fine-looking man. She'd be happy to watch him move around naked all day long.

"Bubble bath?" he asked.

"Under the sink. I can get it," she started to hop down.

"No, stay where you are. I want to do this for you," he said, standing up and coming over to her. Wrapped his arms around her waist and tugged her close to him for a hug.

She rested her head against his chest and had the fleeting sensation that this wasn't going to last. Like she should hold on to him as tight as she could right now. She squeezed him to her and he pulled back.

"You okay?"

"Yeah. Ready for this bath."

"Me, too."

He found the bubble bath and poured it into the running water. Soon there was a sea of bubbles as he turned the faucet off. He lifted her up and then stepped into the tub.

He sat down in the water, which was the perfect temperature, and cradled her on his lap.

"Are you okay?"

"Yes, why wouldn't I be?" she asked.

"I was like an animal out there. You turned me on and I couldn't think of anything except having you. Damn, just thinking about it is getting me hard again," he said.

"I thought men of a certain age took a little longer to recover," she said.

"Not with you around," he admitted. He pulled her back against her, moving his hands over her body.

"Why aren't you staying here?" he asked after a moment. "The real reason."

"I told you…it doesn't feel like home," she said. "And to be honest every time I'm here I remember all the bad things that happened. It makes me feel guilty and sad."

He hugged her close, and he was so sweet in that moment that she felt her heart start to melt. She knew she couldn't give in to that and let herself start to care for him—hell, who was she kidding, she already cared for him or she wouldn't have cooked for him. She was starting to fall for him and that was more dangerous than anything else she could do.

"I hope you will be thinking of me in this place now," he said.

"I definitely will be," she said. And that was a big part of her problem. He was slowly making himself a part of her time here. Making her want to stay in the one place she vowed she'd never make her home again.

They finished their bath with lots of caressing and

touching and Selena felt very mellow after they dried off. She found the dressing gowns that her grandmother kept in the closet for guests who rented the house and they put them on. He led her back outside to the pool and she wasn't surprised when he offered to clean up the dinner dishes for her.

"You don't have to do that. Why don't you mix us some drinks while I take care of those," she said.

He went to the bar, stopping along the way to pick up his cell phone. She suspected he was checking his email and she didn't like it. It was like he was going back to the businessman he essentially was.

She wondered if the sweet guy stuff was an act. Was that part of how he was playing her to make sure that she went along with all of his suggestions?

She piled their dinner dishes on a tray and took them inside to the kitchen putting them away before rejoining Justin.

When she got out on the patio, Justin had put his pants back on and was buttoning his shirt.

"I'm sorry but something has come up and I have to go."

She nodded. "No problem."

He stared at her for a minute. "Okay, good. So I will see you in a couple of days to start our meetings with the tenants of the marketplace."

"Sure."

It felt to her like he was running away and she didn't want to let it upset her but it did. It bothered her that she'd spent the evening with him, seduced him and shared the secrets of her past with him and now he was running out the door as fast as he could.

"I wish I could stay," he said.

"It's not a big deal," she replied. If he truly wanted to stay he'd stay.

"It is. Listen, I can't ignore this page," he said. "Are you spending the night here or at the hotel?"

"The hotel, why?"

"Let's meet for a nightcap. Say, eleven?"

"Why?" she asked again.

"I don't want you to think I'm the kind of man who runs away."

She wrapped her arm around her waist and then realized what it was she was doing and dropped it. "I don't know what kind of man you are."

"Yes, you do," he said. "I will remind you when I see you later tonight."

He kissed her hard on the lips and walked through her house and out the front door.

Justin didn't have an emergency waiting for him—he was a businessman not a surgeon—but he'd had to get out of there. Had to breathe and remind himself that as far as Selena was concerned they were having a vacation affair.

And he needed to remember that. He wasn't looking for the future Mrs. Justin Stern. He wasn't getting married ever and if he did change his mind...well, that wasn't going to happen, at least not now.

He drove aimlessly, finding himself in the parking lot of Luna Azul. Sitting in his car he wondered why he was still here. Cam didn't need him in Miami to continue helping to run the company. Not like he had in the beginning when they'd all three bonded together and did every job they could themselves to cut costs.

He could be anywhere else he wanted to, even New

York. But he knew he wouldn't leave. He couldn't leave. This place was in his blood. This was home.

Someone knocked on his window and he glanced up to see Nate standing there. He turned off the car engine and got out.

"What are you doing?"

"Thinking."

"I guess I can see why you were alone. Takes all your concentration, right?"

"Ha."

"Ha? Damn, man, you don't sound like yourself. What's up?"

He shook his head. No way was he going to tell his little brother that he was confused and a woman was responsible. Nate would laugh himself into a stupor if Justin admitted such a thing.

"Do you ever miss baseball?"

Nate shrugged his muscled shoulders. "Some days, but I don't dwell on it. It's not like I'm going to ever be able to go back."

"What about that high school coach from Texas who made the majors in his forties?"

"He was a pitcher, Jus. I'm not. Plus I like this life. I don't know that I'd be committed enough to work out every day and do all the traveling," Nate said then tipped his head to the side. "Besides, you'd miss me."

Justin smiled at his little brother. "I would. I never thought we'd all end up working together."

"I didn't either, but I bet Cam knew," Nate said.

"What are you doing out here?"

"I …I have a date."

"With Jen? I thought you were engaged, so dating was a thing of the past."

"She likes it when we meet up after she gets done with work and then we have a little alone time."

"Alone time? Seriously. You crack me up," Justin said but to be honest he was envious of his brother and his fiancée. Until this moment he hadn't realized that he wanted what Nate had found. And he knew it was because of Selena.

"I still have to head out after our 'date' to schmooze more celebs but this gives us a little time together."

"Sounds nice," Justin admitted.

"Thanks, bro. So are you going inside?"

"No. I have to head back to my office. I want to review some notes I made earlier."

"At this time of the night? I know Cam is a bit of a pain about this marketplace project but I think he'd let you have a night off."

"You know he doesn't want me to take any time until this is all wrapped up."

Nate arched one eyebrow at him. "You're not big on vacations."

"No, I'm not. I'm a workaholic so I guess it shouldn't surprise you that I'm heading to the office."

"Normally no, but I've never caught you sitting in the parking lot before."

Justin realized that his brother was now concerned. "I'm just looking at all we've accomplished."

"It always makes me proud, too," Nate said, glancing at his watch. "I've got to get inside. I'm hosting that group from the marketplace for drinks after the last show and I don't want to be late to meet with Jen."

"Don't let me keep you. I'm heading to my office."

Justin hugged his brother and then got back in his car and drove away. He needed to pay attention to the deal with the Luna Azul Mercado and get that finalized. Then he'd figure out what to do with Selena.

He wasn't going to allow her to continue to control him the way she had tonight. The only thing that made her power over him acceptable was the fact that she seemed unaware of it.

He pulled into the parking lot of their office building and didn't want to get out. For the first time in his adult life he wasn't interested in working. In fact, only one thing was on his mind and it was Selena.

He'd been an idiot to leave when he had. What had he proved?

He realized he'd proved to himself that he could be the one to leave.

And that was important. His father had never been able to leave their mother and that had been his greatest flaw. It had made the old man weak and Justin had decided at a very young age that he wasn't going to be like his old man. At least not when it came to love.

He wasn't going to fall for the wrong kind of woman. To be honest he'd vowed to never let any woman mean more to him than business.

He forced himself to get out of the car and go up to his office. He spent two hours going over numbers and sending detailed notes to his assistant for the meetings they'd be having over the next few days. By the time he'd left the office, he knew he was a much stronger man than his father had ever been and that Selena Gonzalez wasn't going to find the same flaw in him that his mother had found in his father.

Twelve

Selena changed her outfit about six times but finally went down to the lobby bar a little after eleven. If Justin weren't there, she'd know he was a bit of a con man just like Raul had been. But instead of going after her grandparents' money, Justin was going after—what?

That was the question she didn't know how to answer. She was pretty sure he wasn't after her heart, which she'd like to know more about. She knew most men were commitment-phobes but he took it to extremes, from what she'd observed.

Why then was she standing at the entrance to the mood-lit bar so tentatively? Hoping for…

Justin.

He'd come. To be honest, until she saw him she'd been afraid to hope that he would be here. She just had figured he wouldn't show up.

He waved her over to the intimate banquette where

he was sitting. She sat down and slid around the bench until she was next to him.

He leaned over and kissed her cheek. He'd had time to go and change and he'd put on aftershave but he hadn't shaved because a five o'clock shadow darkened his jaw.

She didn't to talk about the way he'd left. She'd spent most of the night reliving those moments and trying to ascertain if it had been something she'd done.

"Business emergency handled?"

He flushed and nodded. "It wasn't a big deal—just some paperwork that needed signing."

That didn't sound like a reason for him to rush out of her house but she wasn't going to call him on it. She'd see how the rest of the evening went and then make up her mind if he was playing her for a fool or just in over his head like she was.

But Justin didn't seem like the type of man to be overwhelmed by anything.

"What do you want to drink? They make a nice Irish coffee here, but I've always been partial to cognac."

"Me, too," she said. "My *abuelito* used to pour me a small snifter after I turned sixteen to share with him on Sundays when we'd go over to his house for dinner. I always felt very grown-up drinking it."

"My dad always had cigars with cognac, but I don't think we can smoke in here."

"Not at all. Do you smoke?" she asked, realizing that she really didn't know him all too well.

"No. I mean, the occasional cigar. When we first opened Luna Azul it was right at the height of the cigar club phase and we toyed with making it one, but in the end we wanted something that would stay in fashion."

"Good call."

"It was Nate who pointed out it was a fad. That guy has his finger on the pulse of what's hot and what's not."

"I would imagine so—I see him on the society page of the newspaper almost every day."

Justin signaled the waiter and ordered their drinks. "Nate does a lot of that socializing for the club. We get a lot of tourists and locals in the club because they want to catch a glimpse of Nate and his A-list friends."

"I noticed that you and your brothers are close, what about your parents?" she asked. She wanted to know everything about him, the personal stuff that she hadn't thought was important before. She knew from Cam that his parents were gone but she wanted to know more about the brothers' relationship with them.

"My parents are both dead."

"I know—Cam told me. I'm sorry. I know how it is to lose your parents."

"It wasn't that bad. I had a little bit of high school left and Cam stepped in to fill the void."

"I guess you weren't that close to them, then," she said.

"No, I wasn't. Well, my dad. He always took my brothers and I out all the time."

"Where did he take you? Were you rough-and-tumble boys?" she asked.

"He mainly took us to the golf course or out on his boat. Just out of the house. My mother was often socializing and didn't want noisy boys in the way."

It didn't really sound bitter when he said it but she was surprised and a little hurt for him. "My mother loved having us in the house and under her feet. My brother is ten years younger than I was so to keep me from being lonely my mom would always have my cousins over for me to play with," Selena said, remembering the crazy games she used to play with her cousins and how much fun it had been.

"My brothers and I are all two years apart, I guess it was too much for my mother. My dad enjoyed having us with him. I think we learned about living from him."

Their drinks arrived.

"Salud!" she said raising her glass toward him.

"Cheers," he replied.

They both took a sip of their drinks. She set her glass on the table in front of her.

"What did you think of your dad being a pro golfer?"

"Why are you asking me so many questions?"

She didn't know how to answer that. The truth was it had hurt when he left and she wanted to figure out what made him tick so he'd never hurt her again. Frankly, there was no way she was going to tell him that. "You know my family but I really don't know much about yours."

"Fair enough."

"What was your dad's name?"

"Kurt Stern."

"I've never heard of him."

"Most people who aren't very familiar with golf haven't. But he made a very good living playing for all of his life. He and my mother were killed when their private plane crashed on the way to a golf tournament."

Suddenly she did know who his father was. She remembered reading the story about the tragedy. "Of course. I remember seeing that in the news."

"I should have led with that part. He was more famous in death than he was in life."

"I'm sorry I didn't realize who he was."

He took her hand in his. "It's okay. Most people don't."

Justin felt like today had gone on too long. He was ready for it to end but not ready to leave Selena. Yet he knew he'd have to. Spending the night with her when they were on his yacht was one thing, spending the night with her here at the hotel something else. He just wasn't ready for it tonight. He didn't trust himself.

"Thanks for meeting for this drink," he said.

"I guess you are done talking about your family?"

"Way done. I don't like to talk about the past. I prefer to look to the future, which we are doing with our partnership."

"Which one?"

That was the question. "The Mercado is what brought us together."

"That is so true. If my *abuelito* hadn't thought you were a silver-tongued devil our paths never would have crossed."

He frowned as he realized how right she was. It had been chance that had put their paths on a collision course. "I guess it was fate."

She smirked. "Only if you count me falling for Raul as part of fate's ultimate plan. And I'm not sure that our destinies are that spelled out."

He wasn't either. "I've made everything in my life happen by hard work and determination, so I'd have to agree with you."

"Still…for me it would be reassuring if I thought all the heartache and trouble with Raul was so that my grandparents could have an even better place now. I mean that would be worth it."

He wondered if she thought he'd be worth it. What was the man of her dreams? Or had those died when she'd been twenty and betrayed by love? Tonight wasn't the night for asking that type of question.

"It would be worth it. I hope you know it was never my intent to swindle anyone out of anything."

"I think I do know that now. At first I wasn't too sure what to think of you."

"Why?"

She took a deep breath and then leaned forward, crossing her arms on the table. Her arms framed her breasts—he tried to keep his gaze on her face but he was distracted. He liked this woman. He loved her body and he wanted nothing more than to spend every night wrapped in her arms.

"I guess it was the way you came on to me. I thought 'this guy has got to be after something.'"

"Selena," he said, taking her hands in his and looking into those deep chocolate-colored eyes of hers. "I was after you. I didn't know who you were when we were sitting next to each other. I only knew that I wanted you."

"Lust," she said. "The mighty Justin Stern was floored by lust."

He squeezed her hand and lifted it to his lips to kiss the back of it. "I wasn't floored."

"Oh, what were you then?"

"Enamored. I had never seen a woman as beautiful as you," he said, meaning those words more than any he'd ever spoken before. There was something about Selena that struck him deep in his soul. He wasn't the kind of man who made soul connections or thought he'd find his other half but a part of him—the part that had run away from her house earlier—knew that he had. That there was something between the two of them that just couldn't be stopped.

"It was a force of nature," he said.

"You do have a silver tongue."

He didn't like that she thought so. "I don't. I'm known for being blunt and to the point. There is something about you that has captivated me."

"I wish I could believe you," she said, her eyes big and almost sad.

"Why can't you?"

"Men—"

He knew she was going to make a blanket statement that wouldn't be flattering. He knew he should let it go, it was late, they both had a full day of meetings tomorrow and to be fair she'd let him escape her house earlier without asking too many questions. But he wanted to know what she thought of men. Wanted to know the exact company he was keeping.

"Men what?"

"Some men lie. And they do it so well that a person never knows that they aren't telling the truth," she said. She shook her head. "I'm sorry, Justin. I wish I was a different woman who didn't have baggage."

"I don't," he said. He knew she'd been badly used and that the effect was one she still hadn't shaken. Raul's betrayal wasn't just of Selena and her heart but also of her family and he suspected that hurt her even more.

"Why not?"

"You wouldn't be the woman you are today without the past."

She leaned over and hugged him. "Thanks for saying just the right thing."

"Ha, I knew if I blundered around long enough I'd come off as suave."

"I didn't say you were suave."

"You implied it," he said. "I think we should call it a night before you change your mind."

She nibbled on her lower lip and he wondered if she was hesitating over tonight the way he was. When she didn't offer for him to come up to her room, he realized she was just as shy about where this was heading.

"I've got an early meeting so maybe we could have lunch?"

She shook her head. "I can't. I'm due to be grilled by my grandparents for lunch."

"Grilled about what?"

"You. Everyone on the committee guessed I had a date since I didn't come with them to the club and now I'm being called back home to answer for myself."

"Are you going to tell them your date was with me?" he asked.

"Definitely, I'm not lying to them."

"Would you like me to come with you?" he asked.

"That's sweet but I think I better handle this one alone."

"Very well, but let's meet for breakfast."

She nodded and they went their separate ways at the elevator. He down to his suite and she down to hers. He felt like he'd created a barrier between them tonight by running away. And as he fell asleep he realized that he wanted her in his arms. He needed her in his arms and he was going to make sure she was back there as soon as possible.

Selena woke up with the sun streaming through the windows and her thoughts on Justin. He knocked on her door at seven-thirty and she was surprised to see he wore his robe and was pushing a room service cart.

"This is as close as I could get to breakfast in bed, considering that you didn't invite me to spend the night," he said.

"You didn't seem like you were interested," she said.

"My mistake," he said, pulling her into his arms. He walked her back toward the bed.

He didn't say anything but pulled her under him. His robe fell open and he shrugged it off his shoulders revealing his nakedness. He pushed her nightgown up to her waist and slid into her body. He rocked them slowly together.

The sensation of having him inside of her again was exquisite.

She'd grown accustomed to his touch and it felt right to have him here between her legs. In her again. She no longer felt like she was alone.

She knew she was drawn to the feel of him. His body under her fingers, his chest rubbing against her breasts and the feel of his mouth on her neck with that early morning stubble abrading her. She shivered as he whispered darkly sexual words against her skin and rocked his hips leisurely against hers.

The first time they'd made love had been intense and explosive, the second time sweet and sensual, but this morning it felt like coming home. She was awash in feelings of Justin as they slowly moved together.

She scraped her nails down his back until she could cup his butt and pull him closer to her. He paused buried hilt-deep inside of her.

He lifted his head and looked down at her. "Good morning."

"Yes, it is," she said, feeling more relaxed than she

had in a long time. There was something nice about making love first thing in the morning.

"I like the feel of your hands on me."

"Me, too," she admitted. "From the moment I saw you in the lobby of the zoning office I wanted to touch your butt."

He gave her a wicked smile. "I wanted to touch your breasts."

He lowered his head and took the tip of one of her nipples between his lips, suckling her softly in the early morning light.

His hands moved over the sides of her torso and he cupped her other breast in his hand then rotated his palm over it. Stimulating it until the nipple hardened.

She shifted her shoulders as he started to suckle more strongly. She put her heels on the bed trying to get him to move in her but he wouldn't be budged. This morning he was determined to take his time and drive her slowly out of her mind.

"Please…"

"Please what? Doesn't this feel good?"

"Yes, it feels too good," she said.

"How can something feel too good?" he asked, tracing the edge of her areola with his tongue.

She couldn't think. The humid warmth of his tongue contrasted with the slight abrasion of his stubble and it was driving her mad.

"Just please…"

"Please what?" he asked.

"Make love to me," she said at last, looking into those clear blue eyes of his.

"My pleasure," he said. He started moving his hips again and the movement this time was more purposeful. He wasn't teasing the both of them now. The beast within him had been woken and he held her hips with the strong grasp of his hand as he drew in and out of her body.

He did it slowly, letting her feel each inch as he pulled it out, then plunged back in until he was buried inside of her.

"Is that what you wanted?" he asked, his raspy voice sending chills down her spine.

"Yes, but more. Yesss…"

"Selena, you feel so good to me," he said, then lowered his head and kissed her deeply, his tongue thrusting into her mouth with the same rhythm of his hips. She held on to his shoulders to lift herself more fully into his embrace.

Every particle of her being was crying out for release but he was keeping her right on the edge. So that little climaxes feathered through her, making him thrust faster and harder. Plunging into her and driving her over the edge. She tore her mouth from his and screamed his name as her orgasm rushed through her.

Justin held her hips and drove into her three more times before shuddering in her arms and emptying himself in her body. She lifted herself against him once more to draw out the exquisite feeling of pleasure.

He leaned off her body to the side but still held her close and she liked it.

She turned her head to look up at him. "I…"

"Don't," he said. "Don't say anything."

"Is this a mistake?"

He rolled over and pulled her into his arms so she rested on his chest, right over his heart. It beat loudly under her ear. "You don't feel like a mistake to me. But I think objectivity is gone."

She knew he was right. "We can't pretend we are just vacation lovers."

"No, we can't. I've never been good at lying, even to myself and you feel like more than a temporary affair."

It felt the same to her. She wanted more.

Thirteen

A week later, Selena still hadn't made sense of anything with Justin. He was keeping his distance and on some levels, that worked for her. Her grandparents and the other vendors had all had their meetings with him at Luna Azul. Selena had participated in some of them but for the most part had stayed back.

She needed to read every contract that was offered and go over the details very carefully. She'd also spent a fair amount of time at the zoning office and realized that Justin already knew that as long as he hired a local contractor he was within his rights to start construction.

Selena advised everyone of this fact so that they realized at some point they needed to concede some of their dream-list demands.

Her cell phone rang just as she was driving away from her grandparents' store. She glanced at the caller ID and saw that it was Justin.

"Hello." She put him on her Bluetooth speaker-phone.

"Put on your dancing shoes tonight, I'm taking you out."

"Really? Don't you think you should ask me first?"

"Nah, you'd just debate about it and then agree. I'm saving us a little time."

"Okay, then I guess I'll agree to go out with you. Where are we going?"

"Luna Azul. It's celebration time and you and I have never been to the club."

"Celebration?" she asked.

"Yes, ma'am. I finished the last of the appointments ten minutes ago and everyone is on board. Thank you for your hard work in making this happen."

"Not a problem. It is as important to you as it is to me."

"I know," he said. "That's why we need to celebrate. I will pick you up at seven and we can have dinner at my favorite restaurant first."

"Wait a minute. I can't do this," she said abruptly.

"Why not?"

She realized she was shaking and pulled the car over. "We were just a vacation fling, remember? We can't mix business and pleasure. We just can't."

"Why not?"

"Because if we do, I'm going to lose myself. I'm going to fall right back into the girl I used to be. I can't do that."

"You aren't going to turn into the girl you used to be. You're a woman now, Selena, successful and sure of yourself. There is no way you'd ever fall for a con again. And I'm not conning you. I've been nothing but honest with you."

That was true. "You have. But I haven't been honest with myself. I can't pretend that you mean nothing to me and I know we have no future. I can't stay here."

"Why not?"

"Because I have a life that I enjoy."

"Fair enough. Let's talk about this over dinner. I want to celebrate what we both worked so hard for. At least give me that," he said.

She realized that if she saw him again she was never going to be able to leave. He wouldn't let her and she was weak where he was concerned.

"Sounds good," she said, knowing that it was a lie. She wasn't going to meet Justin. In fact, if she played her cards right she'd never see him again. A clean break and she'd be back in New York in the heart of her safe life. Staying here...that wasn't an option no matter how tempting it might be.

She disconnected the call. She already knew about her grandparents' agreement with Luna Azul. There were only a few things left for her to do and then she could head home.

It was beyond time for her to leave. She was beginning to forget she had a life somewhere else. She'd fallen back into her old Miami routines but it wasn't the way she'd been before. She was eating breakfast with her grandparents, spending the afternoons with her brother and enjoying an idyllic life. But that wasn't realistic. If she moved back here, she'd be working all the time like she did back north. And why would she move here...for her family or for Justin?

She shook her head as she drove up to her hotel. It

had helped her keep her perspective that she was here temporarily, or had it? It was hard to stay because Justin had changed the way she looked at life here.

Granted, she was no longer the twenty-year-old woman who had left home with her tail between her legs. Helping her grandparents reclaim their grocery store and have a say in the new Mercado had helped resolve her leftover feelings of guilt.

She pulled the car over as the emotions she'd been burying for so long came to the surface. She started to cry.

She put her head down on the steering wheel. The flood of tears was gone and she felt vulnerable now. Justin had done this to her. He'd helped her make things right for her grandparents and for herself. She knew no one had blamed her for what Raul had done. But his actions had been a black specter over her for too many years and finally she was free.

She wiped her tears as she lifted her head. She had to get back to the hotel and get changed if she was going to actually go through with it and be on time to meet with Justin.

Justin.

He made her feel things she'd never experienced before. Not just sexually, she realized. Sex she could handle because that was lust and hormones—she could explain her attachment sexually to him. But the other bonds. The way she'd missed sleeping in his arms after only doing it one night—that wasn't right.

She was falling in love with him.

Love.

Oh, God, no. She wasn't ready to be in love with Justin Stern. She wasn't ready to face the future with him by her side…if he even wanted that. And what if he didn't?

She needed to get away. She drove to her hotel and handed her keys to the valet. Telling him to keep the car up front because she was checking out.

She went up to her room, packed her bags and called for a bellman. She wanted—no, needed—to get back to New York. Once she was away from Miami, the tropical fever that had been affecting her would go away. She'd be back to normal and whatever emotions she thought she was experiencing would go away.

It was just the vacation mind-set that was making her feel this way. She jotted a short note to Justin on the hotel stationery telling him she was needed at her job and left it at the front desk for him after she checked out.

Ten minutes later she was back in her car and headed to the airport. She knew that Justin would be upset that she left him that way but hey, he'd done it to her the other night, so…

She knew that leaving town wasn't the same as leaving her after a dinner. But at this moment it felt pretty darn close and though she knew her grandparents would be upset that she'd left again, she knew it was time to get out of here. And they at least would always love her.

Justin hung up the phone and leaned back in his leather executive chair. He glanced up at the portrait on the wall of him and his brothers with their father. It was the one thing he'd used as a talisman to keep himself focused on business.

But no matter how long he stared at it now, he knew that he'd been changed by this Mercado deal. He also realized that now that most of their business was concluded there was no real reason for Selena to stay in Miami, but he decided that he was going to ask her to stay. He had tried to keep things light but to be honest it wasn't his nature to be so casual. That was the main reason why he'd always limited himself to short-term affairs. But Selena wasn't that type of woman and with her at least he wasn't that kind of man.

He knew he wasn't ready for marriage…because he'd promised himself to never take that step. But he already knew that Selena meant more to him than any woman ever had.

She made him feel the same loyalty and devotion that he felt for his brothers but there was more than that where she was concerned. He didn't want to admit it to himself but he had fallen for her. He refused to say that it was love because he wouldn't be that weak. But it was pretty damned close.

Maybe knowing that was the key to not being like his father. The last thing he wanted was for Selena to realize how much she meant to him and how much control that gave her.

He got to his feet and walked to his office window. Miami was his hometown but he had seen a different side of it while he'd been with Selena. A side that made him realize that he'd been missing out on a few things.

Important things. He'd isolated himself here in the office. Tonight he was going to take the first step to break down the walls he'd used to shield himself all these years.

It was silly really but being a workaholic had meant that no one expected anything from him when it came to family. His brothers knew they'd have to call him at the office; his "friends" had all been colleagues. Until Selena. Now he was getting to know Enrique and Tomas and Paulo as friends.

He owed that all to Selena. Even though she thought she was no longer entrenched in her family, he'd seen that she was and she'd brought him into that group as well.

There was a knock on his door.

"Come in," he said.

Cam stood there looking tired but holding a bottle of Cristal in one hand and two champagne glasses in the other. "I figured it was time to celebrate."

"Definitely. I sent the last contract to legal and have a verbal confirmation from all of the vendors. To be honest, things worked out even better than I anticipated."

"I knew they would," Cam said. He put the glasses on the desk and opened the bottle of champagne.

"Is Nate coming?"

"No. He… I'm not sure what's going on with him. I think that he is doing something with Jen."

"Doesn't he always these days? He's taken to being a committed man like a fish to water."

"Yes, I hope he doesn't run into the Curse of the Stern men. We just aren't good with women and relationships," Cam said.

Justin took the champagne flute that Cam gave him. "To our success."

They both took a sip of the drink. Justin wished he could say that his mind was still on business but he knew that he was thinking of Selena and the Stern curse.

What if he was destined to screw up the relationship with her?

"Now about the tenth anniversary celebration…"

"Yes, we can get to work planning the details of the ground-breaking. Nate tells me most of the pieces are falling into place for the outdoor festival and concert."

"Excellent," Cam said. "That's exactly what I was hoping you'd say."

"I know. You are an even worse workaholic perfectionist than I am," Justin said.

"I'm not a workaholic," Cam said. "I just put the club and our company first."

Justin reached over and squeezed his brother's shoulder. "I know you do, but you're not on your own supporting us anymore. We are wealthy men, we're here to help. You could relax."

Cam nodded. "I don't know how to relax…or so I've been told."

"That's BS. I've heard the same thing said about myself. The problem with people who make those comments is that they don't understand what it's like to work hard to make their own business successful."

"I see your point, but I am almost always at work or at the club. I was thinking I might take a few days off."

Justin looked at his brother shrewdly. "Is there a woman involved?" Not because Justin was psychic or anything but Selena had made *him* behave that way.

"Maybe. Not sure. Why?"

"Don't you remember me moving into the Ritz?"

"Hell, yes. A woman?"

Justin nodded. "Selena Gonzalez."

"I like her," Cam said. "She's smart and funny. Is she staying in Miami?"

"I hope so. Now that our business is over I can concentrate on her…but I'm not sure that is the wisest thing to do."

"Why not?"

"The Stern curse. Look at Dad."

Cam shook his head. "You're not like Dad. Dad married our mother for business reasons. Even though they didn't get along, I think he liked not having a woman who'd take up his time."

"Why did he stay with her?"

Cam looked over at Justin. This was a subject they'd never spoken of before. "I think he stayed for us. I think having sons was something he hadn't expected."

"How do you know?"

"Just an educated guess. And I know you aren't like Dad when it comes to women," Cam said.

"I don't even know that."

"Jus, look at the life you have led," Cam said. "Then look at the fact that you went through a tough negotiation with Selena and kept your personal life separate. You got the job done. That takes a strong man. And I've always known you were that."

"Thanks, Cam. I…I'm scared to admit how much I need her."

"If she's half the woman I think she is, that won't be a problem. It wasn't Dad's devotion that was the issue with our parents but rather Mother's coldness. Selena isn't like that, is she?"

Justin thought about that after his brother left. If there was one thing he knew for sure it was that Selena wasn't cold. And he wasn't a man who gave up when he wanted something as badly as he wanted her.

* * *

As much as Selena wanted to just escape to the airport and head back to New York, she knew she had to at least read over the contracts with all the vendors for the Mercado one last time. So she was sitting in the back room of her grandfather's grocery store, poring over the documents.

She'd gotten lucky that her grandfather was busy with customers and hadn't had a chance to notice her suitcases in the rental car. She knew she'd have to tell him that she was leaving, but right now she just needed to focus on business. So she read the contracts and existed in a world where emotions weren't a part of the equation. The Stern brothers had been more than fair in the agreements, but she refused to let herself dwell on that or on Justin.

She had had to pay an insane amount of money for the ticket and even then her flight didn't leave for another six hours. Once she was on the plane and back in her Upper West Side apartment, she'd relax. Until then she was swamped with an overwhelming sense of panic. She was afraid. Not of her family or Justin or even how they'd react when they realized she'd left, but of herself.

She didn't want to go. Last time she'd left she wanted to leave. Couldn't have gotten out of Miami fast enough. But this time she wanted to stay and that was even more dangerous.

She knew that the life she'd been living here wasn't real and that getting back to her routine was the only thing that would wake her up. Smiling and laughing and doing things that made no sense like sleeping with Justin Stern…that wasn't her and she needed to get back to New York where she could remember who she was.

"Selena?"

She started as she heard her name and turned to see Paulo standing there. She got up and gave her cousin a hug.

"I think I already reviewed your contract," she said.

"You did," he said. "I noticed your suitcase in the car. Are you leaving?"

"Yes, I am. I was just here to make sure that Luna Azul didn't take advantage of you all in the fine print. I'm almost done."

"I must have missed *abuelita*'s call. I thought she was going to have everyone over before you went back home."

Selena flushed as a weird sensation made her stomach feel like it was full of lead. "Uh, I kind of haven't told her I'm leaving yet."

"What? What's going on? Are you okay?" he asked.

"Nothing is going on. I just got word that all of the vendors at the Mercado were ready to sign their contracts and there is no reason for me to stay anymore."

"No reason…what about family?" Paulo asked.

"I am not leaving the family, Paulo. I'm—"

"Is this about that guy you were dating?" he asked.

"No. The guy—Justin—he's not responsible for this," she said. She needed to make sure her family understood that what was going on had nothing to do with Justin and everything to do with her. "I have to get back to my job, that's all."

"Your job?" Paulo asked. "Maybe if I hadn't known you since we were in diapers I'd believe that. But to leave without saying anything to our grandparents… *Tata*, that is not like you. Even after Raul you said goodbye to them."

She shook her head. "If I don't leave now, Paulo, I think I'm going to make an even bigger mistake than I did before."

He hugged her close to him. "What kind of mistake? I can help you."

She pulled back and realized how much she really loved her family. "You can't. I wish you could."

"There is nothing that is so big that you have to run away."

"I know it seems like I'm running away, but truly I'm not, Paulo, I'm simply going home."

"Is New York really your home?" he asked.

"Yes," she said with all the confidence she could muster. She wanted Paulo to believe it because maybe if he did, she would.

"That's a lie, *tata,*" he said. "When you came down here you were buttoned up, wearing all black and looking like anyone else from up there. But after a few days your hair was down and you blossomed back into the woman you really are."

"I haven't changed," she said.

"Then you aren't being honest with yourself. I hope you wake up to the fact that you can't ever really be comfortable in your own skin unless you acknowledge that your family is a huge part of who you are," he said.

Paulo was being hard on her. Almost as hard as she was sure her grandparents would be. "I'm not going to change my mind."

"I hope someday you do. When are you calling *abuelita?*"

"I will do it in a few minutes when I've finished reviewing this last contract."

"Make sure you do. I don't want to keep secrets for you."

Paulo walked away and she shivered. If she wasn't so afraid she'd try to find a way to stay, but there were no doubts in her mind that she needed to go back home and get some perspective. But Paulo had a point and for the first time she'd seen how badly it had hurt her family the way she'd left before, but they had understood. If Paulo was that mad, how would Enrique and her grandparents react?

How would Justin?

What was she running from? Was she making a huge mistake?

She rubbed the back of her neck. She shouldn't leave without at least saying goodbye to her grandparents. She couldn't. "Paulo!"

"Si, tata?"

"Will you come with me to *abuelita*'s?"

"Definitely. I think this is the right thing to do."

"Paulo, I'm so confused. No one has ever made me feel this way."

"You mean Justin?"

"Yes. And he's not…he's not like anyone else I've ever known. I'm afraid to trust myself."

"You shouldn't be. You are a very smart woman, *tata*," Paulo said. A few minutes later they were in his car driving toward her grandparents' house.

Selena wanted to pretend that she was still getting on that airplane and leaving Miami but a part of her no longer wanted to go.

* * *

Justin arrived at the Ritz twenty minutes before he was supposed to pick Selena up. He went to his room and packed up his luggage and had it taken to his car before he went to check out. Selena was going to look right at home in his waterfront house on Fisher Island. It would be nice to see her there.

"How can I help you, sir?"

"I'm checking out," he said. "Justin Stern."

The front desk hostess nodded and started working on her computer and a minute later glanced up and smiled at him. "It says we have a letter for you. Let me grab that while you look over the folio."

She handed him his resort bill and he glanced down at it before signing his name. Then she passed him an envelope and told him to have a nice day.

The handwriting on the front was Selena's and he knew what it said before he even opened it.

But he tore it open anyway. He glanced down at the note on the hotel stationery.

Justin,
I have an emergency back in New York and had to catch a flight out today. Thank you for all of your hard work on making the Luna Azul Mercado a true part of the Cuban American community. I wish you much success with this endeavor.

On a personal note, I'm sorry to leave without seeing you again but I think this might be easier. I have come to care for you and am questioning my own judgment where you are concerned. Forgive me. I know deep down you'll understand.

Please accept my apology for not calling you but I was afraid to hear your voice again before I left.

Take care,
Selena

Justin refolded the letter and put it in his pocket as he walked out of the club. He got in his Porsche 911 and drove like a madman away from the Ritz. He had no real destination in mind until he found himself parked in front of Selena's house.

He remembered the night they'd made love by her pool. The night that had changed everything between them and though he'd thought he had the luxury of time to make up his mind about her and what he wanted from their relationship, he just realized that Selena was battling the same things he had been. And she'd decided that a quick, clean break was the simplest solution.

But he knew it wasn't. She thought that now that she'd gotten everything she wanted that she could walk away from him, and he felt used.

He'd been the one who'd started this and he'd be the one to end it. Justin Stern wasn't her lapdog…he wasn't about to let Selena get what she wanted and then walk away.

He fired up the engine of his car and drove back to his office building. If that was the way she wanted to play things then he would show her that he was more than willing to play her game. And he would beat her at it.

He pulled out the contracts and then had his assistant bring him the list of other local business owners who weren't in the Mercado. The zoning ordinance simply said that it had to be a local vendor, not that it had to be the same ones.

He drew up a list of comparable businesses and then called Cam to tell him to hold off on celebrating.

"Why?" Cam asked.

"Because we're not going to be lying down for the committee. If they want to be a part of the Mercado they will have to meet our terms," Justin said.

"What has changed in the last two hours? And how much is it going to cost us to break the contracts with our current vendors?"

Justin knew he had to tell his brother something but he didn't have the words right now. "I will tell you later. Let's just say that I think an expert played us. And that makes me mad."

"What does Selena say?"

"I have no idea, she's gone back to New York."

There was silence on the line and Justin knew he'd said too much.

"You can't go back on the deals we have in place. I know you are angry. Hell, I'm pissed for you, but there is no way we are going to let a woman ruin the good thing we have going."

"I know. I really know that it's not the best idea, but I want to hurt her, Cam."

"I understand that," Cam said. "I'm coming back to the office. Don't do anything rash."

When Cam ended the call, Justin stood up, trying to get rid of the restless energy that was making him feel like he was going to punch something. He wasn't in the right frame of mind to work right now, he knew that, but he had no idea where he would go.

The gym. He needed physical exercise and a lot of

it. He would love it if he could go to a boxing ring but the closet one was thirty minutes away and he wasn't in any shape to drive right now.

He kept a bag of workout clothes at the office and grabbed them and his iPod and left. The gym was only a block away and he walked there, got changed and was on the treadmill in less than twenty minutes.

He put his headphones on and ran. It took about two miles for his mind to settle down and he realized that revenge was not the smartest reaction to have to her leaving.

He cared too much for Selena. He knew that he wanted to hurt her the way she'd hurt him by leaving with only a note to explain her actions. But he also liked Tomas and Paulo and all of the other business owners. Hurting them might succeed in getting Selena's attention but he wasn't interested in ruining Luna Azul and his new friends in the process.

"Want some company?" Cam asked as he walked up. He got on the treadmill next to Justin and started running.

"No, but I don't think you are going to listen to me."

"I'm not," Cam said.

"How did you find me here?"

"You're pretty predictable, bro." Cam took a long look at Justin before he started up the machine. "Are you still thinking like a knucklehead?"

"No. I know I can't throw away everything we've worked for because of a woman."

"Good. What else have you figured out?"

"I still want her, Cam. Maybe this is what Dad felt

about Mother. Maybe he realized that he couldn't live without her."

"Maybe, little brother, I never understood the two of them. But this is about you."

How true. He didn't care about his parents' relationship; it was time to break the cycle. He realized he wasn't interested in doing anything that was going to harm Selena. He wanted her back. When he had her in his arms again, he'd make damned sure she never left.

Selena was his. She'd made that choice when she'd given herself to him on his yacht. He hadn't realized it at the time but a bond had been formed.

It took him two more miles of running on the treadmill until he had the seeds of a plan. Normally he'd play his cards close to his chest and keep this wound private but he knew to win Selena he was going to have to pull out all of the stops and involve not only his family but hers as well.

As Justin stepped off the treadmill, he turned to Cam with a smile on his face.

Fourteen

Selena was cold. It was almost April and though spring had definitely been present in Miami, it wasn't very warm here in Manhattan. She'd been back for one weekend. That was it, even though it felt like a lifetime.

She pulled her coat a little closer as she exited the subway station nearest her office and started walking. There were a lot of people on the street but she kept her head down and just walked.

Selena's talk with her grandparents and brother the day she left had been…somber, but she'd done what needed doing. Her boss had been very happy to see her back from her leave of absence so soon and had immediately put her on a project.

The kind of project she loved, one where she just worked 24/7 and was consumed with all the research she had to do. Being a corporate lawyer meant lots of time reading case studies and finding precedence.

She wanted to believe she'd made the right choice but she felt alone and missed Justin. He hadn't called her and to be honest she hadn't expected him to. She hadn't really given him an opening to.

She entered her office and walked past the security guard flashing her badge. He smiled at her as he did every day and called good morning to her. But she didn't smile back. She just didn't have it in her to pretend to be happy when she wasn't.

She took the elevator to the seventh floor where her office was and when she was seated behind her desk she looked around.

She shook her head as she waited for her computer to boot up.

What was she doing here?

Waiting.

She'd spent her entire life waiting.

Her phone rang and she glanced at the caller ID. It was her brother.

She picked up and said, "Hi, Enrique."

"I'm sorry to bother you at work but we need you back in Florida."

"Why? What is going on?"

"The Stern brothers have offered me a gig. I want you to be here. It's my first legit gig," Enrique said.

"When is it?"

"This weekend. I know you said you needed to be back in New York, but I really want you here for this."

"Let me see what I can do," she said. She couldn't avoid the important events in her brother's life. "I will let you know if I'm coming."

"*Tata,* I need my sister there. We are all each other has."

"Enrique, you have *abuelito* and *abuelita* there."

"It's not the same. I want my big sister to be here."

"Okay, I'll do it."

"Good."

They hung up and she stared at the phone. It was odd that her grandfather hadn't told her about the gig when they spoke on the phone last night. But he was still mad she'd left and had refused to tell her anything about the Mercado, so that might explain it.

She went online to research airfares and almost booked her flight, but she realized if she was going back she wanted to see Justin. She needed to see him. She picked up the phone and dialed Justin's number. Something she'd done numerous times in the past. But this time she hung up before he answered. The same thing stopped her now, as had each time over the last several days.

What was she going to say to him? She honestly had no idea what he was going to be like when she phoned. If she knew she'd get his voice mail she'd stay on the line even if just to listen to his voice. And if he answered she could make up some excuse about wanting to read Enrique's contract for him or find out how the Mercado was progressing but that wasn't the truth.

She missed him.

There, she'd said it.

Since she'd been back, she'd been existing.

Existing…hadn't she always wanted more from her life?

Her boss walked by and paused in the doorway.

"You look like you are pondering something big."

"I am. I think I am going to resign."

"Why?"

"I don't belong here, Rudy, I need to be back in Miami."

He shook his head. "I knew I shouldn't have let my best lawyer go to Miami in March."

"It's not the weather," she said.

"What is it then?"

No way was she going to tell her boss that it was a man. A man who might not even want her after the way she'd left. She'd made a mistake but if Justin had cared for her even a tenth as much as she loved him, then he would at least listen to her and that was all she needed.

Her time in Miami had reawakened her fighting spirit.

"It's my heart. I left it down there and I don't think I'm surviving very well without it."

He nodded. "That I understand. Can you at least finish the case you are working on?"

If she worked around the clock she could get her research finished and her notes in order so that she could pass it on to another attorney. She nodded and got to work.

Suddenly she didn't feel so lethargic. She looked out the window, realizing soon she'd be back home in Miami and that was really all she needed.

She decided she'd go to Miami for Enrique's gig this coming weekend. It would give her a chance to find Justin and try to make amends before she moved back there permanently. And if she hustled, she could finish her move by the time Luna Azul's tenth anniversary party rolled around.

She didn't want to waste any more time now that she'd decided what she wanted. She felt silly that it had taken her so long to realize that Justin owned her heart. She suspected she'd known it when she'd gotten on that plane in Miami to fly back here.

When Justin got off the private plane Hutch Damien had loaned him and walked across the tarmac to the heliport, he thanked his lucky stars. Nate's celebrity friends sure came in handy.

Flying to New York City had been his last resort. At first he'd harbored a few fantasies of Selena coming crawling back to him but those had died quickly.

Given her past with men, he knew he was going to have to compromise and be the one to make the first move. He was still mad at the way she'd run off. But he loved her. He'd known that almost the instant he'd read her letter and realized that she was leaving him.

It had taken him one lonely night before he was able to admit it out loud and then he knew that he had to get her back. On his own. He knew her family was more than willing to help him get her to come back, but this was strictly between him and her.

There was no way he could spend the rest of his life without her.

His cell phone rang before he got on the chopper for his ride to midtown Manhattan and Selena's office.

"Stern."

"It's Tomas. Enrique called Selena this morning and… told her about the gig. I think she is coming home."

"Dammit. I told Enrique I could do this without his help," Justin said.

"He loves his sister and he wants her to be happy."

Of that Justin had no doubt. "I thought I said I was handling this."

"You did but our family doesn't want to leave anything to chance."

Justin shook his head. "Thanks for letting me know. I will call as soon as I have some news."

"Just bring our *tata* home," Tomas said.

Justin had every intention of doing just that. Selena belonged by his side. Together they had made a good team but they had also completed each other. This wasn't some big show to convince her to overlook his flaws. She hadn't changed who he was at his core; she'd just shown him that the right woman was all he needed to be happy.

Years of short-term affairs had left him with the feeling that he was just like his father. But one month with the right woman had convinced him that he had been wrong.

He needed Selena the way he needed to breathe.

He got on the chopper and watched the views as he flew over Manhattan. Not bad. What he hadn't told her family but had told his brothers was that if Selena wouldn't come back to Miami, he was going to move here. He even had a possible apartment lined up just in case.

The chopper landed at the heliport and his driver met Justin. Soon they were on their way to Selena's office.

He knew her well enough to know that she would be at work even though it was almost six in the evening. She was the kind of person who poured herself into whatever task she took. But more than that, she'd run away not only from him but also from her family. It was going to take a lot of work to keep her mind busy so she wouldn't have to think of all she'd left behind.

Tonight she was going to have no choice but to think about it. He was back. And he was going to get the answers he needed from her about her actions and then he was going to find the key to both of their happiness.

He was sure it was in the both of them. That they belonged together. Now all he had to do was convince her of that.

His phone buzzed and he glanced down to see a text message from his brother.

Cam: Are you there?

Justin: Just.

Cam: Let me know how it goes.

Justin had to laugh. One would think a make-or-break business deal hung in the balance the way Tomas and Cam were anxiously awaiting news. But he knew that both men had his best personal interest at heart. This wasn't about business.

Justin: I will.

Cam had been worried, angry and then understanding when Justin had come to him and told him that he had to go to Manhattan and that there was a chance he was going to move there.

It had taken Cam less than twenty-four hours to figure out a plan to keep Justin in the business no matter where he ended up. He wanted to bring what he called "a taste of Miami Latin to the club scene in Manhattan" and Justin would be in charge of finding a new location and getting it up and running if he decided to stay in New York.

When the driver pulled to a stop in front of Selena's

building, Justin jumped out of the car. He entered the skyscraper and went right up to the security guard at the reception desk.

"Can I help you, sir?"

"I'd like to see Selena Gonzalez," he said, and gave the man the name of her law firm.

"Is she expecting you?" the guard asked.

"No, she isn't." Never in a million years. But then he figured she didn't know him as well as she should have. How much he needed her. If she had, she might not have ever left him in Miami.

"Have a seat over there, sir."

Justin walked a few feet from the desk but couldn't sit down. Not now. He was ready to see Selena and no matter what happened he wasn't leaving this building until he did.

The guard hung up the phone and motioned for him to come over. Justin did and was handed a pass and given instructions on how to get to Selena's office.

Selena hung up the phone and immediately pulled out her compact and checked her makeup. It was shallow, she knew, but she wanted to be looking her best when Justin got up here. She reapplied her lipstick but there was no disguising the dark circles under her eyes. She was tired and he was going to be able to tell without much effort.

She could hardly believe he was here. What if she'd imagined the call? All day she'd thought about the fact that if she moved back to Miami there was a very real chance for her to reconcile with him.

Reconcile? She would probably have to get down on her knees and beg him to give her another chance. And she was in a place in her life right now to do that. She wanted Justin. He was the reason she was quitting her job and moving back to Miami.

She heard the outer door of her office open and got to her feet, poking her head around the corner.

Justin.

He looked better than she'd remembered. His hair was casually tousled, his skin tanner than the last time she'd seen him and his eyes very intense.

She had to force herself to stay in the doorway and not run to him. But she wanted a hug. She needed one. She hadn't had a single good night's sleep since she left him and she craved the feeling of those big strong arms around her.

"Hello," she said.

"Thanks for agreeing to see me," he said.

She stepped back and retreated behind her desk as he walked toward her. But when he entered the room she realized she wasn't in a position of power, not anymore. She'd tried to protect herself by leaving Miami but she was completely vulnerable where Justin was concerned.

She'd give him whatever he wanted if he forgave her.

"I figured it was the least I could do."

He tipped his head to the side. "The very least…why did you run away?"

"I was scared. I guess I didn't want to take a chance on staying and letting you hurt me."

"Why would I have hurt you?"

"Because all the men in my life have. Maybe not my *abuelito*. But my papa died when I needed him the most and Raul took my heart and my money and then he left. I didn't want to give you the chance to do the same thing to me. So when I realized our business was done and that I had a small window of time to get out of Miami—I took it."

"Have I ever done anything to make you think I would leave you like that?" he asked.

"You suggested we have a vacation affair. That we pretend that our lives were separate. That isn't exactly a ringing endorsement for giving your heart to someone."

"You were afraid of me and what I made you feel. From the beginning it was me coming on strong and you backing up. I guess I should have expected you to run."

Selena looked at him and saw the man she loved. Saw the pain she'd caused him when she'd left. If she had to guess, she'd say it wasn't just the leaving but the way she'd done it. Sneaking out of Miami the way Raul had done to her.

"I'm sorry."

"Me, too."

"Why are you sorry?"

"That you felt you had to leave like that."

"I care for you—hell, I love you, Justin, but I'm not sure I can trust any man with my heart. I ran away from everyone because the desire to stay was so strong I couldn't trust it."

"You love me?" he asked her.

She nodded. There was no way she was going to deny it. She wanted Justin back in her life and he realized it would take a lot for him to trust her again but it was what she wanted more than anything else.

"Yes, I do."

"I'm still angry at you for running away," he said.

"I expected as much. I don't know if I'd be able to forgive myself."

"I can forgive you, I understood why you left even as you were running away. But the anger is still there."

She nodded. "I understand. By the way, why are you here? Enrique said you gave him a gig. I was going to call you and tell you I'm coming back to Miami."

"That is good to hear. Enrique is trying to be helpful. I guess I didn't move fast enough for your family. They want you back."

"Of course they do," she said, relieved that Justin was the kind of man she'd believed him to be. Not a man who would try to hurt her family because she hurt him. "But do you?"

"I wouldn't be here if I didn't."

She smiled over at him. "Thank God. I know it's going to take time before you and I can be back to the way we were...I've already talked to my boss about resigning and moving home. I think—"

"No. You don't have to resign and move back to Miami. I am here because I can't stand another day without you. Together we will figure out what works for both of us because I'm not letting you leave me again."

"Why?"

"Because I love you."

She jumped up and ran around her desk and threw herself into his arms, kissing him. He squeezed her tightly to him and she almost started crying. She'd thought she could control her emotions but she couldn't.

"I was afraid to dream this could happen. I really didn't know what to expect."

"I knew what was going to happen. I have fallen in love with one woman in my life and that's you. There was no way I was going to let you go. I need you, Selena. You are the one person who grounds me."

She cupped his face with her hands and kissed him again. "I need you, too, Justin. You make it possible for me to believe in my dreams again."

"Good. Now what do you say we get out of here so I can make love to you."

"Sounds like a very good idea," she said.

Justin took her hand in his but stopped. "I am not leaving here until you answer one more question."

She took a deep breath. "Yes."

"Will you marry me?"

Justin wasn't playing around. He wasn't about to get Selena back in his life only to let her walk away again. He needed her to not only be his but to show the world that she was.

"Are you sure?"

"I wouldn't have asked if I wasn't," he said. He reached into his pocket and pulled out the ring box. He opened it and took the ring out. "I know that proper form means I should be down on one knee, but I wanted to look into your eyes when you answer me." He'd had it specially made for her. A marquis-cut diamond that he knew would look perfect on her hand.

She nodded. "Yes, I will marry you."

He slipped the ring onto her finger and then pulled her close for a kiss. She moved against him.

And he leaned back against the door pulling her closer to him. He wanted this woman. She'd turned his world upside down and now that he had her back in his arms, he needed to reinforce those bonds by making her his.

"Are you really mine?" he asked.

She smiled up at him, grinning ear-to-ear. "I am."

She shifted against him and he hardened instantly. "Then let's get out of here and find a proper bed so I can make love to you."

She flushed and raised an eyebrow at him. "You drive a hard bargain. Give me a minute to get my bag and shut down my computer and we'll go to my place."

"Okay," he said. "Are you ready to go yet?"

"I am."

The ride across town to her apartment took too long and he held her on his lap and kissed her the entire time. He didn't want to stop touching her and luckily didn't have to.

She shifted around so that she was facing him instead of lying in his arms. "Thank you for coming after me. I mean, I was going to come to you, but thanks."

"You're welcome. I was angry at first and wanted revenge. But that just made me realize how much I love you—because I could never do anything to hurt you or your family."

She hugged him close. "I know you couldn't. Even though you are tough in business, you have a good heart."

"Selena, I thought I was the Tin Man until you came along and showed me that I had one."

The car came to a stop. "This is my place."

"About damned time," he said.

The doorman came and opened the door for them. Justin followed Selena into the lobby and onto the elevator. He couldn't resist caressing the curve of her hips and pulling her into his arms for another kiss. Then he lifted her in his arms as the elevator doors opened and carried her down the hallway, following her directions.

As soon as she unlocked her apartment door and then stepped inside he leaned back against it and kissed her with all the carnality he'd been bottling up since she'd agreed to be his wife.

She dropped her bag and kicked off her shoes as he walked into the apartment.

"Bedroom?"

"Down the hall. Take your jacket off," she said.

"I'd have to put you down and I'm not ready to do that yet."

He walked into her bedroom and set her in the center of her king-size bed. It was covered with pillows. When she turned on the bedside lamp he saw that her room was done in warm hues of green and gold.

He toed off his shoes and socks and then took off his jacket. She reached for the buttons at the front of her blouse but he brushed her fingers aside and undid them himself.

He took his time stripping her. Each new bit of skin that was revealed he took the time to caress first with his hands, then with his mouth.

He lingered over her breasts and when she got restless and tried to hurry him, he refused. This time he wanted it to last and knowing that he had the right to make love to her for the rest of his life gave him the willpower to take his time.

"Now you are mine," he said.

She unbuttoned his shirt and pushed it off his shoulders onto the floor. Her hands roamed over his chest and traced the path of hair down to his belly button. She ran the edge of her nail around the circumference of it again and again. Each circle she completed made him harden even more. She reached for his pants and quickly had them open.

"Now *you're* mine, Justin."

Luckily, they would have a lifetime to work through the fine points of this negotiation.

Epilogue

At the end of May, after Selena had tied up all the loose ends in New York, she and Justin flew down to Miami for the ground-breaking of the Mercado and Luna Azul's tenth anniversary party. The guest list consisted of a glittering array of celebrities. But Selena didn't really care about that. This afternoon, she was enjoying herself in the warm Miami sunshine. They were having a party at her grandparents' house to celebrate her engagement to Justin.

"How's my fiancée?" he asked, coming up behind her and wrapping his arm around her waist.

"Good. I never thought I'd feel this at home in Miami, but moving back here with you…it feels right."

"We can always go back to New York. I'm up to the challenge of opening a Luna Azul club there."

"No, Justin. I'm here to stay." Selena was quiet for

a moment. Then, looking deep into his eyes, she said, "Thank you."

"For what?"

"For giving me back what I thought I'd lost forever."

"What was that?"

"My family and my heritage," she said.

"I didn't give it back to you, you helped me find it and now we can share that. I think we both ended up winning."

"I think so, too," Selena said, going up on her tiptoes and kissing Justin.

"I told you he was a good man," her *abuelita* said as she came up behind her.

"That's not all you said," Selena said with a grin.

"What else did she say?" Tomas asked.

"That he had a nice butt, *abuelito!*"

Justin flushed and everyone standing around them started laughing.

"Well, he does," her grandmother said.

"I guess you are part of the family now," Cam said to Justin. "They definitely like you."

"I like them, too," Justin admitted. He pulled Selena close and whispered in her ear. "I love you."

"I love you, too, Justin Stern."

* * * * *

A REPUTATION FOR REVENGE
JENNIE LUCAS

CHAPTER ONE

TWO DAYS AFTER Christmas, in the soft pink Honolulu dawn, Josie Dalton stood alone on a deserted sidewalk and tilted her head to look up, up, up to the top of the skyscraper across the street, all the way to his penthouse in the clouds.

She exhaled. She couldn't do this. *Couldn't*. Marry him? Impossible.

Except she had to.

I'm not scared, Josie repeated to herself, hitching her tattered backpack higher on her shoulder. *I'd marry the devil himself to save my sister.*

But the truth was she'd never really thought it would come to this. She'd assumed the police would ride in and save the day. Instead, the police in Seattle, then Honolulu, had laughed in her face.

"Your older sister wagered her virginity in a poker game?" the first said incredulously. "In some kind of lovers' game?"

"Let me get this straight. Your sister's billionaire ex-boyfriend *won* her?" The second scowled. "I have real crimes to deal with, Miss Dalton. Get out of here before I decide to arrest *you* for illegal gambling."

Now, Josie shivered in the cool, wet dawn. No one was coming to save Bree. Just her.

She narrowed her eyes. Fine. She should take responsibility. She was the one who'd gotten Bree into trouble in the first place. If Josie hadn't stupidly accepted her boss's invitation to the poker game, her sister wouldn't have had to step in and save her.

Clever Bree, six years older, had been a childhood card prodigy and a con artist in her teens. But after a decade away from that dangerous life, working instead as an honest, impoverished housekeeper, her sister's card skills had become rusty. How else to explain the fact that, instead of winning, Bree had lost everything to her hated ex-boyfriend with the turn of a single card?

Vladimir Xendzov had separated the sisters, forcibly sending Josie back to the mainland on his private jet. She'd spent her last paycheck to fly back, desperate to get Bree out of his clutches. For forty-four hours now, since the dreadful night of the game, Josie had only managed to hold it together because she knew that, should everything else fail, she had one guaranteed fallback plan.

But now she actually had to fall back on the plan, it felt like falling on a sword.

Josie looked up again at the top of the skyscraper. The windows of the penthouse gleamed red, like fire, above the low-hanging clouds of Honolulu.

She'd caused her sister to lose her freedom. She would save her—by selling herself in marriage to Vladimir Xendzov's greatest enemy.

His younger brother.

The enemy of my enemy is my friend, she repeated to herself. And, considering the way the Xendzov brothers had tried to destroy each other for the past ten years, Kasimir Xendzov must be her new best friend. Right?

A lump rose in her throat.

I would marry the devil himself...

Slowly, Josie forced her feet off the sidewalk. Her legs wobbled as she crossed the street. She dodged a passing tour bus, flinching as it honked angrily.

There was no backing out now.

"Can I help you?" the doorman said inside the lobby, eyeing her messy ponytail, wrinkled T-shirt and cheap flip-flops.

Josie licked her dry lips. "I'm here to get married. To one of your residents."

He didn't bother to conceal his incredulity. "*You?* Are going to marry someone who lives *here?*"

She nodded. "Kasimir Xendzov."

His jaw dropped. "You mean His *Highness?* The *prince?*" he spluttered, gesticulating wildly. "Get out of here before I call the police!"

"Look, please just call him, all right? Tell him Josie Dalton is here and I've changed my mind. My answer is now yes."

"*Call* him? I'll do nothing of the sort." The doorman pinched his nose with his thumb and finger. "You must be delusional…if you think you can just walk in off the street…"

Josie rummaged through her backpack.

"His Highness's presence here is secret. He is here on *vacation…*"

"See?" she said desperately, holding out a business card. "He gave me this three days ago. When he proposed to me. At a salad bar near Waikiki."

"Salad bar," the doorman snorted. "As if the prince would ever…" He saw the embossed seal, and snatched the card from her hand. Turning over the card, he read the hard masculine scrawl on the back: *For when you change your mind.* "But you're not his type," he said faintly.

"I know," Josie sighed. Twenty pounds overweight, frumpy and unstylish, she was painfully aware that she was no man's type. Fortunately Kasimir Xendzov wished to marry her for reasons that had nothing to do with love—or even lust. "Just call him, will you?"

The man reached for the phone on his desk. He dialed. Turning away, he spoke in a low voice. A few moments later, he faced Josie with an utterly bewildered expression.

"His bodyguard says you're to go straight up," he said in

shock. He pointed his finger towards an elevator. "Thirty-ninth floor. And, um, congratulations, miss."

"Thank you," Josie murmured, tugging her knapsack higher on her shoulder as she turned away. She felt the doorman watching her as she crossed the elegant lobby, her flip-flops echoing against the marble floor. She numbly got on the elevator. On the thirty-ninth floor, the door opened with a ding. Cautiously, she crept out into a hallway.

"Welcome, Miss Dalton." Two large, grim-looking body-guards were waiting for her. In a quick, professional motion, one of them frisked her as the other one rifled through her bag.

"What are you checking for?" Josie said with an awkward laugh. "You think I would bring a hand grenade? To a wedding proposal?"

The bodyguards did not return her smile. "She's clear," one of them said, and handed her back the knapsack. "Please go in, Miss Dalton."

"Um. Thanks." Looking at the imposing door, she clutched her bag against her chest. "He's in there?"

He nodded sternly. "His Highness is expecting you."

Josie swallowed hard. "Right. I mean, great. I mean…" She turned back to them. "He's a good guy, right? A good employer? He can be trusted?"

The bodyguards stared back at her, their faces impassive.

"His Highness is expecting you," the first one repeated in an expressionless voice. "Please go in."

"Okay." *You robot,* she added silently, irritated.

Whatever. She didn't need reassurance. She'd just listen to her intuition. To her heart.

Which meant Josie was *really* in trouble. There was a reason her dying father had left her a large parcel of Alaskan land in an unbreakable trust, which she could not receive until she was either twenty-five—three years from now—or married. Even when she was a child, Black Jack Dalton had known his naive, trusting younger daughter needed all the help she could get. To say she could be naive about people was an understatement.

But it's a good quality, Bree had told her sadly two days ago. *I wish I had more of it.*

Bree. Josie could only imagine what her older sister was going through right now, as a prisoner of that other billionaire tycoon, Kasimir Xendzov's brother. Closing her eyes, she took a deep breath.

"For Bree," she whispered, and flung open the penthouse door.

The lavish foyer was empty. Stepping nervously across the marble floor, hearing the echo of her steps, she looked up at a soaring chandelier illuminating the sweeping staircase. This penthouse was like a mansion in the sky, she thought in awe.

Josie's lips parted when she saw the view through the floor-to-ceiling windows. Crossing the foyer to the great room, she looked out at the twinkling lights of the still-dark city, and beyond that, pink and orange sunrise sparkling across the Pacific Ocean.

"So...you changed your mind."

His low, masculine purr came from behind her. She stiffened then, bracing herself, slowly turned around.

Prince Kasimir Xendzov's incredible good looks still hit her like a fierce blow. He was even more impossibly handsome than she remembered. He was tall, around six foot three, with broad shoulders and a hard-muscled body. His blue eyes were electric against tanned skin and dark hair. The expensive cut of his dark suit and tie, and the gleaming leather of his black shoes spoke of money—while the ruthlessness in his eyes and chiseled jawline screamed *power*.

In spite of her efforts, Josie was briefly thunderstruck.

Normally, she had no problems talking to people. As far as she was concerned, there was no such thing as a stranger. But Kasimir left her tongue-tied. No man this handsome had ever paid her the slightest notice. In fact, she wasn't sure there *was* any other man on earth with Kasimir's breathtaking masculine beauty. Looking into his darkly handsome face, she almost forgot to breathe.

"The last time I saw you, you said you'd never marry me." Kasimir slowly looked her over, from her flip-flops to her jeans and T-shirt. "For *any* price."

Josie's cheeks turned pink. "Maybe I was a bit hasty," she stammered.

"You threw your drink in my face."

"It was an accident!" she protested.

He lifted an incredulous dark eyebrow. "You jumped up and ran out of the restaurant."

"You just surprised me!" Three nights ago, on Christmas Eve, Kasimir had called her at the Hale Ka'nani Hotel, where she was working as a housekeeper. "My sister told me to never talk to you," she'd blurted out when he introduced himself. "I'm hanging up."

"Then you'll miss the best offer of your life," he'd replied silkily. He'd asked her to meet him at a hole-in-the-wall restaurant near Waikiki Beach. In spite of knowing he was forbidden—or perhaps because of it—she was intrigued by his mysterious proposal. And then she'd been even more shocked to find out he'd meant a real proposal. *Marriage.*

"You ran away from me," Kasimir said quietly, taking a step towards her, "as if you were being chased by the devil himself."

She swallowed.

"Because I did think you were the devil," she whispered.

His blue eyes narrowed in disbelief. "This is your way of saying you'll marry me?"

She shook her head. "You don't understand," she choked out. "You…"

Her throat closed. How could she explain that even though he and his brother had ruined their lives ten years ago, she'd still been electrified by Kasimir's bright blue eyes when he'd asked her to marry him? How to explain that, even though she knew it was only to get his hands on her land, she'd been overwhelmed by too many years of yearning for some man, any man, to notice her—and that she'd been tempted to blurt out *Yes,* betraying all her ideals about love and marriage?

How could she possibly explain such pathetic, naive stupidity? She couldn't.

"Why did you change your mind?" he asked in a low voice. "Do you need the money?"

They did need to pay off the dangerous men who'd pursued them for ten years, demanding payment of their dead father's long-ago debts. But Josie shook her head.

"Then is it the title of princess that you want?"

Josie threw him a startled glance. "Really?"

"Many women dream of it."

"Not me." She shook her head with a snort. "Besides, my sister told me your title's worthless. You might be the grandson of a Russian prince, but it's not like you actually own any land—"

Whoops. She cut off in midsentence at his glare.

"We once owned hundreds of thousands of acres in Russia," he said coldly. "And we owned the homestead in Alaska for nearly a hundred years, since my great-grandmother fled Siberia. It is rightfully ours."

"Sorry, but your brother sold your homestead to my father fair and square!"

He took a step towards her.

"Against my will," he said softly. "Without my knowledge."

Josie took an unwilling step back from the icy glitter in his blue eyes. A self-made billionaire, Kasimir Xendzov was known to be a ruthless, heartless playboy whose main interest, even more than dating supermodels or adding to his pile of money, was destroying his older brother, who had cheated him out of their business partnership right before it would have made him hundreds of millions of dollars.

"Are you afraid of me?" he asked suddenly.

"No," she lied, "why would I be?"

"There are...rumors about me. That I am more than ruthless. That I am—" he tilted his head, his blue eyes bright "—half-insane, driven mad by my hunger for revenge."

Her mouth went dry. "It's not true." She gulped, then said weakly, "Um, is it?"

He gave a low, threatening laugh. "If it were, I would hardly admit it." He turned away, pacing a step before he looked back at her. "So you've changed your mind. But has it occurred to you," he said softly, "that I might have changed my mind about marrying *you?*"

Josie looked up with an intake of breath. "You—wouldn't!"

He shrugged. "Your rejection of me three days ago was definitive."

Fear, real fear, rushed through Josie's heart. She'd gambled her last money to come here. Without Kasimir's help, Bree would be lost. She'd be Vladimir Xendzov's possession. His *slave.* Forever. Her shoulders felt tight as hot tears rushed behind her eyes. Desperately, she grabbed his arm.

"No—please! You said you'd do anything to get the land back. You said you made a promise to your dying father. You—" She frowned, suddenly distracted by the hard muscle of his biceps. "Jeez, how much weight lifting do you do?"

He looked at her. Blushing, she dropped his arm. She took a deep breath.

"Just tell me. Do you still want to marry me?"

Kasimir's handsome face was impassive. "I need to understand your reason. If it's not to be a princess..."

She gave a choked laugh. "As if I'd marry someone for a worthless title!"

His dark eyebrow lifted. "For your information, my title

isn't worthless. It's an asset. You'd be surprised how many people are impressed by it."

"You mean you use it as a shameless marketing tool for your business interests."

His lips curved with amusement. "So you do understand."

"I hope you're not expecting me to bow."

"I don't want you to bow." He looked up, his blue eyes intent. "I just want you to marry me. Right now. Today."

Staring at his gorgeous face, Josie's heart stopped. "So you do still want to marry me?"

He gave her a slow-rising smile that made his eyes crinkle. "Of course I want to marry you. It's all I've wanted."

He was looking down at her...as if he cared.

Of course he cares, she told herself savagely. *He cares about getting his family's land back. That's it.*

But when he looked at her like that, it was too easy to forget that. Her heart pounded. She felt...desired.

Josie tried to convince herself she didn't feel it. She didn't feel a strange tangle of tension and breathless need. She *didn't*.

Kasimir reached out a hand to touch her cheek. "But tell me what changed your mind."

The warm sensuality of his fingers against her skin made her tremble. No man had touched her so intimately. His fingertips were calloused—clearly he was accustomed to hard work—but they were tapered, sensitive fingers of a poet.

But Prince Kasimir Xendzov was no poet. Trembling, she looked down at his strong wrist, at his tanned, thick forearm laced with dark hair. He was a fighter. A warrior. He could crush her with one hand.

"Josie."

"My sister," she whispered, then stopped, her throat dry.

"Bree changed your mind?" Dropping his hand, he walked around her. "I find that hard to believe."

She took a deep breath.

"Your brother kidnapped her," she choked out. "I want you to save her."

She waited for him to express shock, elation, rage, *something*. But his expression didn't change.

"You…" He frowned, narrowing his eyes. "Wait. Vladimir *kidnapped* her?"

She bit her lip, then her shoulders slumped. "Well, I guess technically," she said in a small voice, "you could say she wagered herself to him in a card game. And lost."

His lip curled. "It was a lovers' game. No woman would wager herself otherwise." His eyes narrowed. "My brother always had a weakness for her. After ten years apart, they're no doubt deliriously happy they've made up their quarrel."

"Are you crazy?" she cried. "Bree hates him!"

"What!"

Josie shook her head. "He *forced* her to go with him."

His handsome face suddenly looked cheerful. "I see."

"And it's all my fault." A lump rose in her throat, and she covered her eyes. "The night after you proposed, my boss invited me to join a private poker game. I hoped I could win enough to pay off my father's old debts, and I snuck out while Bree was sleeping." She swallowed. "She never would have let me go. She forbade me ever to gamble, plus she didn't trust Mr. Hudson."

"Why?"

"I think it was mostly the way he hired us from Seattle, sight unseen, with one-way plane tickets to Hawaii. At the time, we were both too desperate to care, but…" She sighed. "She was right. There was something kind of…weird about it. But I didn't listen." She lifted her tearful gaze to his. "Bree lost everything on the turn of a single card. Because of me."

He looked down at her, his expression unreadable. "And you think *I* can save her."

"I know you can. You're the only one powerful enough to stand up to him. The only one on earth willing to battle

with Vladimir Xendzov. Because you hate him the most."
She took a deep breath. "Please," she whispered. "You can
take my land. I don't care. But if you don't save Bree, I don't
know how I'll live with myself."

Kasimir stared at her for a long moment.

"Here." He reached for the heavy backpack on her shoulder. "Let me take that."

"You don't need to—"

"You're swaying on your feet," he said softly. "You look
as if you haven't slept in days. No wonder. Flying to Seattle
and back…"

Without her bag weighing her down, she felt so light she
almost felt dizzy. "I told you I went to Seattle?"

He froze, then relaxed as he looked back at her. "Of course
you did," he said smoothly. "How else would I know?"

Yes, indeed, how would he? After almost no sleep for two
days, she was starting to get confused. Rubbing her cheek
with her shoulder, she confessed, "I am a little tired. And
thirsty."

"Come with me. I'll get you a drink."

"Why are you being nice to me?" she blurted out, not
moving.

He frowned. "Why wouldn't I be nice to you?"

"It always seems that the more handsome a man is, the
more of a jerk he is. And you are very, very…"

Their eyes locked, and her throat cut off. Her cheeks
burned as she muttered, "Never mind."

He gave her a crooked grin. "Whatever your sister might
have told you about me, I'm not the devil. But I am being re-
miss in my manners. Let's get you that drink."

Carrying her backpack over his shoulder, he turned down
the hallway. Josie watched him go, her eyes tracing the muscular shape of his back beneath his jacket and chiseled rear
end.

Then she shook her head, irritated with herself. Why did

she have to blurt out every single thought in her head? Why couldn't she just show discipline and quiet restraint, like Bree? Why did she have to be such a goofball all the time, the kind of girl who'd start conversations with random strangers on any topic from orchids to cookie recipes, then give them her bus money?

This time wasn't my fault, she thought mutinously, following him down the hall. He was far too handsome. No woman could possibly manage sensible thinking beneath the laser-like focus of those blue eyes!

Kasimir led her to a high-ceilinged room lined with leather-bound books on one side, and floor-to-ceiling windows with a view of the city on the other. Tossing her backpack on a long table of polished inlaid wood, he walked over to the wet bar on the other side of the library. "What will you have?"

"Tap water, please," she said faintly.

He frowned back at her. "I have sparkling mineral water. Or I could order coffee…"

"Just water. With ice, if you want to be fancy."

He returned with a glass.

"Thanks," she said. She glugged down the icy, delicious water.

He watched her. "You're an unusual girl, Josie Dalton."

Unusual didn't sound good. She wiped her mouth. "I am?" she echoed uncertainly, lowering the glass.

"It's refreshing to be with a woman who makes absolutely no effort to impress me."

She snorted. "Trying to impress you would be a waste of time. I know a man like you would never be interested in a girl like me—not *genuinely* interested," she mumbled.

He looked down at her, his blue eyes breathtaking.

"You're selling yourself short," he said softly, and Josie felt it again—that strange flash of heat.

She swallowed. "You're being nice, but I know there's no

point in pretending to be something I'm not." She sighed. "Even if I sometimes wish I could."

"Unusual. And honest." Turning, he went to the wet bar and poured himself a short glass of amber-colored liquid. He returned, then took a slow, thoughtful sip.

"All right. I'll get your sister back for you," he said abruptly.

"You will!" If there was something strange about his tone, Josie was too weak with relief to notice. "When?"

"After we're wed. Our marriage will last until the land in Alaska is legally transferred to me." He looked straight into her eyes. "And I'll bring her to you, and set you both free. Is that what you want?"

Isn't that what she'd just said? "Yes," she cried.

Setting down his drink on the polished wooden table, he held out his hand. "Deal."

Slowly, she reached out her hand. She felt the hot, calloused hollow of his palm, felt his strong fingers interlace with hers. A tremble raced through her. Swallowing, she lifted her gaze to his handsome face, to those electric-blue eyes, and it was like staring straight at the sun.

"I hope it won't be too painful for you," she stammered, "being married to me."

His hand tightened over hers. "As you'll be my only wife, ever," he said softly, "I think I'll enjoy you a great deal."

"Your only wife *ever*?" Her brow furrowed. "That seems a little pessimistic of you. I mean—" she licked her lips awkwardly "—I'm sure you'll meet someone someday…"

Kasimir gave a low, humorless laugh.

"Josie, my sweet innocent one—" he looked at her with a smile that didn't reach his eyes "—you are the answer to my every prayer."

Prince Kasimir Xendzov hadn't started the feud ten years ago with his brother.

As a child, he'd idolized Vladimir. He'd been proud of

his older brother, of his loving parents, of his family, of his home. Their great-grandfather had been one of the last great princes of Russia, before he'd died fighting for the White Army in Siberia, after sending his beloved wife and baby son to safety in Alaskan exile. Since then, for four generations, the Xendzovs had lived in self-sufficient poverty on an Alaskan homestead far from civilization. To Kasimir, it had been an enchanted winter kingdom.

But his older brother had hated the isolation and uncertainty—growing their own vegetables, canning them for winter, hunting rabbits for meat. He'd hated the lack of electricity and indoor plumbing. As Kasimir had played, battling with sticks as swords and jousting against the pine trees, Vladimir had buried his nose in business books and impatiently waited for their twice-a-year visits to Fairbanks. "Someday, I'll have a better life," he'd vowed, cursing as he scraped ice off the inside window of their shared room. "I'll buy clothes instead of making them. I'll drive a Ferrari. I'll fly around the world and eat at fine restaurants."

Kasimir, two years younger, had listened breathlessly. "Really, Volodya?" But though he'd idolized his older brother, he hadn't understood Vladimir's restlessness. Kasimir loved their home. He liked going hunting with their father and listening to him read books in Russian by the wood-burning stove at night. He liked chopping wood for their mother, feeling the roughness of an ax handle in his hand, and having the satisfaction of seeing the pile of wood climb steadily against the side of the log cabin. To him, the wild Alaskan forest wasn't isolating. It was freeing.

Home. Family. Loyalty. Those were the things Kasimir cared about.

Right after their father died unexpectedly, Vladimir got news he'd been accepted to the best mining college in St. Petersburg, Russia. Their widowed mother had wept with joy, for it had been their father's dream. But with no money for tuition, Vladimir had put off school and gone to work at a northern mine to save money.

Two years later, Kasimir had applied to the same college for one reason: he felt someone had to watch his brother's back. He didn't expect that he'd have the money to leave Alaska for many years, so he'd been surprised tuition money for them both was suddenly found.

It was only later he'd discovered Vladimir had convinced their mother to sell their family's last precious asset, a jeweled necklace hundreds of years old that had once belonged to their great-grandmother, to a collector.

He'd felt betrayed, but he'd tried to forgive. He'd told himself that Vladimir had done it for their good.

Right after college, Kasimir had wanted to return to Alaska to take care of their mother, who'd become ill. Vladimir convinced him that they should start their own business instead, a mining business. "It's the only way we'll be sure to always have money to take care of her." Instead, when the banks wouldn't loan them enough money, Vladimir had convinced their mother to sell the six hundred and thirty-eight acres that had been in the Xendzov family for four generations—ever since Princess Xenia Petrovna Xendzova had arrived on Alaskan shores as a heartbroken exile, with a baby in her arms.

Kasimir had been furious. For the first time, he'd yelled at his brother. How could Vladimir have done such a thing behind his back, when he knew Kasimir had made a fervent deathbed promise to their father never to sell their land for any reason?

"Don't be selfish," Vladimir said coldly. "You think Mom could do all the work of the homestead without us?" And the money had in part paid for their mother to spend her last days at a hospice in Fairbanks. Kasimir's heart still twisted when he thought of it. His eyes narrowed.

The real reason they'd lost their home had been Vladimir's need to secure the most promising mining rights. What mattered: a younger brother's honor, a mother's home, or his need to establish their business with good cash flow and the best equipment?

"Don't worry," his brother had told him carelessly. "Once we're rich, you can easily buy it back again."

Kasimir set his jaw. He should have cut off all ties with his brother then and there. Instead, after their mother died, he'd felt more bound than ever to his brother—his only family. They strove for a year to build their business partnership, working eighteen-hour days in harsh winter conditions. Kasimir had been certain they'd soon earn their first big payout, and buy their home back again.

He hadn't known that Black Jack Dalton, the land's buyer, had put the land in an irrevocable trust for his child. Or that, as recompense for Kasimir's loyalty, hard work and honesty, at the end of that year Vladimir would cut him out of the partnership and cheat him out of his share of half a billion dollars.

Now, even though Kasimir had long since built up his own billion-dollar mining company, his body still felt tight with rage whenever he remembered how the brother he'd adored had stabbed him in the back. Even once Kasimir regained the land, he knew it would never feel like home. Because he'd never be that same loyal, loving, idealistic, stupid boy again.

No. Kasimir hadn't started the feud with his brother.

But he would end it.

"I'm the answer to your prayer?" a sweet, feminine voice said, sounding puzzled. "How?"

Kasimir's eyes focused on Josie Dalton, standing in front of him in the library of his Honolulu penthouse.

Her brown eyes were large and luminous, fringed with long black lashes—but he saw the weary gray shadows beneath. Her skin was smooth and creamy—but pale, and smudged on one cheek with dust. Her mouth was full and pink—but the lower lip was chapped, as if she'd spent the last two days chewing on it in worry. Her light brown hair, which he could imagine thick and lustrous tumbling down her shoulders, was half pulled up in a disheveled ponytail.

Josie Dalton was not beautiful—no. But she was attractive in her own way, all youth and dewy innocence and overblown curves. He cut off the thought. He did not intend to let himself explore further.

He cleared his throat. "I've wanted our land back for a long time." His voice was low and gravelly, even to his own ears. "I'll make the arrangements for our wedding at once."

"What kind of arrangements?" She bit her lip anxiously, her soft brown eyes wide. "You don't mean a—a honeymoon?"

He looked at her sharply. She blushed. Her pink cheeks looked very charming. Who blushed anymore? "No. I don't mean a honeymoon."

"Good." Her cheeks burned red as she licked her lips. "I'm glad. I mean, I know this is a marriage in name only," she said hastily, holding up her hand. "And that's the only reason I could agree to…"

Her voice trailed off. Looking down, he caught her staring at his lips.

She was so unguarded, so innocent, he thought in wonder. Soft, pretty. Virginal. It would be very easy to seduce her.

Fortunately, she wasn't his type. His typical mistress was sleek and sophisticated. She lavished hours at the salon and the gym as though it was her full-time job. Véronique, in Paris. Farah, in Cairo. Oksana, in Moscow. Exotic women who knew how to seduce a man, who kept their lips red and their eyes lined with kohl, who greeted him at the door in silk lingerie and always had his favorite vodka chilled in the freezer. They welcomed him quickly into bed and spoke little, and even then, they never quite said what they meant. They were easy to slide into bed with.

And more importantly: they were very easy to leave.

Josie Dalton, on the other hand, expressed every thought—

and if she forgot to say anything with words, her face said it anyway. She wore no makeup and clearly saw her hair as a chore, rather than an asset. In that baggy T-shirt and jeans, she obviously had no interest in fashion, or even in showing her figure to its best effect.

But Kasimir was glad she wasn't trying to lure him. Because he had no intention of seducing her. It would only complicate things that didn't need to be complicated. And it would hurt a tenderhearted young woman whom he didn't want to hurt—at least not more than he had to.

No. He was going to treat Josie Dalton like gold.

"So what other…arrangements…are you talking about?" she said haltingly. She lifted her chin, her eyes suddenly sparkling. "Maybe a wedding cake?"

This time, he really did laugh. "You want a cake?"

"I do love a good wedding cake, with buttercream-frosting roses…" she said wistfully.

"Your wish is my command, my lady," he said gravely.

Her expression drooped, and she shook her head with a sigh. "But I'd better not."

He rolled his eyes. "Don't tell me you're on a diet."

"Do I look like I watch my weight?" she snapped, then flushed guiltily. "Sorry. I'm a little grumpy. My flight ran out of meals before they reached my aisle, and I haven't eaten for twelve hours. I would have bought something at the airport but I only have three dollars and thought maybe I should save it."

Her voice trailed off. Kasimir had already turned away, crossing to the desk. He pressed the intercom button.

"Sir?"

"Send up a breakfast plate."

"Two, Your Highness?"

"Just one. But make it full and make it quick." He glanced back at Josie. "Anything special you'd like to eat, Miss Dalton?"

She gaped back at him, her mouth open.

He turned back to the intercom and said smoothly, "Just send everything you've got."

"Of course, sir."

Taking her unresisting hand, Kasimir led her to the soft blue sofa and sat beside her. She stared at him, apparently mesmerized, as if he'd done something truly shocking by simply ordering her some breakfast when she said she was hungry.

"You were saying," he prompted.

"I was?"

"Wedding cake. Why you don't want it."

"Right." Ripping her hand away nervously, she squared her shoulders and said in a firm voice, "This is just a business arrangement, so there's no point to wedding cake. Or a wedding dress. I think it's best for both of us—" she looked at him sideways, not quite meeting his eyes "—to keep our marriage on a strictly professional basis."

"As you wish." He lifted an eyebrow. "You are the bride. You are the boss."

She swallowed, turning her head to look at him nervously. "I am?"

He smiled. "I know that much about how a wedding works."

"Oh." Josie's face was the color of roses and cream as she chewed on her full, pink bottom lip. "You're being very, um—" her voice faltered and seemed to stumble "—nice to me."

Kasimir's smile twisted. "Will you stop saying that."

"But it's true."

"I'm being strictly professional, just as you said. Courtesy is part of business."

"Oh." She considered this, then slowly nodded. "In that case…"

"I'm glad you agree." He wondered if she would still accuse him of kindness if she knew the truth about what he intended to do with her. Or exactly why she was the answer to his prayer.

An hour ago, he'd been on the phone in his home office, barely listening to his VP of acquisitions drone on about how they could sabotage Vladimir's imminent takeover of Arctic Oil. He'd been too busy thinking about how his own recent plan to embarrass his brother had blown up in his face.

Kasimir had long despised Bree Dalton, the con artist he blamed for the first rift between the brothers ten years ago. All this time, he'd kept track of her from a distance, waiting for her to go back to her old ways (she hadn't) or to agree to let Josie marry him to get the land (she wouldn't, and he could go to hell for asking).

Kasimir had finally decided to try another way: Josie herself.

Until they'd met at the Salad Shack a few days ago, all he'd known of Josie was in a file from a private investigator, with a grainy photograph. Six months ago in Seattle, the man had tested her by dropping a wallet full of cash in the aisle of a grocery store in front of her. Josie had run two blocks after the man's car, catching up with him at a stoplight, to breathlessly give the wallet back, untouched. "Girl's so honest, she's a nut," the investigator had grumbled.

So finally, Kasimir had come to a decision. Knowing his brother was recuperating from a recent car-racing injury in Oahu with a private weekly poker game at the Hale Ka'nani, he'd bribed the general manager of the resort, Greg Hudson, to hire the Dalton sisters as housekeepers. He'd hoped Vladimir would have a run-in with Bree Dalton, causing him a humiliating scene, but that was just an amusement. Kasimir's real goal in coming here had been to try to negotiate for the land, and the requisite marriage, directly with Josie Dalton.

He shouldn't have been surprised that she'd flung her soda at him and run out. Or that, according to the report he'd gotten from Greg Hudson, not only had there been no screaming match between Vladimir and Bree, they'd apparently fallen into each other's arms at the poker game. Bree had won back the entire amount of her sister's wager, then promptly accepted Vladimir's offer to a single-card draw between them—a million dollars versus possession of Bree.

Reintroducing the formerly engaged couple to happiness after ten years of estrangement, had never been Kasimir's plan. For the past day and a half, he'd been grinding his teeth in fury. He'd spent last night dancing at a club, women hitting on him right and left, until even that started to irritate him, and he'd gone home early—and alone.

Then, like a miracle, he'd been woken from sleep with the news that Josie Dalton was here and wished to marry him after all.

And now, here she was. He had her. She'd just changed his whole world—forever.

He could have kissed her.

"I will be happy to get you a cake," he said fervently. "And a designer wedding gown, and a ten-carat diamond ring." Reaching for her hand, he kissed it, then looked into her eyes. "Just tell me what you want, and it's yours."

Her cheeks turned a darker shade of pink. He felt her hand tremble in his own before she yanked it away. "Just bring my sister home. Safely away from your brother."

"You have my word. Soon." He rose to his feet. "I must call my lawyer. In the meantime, please take some time to rest." He gestured to the bookshelves of first-edition books. "Read, if you like. Your breakfast will be here at any moment." He gave a slight bow. "Please excuse me."

"Kasimir?"

He froze. Had Josie somehow guessed his plans? Was it possible her expressive brown eyes had seen right through his twisted, heartless soul? Hands clenched at his sides, body taut, Kasimir turned back to face her.

Josie's eyes were shining, her expression bright as a new

penny, as she leaned back against the sofa pillows. His gaze traced unwillingly over the patterns on her skin, along the curve of her full breasts beneath her T-shirt, left by the soft morning light.

"Thank you for saving my sister," she whispered. She took a deep breath. "And me."

Uneasiness went through him, but he shook it away from his well-armored soul. He gave her a stiff nod. "We will both benefit from this arrangement. Both of us," he repeated stonily, squashing his conscience like a newly sprouted weed.

"But I'll never forget it," she said softly, looking at him with gratitude that approached hero-worship. Her brown eyes glowed, and she was far more beautiful than he'd first realized. "I don't care what people say. You're a good man."

His jaw tightened. Without a word, he turned away from her. Once he reached his home office, he phoned his chief lawyer to arrange the prenuptial agreement and discuss ways to break Josie's trust as quickly as possible. The discussion took longer than expected. When Kasimir returned to the library an hour later, he found Josie curled up fast asleep on the sofa, with a cold, untouched breakfast tray on the table beside her.

Kasimir looked down at her. She looked so young, sleeping. Had he ever been that young? She couldn't be more than twenty-two, eleven years younger than he was, and more stupidly innocent than he'd been at that age. In spite of himself, he felt an unwelcome desire to take care of her. To protect her.

His jaw set. And so he would. For as long as she was his prisoner—that was to say, his wife.

He reached a hand out to wake her, then stopped. He looked down at the gray shadows beneath her eyes. No. Let her sleep. Their wedding could wait a few hours. She deserved a place to rest, a safe harbor. And so he would be for her....

Carefully, he picked her up into his arms, cradling her against his chest. He carried her upstairs to the guest room.

Without turning on the light, he set her gently on the mattress, beside the blue silk pillows. He stepped back, looking down at her in the shadowy room.

He heard her sweetly wistful voice. *I do love a good wedding cake with buttercream-frosting roses.*

Kasimir had told her the truth. She would be his only wife. He never intended to have a real marriage. Or trust any human soul enough to give them the ability to stab him in the back. This would be as close as he'd ever get to holy matrimony. For the few brief weeks of the marriage, Josie Dalton would be the closest he'd ever have to a wife. *To a family.*

He took a deep breath. She'd make an exceptional wife for any man. She was an old-fashioned kind of woman, the kind they didn't make anymore. From his investigator's reports, he knew Josie was ridiculously honest and scrupulously kind. Six months ago, a different private investigator had her under surveillance in Seattle. He'd dressed as a homeless street person, which should have rendered him invisible. Not to Josie, though. "She came right up to me to ask if I was all right," the man reported in amazement, "or if I needed anything. Then she insisted on giving me her brown-bag lunch." He'd smiled. "Peanut butter and jelly!"

What kind of girl did that? Who had a heart that unjaded and, well—soft?

Unlike Vladimir and Bree, unlike Kasimir himself, Josie deserved to be protected. She was an innocent. She'd done nothing to earn the well-deserved revenge he planned for the other two.

Even though it would still hurt her.

He felt another spasm beneath his solar plexus.

Guilt, he realized in shock. He hadn't felt that emotion for a long time. He wouldn't let it stop him. But he'd be as gentle as he could to her.

Turning away from Josie's sleeping form, he went back downstairs to his home office. He phoned his head secretary, and ten minutes later, he was contacted by Honolulu's top wedding planner. Afterward, he tossed his phone onto his desk.

Swiveling his chair, he looked out the window overlooking the penthouse's rooftop pool. Bright sunlight glimmered over the blue water, and beyond that, he could see the city and the distant ocean melting into the blue sky.

For ten years, he'd been wearing Vladimir down, fighting his company tooth and claw with his own, getting his attention the only way he knew how—by making him pay with tiny stings, death by a thousand cuts.

But getting Bree Dalton to betray Vladimir would be the deepest cut of all. The fatal one.

Rising to his feet, Kasimir stood in front of the window, hands tucked behind his back as he gazed out unseeingly towards the Pacific. He'd give his lawyer a few weeks to transfer possession of Josie's land back to his control. By then, once the two little lovebirds were enmeshed in each other, Kasimir would blackmail Bree into stealing his brother's company away.

He narrowed his eyes. Bree would crush Vladimir's heart beneath her boot, and his brother would finally know what it felt like to have someone else change his life, against his will, when Bree betrayed him.

She'd have no choice. Kasimir had all the ammunition he needed to make Bree Dalton do exactly as he wanted. A cold smile crossed his lips.

He had her sister.

CHAPTER TWO

JOSIE'S EYELIDS FLUTTERED, then flew open as she sat up with a sharp intake of breath.

She was still fully dressed. She'd been sleeping on an enormous bed, in a strange bedroom. The masculine, dark-floored bedroom was flooded with golden light from the windows.

How long had she been sleeping? She yawned, and her mouth felt dry, as if it was lined with cotton. Who had brought her here? Could it have been Kasimir himself?

The thought of being carried in those strong arms, against his powerful chest, as she slept on unaware, caused her to tremble. She looked down at the mussed white bedspread.

Could it possibly be his bed…?

With a gulp, Josie jumped up as if it had burned her. The clock on the fireplace mantel said three o'clock. Gracious! She'd slept for hours. She stretched her arms above her head with another yawn. It had been nice of Kasimir to let her sleep. She felt so much better.

Until she saw herself in the full-length mirror on the other side of the bedroom. Wait. Was that what she looked like? She took three steps towards it, then sucked in her breath in horror, covering her mouth with her hand.

Josie knew she wasn't the most fashionable dresser, and that she was a bit on the plump side, too. But she'd had no idea she looked *this* bad. She'd crossed the Pacific twice in the same rumpled T-shirt and wrinkled, oversize men's jeans that she'd bought secondhand last year. In her flight back from Seattle, she'd been crushed in the last row, in a sweaty middle seat between oversize businessmen who took her armrests and stretched their knees into her personal space. And she hadn't had a shower or even brushed her teeth for two days.

Josie gasped aloud, realizing she'd been grungy and gross like this when she'd been face-to-face with Kasimir. Picturing his sleek, expensive clothes, his perfect body, the way he looked so powerful and sexy as a Greek god with those amazing eyes and broad shoulders and chiseled cheekbones, her cheeks flamed.

She narrowed her eyes. She might be a frumpy nobody, but there was *no way* she was going to face him again, possibly on her fake wedding day, without a shower and some clean clothes. *No way!*

Looking around for her backpack, she saw it sitting by the door and snatched it up, then headed for the large en suite bathroom.

It was luxurious, all gleaming white marble and shining silver. Tossing her tattered backpack on the marble counter, where it looked extremely out of place, she started to dig through it for a toothbrush. Some great packing job, she thought in irritation. In the forty seconds she'd rushed around their tiny apartment in Honolulu, trying to flee before Vladimir Xendzov could collect Bree as his rightful property, Josie had grabbed almost nothing of use.

The top of a bikini—just the top, no bottom. Her mother's wool cardigan sweater, now frayed and darned. Some slippers. She hadn't even remembered to pack underwear. Gah!

Desperately, she dug further. A few cheap souvenirs from Waikiki. Her cell phone, now dead because she'd forgotten to pack the charger. A tattered Elizabeth Gaskell novel which had belonged to her mother when she was a high-school English teacher. A small vinyl photo album, that flopped open to a photo of her family taken a year before Josie was born.

Her heart twisted as she picked it up. In the picture, her mother was glowing with health, her father was beaming with pride and five-year-old Bree, with blond pigtails, had a huge toothless gap in her smile. Josie ran her hand over their faces. Beneath the clear plastic, the old photo was wrinkled at the edges from all the nights Josie had slept with it under her pillow as a child, while she was left alone with the babysitter for weeks at a time. Her parents and Bree looked so happy.

Before Josie was born.

It was an old grief, one she'd always lived with. If Josie had never been conceived, her mother wouldn't have put off chemotherapy treatments for the sake of her unborn child. Or died a month after Josie's birth, causing her father to go off the deep end, quitting his job as a math teacher and taking his seven-year-old poker-playing prodigy daughter Bree down the Alaskan coast to fleece tourists. Josie blinked back tears.

If she had never been born…

Her parents and Bree might still be happy and safe in a snug little suburban home.

Squaring her shoulders, she shook the thought away. Tucking the photo album back into her bag, she looked at her own bleak reflection, then grabbed her frayed toothbrush, drenched it in minty toothpaste and cleaned her teeth with a vengeance.

A moment later, she stepped into the steaming hot water of the huge marble shower. The rush of water felt good against her skin, like a massage against the tired muscles of her back and shoulders, washing all the dust and grime and grief away. Using some exotic orange-scented shampoo with Arabic writing—where on earth had Kasimir gotten that?—Josie washed her long brown hair thoroughly. Then she washed it again, just to be sure.

It was going to be all right, she repeated to herself. It would all be all right.

Soon, her sister would be safe.

Soon, her sister would be home.

And once Bree was free from Vladimir Xendzov's clutches, maybe Josie would finally have the guts to tell her what she felt in her heart, but had never been brave enough to say.

As much as she loved and appreciated all that Bree had sacrificed for her over the past ten years, Josie was no longer a child. She was twenty-two. She wanted to learn how to drive. To get a job on her own. To be allowed to go to bars, to date. She wanted the freedom to make mistakes, without Bree as an anxious mother hen, constantly standing over her shoulder.

She wanted to grow up.

Turning off the water, she got out of the shower. The large bathroom was steamy, the mirrors opaque with white fog. She wondered how long she'd been in the water. She didn't wear a watch because she hated to watch the passage of time, which seemed to go far too slowly when she was working, and rushed by at breakneck speed when she was not. Why, she'd often wondered, couldn't time rush by at work, and then slip into delicious slowness when she was at home, lasting and lasting, like sunlight on a summer's day?

Wrapping a plush white towel around her body, over skin that was scrubbed clean with orange soap and pink with heat, she looked at the sartorial choices offered by her backpack. Let's see. Which was better: a wool cardigan or a bikini top?

With a grumpy sigh, she looked back at the dirty, wrinkled T-shirt, jeans and white cotton panties and bra crumpled on the shining white tile of the bathroom floor. She'd worn those clothes for two days straight. The thought of putting them back over her clean skin was dreadful. But she had no other option.

Or did she…?

Her eyes fell upon something hanging on the back of the bathroom door that she hadn't noticed before. A white shift dress. Going towards it, she saw a note attached to the hanger.

Every bride needs a wedding dress. Join me at the roof-top pool when you're awake.

She smiled down at the hard black angles of his hand-writing. She'd thought she hadn't wanted a dress, that she wanted to keep their wedding as dull and unromantic as pos-sible. But now...how had he known the small gesture would mean so much?

Then she saw the dress's tag. Chanel. Holy cow. Maybe the gesture wasn't so small. For a moment, she was afraid to touch the fabric. Then she stroked the lace softly with her fingertips. It felt like a whisper. Like a dream.

Maybe everything really was going to be all right.

Josie exhaled, blinking back tears. She'd taken a huge gam-ble, using her last paycheck to come back to Honolulu, trust-ing Kasimir to help her. But it had paid off. For the first time in her life, she'd done something right.

It was a strangely intoxicating feeling.

Josie had always been the one who ruined things, not the one who saved them. She'd learned from a young age that the only way to make up for all the pain she'd caused everyone was just to take a book and go read quietly and invisibly in a corner, making as little trouble or fuss as possible.

But this time...

She tried to imagine her sister's face when Josie burst in with Prince Kasimir and saved her. Wouldn't Bree be sur-prised that her baby sister had done something important, something difficult, all by herself? *Josie,* her usually un-flappable sister would blurt out, *how did you do this? You're such a genius!*

Josie smiled to herself, picturing the sweetness of that mo-ment. Then she looked down at her naked body, pink with heat from the shower. Time to do her part, but maybe it wouldn't be so awful after all. How hard could it be, to get dressed in a fancy wedding gown, and marry a rich, handsome prince?

Pulling the white shift dress off the hanger, she stepped into it. Pulling it up her thighs, she gasped at the feel of the sensual fabric against her skin. It was a little short, though.

Josie frowned, looking down. It only reached to her mid-thigh. Maybe it would be all right, though. She reached back for the zipper. As long as it wasn't…

Tight. She stopped. The zipper wouldn't zip. Holding her breath, she sucked in her belly. Nervously, she moved the zipper up inch by inch, afraid she'd break it and ruin the expensive dress. Finally the zipper closed. She looked at herself in the mirror.

Her full breasts were pushed up by the tight dress, practically exploding out of the neckline. She looked way too grown-up and, well, *busty*. Bree would never have let her leave the house like this in a million years.

But it was either this or the dirty clothes. She decided she could live with tight. She'd just have to be careful not to bust a seam every time she moved.

Going to her backpack in mincing steps, she grabbed a brush and brushed her wet brown hair down her shoulders, leaving traces of dampness against the silk. She put on her pink flip-flops—it was either that or fuzzy slippers, and she was in Hawaii, after all—and some tinted lip balm. She left the bedroom with as much elegance as she could muster, her head held high.

Tottering down the stairs to the bottom floor of the penthouse, Josie went through the rooms until she finally found her way to the rooftop pool, with the help of the smiling housekeeper she'd found in the big kitchen. "That way, miss. Down the hall and through the salon."

The salon?

Josie went through a large room with a grand piano, then through the sliding door to the rooftop pool. She saw Kasimir at a large table, still dressed in his severely black suit, leaning back in his chair. He was talking on the phone, but when he saw her, his eyes widened.

Nervously, Josie walked along the edge of the pool towards him. She had to sway her hips unnaturally to move forward, and she felt a bead of sweat suddenly form between her breasts. The sun felt hot against her skin.

Or maybe it was just the way her bridegroom was looking at her.

"I'll talk to you later," he breathed to the person on the phone, never looking away from Josie, and he rose to his feet. His gaze seemed shocked as it traveled up and down her body. "What are you wearing?"

"The wedding dress. That you gave me. Should I have not?"

"That—" his voice sounded strangled "—is the dress I left you?"

"Yeah, um, it's a little tight," she said, her cheeks burning. She wasn't used to being the center of any man's attention, let alone a man like Prince Kasimir Xendzov. Then she bit her lip, afraid she'd sounded like she was complaining. "But it was really thoughtful of you to get me a wedding dress," she added quickly.

He slowly looked her up and down. "You look…"

She waited unhappily for his next word.

"…*fine*," he finished huskily, and he pulled out a chair for her. "Please sit."

Fine? She exhaled. Fine. She could live with *fine*. "Thanks."

But could she sit down? Clutching the edges of the short hem, she sat down carefully. The expensive craftsmanship paid off. The seams held. She exhaled.

Until, looking down, she saw she was flashing way too much skin. With the dress tugged so hard downward, her breasts were thrust up even higher, and the fabric now just barely covered her nipples for decency. Trying to simultaneously pull the dress higher over her breasts and lower over her thighs, she bit her lip, glancing up in chagrin.

Fortunately, to her relief, as he sat down across the table from her, Kasimir's gaze seemed careful not to drop below her eyes. He indicated the lunch spread across the table. "You've come at the perfect time."

She looked at the chicken salad, fresh fruit and big rolls of crusty bread. It all looked delicious. But even Chanel craftsmanship would only go so far. "I probably shouldn't," she said glumly.

"Don't be ridiculous. You must be starving. You fell asleep before breakfast. You've not had a decent meal for days." Taking a plate, he started to load it with a bit of everything. "We can't have you fainting during our wedding this afternoon."

She almost laughed aloud. Her? Faint from hunger?

Food had always been Josie's guilty pleasure. She felt self-conscious about the extra pounds she carried around, sure, but not enough to give up the pastries and candy she loved. Unlike Bree, who boringly ate the same healthy salad and nuts and fish every day, Josie loved trying exotic new cuisine. Maybe she didn't have the money or courage to travel around the world, but eating at a Thai or Mexican or Indian restaurant was almost as good, wasn't it? Especially when she found a half-price coupon. She looked at the delicious meal in front of her. And this was even better than half price!

She gave him a sudden grin. "Who says there's no such thing as a free lunch, huh?"

"Glad you understand." Placing the full plate in front of her, Kasimir gave her a wicked grin. "You are going to be my wife, Josie. That means, as long as you are mine, all you will know—is pleasure."

Their eyes locked, and she felt that strange flutter in her belly—a flutter that had nothing to do with cookies, couscous or even chocolate. "Okay," she whispered as heat pulsed through her body. She unconsciously licked her lips. "If you insist."

"I'll admit the dress is a bit tight. Women's fashions are often a mystery to me," he said huskily. "I very rarely pay attention to them—except when I'm taking them off."

"I bet," she said shyly, shaking a little. Could he see that she was a virgin with zero sexual experience? Could he tell? Suddenly unable to meet his eyes, she dropped her own back to her plate. Even across the table, he felt so close to her. And too good-looking. Why did he have to be so good-looking? Not to mention sophisticated and powerful. He looked like a million bucks in that dark vested suit.

Sitting back in his chair, he filled himself a plate, then pushed a pile of papers towards her. "You need to sign this."

"What is it?"

"Our prenuptial agreement."

"Fantastic," she said, looking up in relief.

His eyebrows raised. "Not the usual reaction I'd expect."

"Remember, I want to keep our arrangement nice and official." She started reading through the first pages, pausing to sign and initial in places. As she read, she took a bite of a crusty bread, then a nibble of the ginger chicken salad. It was surprisingly good, with carrots, lettuce and cilantro. She ate some more. "Have you found my sister yet?"

"I might have an idea where Vladimir could have taken her."

"Where?"

"I'll look into it further." He tilted his head. "*After* we are married."

"Oh. Right. The deal." She took a deep breath. "But she's safe?"

He snorted. "What do you think?"

She looked up. "You think she is?"

"She is crafty. And sly. I doubt even my brother will be

able to control her," he said dryly. "It's more likely she'd be putting him through hell."

Feeling reassured, she leaned her elbows against the table. "You don't like my sister, do you?"

"She's a liar," he said evenly. "A con artist."

"Not anymore!" Josie cried, stung.

"Ten years ago, she told my brother your land was legally hers to sell. Then she tried to distract him from doing his due diligence with her big weepy eyes and a low-cut blouse."

Josie licked her lips. "We were desperate. My father had just died, and violent men were demanding repayment of his debts—"

"Of course." He shrugged contemptuously. "Every criminal always has some hard-luck story. But our company was still new. We wanted our family's land back, but we could little afford to lose the thousands of dollars in earnest money she planned to steal from us. She had Vladimir so wrapped around her finger, she would have succeeded…"

She shook her head vehemently. "She told me the whole story. By then she'd already fallen in love with your brother, and was planning to throw herself on his mercy."

"On his mercy? Right. I told him the truth about her, and he refused to believe me." He looked away. "I decided to fly back to our site in Russia, alone. At the airport, I drunkenly told a reporter the whole story. The next morning, when my brother found himself embarrassed in front of all the world, he pushed me out of our partnership. And out of a Siberian deal he signed two days later worth half a billion dollars."

"I'm sorry about the problems between you and your brother, but it wasn't Bree's fault!"

"No. It was Vladimir's. And mine." He narrowed his eyes. "But she still deserves to be punished."

"But she has been," Josie said, looking down unhappily at her empty plate. "She was going to tell your brother everything. To be honest, at any price. But he never gave her the chance. He deserted her without a word. And he left her to the wolves. Alone, and in charge of a twelve-year-old child." She lifted her gaze. "My sister has been punished. Believe me."

As he stared at her, his angry gaze slowly softened. "You alone are innocent in all this. I will bring her back to you. I swear it."

She gave an awkward laugh. "Stop it, will you? Stop being so—"

"You'd better not say *nice,*" he threatened her.

She took a deep breath. "Just stop reminding me!"

"Of what?"

She spread her arms helplessly. "That you're a handsome, charming prince, and I—" She stopped.

"And you what?"

She blurted out, "I'm a total idiot who can't even remember to pack underwear!"

Oh, now she'd really done it. She wished she could clap a hand over her mouth, but it was too late. His eyes widened as he sucked in his breath.

"Are you telling me," he said in a low voice, "that right now, you're not wearing any underwear?"

Miserably, she shook her head, hating herself for blurting out every thought. Why, oh why, had she ever mentioned underwear? Why couldn't she keep her mouth shut?

His blue eyes moved slowly over her curves in the tight white dress. A muscle tightened in his jaw. "I see." He turned away, his jaw clenched. "We'll have to buy you some. After the wedding."

His voice was ice-cold. She'd offended him, she thought sadly. She buttered a delicious crusty roll, then slowly ate it as she tried to think of a way to change the subject. "Your Highness…"

He snorted. "I thought you said it was a worthless title."

"I changed my mind."

"Since when?"

She tried to grin. "Since I'm about to be a princess?"

"Just call me by my first name."

She hesitated… "Um, I'd rather not, actually. It just feels a little too personal right now. With you being so irritated…"

"I'm not irritated," he bit out.

"Your Highness…"

"Kasimir," he ordered.

She swallowed, looking away. But he waited. Taking a deep breath, she finally turned back to face him and whispered, "Kasimir."

Just his name on her lips felt very erotic, the *K* hard against her teeth, the *A* parting her lips, the *S* vibrating, sibilant against her skin as the *M-I-R* ended on her lips like a kiss.

He looked at her in the Hawaiian sunlight.

"Yes," he said softly. "Like that."

She swallowed, feeling out of her depth, drowning. "I like your name," she blurted out nervously. "It's an old Slavic name, isn't it? A warrior's name. 'Destroyer of the Peace.'" She was chattering, something she often did when she was nervous. "Very different from the meaning of your brother's…" *Uh-oh.* That topic wouldn't end well. She closed her mouth with a snap. "Sorry," she said weakly. "Never mind."

"Fascinating." His body was very still on the other side of the table, his voice cold again. "Go on. Tell me more."

She shrugged. "I've worked as a housekeeper for hotels for years, since I turned eighteen, and I listen to audio books from the library while I clean. It's amazing what you can learn," she mumbled. She gave him a bright smile. "Like about…um… botany, for instance. Did you know that there are only three types of orchid native to Hawaii? Everyone always thinks tons of orchids grow here in the rain forest, while the truth is that another place I once lived, Nevada, which is nothing but dry desert, has *twelve* different wild orchids in two distinct varieties. There was this, um, flower that…"

But Kasimir hadn't moved. He sat across from her beneath the hot Hawaiian sunshine, his arms folded as the water's reflection from the pool left patterns of light on his black suit. "You were telling me about the meaning of my brother's name."

She gulped. There was no help for it. "Vladimir. Well. Some people think it means 'He on the Side of Peace,' but most of the etymology seems to indicate the root *mir* is older still, from the Gothic, meaning 'Great in His Power.' And Vladimir is..." She hesitated.

Kasimir's eyes were hard now. She took a deep breath.

"'The Master of All,'" she whispered.

Hands clenched at his sides, Kasimir rose to his feet. Frightened by the fierce look in his eyes, she involuntarily shrank back in her chair. His hands abruptly relaxed.

"My brother is not all-powerful," he said simply. "And he will know it. Very soon."

"Wait." As he started to turn away, she jumped to her feet, grabbing his arm. "I'm sorry. I'm so stupid, always letting my mouth get ahead of my brain. My sister always says I need to be more careful."

"I'm not offended." Looking down at her, he gave her a smile that didn't quite meet his blue eyes. "You shouldn't listen to your sister. I respect a woman who speaks the truth without fear far more than one who uses silence to cover her lies."

"But I told you—she's not like that. Not anymore." With a weak laugh, she looked away. "If she were, we'd be rich right now, instead of poor. But she gave up gambling and con games to give me an honest, respectable life. And just look at the trouble I've caused her." She looked down at the floor. "I gambled at that poker game, and she had to sacrifice herself for me. Again."

He touched her cheek, forcing her to meet his gaze. "Josie." His eyes were deep and dark as a winter storm on a midnight sea. "The choice she made to sacrifice herself to my brother was not your fault. It was never your fault."

"Not my fault?" she repeated as, involuntarily, her eyes fell to his sensual lips. He seemed to lean towards her, and her own lips tingled, sizzling down her nerve endings with a strange, intense need. Somewhere in her rational mind, she heard a warning that she couldn't quite hear; her brain had lost all power over her body. Her traitorous heart went thump, thump in her chest. Still staring at his cruelly sensual mouth, she whispered, "How can you say it's not my fault?"

"Because I know your sister. And I know you." Cupping her face, he tilted her head back. "And other than my mother, who died long ago, I think perhaps you are the only truly decent woman I've known. And not just decent," he said softly. "But incredibly beautiful."

Josie's mouth fell open as she looked up. Her? Beautiful? Was he—cripes—was it possible he was *flirting* with her?

Don't be ridiculous, she told herself savagely. *He's being courteous. Nothing more.* She had no experience with men, but she did know one thing: a devastatingly handsome billionaire prince would have no reason to flirt with a girl like her. But still, she felt giddy as she looked up at him, mesmerized by his blue eyes, which seemed so warm now, warm as a June afternoon, warm as one of the brief summers of her childhood in Alaska.

"Don't do that," he said.

"Don't what?"

"Look at me like that," he said softly.

She swallowed, lifting her gaze to his. "Then don't tell me I'm beautiful. It's…it's not something I've ever heard before."

"Then all the other men in the world are fools." His blue eyes burned through her. "Our marriage will be short, but for the brief time you are mine…" He put his hand over hers. "I am not going to stop telling you that you're beautiful. Because it's true." His lips curved up at the corners as he said softly, "And didn't I just say that one should always speak the truth?"

Stop, Josie ordered her trembling heart as she looked up at his handsome face. There would be no schoolgirl crushes on her soon-to-be husband! Absolutely none!

But it was too late. The deed was done.

"Are you ready?"

"Ready?" she breathed.

He smiled, as if he could see the sudden brutal conquest of her innocent heart. "To marry me."

"Oh. Right." She bit her lip. "Um, yeah. Sure."

Pulling her into the foyer, he took a bouquet of white flowers out of a waiting white box. He placed a bridal bouquet in her hand. "For you, my bride."

"Thank you," she whispered, fighting back tears as she pressed her face amid the sweetly scented flowers.

He scowled. "Don't you dare tell me no man has ever given you flowers before."

She hesitated. "Well…"

"You're killing me," he groaned. "The men you know must be idiots."

She gave him a wan smile. "Well, I don't really know any men. So it would be unreasonable to expect them to buy me flowers."

"You don't know any men?" He stared at her incredulously. "But you're so friendly. So chatty."

"I don't talk to cute ones. I'm too nervous. Besides—" she gave her best attempt at a casual shrug "—Bree won't let me date. She's afraid I'll get hurt."

His lips parted. "You've never been on a date?"

She shook her head. "I did have a sort of boyfriend once," she added hastily. "In high school. We met in chemistry class. He was…nice."

"Nice," he snorted. "With your rose-colored glasses, he

probably had a mohawk, a spiked dog collar and a propensity for stealing," he muttered.

"That's not fair," she protested. "After all, I think you're nice. And you're not a thief."

Looking uncomfortable, Kasimir cleared his throat. "Go on."

"We went out a few times for ice cream. Studied together at the library. Then he asked me to prom. I was so excited. Bree helped me fix up a thrift-shop dress, and I felt like Cinderella." She stopped.

"What happened?" he asked, watching her.

She looked away. "He never showed up," she whispered. "He took another girl instead, a girl he'd just met." She lifted her gaze in a trembling smile. "But she put out. And I... didn't."

A low growl came from the back of Kasimir's throat.

Clutching the bouquet of white flowers, Josie stared down at the pattern of the polished marble floor. "I just think kissing someone should be special. That you should only share yourself with someone you love." She shuffled her pink flip-flops, echoing the sound across the high-ceilinged foyer. "I expect you think it's stupid and old-fashioned."

"No." Kasimir's voice was low. "I used to think the same."

Her jaw dropped as she looked up. "What?"

He gave a humorless smile. "Funny story for you. I was a virgin until I was twenty-two."

"You?" Josie breathed. The fact that he'd told her something so intimate caused a shock wave through her. "The international playboy?"

He snorted. "Everyone has a first experience. Mine was Nina. She worked at a PR firm in Moscow, and we hired her to help our new business. She was far older than me—thirty. We dated for a few months. After I lost my half of Xendzov Mining, I went back to Russia to see her. I was floundering. I had some half-baked idea that I'd ask her to marry me." He gave her a crooked smile. "Instead, I found her in bed with a fat, elderly banker."

Josie gasped aloud.

He looked away. "I thought I was in love with her." He gave her a crooked smile. "Virgins usually think that, their first time. But Nina just thought of me as a client. To her, sex was 'networking.' And when I no longer was a potentially lucrative PR account, she no longer had reason to see me."

"Oh," Josie whispered. Her brown eyes were luminous with unshed tears. "I'm so sorry."

He shrugged. "She did me a favor. Taught me an important lesson."

She swallowed, looking up at him. "But just because one woman hurt you, that's no reason to give up on love forever."

His lips twisted sardonically. "You wouldn't say that if you'd seen me standing outside her apartment in the snow and ice, with an idiotic expression on my face."

"But—"

"You'll be my only wife, Josie. Because you're temporary. And this sham marriage will be over in weeks." Giving her a smile that didn't meet his eyes, Kasimir held out his arm. "Come, my beautiful bride," he said softly. "Our wedding awaits."

An hour later, Kasimir and Josie exchanged wedding rings, speaking their vows in a simple ceremony in the office of a justice of the peace in downtown Honolulu. Kasimir couldn't look away from the radiant beauty of his bride.

Or believe that he'd told her so much about his past. He'd told her about his first experience with love. He'd told her he'd been a virgin at twenty-two. What the hell had possessed him?

He didn't care if she looked at him with her weepy eyes and vulnerable smile. He'd never try to comfort her again with a little piece of his soul.

From now on, he'd keep his damned mouth shut.

"And do you, Josephine Louise Dalton, take this man to be your lawfully wedded husband, to have and to hold, in sickness and in health, for richer or poorer, as long as you both shall live?"

Josie turned to look at Kasimir, her soft brown eyes glowing as she whispered, "I do."

Kasimir's gaze traced downward, from her beautiful face to her slender neck, to those amazingly sexy curves in the tight, clinging white sheath.

And he'd keep his hands off her. His forehead burst out in a hot sweat as he repeated the rule to himself again.

He wasn't going to seduce Josie. He *wasn't*.

He had good reasons. All reasons he'd thought of before he'd seen her in this dress.

Who'd known she was hiding all those curves beneath her baggy clothes?

He'd nearly gasped the first time he saw her, when he'd been talking on the phone near his rooftop pool, tying up loose ends with Greg Hudson. The man was taking full credit for the way Bree Dalton and Vladimir had left together after the poker game, and wanted a bonus on top of the agreed-upon bribe. "I went to a lot of work," Hudson whined. "I didn't just hire the Dalton girls, I got them to trust me. And I managed to get your brother to leave with her. I think I deserve double." Kasimir had been rolling his eyes when he'd looked up and seen Josie in that tight white dress. "I'll talk to you later," he'd said, hanging up on the man in midsentence.

But he knew the whole story now. Bree had taken Josie's place at the poker table to try to win back her little sister's debt. She'd succeeded, and had been walking away from the table free and clear, when Vladimir had taunted her into one last game.

It was Bree's fault she was in Vladimir's hands. Her own pride had been her downfall.

And it irritated Kasimir beyond measure that Josie blamed

herself for her sister's predicament. No wonder her father had established the land trust for her. She'd give undeserving people the very shirt off her back. She needed to be protected—even from her own soft heart.

Although he wouldn't mind taking the shirt off her back. He looked at the way her full breasts plumped above her neckline, and the white lace clung tightly to her tiny waist and hips. He looked at the curvaceous turn of her bare legs all the way to her casual pink flip-flops, and realized she might need to be protected from him, as well.

Because he wanted her in his bed.

He hadn't planned to want her, but he did. And seeing the glow of hero-worship in her big brown eyes made it even worse. It made him want her even more. She was so different from his usual type of woman. She wasn't sarcastic or snarky or ironic. Josie actually cared.

I just think kissing someone should be special. That you should only share yourself with someone you love.

She clearly had no idea how powerful lust could be. Her first experience would hit her like a tidal wave. It would be so easy to seduce her, he thought. One kiss, one stroke. She would be totally unprepared for the fire. But she would be an apt student. He felt that in the tremble of her hand as he slid the ten-carat diamond ring on her finger. Saw it in the rosy blush on her cheeks as she placed the plain gold band on his. All he would have to do would be to kiss her, touch her, and she'd be lost in a maelstrom of pleasure she would not know how to defend herself against. She'd fall like a ripe peach into his hands.

Except he couldn't. *Wouldn't.*

Unlike anyone else he'd met for a long while, Josie was a good person with a trusting heart. It was bad enough that he'd be virtually holding her hostage over the next few weeks in order to blackmail her sister and get revenge on his brother.

Kasimir could be ruthless, yes, even cruel. But to people

who deserved it. Not to a sweet, trusting, old-fashioned young woman like Josie. She deserved better.

So he wouldn't take his wife to bed. He would control himself. No matter how difficult it might prove to be.

"I now pronounce you man and wife." Adjusting the flower lei around his neck, the officiant looked between them. "You may now kiss the bride."

With an intake of breath, Josie looked up at Kasimir with a tremulous smile.

He hesitated. It would be appropriate to kiss her, wouldn't it? It would almost be weird *not* to kiss her.

But he feared taking even one taste of what was forbidden. Undecided, he leaned forward, torturing himself as he breathed in the scent of her hair, like summer peaches. He wanted to wrap his hands in her hair, lower his mouth to hers and plunder those pink lips, and see if they were as soft and sweet as they looked...

He couldn't seduce her. *Couldn't.*

Kasimir turned his head, giving her a brief, chaste peck on the cheek, before he drew away.

She blinked, then reached for her bouquet, giving Kasimir a small smile, as if she were tremendously relieved he hadn't given her a proper kiss. As if she hadn't been waiting breathlessly for one.

Neither of them were glad he hadn't properly kissed her. Even the officiant looked bewildered as he cleared his throat. "Sign here," he told Kasimir's attorney, who was their witness. They posed for photographs, to make their wedding look real, and they were done.

"Get busy," Kasimir told his attorney, handing him the marriage license and the camera. "I expect the land in Alaska to be in my name before the end of January."

Today was December twenty-seventh. The man looked flummoxed beneath his wire-rimmed glasses. "But sir...the legal formalities of getting the trust to transfer the land to

Miss Dalton, and then having her sell it to you are complicated. It could easily take three or four months…."

"You have four weeks," he cut the man off. Plenty of time to blackmail Bree Dalton into handing over his brother's company. And too much time of having Josie—now his wife—enticing him with her body and the latent passion in her deep brown eyes. The first man to take her might be consumed by it.

But it wouldn't be him. Kasimir set his jaw. He wouldn't touch her.

At all.

Even if it killed him.

"Kasimir?" Josie's brow furrowed. "What's wrong?"

She saw too much. "Nothing," he said shortly.

"Do you…" She paused, biting her lip. "You don't already regret marrying me…do you?"

"No," he said shortly. "I just don't want to make this marriage any harder for you than it has to be."

She glanced down at her Chanel gown, her beautiful bouquet, her enormous diamond ring. Her pink lips curved. "Well," she said teasingly, "this *has* been pretty tough to take."

"And I saved the best for last. Your cake."

"You didn't!" she cried happily. "What kind?"

"Three layers, with buttercream roses. You were sleeping, so I couldn't ask your favorite flavor. So each layer is different—white, yellow and devil's food."

Her eyes looked luminous. "You are so kind," she whispered.

He frowned at her.

"Don't you dare cry," he ordered.

"Don't be silly," she said, wiping her eyes. "Of course I'm not crying."

Kasimir cursed aloud. "How can the small kindness of cake make you weep?"

"You listened to me," she said, giving him a watery smile. "I'm not used to anyone actually listening to me. Even Bree just talks at me, telling me what I should want."

"No more. Remember, now you're a princess." He gave her a sudden cheeky grin. "Princess Josephine Xendzov." Reaching down, he stroked her cheek as he looked into her eyes. "Princess Josie, you're perfect."

"Princess." She gulped, then shook her head with a laugh. "If only the girls who teased me in high school could see me now!"

Setting his jaw, he looked down at her. "If any girls who teased you were here right now, I'd make them regret they were born."

Looking up at him, she gave a shocked laugh.

Then she blinked fast. She gave a sudden tearful sniff.

"Don't start that again," he said in exasperation. Grabbing her hand, he pulled her out of the justice of the peace's office and into the sunshine. The sky was a brilliant blue against the soaring skyscrapers of downtown Honolulu. Holding Josie's hand, Kasimir led her to the Rolls-Royce waiting for them at the curb.

"Kiss her!" Some rowdy tourists shouted from a nearby bus, spotting him in a black suit and Josie with her white dress and bouquet, standing beside a chauffeured black Rolls-Royce.

Kasimir looked back at her. "They want me to kiss you."

Josie looked back at him breathlessly, her eyes huge with fear. "It's all right," she said awkwardly. "I know you don't want to. It's okay."

"Since this is my only wedding—" his hand tightened over hers as he pulled her closer "—this is my only chance to properly fulfill the traditions."

He felt her tremble in his arms, saw her lips part as she looked up at him, ripe for plunder. And he knew it would be easy, so easy, to possess her. Not just her lips, but her body. Her heart. Her soul.

"Josie," he said hoarsely, looking at her lips.

"Yes?"

He lifted his gaze. "You'll remember that our marriage is in name only. You know that. Don't you?"

Her cheeks went pale, and she dropped his hand with an awkward laugh. "Of course I know that. You think I don't know that? I know that."

"Good," he said, exhaling. Now he just had to keep on reminding himself. Turning away, he opened the door of the Rolls-Royce.

"I'm know I'm not your type," she chattered, climbing into the backseat of the car. "Of course I'm not your type."

"No," he growled. He climbed in beside her as his chauffeur closed the door. "You're absolutely not."

Her lips tugged downward, and she abruptly fell silent. But as the Rolls-Royce drew away from the curb, she turned to him suddenly in the backseat with pleading eyes. "So what *is* your type?"

His type. Kasimir's jaw clenched. It was time to draw a line in the sand. To end the strange emotional connection that had leapt up between them since he'd told her about Nina. He'd never told anyone about that. But Josie had looked so sad, so vulnerable, he'd wanted to comfort her.

He'd overshot the mark. Because for the last hour she'd been looking at him as if he were some kind of damned hero just for some flowers and cake and sharing a story from his past. Enough. The way his body was fighting him now, he needed Josie to be on her guard against him. To remind them both that he was exactly what the world thought he was—a heartless playboy—he opened his mouth to tell her frankly about Véronique, Oksana and all the rest.

Taking her hand, Kasimir looked straight into her eyes.

Then he heard himself say huskily, "My usual type isn't half as beautiful as you."

He sucked in his breath. Why had he said that? How had it slipped past his guard? Was he picking up the habit from Josie—randomly blurting things out? He risked a glance at her.

Josie's jaw had dropped. Her hand trembled in his own. Her eyes were shining.

He pulled his hand away. "But I'm heartless, Josie. You should know I'm not the good man you think."

"You're wrong," she whispered. "I can tell—"

He turned away, clawing back his hair as he stared out the window at the passing city. "I don't want to hurt you," he said in a low voice. "But I'm afraid I will."

The truth was, he was starting to like the glow of admiration in her eyes. Josie had a good heart. He saw that clearly. But oddly, she seemed to think he had a good heart, as well—which was an opinion that no one on earth shared, not even Kasimir himself. But some part of him didn't want to see that glow in her eyes fade.

Although it would. Once she found out the truth about him, no amount of cake or diamonds or flowers would ever convince Josie to forgive the man who'd blackmailed her sister.

It doesn't matter, he told himself harshly. He was glad she admired him. That delusion would keep her close. She would have no reason to try to leave. Not that she could. Turning to her, he asked abruptly, "Why did you use your passport as ID for the wedding license? Don't you drive?"

She shook her head with a sigh. "Bree is too afraid I'll get distracted by a sunset and crash, or forget where I parked, or maybe even give the car away to some beggar on the street. Not that we have a car," she said wistfully. "Our clunker that we drove south from Alaska died when we crossed the Nevada border."

"How can you not know how to drive?"

She bit her lip. "I would like to, but…"

"You are a grown woman. If you want to learn, learn. Nothing is stopping you."

"But Bree—"

"If she treats you like a child, it's because you still act like one. Mindlessly obeying her. I'm surprised she even let you get a passport," he said sardonically. "Isn't she afraid you might fly off to Asia and wreak havoc? Crash international stock markets in South America?"

She stared at him, wide-eyed. "How would I even do that?"

"Forget it," he bit out, looking out the window. "It just irritates me, how you've allowed her to control you. I can hardly believe you've bought into it for so long, looking up to her as if she's so much smarter than you, thinking that eventually, if you tried hard enough, you'd be able to earn her trust and respect—"

His voice cut off as he realized it wasn't Josie's sister he was talking about. Jaw tight, he glanced at her, hoping she hadn't noticed. His usual sort of mistress, who focused only on herself, wouldn't have registered a thing.

Josie was staring at him, her eyes wide.

"But Bree *is* smarter than me," she said in a small voice. "And it's okay. I don't mind. I love her just the same." She tilted her head. "Just as you love your brother. Don't you?"

Damn her intuitive nature. He turned away, his shoulders tight. "Loved. A long time ago. When I was too stupid to know better."

"You shouldn't give up on him. You should—"

"Leave it alone," he ground out.

"But you've spent the last ten years trying to destroy him—in this internecine battle—"

"Internecine?"

"Mutually destructive."

"Ah." His lips tugged up at the edges. "Well. Our rivalry has certainly been that. We've both lost millions of dollars bidding up the same targets for acquisition, sabotaging each other, planting rumors, political backstabbing. All of which Vladimir deserves. But I can hardly expect him just to take it without fighting back. No. In fact—" he tapped his knuckles aimlessly against the side of the car "—I'd have been very disappointed if he had."

"Oh," Josie breathed. "Now I get it."

Frowning, he looked at her. "Get what?"

"You're like little boys in some kind of quarrel, wrestling and punching each other till you're bloody. Till someone says 'uncle.' The reason you're fighting him so hard…is because you miss him."

Kasimir gave an intake of breath, staring at her. His shoulders suddenly felt uncomfortably tight. He was grateful when his phone rang. "Xendzov," he answered sharply.

"It's happened, Your Highness," his investigator said. "Even sooner than you expected. Your brother has started looking for Josie."

"Do you know why?" he bit out, extremely aware of Josie watching him anxiously in the back of the car.

"It could be at her sister's request. Or for some reason of his own. He tracked her commercial flight from Seattle to Honolulu. It's just a matter of time until he finds her on this island. With you."

Kasimir's hand tightened on his phone. "Understood."

"Who was that?" Josie asked after he hung up. "Was it about my sister?"

His lips tightened. "Change of plan." He turned to her. "We'll have to skip the cake."

"Did you find her?" she cried. "Where is she?"

"How would you like a surprise honeymoon?" he said evasively.

Josie scowled. "Why would I want that?"

Ouch. He tried to ignore the blow to his masculine pride. "You've never wanted to go to Paris?" he said lightly. "To stay at the finest hotels, to have a magnificent view of the Eiffel Tower, to shop in designer boutiques, to…"

His voice trailed off when he saw Josie shaking her head fiercely. "I just want my sister—home safe. As you promised!"

Kasimir sighed, telling himself they'd have been tracked to Paris, anyway, when he was surrounded by the inevitable paparazzi. He flashed her a careless smile. "Fine. No honeymoon."

"But do you know where Bree is?" she persisted.

"I might have a slight suspicion." It wasn't a lie. He knew exactly where Bree was, and he'd known since yesterday. She was at Vladimir's beachfront villa on the other side of Oahu. Too damned close for comfort. It was a miracle that for almost a week now, Kasimir had managed to keep it quiet that he was in Honolulu.

"Is she safe?" Josie grabbed his hand anxiously. "He hasn't—hurt her—in any way?"

Hurt her? Kasimir snorted. His investigator had seen Vladimir kissing her on a moonswept beach last night, while Bree, wearing a bikini, had been enthusiastically kissing him back. But at Josie's pained expression, he coughed. "She's fine."

"How can you know?"

"Because I know." Rubbing his throbbing temples, Kasimir leaned forward to tell his chauffeur, "The airport."

They'd already turned down the street of his penthouse as the driver nodded.

"Airport?" Josie breathed. "Where are we going?"

Kasimir smiled. "Let's just say I'm glad you have your passport…"

His voice trailed off as he saw Greg Hudson pacing on the sidewalk outside his building. He'd come to demand payment in person. A snarl rose to Kasimir's lips. *Damn his greedy hide.* If Josie saw her ex-boss, it would ruin everything. Intuitive as she was, she'd quickly figure out who'd bribed him to hire the two Dalton girls. And why. Then, married or not, she'd likely jump straight out of Kasimir's car, and that would be the end of his revenge.

Josie blinked. "Wait, are we back on your street?" She turned towards the chauffeur. "Could we please just stop for a moment at the penthouse, so I can pick up my bag before we go?" She glanced at Kasimir with a dimpled smile. "And I'll grab the cake."

The chauffeur looked at Kasimir in his rearview mirror, then said gravely, "Sorry, Princess."

"Tell him to stop," Josie said imploringly to Kasimir. She started to turn towards the window, her hand reaching instinctively for her door. In another two seconds, she'd see her ex-boss waiting outside the building, and Kasimir's plans would be destroyed.

He didn't think. He just acted. That was the reason, he told himself later, the only possible reason, for what he did next.

Throwing himself across the leather seat of the Rolls-Royce, he pulled her roughly into his arms. He heard her gasp, saw her eyes grow wide. He saw panic mingle with tremulous, innocent desire in her beautiful face. He saw the blush of roses in her pale cheeks, breathed in the sweet peaches of her hair. His hands cupped her face as he felt the softness of her skin.

And then, with a low growl from the back of his throat, Kasimir did what he'd ached to do for hours.

He kissed his wife.

CHAPTER THREE

JOSIE TRULY DIDN'T believe he was going to kiss her. Not until she felt his mouth against her own. As he lowered his head to hers, she just stared up at him in shock.

Then she felt his lips against hers, rough and hot, hard and sensual as silk. She gasped, closing her eyes as she felt the caress of his embrace like a thousand shards of light.

In the backseat of the Rolls-Royce, Kasimir pulled her more tightly against him, and she felt his power, his strength. He tilted her head back, deepening the kiss as his hands twined in her hair. Her eyes squeezed shut as she felt the hot, plundering sweep of his tongue, felt the velocity of the world spinning around her, as if they were at the center of a sandstorm. She was lost, completely lost, in sensations she'd never felt before, in his lips and tongue and body and hands. When he finally pulled away, she sagged against him, dazed beneath the force of her own surrender.

But Kasimir just sat back against the seat, glancing out the car window calmly. As if he hadn't just changed her whole world—forever.

"Why…" she whispered, touching her tingling, bruised lips. "Why did you kiss me?"

Kasimir glanced back at her. "Oh, that?" He shrugged, then drawled, "The justice of the peace did tell me I was allowed to kiss you now."

Her heart was pounding. She tried to understand. "You

did it to celebrate our wedding?" she said faintly. "Because you were overcome...by the moment?"

He gave a hard laugh. As the chauffeur drove the Rolls-Royce onto the highway, Kasimir looked away from her, as if he were far more interested in the shining glass buildings and palm trees and blue sky. "Exactly." His tone was sardonic. "I was overcome."

And she imagined she saw smug masculine satisfaction in his heavy-lidded expression.

Josie had never thought of herself as a violent person. If anything, she was the type to hide and quiver from conflict. But in this moment, she suddenly felt a spasm of anger. "Then tell me the real reason."

He looked at her. "You were handy."

She gasped. He hadn't kissed her to share the sacredness of the moment, or because he was overwhelmed by sudden particular desire for Josie. Oh, no. He'd kissed her just because she was *there*.

I'm heartless, Josie, he'd told her. *You should know I'm not the good man you think.*

Apparently he'd felt that words weren't enough of a warning. He'd decided to show her, and this was exhibit A.

And for that, he'd ruthlessly stolen her first kiss away.

"It meant nothing to you?" she choked out. "You were just using me?"

"Of course I was," he said coldly. "What else could a kiss be? You know the kind of man I am. I don't do commitment. I don't do hearts and flowers and sappy little poems so dear to the innocent souls of tender little virgins," he ground out. His eyes were fierce as he glared at her. "So get that straight—once and for all."

She stared at him, her mouth wide-open.

Then emotion tore through her, like fire through dry brush. It was an emotion she barely recognized. She'd never felt it before.

Rage.

Hot burning tears filled her eyes. Drawing back her hand, she slapped his face—hard.

The ringing sound of the blow echoed in the car. Even the chauffeur in the front seat flinched.

Blinking in shock, Kasimir instinctively put his hand to his rugged, reddened cheek as he stared down at her.

"I dreamed about my first kiss for my whole life," she cried. "And you stole it from me. For no reason. Just to prove your stupid point!"

He narrowed his eyes. "Josie—"

"I get it. You don't want me to fall in love with you. No worries about that!" A lump rose in her throat. "You turned a memory that should have been sacred into a mockery," she whispered. Tears spilled over her lashes as she looked away. "Don't ever touch me again."

Silence fell in the backseat of the limo. She waited for him to apologize, to say he was sorry.

Instead, he said in a low voice, "Fine."

She whirled to face him, eyes blazing. "I want your promise! Your word of honor!"

"You think I have a word of honor?" His handsome face was stark, his blue gaze oddly vulnerable as he looked down at her, his arms folded over his black vest and tie.

"Stop joking about this!" Her voice ended with a humiliating sob. "I mean it!"

Seeing her tears, he released his arms. He touched her gently on the shoulders.

"All right. I will never kiss you again," he said in a low voice. His blue gaze burned through her like white fire. "I give you my word of honor."

She swallowed, then wiped her eyes roughly with the back of her hand. "I don't like being used," she whispered. Squaring her shoulders, she looked up. "Just stick to our original deal. A professional arrangement. You get your land. I get my sister back safe."

"Yes." Matching her tone, he said, "We'll be at the airport in a few moments."

She suddenly remembered. "My backpack—"

"I'll have my housekeeper bring it to the airport." Pulling out his phone, he dialed and gave his orders. After he hung up, he asked Josie quietly, "What is so important in the backpack, anyway?"

"Nothing much," she said, looking down at her hands, now tightly folded over the white lace of her dress. "An old photo of my family. A sweater that used to belong to my mother. Before she—" Josie's lip trembled "—died. Right after I was born."

Silence fell.

"I'm sorry," he said gruffly. "I lost my own mother when I was twenty-two. I still miss her. She was the only truly good, decent woman I've ever known. At least until—"

His voice cut off.

"Until?"

"Never mind," he muttered.

Josie stared at him. Then her hand reached out for his.

Kasimir looked down at her hand. "You're trying to make me feel better?" he said slowly. He looked up. "I thought you were ready to kill me."

"I was—I mean, I am." She swallowed, then whispered, "But I know how it feels to lose your parents. I know what it's like to feel orphaned and alone. And I wouldn't wish it on my worst enemy." She tried to smile. "Though I guess you've done all right, haven't you? Being a billionaire prince and all."

He stared at her for a long moment. "It's not always what it's cracked up to be." He looked away. "You asked me where we're going? I'm taking you home."

"To Alaska?"

He snorted, then shook his head. "Not even close." He

looked down at her tight white dress. "We'll need to get you some new clothes."

She followed his gaze. Sitting down, her body was squeezed by the white sheath like a sausage, pressing her full breasts halfway to her chin. Her nipples were barely tucked in for decency. She gulped, fighting the urge to cover herself with her bouquet of flowers. She cleared her throat. "I was planning to wash all my dirty clothes today. Does this place we're going to happen to have a washer and dryer...?"

Her voice trailed off when she saw his gaze roaming from her breasts, to her hips, and back again. Her cheeks colored.

"I wish I'd never told you," she said grumpily, folding her arms and turning away.

"Told me what?"

"About the underwear."

Silence fell in the backseat of the car.

"Me, too," he muttered.

Josie craned her neck to look right, left, then up. And up some more.

"Unreal," she muttered.

Kasimir flashed her a grin. "I'm glad you like it."

"This is your *home?*"

"No." He smiled at her, looking sleek and shaved in a clean suit, having showered on their overnight flight. "My home is in the desert, a two-hour helicopter ride away. But this..." He shrugged. "It's just a place to do business. I come here as little as possible. It's a bit too...civilized."

Too civilized?

Josie shook her head as she looked back up at the beautiful Moorish palace, two stories tall, surrounded by gently swaying palm trees and the glimmer of a blue-water pool.

It was like a honeymoon all right, she thought. If you were really, really rich.

After sleeping all night on a full-size bed in the back cabin of Kasimir's private jet, she'd woken up refreshed. She'd looked out the jet's small windows to see a golden land rising beyond the sparkling blue ocean, and past that, sunlight breaking over black mountains.

"Where are we?" she'd breathed.

Kasimir had looked at her, his eyes shining. "Morocco." His smile was warm. "My home."

Now, they were standing in front of his palace in the desert outside Marrakech. She could see the dark crags of the Atlas Mountains in the distance, illuminated by the bright morning sun. Birds were singing as they soared across the wide desert sky. The pool glimmered darts of sunlight, like diamonds, against the deep green palm trees.

It was an oasis here. Of beauty, yes. She glanced behind her at the guardhouse beside the wrought-iron gate. But also of money and power.

"It's beautiful." She exhaled, then could no longer keep herself from blurting out, "So is she here?"

He looked at her blankly. "Who?"

"Bree." She furrowed her brow. "You said she was here!"

"I never said that. I said I had a slight suspicion of where she might be."

"Do you think she's in Morocco?"

His lips twisted. "Unlikely."

Josie glared at him. "Then why on earth did we come all the way here?"

"Hawaii was getting tiresome," he said coldly. "I wanted to leave. And I told you. This is where I do business…"

"Business!" she cried. "Your only business is finding Bree!"

"Yes." He tilted his head. "Once I have your land."

She gasped. "You said as soon as we were married, you'd save her!"

"No." He looked at her. "I said I'd save her *after* we got married. When I had possession of your land."

She shook her head helplessly. "You can't intend to wait for some stupid legal formalities…"

"Can't I?" Kasimir said sharply. "It would be easy for you to decide, after your sister is safely home, that you'd prefer not to transfer your land to me at all. Or to suddenly insist that I pay you, say, a hundred million dollars for it."

"A hundred million…" She couldn't even finish the number. "For six hundred acres?"

"You know what the land means to me," he said tightly. "You could use my feelings against me."

"I wouldn't!"

"I know you won't. Because you won't have the chance."

"Getting the land could take months!"

"I have the best lawyers in the country working on it. I expect to have it in my possession within a few weeks."

A few weeks? She forced herself to take a deep breath, to calm the frantic beating of her heart, so she could say reasonably, "I can't wait that long."

His lips pursed. "You have no choice."

"But my sister's in danger!" she exploded.

"Danger?" He looked at her incredulously. "If anyone's in danger, it's Vladimir."

Josie frowned. "What do you mean by that?"

He blinked. "She's always been his weakness, that's all," he muttered. He reached for her hand. "Come inside. I want to show you something."

He led her through the exotic green garden towards the palace, and as they walked past the soaring Moorish arches, she looked up in amazement. The foyer was painted with intertwined flowers and vines and geometric motifs in gold leaf and bright colors. Raised Arabic calligraphy was embedded into the plaster on the walls. She'd never seen anything quite so beautiful, or so foreign.

Josie's lips parted as, in the next room, she saw the ornamental stucco pattern of the soaring ceiling, which seemed to drip stalactites in perfect symmetry. "Are those *muqarnas?*" she breathed.

He looked at her with raised eyebrows.

"I love architecture coffee-table books," she said, rather defensively.

"Of course you do." He sounded amused.

Her eyes narrowed, and she tilted her head. "It's beautiful. Even though it's fake."

"Fake?" he said.

"The builder tried to make it look older, Moorish in design, but with those art-nouveau elements in the windows... I'm guessing it was built in the 1920s?"

He gave her a surprised look. "You got all that from a single coffee-table book?"

Her cheeks colored slightly. "I might have spent a few hours lingering over books at my favorite couscous restaurant."

He grinned at her. "Well, you're right. This was built as a hotel when Morocco was a French protectorate." He looked at her approvingly. "There's no way Bree is smarter than you."

Her heart fluttered. In spite of her best efforts, she was still beaming foolishly beneath his praise as he led her past a shadowy cloistered walkway to the open courtyard at the center of the palace. The white merciless sun beat down in the blue sky, but the center courtyard garden was cool, with lush flowers and an orange tree on each corner. Soft breezes sighed through palm trees, leaving dappled shadows over the burbling stone fountain.

"Josie?" Kasimir was staring at her.

She realized she'd stopped in the middle of the courtyard, her mouth open. "Sorry." Snapping her lips shut, she followed him across the courtyard to a hallway directly off the columned stone cloister.

He held a door open for her.

"This will be your room," he murmured. She walked past

him to find a large bedroom with high ceilings, sumptuously decorated, with two latticed windows, one facing the courtyard, the other the desert. "You will need something to wear while you're here."

"No, really," she protested. "All I need is a washer and a dryer—"

He opened a closet door. "Too late."

Peeking past him, she saw a huge closetful of women's clothes, all with tags from expensive designers. She said doubtfully, "Whose are these?"

"Yours."

"I mean, where did they come from? Were they...left here by your other, um, female guests?"

"Female guests." His lips quirked. "Is that what you call them?"

"You know what I mean!"

"I wouldn't come all the way to Marrakech for a one-night stand." His smile lifted to a grin. "Why would I bother going to the trouble?"

"Yeah, why," she muttered. Her husband could seduce any woman with a smile. He'd melted Josie into an infatuated, delusional puddle with a single careless, stolen kiss.

She scowled. "Look. I just want to know if I'm wearing clothes you bought for someone else."

He gave an exaggerated sigh. "They were purchased in Marrakech for you, Josie. Specifically for you. And if you don't believe me..." He gave her a wicked grin as he opened a drawer. "Check this out."

Her lips parted as she looked down at all the lacy unmentionable undergarments.

"You'll never have to go commando again," he said smugly. His eyes met hers. "Unless you want to."

She swallowed, then turned away as her cheeks burned. "Great... Thanks."

"And for your information," he said behind her, "I would never bring a female guest here."

She didn't meet his eyes. She was afraid he would notice how she was trembling. "I'm the first?"

"Ah," he said softly. "But you're more than a guest." Reaching over, he tucked a tendril of her hair off her face. "You are my wife."

As his fingertips stroked her skin, she felt his nearness, felt his powerful body towering over hers. Swallowing, she turned away, pretending to look through the expensive items in the closet to hide her confusion.

"Well?" he said huskily. "Do you see anything you like?"

Her heart gave an involuntary throb as she looked back at him.

"Yes," she said in a low voice. "But nothing that's right for me."

His blue eyes narrowed as he frowned. "But they're your size."

"That's not what I meant."

"Then what?"

She swallowed. "Look, I appreciate the gesture, but…" She stopped herself in her tracks, then blurted out, "They're all just too—fancy."

He drew back, blinking in surprise. "Too fancy?"

She nodded. "I like clothes I can be comfortable in. Clothes I can work in."

He looked at her. "But you wore that all night?"

She looked down at her tight wedding dress. "Well. I just put this back on. I slept naked."

Kasimir swallowed. "Naked?" he said hoarsely.

"Look, I really appreciate your sweet gesture, but until I can wash my own clothes, couldn't I just borrow some of your old jeans?" she said hopefully. "Maybe an old T-shirt?"

The shock on his handsome face was almost comical.

"You'd rather wear my old ratty work clothes than Louis Vuitton or Chanel?"

Not wanting to examine too carefully the reasons for that, she just nodded.

He snorted. "You're a very original woman, Josie Xendzov."

Josie Xendzov. Her heart did that strange thump-thump again. "So people have always told me."

"So what work are you planning to do around here, Princess? Dig trenches in the dirt? Change the oil in my Lamborghini?"

"You have a Lamborghini?" she said eagerly.

His lips curved. "You don't give a damn about designer clothes, but you're impressed by a car? You can't even drive!"

She shrugged. "My father had a Lamborghini when I was six years old. He had it shipped up to Alaska, delivered to our house in the middle of winter. The roads were covered with snow. Impossible to drive the Lamborghini with those wide performance tires."

Kasimir nodded. "You'd slide right into a snowbank."

"So Dad let me pretend to drive it in the driveway. For hours. I remember it was dark, except for flashes of the northern lights across the sky, and I drove the steering wheel so recklessly. Pretending to be a race-car driver. We both laughed so hard." She blinked fast. "It was the first time I ever really heard him laugh. Though I heard he used to laugh all the time before my mom died." She looked down at her feet. "I miss my family," she whispered. "I miss my home."

For a moment, he didn't move.

Then his warm, rough hands took her own. With an intake of breath, she looked up, waiting for him to tell her Black Jack Dalton had been a criminal who didn't deserve a Lamborghini. She waited for Kasimir to mock her grief, to tell her she should put the memory of childhood happiness away, like outgrown toys, discarded and forgotten.

Instead, Kasimir put his hand on the small of her back, pulling her close as he looked down at her.

"So you have a fondness for Lamborghinis, do you?" he said softly, searching her gaze. "They're not too fancy?"

Josie looked up at his ruggedly handsome face. Every inch of her body felt his touch on her back. She shook her head. "Nope," she whispered. "Not fancy."

"In that case…" With a wicked smile, he reached out to stroke her cheek as he said softly, "I know just what I'm going to do with you."

CHAPTER FOUR

Two hours later, Josie's body was shaking with fear.

Her hand trembled on the gearshift. "I can't believe you're making me do this."

"I'm not making you do anything."

She'd changed out of her tight dress, but in spite of wearing Kasimir's old rolled-up jeans and a clean, slightly tattered black Van Halen T-shirt, she didn't feel remotely comfortable. She'd showered, too, but that hadn't done her much good, either. Her forehead now felt clammy with sweat. The two of them were in the enormous paved exterior courtyard of the palace. In his Lamborghini.

And for the first time since she was a child, Josie was in the driver's seat.

"You wanted to learn how to drive," Kasimir pointed out.

"Not in your brand-new Lamborghini!"

"Snob, huh? So it's suddenly 'too fancy' for you after all?"

"You're laughing now. You'll be crying when I crash it straight into your pool."

He shrugged. "I'll buy a new one."

"Car or pool?"

"Either. Both."

She gaped at him. "Are you out of your mind? These things cost real money!"

"Not to me." Reaching over, he put his hand on her denim-clad leg. She nearly jumped out of her skin before she realized he was only pressing on her knee. "Push down harder on the clutch. Yes." He put his other hand over hers on the gearshift. "Move it like that. Yes," he said softly as he guided her. "Exactly like that."

Josie gulped, her heart pounding in her throat. She accelerated, then stalled. She stomped on the gas, then the brakes. She spun out, again and again, kicking up clouds of dust.

"You're doing great," Kasimir said for the umpteenth time, even as he was coughing from the dust. He gave her a watery smile, his face encouraging.

"How can you be so patient?" she cried, nearly beating her head against the steering wheel. "I'm terrible at this!"

"Don't be so hard on yourself," he said gruffly. "It's your first time."

Resting her head against the steering wheel, Josie looked at him sideways. Since she'd met Kasimir, it had been her first time for lots of things. The first time she'd ever been recklessly pursued by a man who wanted to marry her. The first time she'd felt her heart pound with strange new desire. The first time she'd ever been wildly, truly infatuated with anyone.

She looked down at the huge diamond ring on her finger, seeing the facets flash in the light. The first time she'd fully realized the depths of her bad luck, that she was married to a handsome prince, whose secretly kind heart would unfortunately never pound that way over her.

Never ever, her brain assured her.

Not in a million years, her heart agreed.

His phone rang, and he looked down at the number. "Excuse me."

"Sure," she said, relieved to take a break from driving, or whatever her tire-screeching, bloodcurdling version of driving might be. She stretched in her seat, yawning.

Then she noticed how Kasimir had turned his body away from her to speak quietly into the phone. He got out of the car altogether, closing the door behind him.

Who on earth was he speaking to? Josie's eyes narrowed. Clearly someone he didn't want her to know about. Was it information about Bree? Or—cripes, could he be talking to another woman, making plans for a romantic getaway as soon as he was safely rid of her?

She quietly got out of the driver's-side door.

Kasimir had turned away to speak into the phone. In a very low voice. *In Russian.* "My brother's private jet left for Russia? You're sure?" He paused. "And she's still with him? Very well. Get out of Oahu and head for St. Petersburg. As soon as you can."

Hanging up, Kasimir turned around. His eyes widened as he saw her standing beside him in the dust-choked driveway.

"What was that about?" she asked casually.

"Nothing that concerns you."

"You haven't found my sister?"

"Nope." He gave her a careless, charming smile. Lying to her. Lying to her face! "You've almost got the clutch down. Ready for more?"

She didn't move. "I studied Russian in school," she ground out. "For six years."

His expression changed.

"You found Bree," she whispered, hands clenching at her sides. "She was on Oahu. And you didn't want me to know."

Kasimir stared at her, then resentfully gave a single nod.

Closing her eyes, Josie took a deep breath as grief filled her heart. "She was on Oahu. All the time we were there, we could have just driven across the island at any time and picked her up?"

"If we'd gone the moment you arrived at my penthouse— yes." Her eyes flew open. His cold blue gaze met hers. "We weren't married then. You could have walked away. I had no reason to tell you."

With a little cry, Josie leapt towards him. She pounded on his chest. "You bastard!"

He didn't move, or try to protect himself. "I don't blame you for being angry," he said softly.

"So that's why you brought me here?" Wide-eyed, she staggered back. "Damn you," she whispered. "How selfish can you be?"

He looked at her. "You already know the answer to that, or else you're a fool."

But she was. She was a fool, because she'd believed in his compliments and lies! Turning on her heel, she started to walk away.

He grabbed her wrist, turning her to face him. "Where do you think you're going?"

"To St. Petersburg," she flashed. "To save her, since you won't!"

"And just how do you intend to do that?" He sounded almost amused. "With no money and nothing to barter?"

She tossed her head. "Perhaps your brother is interested in trading for his old family homestead!"

She heard his ragged intake of breath. "You couldn't do that."

"Why not? It's mine now. Thanks for marrying me."

His hand tightened on her wrist. "That land belongs to me—"

"I signed a prenup, remember? It protected all your possessions and fortune you brought into our marriage. But it also protected mine!"

His blue eyes were like fire. "You—you, the last honest woman—would try to steal my land? And give it to my brother?"

"Why not? You stole my first kiss!" she cried, trembling all over. She looked away, blinking fast. "It should have been something special, something I shared with someone I loved, or might love someday. And you ruined it!" She turned on him fiercely. "You lied to my face from the moment I came back to Honolulu. You won't go save Bree until you legally get my land? You say you can't trust me? Fine!" She tossed her head. "Maybe I won't trust you, either!"

His expression was dark, even murderous. "Yes. I lied to you about your sister's whereabouts. And yes, kissing you was a mistake." His grip on her wrist tightened as he looked down at her. "But don't act like a traumatized victim," he ground out. "You enjoyed our kiss. Admit it."

"What?" She tried to pull away. "Are you crazy?"

He wrapped her in his arms, bringing her tight against his hard body. "Claim what you want. I know what I felt when you were in my arms," he growled. "I felt your body tremble. You looked at me with those big eyes, holding your breath. Parting your mouth, licking your lips. Did you not realize you were giving me an invitation?" Cupping her face, he glared at her. "It is the same thing you are doing now."

She swallowed, yanking her chin away as she closed her mouth with a snap. She blinked fast.

"Maybe I did want you to kiss me. *Then*," she whispered. Wistfully, she looked towards the wrought-iron gate, towards the road to the Marrakech airport. "But I don't anymore. All I want now is for you to let me go."

For a moment, the only sound was the pant of her breath.

"Is being married to me really so awful?" he said roughly. "Was—kissing me—really so distasteful to you?"

She took a deep breath.

"No," she said honestly. She couldn't lie. She pushed away from him. "But I can't just wait around here for weeks, hoping she's all right. If you're in no hurry to save her…I'll make a deal with someone who is."

"You'll never even make it to Marrakech."

"I'll hitchhike into town," she tossed back. "And hock my wedding ring for a plane ticket to St. Petersburg."

"You'll never even be able to talk to him!"

She stopped. "My phone," she breathed aloud. "I'll call my sister's number. Either she will answer it, or Vladimir will.

The battery is dead but I'll plug it in and…" Triumphantly, Josie glanced behind her. Then she saw his face.

With a gasp, she started to run towards the house.

She was only halfway across the inner courtyard, racing for her bedroom, when he came up behind her, scooping her up with a growl. "I won't let you call him."

She struggled in his arms. "Let me go!"

"Vladimir will never have that land." Beneath the swaying palm trees of the sunny courtyard, next to the soft burbling water of the stone fountain, he slowly released her, and she felt the strength of his muscular form as she slid down his body. He gripped her wrists. "It's mine. And so are you."

She shook her head wildly. "You can't keep me prisoner here. I'll scream my head off! One of your servants will…"

"My servants will say nothing. They are loyal."

It was impossible to pull her wrists out of his implacable grip. Tears filled her eyes.

"Someone will talk," she whispered. "Someone will hear me. We're not that far from the city. I'll find a phone that works. Or email. There's no way you can keep me here against my will."

Kasimir looked down at her, then his eyes narrowed. He abruptly let her go.

"You're right."

She rubbed her wrists in relief. "You're letting me go?"

His sensual mouth curled in a devastating smile. He looked every inch a ruthless Russian prince, his blue eyes icy as a Siberian winter. "Wrong," he said softly.

Frightened of the coldness in his eyes, Josie slowly backed away. "Whatever you're planning, it won't work. I'll escape you…"

Their eyes locked, and shivers went through her.

"Will you?" he purred.

And coiling back like a tiger, he sprang.

* * *

Kasimir heard the loud whir of the helicopter flying away as he stood on thick carpets over the packed sand in his own grand tent, the largest and most luxurious in his camp, deep inside the Sahara Desert.

He looked down at his prisoner—that is to say, his dear wife—sitting on his bed. Tied up with a soft silken gag over her mouth, Josie was glaring at him with bright sparks of hatred in her eyes.

His eyes traced down her body. She still wearing his black T-shirt and oversized jeans from Marrakech, but from the flash of lacy bra strap, he knew she was wearing the sexy lingerie he'd given her underneath. His body tightened. He said softly, "What am I going to do with you?"

Josie answered him in a muffled, angry voice, and he had the feeling she was telling him what he should do with *himself,* and that her suggestion was not a courteous one.

Kasimir sighed. He should have guessed Josie might speak Russian—it was sometimes taught in Alaskan schools. He regretted that he'd let himself be caught in such a clumsy lie.

But at the moment, he regretted even more his promise never to kiss her again. A word of honor was a serious thing: unbreakable. He'd unknowingly broken a vow once, to his dying father, when Vladimir had sold their homestead behind his back. Kasimir wouldn't break another.

The truth was he'd been attracted to Josie Dalton from the moment they'd met on Christmas Eve, in the Salad Shack. Kissing her in the back of his Rolls-Royce yesterday, far from satiating his desire, had only made him want her more. Her shy, trembling, perfectly imperfect kiss had punched through him like a hurricane, knocking him over and sucking him down beneath the sensual undertow of her sweet, soft embrace.

Why did she have such power over him?

He felt a sudden hard thwack against his shin.

Exhaling, Kasimir looked down at her, sitting on his bed. "Stop trying to kick me, and I'll untie you."

"Mmph!" Josie responded angrily. If looks could kill, a lightning bolt would have sizzled him on the spot, leaving only the ash of his body to be carried away like smoke on the hot desert wind.

With a sigh, he reached down and untied the white sash from her mouth. "I warned you what would happen if you didn't stop screaming," he said regretfully. "You were driving the pilot crazy. Tark's been in some rough places, flown military missions all over the world. But even he had never heard the kind of curses that came shrieking out of your mouth."

Her mouth now free, Josie coughed. "You kidnapped me, you—" And here she let out a torrent of new invective against his manhood, his intelligence and his lineage in her sweet Sunday-school voice, that left him wide-eyed at her creative vulgarity.

"Ah, my dear." He gave a soft laugh. "I'm beginning to think you are not quite the innocent I thought you were."

"Go to hell!"

He tilted his head. "Who taught you to swear like that?"

"Your *mother*," she bit out insultingly. Then with an intake of breath, Josie looked up, as if she'd just remembered that his mother had died. She bit her lip, abashed. "I'm sorry," she said in a small voice. She held out her wrists. "Would you mind please untying me now?"

Kasimir stared at her. After the way he'd thrown her bodily into his helicopter, ignoring her protests, tying her up—she felt guilty for her single thoughtless insult? She was afraid of causing *him* pain?

Bending to untie her wrists, he muttered, "You are quite a woman, Josie Xendzov."

"So you keep telling me." She looked around his enormous, luxurious white canvas tent, from the four-poster bed to the luxurious Turkish carpets lining the hard-packed sand floor. A large screen of carved wood covered the wardrobe, illuminated by the soft golden light of a solar-powered lamp. "Where are we?"

"My home. In the Sahara."

"Where in the Sahara?"

"The middle," he said sardonically.

"Thanks." Narrowing her eyes she tossed her head. "I'm grateful you're not just going to leave me in chains. As your prisoner."

"It's tempting," he said softly. "Believe me."

As he loosened the knots around her wrists, he tried not to notice the alluring softness of her skin. Tried not to imagine how the white lacy bra and panties looked beneath her clothes. Tried not to think how easy it would be to push her back against his bed, to stretch back her arms, still bound at the wrists, against the headboard. To press apart her knees, still bound at the ankles. He tried not to think how it would feel to lick and caress up her legs, to the inside of her thighs, until he felt her tremble and shake.

No. He wouldn't think about it. At all.

A bead of sweat broke out on Kasimir's forehead. *His word of honor.* That meant his lips and tongue couldn't possibly yearn to suckle her full, ripe breasts. His hands could not ache to part her virgin thighs. He couldn't hunger to stroke and kiss her until he lost himself deep, deep, deep inside her hot wet core.

The bindings on her wrists abruptly burst loose and, as the rope dropped to the floor, Kasimir took a single staggering step back from her. He ran his hand over his forehead, feeling dizzy.

She rubbed her free wrists, looking up at him dubiously. "Are you all right?"

Blinking, he focused on her beautiful brown eyes, expressive and still slightly resentful, in the fading afternoon light. Her voice was like the cool water of an oasis to a man half-dead with thirst. Did she feel the same electricity? He'd been so sure of it in Honolulu. In Marrakech, he'd been absolutely confident of the answering desire in her eyes. But now, he wondered if that had just been a mirage in the desert, an illusion created by his own aching, inexplicable need.

Josie took a deep breath. "Please," she whispered.

"Yes," he said hoarsely. He wanted to please her. He wanted to push her back against the pillows and rip the clothes from her body. He wanted to thrust himself inside her until he felt her scream and explode with joy.

"Please—" she held out her ankles "—finish untying me."

Kasimir exhaled. "Right," he said unsteadily.

Holding himself in check, he knelt at her feet. From where she sat on the bed, her long legs were stretched towards him, her heels on the Turkish carpet. Even in the baggy jeans he'd loaned her, she had legs like a houri—the pinnacle of feminine beauty. As he undid the ropes, his fingertips unwillingly brushed against her calves, against the tender instep of her sole. He felt her shiver, and he stopped, his heart pounding. He looked up her legs, straight past her knees to her thighs, and the heaven that waited there, then to her breasts, then to her face. His body broke out into a hot sweat.

His word of honor.

With a twist and a rip, he yanked the rope off her ankles. His own legs trembled as he rose to his feet. He clenched his hands at his sides, his body tight and aching for what he could not have.

"I shouldn't have tied you up," he said in a low voice. "I should have told Tark to go to hell and just let you scream curses at me for two hours."

"No kidding." She stared at him, waiting, then she gave a crooked smile. "So are you going to say you're sorry?"

"Mistakes were made," he said tightly, and that was the best he could do.

Her smile widened. "You're not used to saying you're sorry, are you?"

"I don't make it a habit."

"Too bad for you. It's a big habit with me. I say it all the time. You should try it."

"It's been a while." Kasimir's throat burned as he remembered the last time he'd apologized. Ten years ago, he'd arrived in St. Petersburg to discover his "interview" was all over the business news. He'd immediately phoned his brother, still in Alaska. Kasimir still writhed to remember the pitiful way he'd groveled. *I'm sorry. I didn't know he was a reporter. Forgive me, Volodya.*

But his brother had just used his confession against him, convincing Kasimir his mistake was a betrayal and they should end their partnership immediately. And all along Vladimir had secretly known a billion-dollar mining deal in Siberia was about to come through.

"How long has it been since you apologized?" Josie asked softly.

Kasimir shrugged. Saying sorry was tantamount to admitting fault, and he'd learned that humbly asking for forgiveness was a useless, self-destructive exercise, like flinging your body in front of a speeding train. It could only end in being flattened. "Ten years."

Her jaw dropped. "Seriously?"

"I have to go." His shoulders felt tight in his suit jacket. "Just stay here, all right? I'll be back in a few minutes."

"Where are you going?"

"To change out of these clothes. And take a quick shower." From the corner of his eye, he saw her immediately glance at her old backpack on the floor. He could almost see the wheels turning in her mind. Fine, let her dig for her phone. Let her try to use it out here—with no way to recharge the dead battery and no connection even if she'd had power. He looked back at her. "Make yourself comfortable. But don't try to leave the encampment," he warned. "You're in the middle of the desert. There is no way for you to escape, so please don't try."

"Right." Josie nodded, her expression blank and bland. "No escape."

"I mean it," he said sharply. "You could die a horrible death, lost in the sand."

"Die a horrible death. Got it."

With a sigh, he tossed back the heavy canvas door, and went to a nearby smaller bathing tent. He knew Josie was up to something, but she'd soon see there was nowhere to go. He twisted his neck to the left, cracking his vertebrae. She'd hopefully spend the next ten minutes trying to get her phone to work. He gave a low laugh.

Taking off his suit, he used silver buckets filled with cool, clean water to wash the grime of civilization off his skin. He exhaled, feeling his shoulders relax, as they always did here. He changed into the traditional male caftan over loose-fitting pants. His body felt more at ease in a lightweight djellaba than he'd ever felt in a suit. He loved the natural wildness of the desert, so much more rational and merciful than the savage corporate world.

As he left the bathing tent, Kasimir looked up at the endless blue sky, at the white-sand horizon stretching to eternity. There were eight large white tents, most of them used by his Berber servants who maintained this remote desert camp, surrounding the deep well of an oasis. On the edge of the camp was a pen for the horses, and farther away still, a helicopter pad. He'd given up trying to drive here. He'd destroyed three top-of-the-line Range Rovers trying to drive over the sand dunes before he'd finally given up on driving altogether and turned to horses and helicopters.

Now, he looked across the undulating sand dunes stretching out to the farthest reaches of the horizon. Sand muffled all sound at this lonely spot on the edge of the Sahara. The sun was falling in the cloudless blue sky.

His oasis in the desert was as far from Alaska as he could possibly get. He had no memories here of the bleak, cold snow. Or of the only promise he'd ever broken.

Yet.

Kasimir sighed. He was starting to think it was a mistake to wait until he had the land before he searched for Bree. Not just because it was making Josie so unhappy, but also because it was growing agonizing for him to be near his wife and unable to touch her.

"Sir." One of his most trusted servants, a man in a blue turban, spoke to him anxiously in Berber. He pointed. "Your woman…"

Kasimir's lips parted as he saw Josie struggling up a nearby dune, kicking off her flimsy flip-flops, her bare feet sinking in the sand to her knees.

A sigh escaped him. He should have known that mere warnings of death wouldn't be enough to stop Josie from trying single-handedly to rush off to save that sister of hers. Irritated, he went after her.

Catching up with her easily, he grabbed her hand and pulled her all the way to the top of the dune. Then he abruptly released her.

"Look where you are, Josie," he raged at her. "Look!"

With an intake of breath, Josie turned in a circle, looking in every direction from the top of the dune. It was like standing in the middle of an ocean, surrounded by endless waves of sand.

"There's a reason why I brought you here," he said quietly. "There is nowhere for you to go."

She went in circles for five minutes before the truth of his words sank in on her, and she collapsed in a heap on the sand. "I can't stay here."

Kasimir knelt on the sand beside her. Reaching out, he tucked some hair away from her face. "I'm still going to save your sister. So stop trying to run away," he said gruffly. "Okay?"

Wiping her eyes, she sat on the sand, looking at him. "You can't just expect me to just sit here and do nothing, and leave her fate in Vladimir's hands. Or yours!"

"I thought you said I was a good man with a good heart."

She hiccupped a laugh, then sniffled. "I changed my mind."

His jaw tightened. "Your sister is in no danger. Vladimir has done nothing worse to her than making her scrub the floor of his villa."

"How do you know?"

"His housekeeper in Hawaii was not pleased to see him treating a female guest so rudely. But Bree has always been my brother's weakness. That is why I—" *Why I arranged for them to cross paths in Hawaii,* he almost said, but cut himself off. He could hardly admit that now, could he? Josie's trust in him was on very tenuous ground already. He set his jaw. "I've just found out he has her at his palace in St. Petersburg, where his company is busy with a merger."

"And he's not—bothering her?"

His lips curved. "From what I've heard, her greatest suffering has involved too much shopping at luxury boutiques with his credit card."

Josie frowned. "But Bree hates shopping," she said uncertainly.

"Maybe you don't know her as well as you think." He stood up, then held out his hand. "Just as she does not truly know you."

She put her hand into his. "What do you mean?" she said softly.

"She's spent the last decade treating you like something fragile and helpless. You are neither." He pulled her up against him, looking down at her. "You are reckless, Josie. Powerful. Fearless."

"I am?" she breathed, looking up into his eyes.

"Didn't you know?" He searched her gaze. "You risk yourself to take care of others. Constantly. In a way I cannot imagine."

She bit her lip, looking down.

His hand tightened on hers. "No more escape attempts. I mean it. I swear to you that she is safe. Just be patient. Stay here with me. From this moment, you will be treated not as a prisoner, but as an honored guest."

"*Honored guest?* You said I was more."

"I cannot treat you as my wife," he said huskily. "Not anymore."

"What do you mean? Of course you…"

"I cannot make love to you." His eyes met hers. "And since we kissed in Honolulu, it's all I can think about."

He heard her intake of breath.

"But I gave you my word of honor. I will not touch you. Kiss you. Make love to you for hours on end." Kasimir's larger hand tightened over hers. He looked down at her beautiful face, devoid of makeup. Her luminous brown eyes were the sort a man could drown in. And her lips… He shuddered. "You are safe, Josie," he whispered. "Until the end."

She slowly nodded. Holding her hand, he turned to lead her down the dune. They walked sure-footedly down the spine of sand, pausing to collect her discarded shoes, until they reached the encampment below. He thought about the cake he'd ordered for her, left behind in Honolulu. He'd order a wedding feast for her tonight. He would do everything he could to treat her as a princess—as a queen. That much he could do.

At the door of his tent, he glanced back to tell her how he planned to make her evening a happy one. Then he saw how her shoulders were slumped in his old black T-shirt, how the jeans he'd loaned her had unrolled at the hem, to drag against the ground. Her face was sad.

Something twisted in Kasimir's chest.

He suddenly wanted to tell her he was sorry. Sorry he'd brought her here. Sorry he'd dragged her into his plans for revenge. And sorry above all that when she discovered the blackmail against her sister, it would be a crime that even Josie's heart would be unable to forgive. She would despise him—forever. And he was starting to realize hers was the one good opinion he'd regret.

But when he opened his mouth to say the words, they caught in his throat.

Clenching his jaw, he turned away, pointing at the wardrobe. "You have fresh clothes here." He gestured towards the large four-poster bed, the sumptuous wall-to-wall Turkish carpets. "I will ask the women to bring you refreshment and a bath. When you are done, we will have dinner." He gave her a smile. "A wedding feast of sorts."

But she didn't smile back. She didn't seem interested, not even in the bath—a rare luxury in the desert. Sitting down heavily on the edge of the bed, she lifted her gaze numbly.

"I don't want to stay here with you," she whispered. She was so beautiful, he thought. His gaze traced from her full, generous mouth down the curve of her long, graceful neck. Like a swan. So unself-conscious, as if she had no idea about her beauty, about the way her pale skin gleamed like cream in the shadows of the tent, or the warmth and kindness that caused her to glow from within, as if there were a fire inside her.

And that fire could be so much more. Standing beside the bed, he felt how alone they were in his private tent. He could push her back against the soft mattress and see the light brown waves of her hair fall like a cascade against the pillows. He could touch her skin, stroke its luminescence with his fingertips and see if it was as soft as it looked.

He had to stop thinking about this. Now.

Kasimir turned away, stalking across the tent. He flung

open the heavy canvas flap of the door, then stopped. Standing in the late-afternoon sun, he heard the sigh of the wind and the distant call of desert birds. Shoulders tight, without turning around, he said in a low voice, "I never should have kissed you."

He heard her give a little squeak. He slowly turned back to face her.

"I was wrong." He took a deep breath. And then, looking into her shocked brown eyes, he spoke the words he hadn't been able to say for ten years. "Josie," he whispered, "I'm sorry."

CHAPTER FIVE

AN HOUR LATER, Josie was in the tent, bathed, comfortable and wearing clean clothes. And more determined than ever to escape.

Okay, so her phone didn't work and her impulsive escape attempt had been laughable. But she couldn't stay here. Whatever Kasimir thought, she couldn't just be patient. She had no intention of abandoning Bree for weeks in her ex-boyfriend's clutches and trusting all would be well.

Why had Kasimir even insisted on keeping her here? There was no reason he couldn't have her sign some kind of letter of intent or something, promising to give him the property. Something just didn't add up. She felt as if she'd become almost as much a prisoner as Bree was. Two prisoners for two brothers, she thought grimly.

And yet…

Josie brushed her long brown hair until it tumbled softly over her shoulders. Somehow, he'd also made her feel free. As if she, of all people, could be daring enough to travel around the world, learn to drive on a Lamborghini and boldly catch a powerful man in a lie.

You are reckless, Josie. Powerful. Fearless.

Could he be right? Could that be the voice inside her, the one she'd ignored for so long, the one she'd been scared to hear?

Dropping the silver-edged brush, she pulled her hair back

into a ponytail. Well, she was listening to it now. And that meant one thing: maybe she would have accepted being in a cage once…

But she'd be no man's prisoner now.

Josie stood up in her pale linen trousers and a fine cotton shirt she'd found in the wardrobe, in her exact size. She'd just come back from the bathing tent, where she'd been delightfully submerged in hot water and rose petals. As she'd watched the Berber servants pour steaming water into the cast-iron bathtub, she'd felt as though she was in another century. In *Africa*. In Morocco.

"He's called the Tsar of the Desert," one of the women had whispered. "He came here with a broken heart."

Another woman tossed rose petals into the fragrant water. "But the desert healed him."

A broken heart? *Kasimir?* If she hadn't already heard his story about his lost love, Josie would have found that hard to believe. With a shiver, she pictured him, all brooding lips and cold eyes…and hard, broad-shouldered, muscular body, towering over her. A man like that didn't seem to have feelings. She would have assumed he didn't have a heart to break.

But now she knew too much. An orphan who'd been stabbed in the back by his beloved older brother. A romantic who'd waited to lose his virginity, then fallen for his first woman, even planning to propose to her. If she'd known Kasimir when he was twenty-two…

Josie shivered. She would have fallen for him like a stone. A man with that kind of strength, loyalty, integrity and kindness was rare. Even she knew that.

She knew too much.

Now, as she left his tent, she looked out at the twilight. *Stop having a crush on him,* she ordered herself. She couldn't let herself get swept up in tenderness for the young man he'd once been—or in desire for the hard-eyed man he'd become. She couldn't get caught up in the romance of the desert, and start imagining herself some intrepid lady adventurer from a 1920s movie matinee. Kasimir was *not* some Rudolph Valentino-style sheikh waiting to ravish her, or love her.

No matter how he'd looked at her an hour ago.

I never should have kissed you. I was wrong. Josie, I'm sorry.

She pushed away the memory of his haunted voice, and hardened her heart. She couldn't completely trust him—no matter how handsome he was, or how he made her feel. There was something he wasn't telling her. And she wasn't going to stick around to find out what it was.

The air was growing cool in the high desert. She saw the darkening shadows of dusk lit up by torches on both sides of the oasis. It looked like magic.

She'd find a chance to escape. And this time, she wouldn't just run off. She'd figure out a plan. She'd seen horses on the edge of the encampment. Perhaps she could borrow one. She'd never been much of a planner. Bree had the organized mind for that. Josie was more of a seat-of-your-pants type of girl.

She'd figure it out. She'd seize her chance. Sometime when Kasimir wasn't looking.

Josie looked for him now, turning her head right and left. She pictured his handsome face, so intense, so ruthless. No wonder, under the magnetic force of his complete attention, she'd once felt infatuated—at least before she'd realized he was a liar and kidnapper. Her brief crush wasn't anything to be embarrassed about. With Kasimir's chiseled good looks, electric-blue eyes and low, husky voice—and the sensual stroke of his practiced fingertips, rough against her skin—any woman would have felt wildly attracted. But her crush was over now. Her hands tightened. She wasn't going to let him stop her from doing what she needed to do.

But it couldn't hurt to be fortified with dinner before her escape. Her stomach growled. Calories would give her energy, which would give her ideas. Josie looked around for the dining tent. The sun was setting at a rapid pace.

A man in an indigo turban bowed in front of her. "Princess," he said in accented English.

Princess...? She blushed. "Oh. Yes. Hello. Could you please tell me where Kasimir—Prince Kasimir—might be?"

The man smiled then gestured across the encampment. "You go, yes? He waits."

"Yes, of course," she stammered. "I'll hurry."

Josie went in the direction he'd pointed. She wasn't sure she was going the right way, until she suddenly saw a path in the sand, illuminated by a line of torches in the dusk.

She followed the path, all the way up the spine of the tallest sand dune. At the top, she discovered a small table and two chairs on a Turkish carpet, surrounded by glimmering copper lanterns.

Kasimir rose from one of the chairs. "Good evening." Coming forward, he bent to kiss her hand. She felt the heat of his lips against her skin before he straightened to look at her with dark, sizzling blue eyes as he said huskily, "You look beautiful."

She gulped, pulling back her hand. "Thank you for the clothes, and the bath," she said weakly. "I hope you haven't been waiting long."

He gave her a warm smile that took her breath away. "You are worth waiting for."

Silhouetted in front of the red-and-orange twilight, Kasimir looked devastatingly handsome in the long Moroccan djellaba with its intricate embroidery on the edges and loose pants beneath. His head was bare, and the soft wind ruffled his black hair as he pulled back her chair. "Will you join me?"

Holding out her chair was such an old-fashioned, courtly gesture. And in this setting, with this particular man, it was extremely romantic. In spite of her best efforts, a tremble rose inside her. *I do not have a crush on him anymore,* she told herself firmly, but apparently her legs hadn't gotten the message, because they turned to jelly.

She fell into her chair. He pushed it back beneath the table, and as she felt his fingertips accidentally brush her shoulders, she couldn't breathe. She didn't exhale until he took his own seat across the small table.

"How lovely," she said, looking around them. "I never would have thought a table could be brought up here. It's enchanting...."

"Yes," he said in a low voice, looking at her. "Enchanting."

Their eyes locked in the deepening twilight, and spirals of electricity traveled down Josie's body to her toes, centering on her breasts and a place low and deep in her belly. Looking at the hard angles of his chiseled face, she felt uneasy. She suddenly wanted to lean across the table, to touch and stroke the rough dark stubble of his jawline, to run both her hands through his wind-tousled black hair....

What was she thinking? Nervously, she looked down at the flickering lanterns that surrounded the carpet. She was relieved to see four servants with platters of food coming up the path illuminated by torches in the dusk.

"I've ordered a special dinner tonight that I hope you'll enjoy," her captor said softly. "Would you care for some white wine?"

She gulped. "Sure," she said, trying to seem blasé, as if drinking wine in the Sahara with billionaire princes was something she did every day. Oh, good heavens. With her billionaire prince *husband.*

Pouring wine from a pitcher into a crystal-and-gold goblet, he handed it to her. Smoothly, she lifted it to her lips. She didn't much like the smell, but she took a big drink anyway.

Then she sputtered, and nearly choked. Making a face, she pulled the glass away from her lips.

"Don't you like it?" Kasimir asked in surprise.

"Like it?" She blurted out. "It tastes like juice that's gone bad!"

He laughed, shaking his head. "But Josie, that's exactly what wine is." He tilted his head, giving her a boyish grin. "Though I don't think the St. Raphaël winery will be using those exact words in their ads anytime soon. No wine, huh?"

"I didn't like it."

"I never would have guessed. You hide your emotions so well."

For an instant, they smiled at each other, and Josie's heart suddenly twisted in her chest. Then, turning away, he lifted his hand in signal. "I'll get you something you'll like better."

He spoke in another language—Berber?—to one of the servants, and the man left. After serving their dinner, the other three, too, departed, leaving Kasimir and Josie to enjoy a private dinner in the Sahara, beneath the shadows of red twilight.

"Ooh." Looking down at the table, Josie saw a traditional Moroccan dinner, full of things she loved: *tajine,* a zesty saffron-and-cumin-flavored chicken stew—pickled lemons and olives, carrot salad sprinkled with orange-flower water and cinnamon and couscous with vegetables. She sighed with pleasure. "You have no idea how often I ate at the Moroccan restaurant, trying to imagine what it would be like to travel here."

"How often?"

"Every time I got my hands on a half-off lunch coupon."

He grinned at her, then the smile slid from his face. His expression grew serious.

"So," he said in a low voice, "does that mean you forgive me? For bringing you here?"

She looked in shock at the vulnerability in his eyes. Something had changed in him somehow, she thought. The warm, generous man sitting across from her in exotic Moroccan garb seemed very different from the cold tycoon in a black suit she'd met in Hawaii. Had the desert really made him so different? Or was it just that she knew too much about the man behind the suit?

"I don't like that you lied to me about Bree," she said slowly. "Or that you brought me out here against my will. But," she sighed, taking a bite of the *tajine* as she looked at the sunset, "at the moment it's a little hard for me to be angry."

He swallowed. Reaching across the table, he briefly took her hand. "Thank you."

She shivered as their eyes met. Then he released her as the servant returned with a samovar of filigreed metal. He left it on the table in front of Kasimir, then disappeared.

"What's that?" Josie said, eyeing it nervously.

He smiled. "You'll enjoy it more than wine. Trust me."

She wrinkled her nose. "I'd enjoy anything more than that," she confessed.

"It's mint tea."

"Oh," she sighed in pleasure. She watched him pour a cup of fragrant, steaming hot tea. "This is kind of like a honeymoon, you know."

He froze. "What do you mean?"

"The bath with rose petals. This wonderful dinner. The two of us, in Morocco. It's like something out of a romantic movie. If I didn't know better, I would have thought…"

Whoa. She cut herself off, biting down hard on her lower lip.

He looked up from the samovar. "You'd have thought what?"

"You were trying to seduce me," she whispered.

His shoulders tightened, then he shrugged, giving her a careless smile belied by the visible tension in his body. "I could only dream of being so lucky, right?" He swept his arm over the horizon, over the tea and the lanterns, with a sudden playful grin. "You can see the tricks I'd use to lure you."

"And I'm sure they'd work," she said hoarsely, then added,

"Um, on someone else, I mean." Looking away quickly, she changed the subject. "How did you find this place?"

He set down the elegant china cup on the table in front of her. Sitting back in his chair, he took a sip of his own wine. "After Nina dumped me, I had the bright idea that I should go see every single place where I held mining options. After our partnership dissolved, I still held the mining rights in South America, Asia and Africa." He gave her a crooked smile. "Vladimir was happy to let those lands go. He didn't believe I'd ever find anything worth digging."

"But you proved him wrong."

"Southern Cross is now a billion-dollar company, almost as wealthy as his." His lips curved. "I left St. Petersburg with total freedom—no family, no obligations, almost no money, nothing to hold me back. Every young man's dream."

"It sounds lonely."

He took a drink from his crystal goblet. "I bought a used motorcycle and got out of Russia, crossing through Poland, Germany, France, Spain—all the way to the tip of Gibraltar. I caught a ferry south to Africa, then in Marrakech, I took roads that were barely roads—"

"You wanted to disappear?" she whispered.

He gave a hard laugh. "I did disappear. My tires blew up, my engine got chewed up by sand. I was dying of thirst when they—" he nodded towards the encampment "—found me. Luckiest day of my life." He took another gulp of wine. "They call this place the end of the world, but for me, it was a beginning. I found something in the desert I hadn't been able to find anywhere."

"What?"

He put his wineglass down on the table and looked at her. "Peace," he whispered.

For a moment, they both looked at each other, sitting alone on an island amid an ocean of sand in the darkening night.

"What would it take to make you give up the war with your brother?" Josie asked softly.

"What would it take?" His eyes glittered in the deepening shadows. "Everything that he cares about."

"It's just so…sad."

He looked at her incredulously. "You're sad? For him? For the man who took your sister?"

She shook her head. "Not for him. For you. You've wasted ten years of your life on this. How much more time do you intend to squander?"

He finished off his wine in a gulp. "Not much longer now."

The brief, cold smile on his face made her shiver. "There," she breathed. "That smile. There's something you're not telling me. What is it?"

Kasimir stared at her for a long time, then turned away. "It's not your concern."

She watched the flickering shadows from the lanterns move like red fire against his taut jaw. He clearly wanted to end the subject. *Fine,* she told herself. What did she care if Kasimir wasted his life on stupid revenge plots? She didn't care. She *didn't.*

She bit her lip, then said hesitantly, "Is hurting your brother really more important to you than having a happy life yourself?"

"Leave it alone, Josie," he said harshly.

Josie knew she should just be quiet and drink her mint tea but she couldn't stop herself from replying in a heated tone, "Maybe if you just talked to him, explained how he'd hurt you—"

"He'd what, apologize?" Kasimir ground out. "Give me back my half of Xendzov Mining, wrapped in a nice gold bow?" His lips twisted. "There must be limits even to your optimism."

She looked up quickly, her cheeks hot. "You keep telling

me to be honest, to be brave and bold, but what have you done lately that was any of those things?"

He looked at her.

"If I weren't bound by my vow," he said, "I'd do the bravest, boldest, most honest thing I can think of. And that's kiss you."

She sucked in her breath.

Exhaling, Kasimir looked up, tilting his head back against his chair. "Look at the stars. They go on forever."

Josie stared at him, her lips tingling, her heart twisting in her chest. Then she slowly followed his gaze. He was right about the stars. They had never looked so bright to her before, like twinkling diamonds above a violet sea. Looking at them, she felt so small, and yet bigger, too, as if she were part of something infinite and vast.

"You really want to kiss me so badly?" she heard herself say in a small voice.

"Yes."

"And it's not just because I'm—handy?"

He groaned. "I never should have said that. I knew I was wrong to kiss you. I was trying to act like it was no big deal." His lips quirked upward. "Hoping maybe you wouldn't notice that it was."

Her own lips trembled. "Oh, I noticed."

Their eyes locked across the table. As they faced each other, alone in the desert, the full moon had just lifted above the horizon. The world seemed suspended in time.

"But why me?" she choked out. "You could kiss any woman you wanted. And we both agreed I'm not your type...."

Tilting his head, Kasimir looked at her. "You keep talking about my type. What is my type?"

She looked down at her plate, which had been filled with enough *tajine* and bread for your average Moroccan lumberjack. It was now empty—and just a moment ago, she'd been considering going back for seconds. She bit her lip. "She's thin and fit. She spends hours at the gym and rarely eats anything at all."

He gave a slow nod. "Go on."

Josie looked down at her linen trousers and plain cotton blouse that had felt so good, but now seemed dowdy and dumpy. "She's very glamorous. She wears tight red dresses and six-inch stiletto heels." She ran a hand over her ponytail. "She has her hair styled every single day in a top salon." She pressed her bare lips together. "And she wears makeup. Black eyeliner and red lipstick."

He gave her a crooked smile. "Yes. Even when I wake up beside her in bed, her lipstick is perfectly applied."

"What, you mean when you wake up in the morning?" Josie blinked, pulled out of her reverie. "How is that even possible? Do magic makeup fairies put lipstick on her in the middle of the night or something?"

He lifted a dark eyebrow. "Obviously, she gets up early, to freshen up her makeup and hair before I wake up."

Josie dropped her fork with a clang against her plate. "Sheesh! What a waste of time!" She thought of how much she loved sleeping in on mornings she didn't have to work. And if she happened to be sharing a bed with a man—a man like Kasimir—there surely would be better ways to wake up. Not that she would know. Her cheeks flared with heat as she pushed away the thought. She scowled, folding her arms. "You would never know the flaws of a woman like that. So long as she's wearing lots of lipstick and a tight red dress, you don't really know her at all."

Kasimir stared at her in the moonlight.

"You're right," he said softly. "And that's why I want you."

Josie dropped her folded arms. "What?"

"More than I've ever wanted any woman." He sat forward in his chair, his eyes intense. "I know your flaws. They're part of what makes you so beautiful."

She swallowed, looking down as she mumbled, "I'm dowdy and frumpy."

"You don't need sexy clothes for your natural, effortless beauty."

"I'm a klutz." She looked down at her empty plate, feeling depressed. "And I eat too much."

"You eat the exact right amount for your perfect body."

"My what?" She gasped out a laugh, even as her throat ached with pain. "You don't have to sugarcoat it. I'm chubby."

"Chubby?" He shook his head. "You drove me insane in your wedding dress. You taunted me in that sliver of white lace, teasing me with little flashes of your breasts and thighs until I thought I'd go mad." Standing up, he walked around the table. "You have the type of figure that men dream about," he said quietly. "And if you haven't noticed, I'm a man."

Kasimir stood over her now, so close their bodies almost touched. Her body sizzled as her lips parted.

"But I'm plain," she whispered. "I'm naive and silly. I blurt out things no one cares about."

He knelt beside her chair. "Your beauty doesn't come from a jar." He took her hand gently in his own. "It comes from your heart."

His palm and fingertips were warm and rough against hers. And Josie suddenly realized that he wasn't just being courteous. He wasn't trying to give compliments to an honored guest. He wasn't even flirting, not really.

He actually believed what he was saying to her.

A lump rose in her throat. How she'd longed to hear those words from someone, anyone, let alone a devastatingly handsome man like Kasimir....

But she couldn't let herself fall for it. *Couldn't.* She swallowed. Her voice was hoarse as she said, "I'm nothing special."

"Are you joking?" His hand tightened over hers. "How many women would have spent their last money to cross an ocean—and agree to marry a man like me—just to save an older sister who's perfectly capable of taking care of herself?"

Josie's whole body was shaking. With an intake of breath, she pulled away. "Anyone would have—"

"You're wrong." He cut her off. "And that is what's different about you. You're not just brave. Not just strong. You don't even know your own power. You are—" he kissed the back of her hand, causing a flash of heat across her body as he whispered "—an elemental force."

Her body felt as if it was on fire. A breeze blew through the desert night, cooling her skin. Her heart pounded in her chest. She looked up at him.

The wind caught at his black hair, blowing it against his tanned skin, against his high cheekbones that looked chiseled out of marble in the silver moonlight and flickering glow of the lanterns.

"Now do you understand? Now do you believe?" he said softly. "I want you, Josie. Only you."

He reached out to stroke her cheek, and the sensuality of that simple touch caused her whole body to shake. Against her will, her gaze dropped to his mouth. Could she…? Did she dare to…?

Kasimir's hand dropped.

"But I will be true to my word. And I am almost glad you bound me by it." He gave her a small, wistful smile. "Because we both know that you are far too good for a heartless man like me."

Searching his gaze, she swallowed. "Kasimir—"

His expression shuttered. "You are tired." Rising to his feet, he held out his hand. "I will take you back to the tent."

But Josie didn't feel tired. Every sense and nerve in her body was aware of the stars, the night, the desert. From a distance, she could hear the call of night birds. She breathed in the exotic scent of spice on the soft warm wind. She'd never felt so alive before. So awake.

Because of him.

Kasimir's handsome face was frosted by moonlight, giving his black hair and high cheekbones a hard edge of silver. He looked like a prince—or a pirate—from a far-off time. Euphoria sang through her body, through her blood. *Like an elemental force.*

As if in a trance, Josie reached for his hand. Without a word, he led her down the sand dune towards the encampment. She was distracted by the feel of his hand against hers, by the closeness of his powerful body. Her feet were somehow as sure-footed as his as they walked lightly over the sand, down past the flickering torches blazing through the night, illuminating their path.

Kasimir led her into his private tent. They faced each other, and as they stood beside the enormous four-poster bed, which suddenly seemed to dominate the luxurious tent, Josie's knees felt weak. Her lips felt dry, her heart was pounding.

He looked down at her with smoldering eyes, as if only a hair's breadth kept him from pushing her back against the bed and covering her body with his own. As if some part of him were waiting—praying for her to say the magic words: *Kasimir, I release you from your promise.*

Josie clenched her hands into fists at her sides. And, in a supreme act of will, stepped back from him.

"Well," she choked out. "Good night."

He tilted his head, frowning. "Good night?"

"Yes," she stammered. "I mean, thank you for our wedding night. I mean, our wedding feast. It was delicious. I'll never forget how you tasted—I mean, how the *tajine* tasted." *Oh, for heaven's sake.* Squaring her shoulders, she cried out, "But good night!"

"Ah." His sensual mouth curved at the edges. He took a step towards her. Josie almost lifted her arms to push him away. That was surely the reason she yearned to put her hands against his chest, to touch the powerful plane of his muscles through his djellaba and see if they could possibly be as hard as they looked. "Josie," he murmured, "I don't think you understand." He leaned his head down towards her with a gleam in his eye. "This is my private tent."

She licked her lips. "And you're giving it to me as your guest? No." She shook her head. "I couldn't possibly accept. I'm not kicking you out of your bed."

"Thank you." His eyebrow lifted as he said evenly, "And I'm not going to allow you to run away."

"What?" She jumped, flushed with guilt. "What makes you think I'm planning to run away?"

He put his hand over his heart in an old-fashioned gesture, even as his eyes burned through her. "If you run out into the desert alone, you will die in the sand."

She swallowed nervously. "I would never..."

"Then give me your word." In the dim light of the tent, lit by only a single lantern, his gaze seemed to see straight through her soul. He put his hand on her cheek.

"My word?" she echoed softly.

"As I gave you mine. Not just a promise. But your sacred word of honor—" his eyes met hers "—that you won't try to leave."

She sucked in her breath, knowing what a word of honor meant—to both of them. Her cheeks were burning as she licked her lips. "What would be the point? Do you really think I'm that much of an idiot to—"

"I think you are an incurable optimist. And when it comes to people you love, you make reckless decisions with your heart. I cannot allow you to put yourself at risk. So I intend to sleep here. With you. All night."

"Here?" she squeaked. She frantically tried to regroup, to think of a way she could still try to escape. Maybe if she waited until he was deeply asleep in the middle of the night... She licked her lips. "So you're going to sleep where—on those pillows? Or on the carpet, across the doorway of the tent?"

"Sorry. I'm not sleeping on the floor." Coming closer to her, he smoothed a tendril of hair off her face, looking down at her with something like amusement. "Not when I have a nice big bed."

She furrowed her brow, then with an irritated sigh, she rolled her eyes. "You mean after all that song and dance about me being your honored guest, you want the bed, while I get the floor?" She folded her arms, scowling.

Then she saw a spot on the floor not too far from the door. He was actually doing her a favor. She brightened. This would be almost too easy! Looking up, she saw his suspicious, searching glance, and tried to rearrange her own face back into a glower. She tossed her head, pretending she was still really, really mad. "Fine. I'll sleep on the floor like a prisoner. Whatever."

"I'm afraid that solution is also unacceptable," Kasimir said gravely, looking down at her with his midnight-blue eyes. "There is only one way I can make sure you do not try to sneak out in the night the moment I am asleep."

She stared at him in dawning horror.

"We are going to share this bed," he said huskily.

CHAPTER SIX

"No way!" Josie exploded. "I'm not sharing a bed with you!"

She folded her arms and stuck out her chin, glaring at Kasimir in a way that told him everything he needed to know.

He'd been right. She'd been planning to escape.

Narrowing his eyes, Kasimir folded his arms in turn and glared right back at her. "If I cannot trust you, I will keep you next to me all night long."

She now looked near tears. "You're being ridiculous!" She unfolded her arms. "Can't you just trust me not to escape?"

His eyebrow lifted. "Sure. I told you. All you need to do is give me your word of honor."

Her eyes widened, and then her shoulders sagged as she looked away.

"I can't," she whispered.

Kasimir brushed back some long tendrils of light brown hair that had escaped her ponytail. "I know."

Her brown eyes were bright with misery as she looked back at him. "How did you guess?"

"Ah, *kroshka*." He looked down at her trembling pink lips, at her cheeks that were rosy with emotion. "I can see your feelings on your face." His jaw tightened. "But you saw how deep we are in the desert. Even with your reckless optimism, you cannot think that running away on foot in the middle of the night is a good idea."

"That wasn't my plan," she mumbled.

"If you try to flee, you'll die. You'll be swallowed up by the desert and never be found again."

Her shoulders slumped further, and she wouldn't meet his eyes. "I wouldn't…" She took a deep breath, then lifted her eyes, shining with unshed tears that hit him like a knife beneath his ribs. "I just can't share a bed with you," she whispered.

His hands clenched.

"Damn you, can't you understand?" He had to restrain himself from shaking her. "It's either share a bed with me, or I'll tie you up as you were before, and leave you to sleep on the floor!"

She didn't answer.

"Well?" he said sharply.

"I'm thinking!"

He exhaled, setting his jaw. "I'm not going to seduce you. Surely you know that by now. What more can I do to prove it to you?"

"You don't have to do anything," she said in a small voice. "I believe you."

"Then what are you so afraid of?"

She looked at him in the dim light of the flickering lantern as they stood alone together in his tent.

"But what if I touch you?" she whispered.

Kasimir's whole body went hard so fast he nearly staggered back from the intensity of his desire. He held his breath, staring down at her as he choked out, "You—"

"Just accidentally, I mean," she said, her cheeks red. "I might roll over in bed in the middle of the night and put my arms around you while I'm sleeping. Or something. You might wake up and, well, get the wrong idea…"

The wrong idea? Kasimir's mind was filled with dozens of ideas, and all of them seemed exactly *right*. He looked at the way she was chewing her full, pink lower lip. A habit of hers. He wanted to lean forward and taste its sweetness for himself. To part her mouth with his own and stroke deep inside with his tongue. To push her back against the blue cushions of the bed, to feel her naked skin against his, and bury himself deep inside her.

"Well, would you?" she said awkwardly. "Or would you know it was all...an innocent mistake?"

Kasimir cleared his throat, forcing the seductive images of her from his mind. "You don't need to worry," he said, hoping she didn't notice the hoarseness of his voice. "I do not make a habit of pouncing on virgins in the middle of the night."

She stared at him, then gave him a sudden, irrepressible smile that caused a dimple in her cheek. "Why? Is there some other time you prefer to do it?"

She was teasing him! His lips parted in surprise, then he gave a low laugh, shaking his head. "For your information, I've never been anyone's first lover."

Josie blinked. "Ever?"

"No," he said softly. "You were my first 'first' kiss."

"I was?"

"And I've changed my mind," Kasimir said in a low voice. "I'm not sorry about kissing you. Because I'll never forget how it felt."

For an instant, they looked at each other in the flickering light.

"Nor will I," she whispered.

The night wind shook noisily against the canvas of the tent, and he forced himself to turn away. "Change for bed."

"Change clothes in the same tent? Forget it!"

"You can change behind the screen. I won't look."

"Can't you please wait outside?"

"And give you the chance to run off in the dark? No."

"But I don't have a nightgown." She choked out a nervous laugh. "Am I supposed to sleep naked?"

Naked. He squeezed his eyes shut, imagining the full, bare curves of her naked body, hot and smooth beneath his hands.

He shuddered, his body aching. He realized he had clenched his hands again. His fists were as hard as the rest of him.

Stop it, he ordered his body, which ignored him. He exhaled.

"Look in that trunk." He waved his hand behind him without looking towards her. "Over there. They should fit."

"Really? Thanks." He heard her go to the trunk and dig through it before she went towards the wooden screen painted with designs of flowers. "I guess I owe you."

"You can pay me back by not getting yourself killed," he growled, still not turning around. "What was your plan of escape, anyway?"

"My plan?" When he heard her voice muffled behind the screen, he knew it was safe to turn around. He saw her arms lifting over the top of the painted wooden panels as she pulled off her shirt. She tossed it over the screen, followed by the white lacy bra he'd given her. He swallowed, feeling hot. She gave a low laugh. "You're right, it was completely stupid. I hadn't figured out the exact details, but I was going to steal a horse from your pen, fling myself on it and ride bareback into the sunset."

"Do you have experience with horses?"

"Absolutely none." She tossed her pants over the top of the screen with a merry laugh. "Now that I'm considering my plan in a more rational light, I'm kind of relieved you figured it out."

Josie was naked behind the screen—or nearly so, just wearing the lacy white panties he'd had purchased for her in Marrakech. He tried not to think about it. Because in a moment, they'd be lying beside each other in his big bed.

He had the sudden feeling that it was going to be a long night.

"Pretty nightgown," she mused behind the screen. "And modest, too."

He was grateful for that, although in his current state of

mind he knew he'd be aroused by her even if she was covered from head to toe. Turning away, he pulled off his djellaba, leaving his chest bare, wearing only his lightweight, loose-fitting pants. "Just so you know," he said, "I generally sleep in the nude."

He heard her gulp.

"But not tonight," he said quickly.

"Good." She breathed an audible sigh of relief. "I've never seen a naked man before, and tonight doesn't seem like the time to start."

He couldn't even disguise the hoarseness of his voice this time. "Never?"

Lifting on her tiptoes, she peeked over the screen, looking at him over the painted wooden panels. Her eyes lingered over his bare chest as she purred, "Never."

Kasimir didn't breathe till she ducked back behind the screen. Her arms lifted as she pulled the nightgown over her head. The loose fit of his pants had never felt so uncomfortably tight before.

"Is it safe to come out?" she called.

"Safe as it will ever be," he muttered.

Josie came around the screen in a silver silk nightgown, bias-cut in a retro style, which went to her ankles, but left her arms bare. "Thanks for this. It's very retro. Nineteen forties."

"I told my staff to ransack the vintage shops, and avoid designer boutiques. Warned them not to get all 'fancy.'"

"I love this." She stroked the silk over her belly. "It's... soft."

His fingers itched to discover that for himself. He didn't let himself move. "Glad you approve."

Their eyes met. His forehead broke out into a sweat. At the same moment, they both abruptly turned towards the water basin, causing their hands to brush.

Josie ripped back her hand as if he'd burned her. "You go ahead."

"No, be my guest."

"All right." Keeping a safe distance, she quickly washed her face and brushed her teeth, then walked a semi-circle around him towards the bed. She was afraid to touch him, which meant she felt the same electricity, after all. Knowing she wanted him made this all the harder.

Or maybe it was just him.

As he brushed his teeth, out of the corner of his eye he watched her climb into bed, watched the silk of her nightgown move as sensuously as water over her curves. Putting down his toothbrush, he splashed cold water on his face, wishing he could drench his whole body with it.

Josie hesitated, biting her lip prettily as she glanced at him. "Do you care which side—"

"No," he ground out.

She frowned. "You don't have to be so rude..."

He looked at her, and something in his face made her close her mouth with a snap. Without another word, she jumped into bed and pulled the covers all the way up to her chin.

"Ready." Her voice was muffled.

He put out the flickering lantern light. Stretching his tight shoulders, he climbed in beside her. They each took opposite sides of the bed in the darkness, neither of them moving as the wind howled against the canvas roof.

"Kasimir?" her soft voice came from the darkness a moment later. "What will you do...when all this is over?"

"You mean our marriage?"

"Yes."

He leaned his head back against the pillow, folding his arms beneath his head. "I'll have everything I ever wanted."

"You mean the land?"

He exhaled with a flare of nostril. "Among other things."

"But you're not planning to live in Alaska, are you?"

Live at the old homestead? He inhaled, remembering nights sharing the cold attic room with his brother. Remembering the constant love of his hardworking parents, and how he'd bounded up eagerly each morning to start his chores.

As a boy, Kasimir had felt so certain of what mattered in the world. Home. Family. Loyalty.

"No, I won't go back," he said quietly.

"Then why do you want it so badly? Just because of your promise to your father?"

"It was a deathbed vow…" He stopped. He'd told himself that same lie for years, but here in the darkness, lying in bed beside her, he couldn't tell it again. "Because I don't want Vladimir to have it. He doesn't deserve a home. Or a brother."

"What about you?" Josie said softly. "What do you deserve?"

Kasimir looked away from her, towards his briefcase, which looked distinctly out of place in the corner of the tent. "Exactly what I will get," he said. Retribution against his brother and the Mata Hari who'd caused their rift. Total ownership of both Xendzov Mining and Southern Cross. That would make him happy. Give him peace.

It would. It had to. Looking at her shadowy form in the darkness, he turned the question back on her. "What will you do? With your life?"

"I don't know." She swallowed. "Bree always talked about sending me to college, but even if we had the money, I'm not sure that's what I want."

"Why not? You'd be good at it."

She gave a regretful laugh. "Bree should have been the one to go. She's a planner. A striver. Though she dropped out of high school to help support me." He could hear the self-blame in her voice. Then she laughed again. "But maybe she was glad. She was impatient with school. She's always had an eye to the bottom line. If not for those old debts threatening us, she'd be running her own business by now."

"I didn't ask about Bree's dreams," he said roughly. "I asked about you. What do *you* want?"

She paused. "You're going to think it's stupid."

"Nothing you want is stupid," he said, then snorted. "Except maybe stealing my horse and riding off alone into the desert."

"Not one of my best ideas," she admitted. For a long moment, they lay silently beside each other in the darkness. Kasimir started to wonder if she'd fallen asleep, then she turned in the darkness. Her voice was muffled as she said, "I never really knew my mother. She died a month after I was born. She was supposed to start chemo, then found out she was pregnant. She didn't want to put me at risk."

"She loved you."

Her voice trembled. "She died because of me," she said softly. "When I was growing up, my father and Bree were always away on their moneymaking schemes. I was mostly alone in a big house, left with a babysitter who got paid by the hour."

Kasimir's heart ached as he pictured Josie as a child—even more tenderhearted and vulnerable than she was now—feeling alone, unwanted, unloved.

"And from that moment, even as a kid, I knew what I wanted someday. And it wasn't college. It wasn't even a career."

"What is it?" he said in a low voice.

He heard her shuddering intake of breath.

"I want a home," she whispered. "A family of my own. I want to bake pies and do piles of laundry and weed our garden behind the white picket fence. I want an honest, strong husband who will never lie to me, ever, and who will play with our kids and mow our lawn on Saturdays. I want a man I can trust with my heart. A man I can love for the rest of my life." She stopped.

Kasimir's heart lurched violently in his chest. For a moment, he couldn't speak.

"See?" she said in a voice edged with tears. "I told you it was stupid."

He exhaled.

"It's not stupid," he said tightly. For a moment, he closed his eyes. Then he slowly turned to face her in the darkness. His vision adjusted enough to see her eyes glimmer with tears in the shadows of the bed.

I want an honest, strong husband who will never lie to me. A man I can trust with my heart.

Kasimir suddenly envied him, Josie's future husband, whoever he might be. He would deserve her, give her children, provide for her. And she would love him for the rest of her life. Because she had that kind of loyalty. The kind of heart that could love forever.

The irony almost made him laugh. Kasimir envied her next husband. Because even though he was married to her now, Kasimir couldn't be that man. He wasn't her partner, or even her lover. Not even, really, her friend.

But he could be.

"After I pay you for the land," he said, "you and your sister will be free of those old debts. You'll be able to pursue your dreams." He ignored the lump in his throat. "Whatever they might be."

"You're going to pay me?" she gasped. "I thought our deal was just a direct trade—the land for my sister."

"And I always intended to pay you full market value," he lied.

He heard her intake of breath. "Really?" she said wistfully.

No. He'd pay her double the market value. "Yes."

"You don't know what this means to me," she choked out. "We won't have to hide from those men anymore. We'll be free. And if there's any money left after the debts, Bree could use it to start her bed and breakfast."

"Is that what will make you happy?" he said. "Using the money so your sister can fulfill her dreams?"

"Yes!" she cried. "Oh, Kasimir..." He felt her hand against his rough, unshaven cheek, turning him towards her. He saw the tearful glitter of her eyes. "Thank you. You are—you are..."

With a joyful sob, she threw her arms around him.

Kasimir's arms slowly wrapped around her as her silken negligee slid against the bare skin of his chest. Their bodies pressed together in the bed, and as he felt her soft body against his own, he became all jumbled inside, twisted up and down and turned around.

He put his hand against her cheek. "Josie..." he said hoarsely.

In the shadowy tent, beneath the covers of the bed, he could see her beautiful eyes. He could barely hear her ragged breathing over the pounding of his own heart.

Her skin felt so soft beneath his fingertips. Her arms were bare and wrapped around his naked back. Their faces were inches apart. He wanted to kiss her, hot and hard and deep. He wanted to take her and let his promises fade like mist into the night.

Using every bit of willpower he possessed, he dropped his hand. He pulled away, rolling to the farthest edge of his bed.

"Good night," he choked out.

Silence fell. Then she said softly behind him, "Good night."

Kasimir heard her move to the other side of the bed. He exhaled, closing his eyes. He could still see her beautiful, innocent face, her curvaceous body sheathed in diaphanous silk, shimmering like waves in the flickering light.

He listened to the wind blowing against the tent, the distant whinny of horses, the call of servants' voices across the encampment. And he still heard Josie's voice, sweet and innocent, filled with the trembling edge between desire and fear.

But what if I touch you? she'd asked.

Kasimir didn't have to touch her to feel her. Lying next to her in the soft bed, with blankets warming them in the cool, arid night, there was a desert of empty space between them, but her slightest tremble was an earthquake.

In just a few weeks, once her land was his, Kasimir would trade her for what he wanted most. He would seize control of Xendzov Mining. He'd get justice against those who'd wronged him. He'd finally win.

He should be glad. Excited. His teeth should have been sharpening with anticipation.

But as he listened to Josie's soft, even breathing, all he could think about was what he would soon lose.

He glanced over at her in the darkness. She didn't care about vengeance or money. She wanted to give away her fortune to make her sister happy. She gave everything she had, without worrying if she'd get anything back in return. She didn't even try to protect her heart.

Thank you, Kasimir. He remembered the joy in her voice when she'd thrown her arms around him. *You are...you are...*

He was a selfish bastard with a jet-black heart. He'd kissed her, kidnapped her, kept her prisoner, but she kept forgiving him, again and again.

Rolling onto his back, Kasimir stared up bleakly at the swoop of the tent's canvas, gray with shadow.

Was there some way to keep her in his life? Some way to bind her to him so thoroughly that she'd have no choice but to forgive him the unforgivable?

Two days later, Josie stared up at him with consternation. "You have to be joking."

"Come on," Kasimir wheedled, holding out his hand beneath the hot afternoon sunshine. "You said you wanted to do it."

Glancing back at the tallest sand dune, she licked her lips. "I said it looked fun in theory."

"You know you want to." Wind ruffled his tousled black hair as he smiled down at her. He was casually dressed, in a well-worn black T-shirt that hugged his muscular chest and large, taut biceps and low-slung jeans on his hips. He looked relaxed and younger than she'd ever seen him. He lifted a dark eyebrow wickedly. "You're not scared, are you?"

Josie licked her lips. When he looked at her with that mischievous smile, he made her want to agree to absolutely anything.

But—this?

Furrowing her brow, she looked behind her. Three young Berber boys, around twelve or thirteen years old, were using brightly colored snowboards to careen down the sand, whooping and hollering in Berber, the primary language of the tribe, but the boys' joyous laughter needed no translation.

Josie and Kasimir had been sitting outside the dining tent, lazily eating an early dinner of grapes, flatbread and lamb kabobs, when the boys had started their raucous race. As Josie sipped mint tea, with Kasimir drinking a glass of Moroccan rosé wine beside her, she'd said dreamily, "I wish I could do what they're doing. Be fearless and free."

To her dismay, Kasimir had immediately stood up, brushing sand off his jeans. "So let's go."

Now, he was looking at her with challenge in his eyes. "I have an extra sandboard. I'll show you how."

She scowled. "You know, saying something looks fun and being brave enough to actually do it, are two totally different things!"

"They shouldn't be."

"It looks dangerous. Bree would never let me do it."

"Another good reason."

Josie stiffened. "I wish you would quit slandering Bree—"

"I don't care about her," he interrupted. "I care about *you*. And what you want. Your sister isn't here to stop you. I'm not going to stop you. You say you want to do it. The only one stopping you is you."

She looked up at the dune. It was very tall and the sand looked very hard. She licked her lips. "What if I fall?"

He lifted an eyebrow. "So what if you do?"

"The kids might laugh, or—" she hesitated "—you might."

"Me?" He stared at her incredulously. "Is that a joke? You'd let fear of my reaction keep you from something you want?" His sensual lips lifted as he shook his head. "That doesn't sound like the Josie I know."

She felt a strange flutter in her heart. Kasimir thought she was brave. He thought she was bold.

And she was, when she was with him. She barely recognized herself anymore as the downtrodden housekeeper she'd been in Hawaii. Tomorrow was New Year's Eve, but for Josie, the New Year—her new life—had already begun.

She'd be able to pay off their debts. She hugged the thought to her heart like a precious gift. They'd be free of the dark cloud of fear that had hung over them for ten years, forcing them to stay under the radar with low-paying, nondescript jobs. Bree would be able to start her business. Josie would never feel like a burden again to anyone.

But it would come at a cost. Josie looked up at Kasimir. He could be a rough man, selfish and unfeeling, and yet beneath it all…he truly was a good man. His generosity would change her life.

But she would never see him again. And that thought was starting to hurt. Because she couldn't kid herself.

She'd stopped thinking of their marriage as a business arrangement long ago.

Yesterday, Kasimir had taught her how to ride a horse. Very patiently, until she lost her fear of the big animals' teeth and sharp hooves, until she started to gain confidence. She was still a little sore from their ride that morning, traveling across the dunes to the nearest village, to bring medicine from Marrakech. As she and Kasimir galloped back together across the desert, his eyes had been as blue and bright as the wide Moroccan sky. She lost a new fragment of her heart every time he looked at her with that brilliant, boyish smile.

Just as he was looking at her now.

"Well?" His hand was still outstretched with utter confidence, as if he knew she would not be able to resist.

"Is it soft? Like powder?"

He laughed. "No. It'll leave bruises."

"Sounds fun," she muttered.

"Do you want to try it or not?"

She swallowed, then looked at the boys zooming down the sand dune at incredible speed, on boards lightly strapped to their feet. Heard their roars of laughter and delight. Maybe it wasn't hard. Maybe it was actually quite easy. All she had to do was make the choice.

Josie's eyes narrowed. She was done being afraid—of anything. Done living a life smaller than her dreams.

Holding her breath, she put her hand in his own.

He pulled her close. "Good," he said in a low voice. "Let's do it. Right now."

His face was inches from her own, and a tremble went through her that had nothing to do with fear. Every time Kasimir looked at her, every time he spoke to her, she felt her heart expand until she felt as if she was flying.

Let's do it. Right now.

His grip on her hand tightened. Then he abruptly turned away, disappearing into a nearby tent. And she exhaled.

It had been torture sleeping next to him the last two nights. She'd been so aware of him beside her, it was a miracle she'd gotten any rest at all. Especially the first night, when they'd been talking so late into the darkness, and he'd told her he meant to pay for her land. She'd been so ecstatic that she'd thrown arms around him. He'd held her so tightly, his eyes dark on hers, and for one moment, she'd thought, really thought, he might break his promise. And here was the really shocking thing...

She'd *wanted* him to.

Her lips had tingled as she'd waited breathlessly for him to lower his mouth savagely to hers and pull her hard against his body. She'd ached to stroke her hands down his hard, tanned chest, laced with dark hair. She'd yearned to feel his pure heat and fire. Her body still shook with the memory of how she'd wanted it. And looking at him, she'd known he felt the same.

But he'd hadn't touched her.

When he'd abruptly turned away, she'd felt bereft— disappointed. Almost heartbroken.

Which made no sense at all. She admired commitment to promises, didn't she? And while they'd been thrown together in a very intimate way, it wasn't as if they had—or ever would have—a real marriage.

She needed to keep reminding herself of that.

Kasimir returned to the table outside the dining tent. He had two snowboards hefted over his shoulders as if they weighed nothing. "Let's go."

Smiling, and far lighter on her feet, she led the way to the top of the dune.

"Like being faster than me, huh?" he said, quirking his eyebrow.

She grinned. "Absolutely."

"We'll see." He answered her with a wicked smile. "Sit down right here."

Obediently, Josie plunked back on the warm sand in her cotton button-down shirt and soft linen pants. As he knelt on the sand in front of her, in his form-fitting T-shirt and loose cargo shorts, she wondered how brave she could really be. He'd promised not to kiss her.

But there was no rule about her kissing him.

"You're going to love this," he said, pulling off her sandals.

She shivered. His hands brushed against the hollows of her bare feet, and her mouth went dry. "I'm sure," she murmured.

He was inches away from her. She could just lean forward

and kiss him. Press her lips against his. Could she do it? Was she brave enough?

Kasimir's blue eyes met hers, and he smiled. She wondered how she'd ever thought him cold in Honolulu. Here, he was warm and bright as the blazing desert sun. "Are you nervous?"

"Yes," she whispered, praying he couldn't guess why.

"Don't be."

She gave a soft laugh. "That's easy for you to say."

He placed her bare feet into the straps attached to the board. Standing up, he grabbed her hands and pulled her upright. Josie swayed a little, getting used to the balance. She hadn't been on a board in a long time. She tested the sand with a slight lean and twist. Without snow boots, the ankle support was nonexistent. Turning corners would be nearly impossible.

Kasimir stepped into his own modified snowboard, and his arm shot out to grab her when she started to tilt. "Ready?"

She felt a flash of dizzying heat with his hand on her arm. "Yes," she breathed. "I just need a second to build my courage."

"So." He gave her a slow-rising grin. "Are you interested in racing me?"

"Racing?" Josie looked dubiously over the edge of the dune. It wasn't as steep as some of the mountains she'd snowboarded in Alaska, but that was ten years ago. To say her skills were rusty was an understatement. And boarding down sand was going to be like sailing down a sheet of ice. "I'm not sure that's a good idea."

"I thought you said you liked being faster than me."

"I do."

"Then racing me should be right up your alley." His masculine grin turned downright cocky. "I'll even give you a head start."

Laughter bubbled up to her lips, barely contained. He clearly believed he would be faster. "Um. Thank you?"

"And if you win, you'll get a prize."

"What do you have in mind?"

"Your own private tent," he said recklessly. "For the rest of the time we're in the Sahara."

Her lips parted. Somehow that prize didn't excite her as much as it once would have. "And what about if you win?"

Kasimir looked down at her, and something in his glance made her hold her breath.

"You'll share my bed," he said softly, "and let me make love to you."

CHAPTER SEVEN

SHARE HIS BED?

Josie's lips parted, her heart beating frantically as she looked up at him.

Let him make love to her?

She'd been trying to build up enough courage to kiss him. What would it be like to have him make love to her?

With a shuddering breath, she looked up at him. "I thought you said our marriage was in n-name only."

"I changed my mind," Kasimir said huskily. "You know I want you. And I've come to enjoy your company. There's no reason we shouldn't be…friends."

"Friends who will divorce in a few weeks."

"We could still see each other." He looked at her. "If you want."

Her lips parted. "If *I* want?"

"I would very much like to still see you, after we are divorced." His blue eyes seared through her soul. "For as long as you are still interested in seeing me."

Josie sucked in her breath. For as long as *she* wished to see him? That would be forever!

She looked back over the edge of the dune. It didn't look so frightening anymore. Not with this new challenge. Not with her very virginity on the line.

But…

What about saving herself for love, for commitment, for a lifetime?

She looked back at him. Was Kasimir the man? Was this the time? Was this how she wanted to remember her first night, for the rest of her life?

Her heart pounded in her throat.

Should she let her husband take her virginity?

"Just so you know," she said hesitantly, "my babysitter taught me to snowboard."

"Even better." He gave her a cheeky grin. "So with your head start, you have pretty good odds."

She couldn't help but smile at his smug masculine confidence. "Bree's the gambler, not me."

He gave her a long look beneath the blazing white sun.

"Are you sure about that?" he said softly.

On the other end of the dune, with a loud shout, the boys pushed off again, going straight down, good-naturedly roughhousing and cutting in front of each other as they skidded down the sand.

Josie closed her eyes, took a deep breath, and made her choice.

"I'll do it."

"Excellent."

His blue eyes were beaming. He clearly expected that this would be no contest and that he would easily overtake her. He didn't know that the entirety of the choice was still hers. Would she let him beat her? Or not?

Before her courage could fail her, she breathed, "Just tell me when to go."

"One…two…three…*go!*"

Hastily, Josie tilted her snowboard and went off the edge, plummeting down the dune. Her body remembered the sport, even though her brain had forgotten, and her board picked up speed. For a glorious instant, she flew, and wild joy filled her heart—joy she hadn't felt for ten years.

Then she remembered: if she won, she would sleep alone.

And if she lost, *he would seduce her.*

Slow down, she ordered her feet, and though they protested, she made them turn, her body leaning to drag the board against sand as hard and glassy as ice. It was hard to slow down, when her body yearned to barrel down the dune, like the reckless child she'd once been.

"You'll never win that way," Kasimir called from the top, sounding amused. "Turn your feet to aim straight down."

Josie choked back a wry laugh. He had no idea how hard she was trying *not* to do that. A bead of sweat formed on her forehead from the effort of fighting her body's desire to aim the snowboard straight down and plummet at the speed of flight. Couldn't he tell? Couldn't he see she was actually forcing herself *not* to win?

"Ready or not…"

Behind her, he pushed off the top of the dune. Smiling, she looked up at him as he glided past her on his snowboard. She saw the joy in his face—the same as when they'd galloped together across the desert that morning.

"You are mine now, *kroshka!*" he shouted, and flew past her.

Let me fly fast, half her heart begged.

Let him seduce you, the other half cried.

Then Josie turned her head when she heard a scream at the bottom of the hill. One of the roughhousing boys had lost control and crashed into the other, sending the smaller one skidding down the hard sand in panicked yells. The smaller boy, perhaps twelve years old, had a streak of blood across his tanned face and a trail of red followed him across the pale sand.

Josie didn't think, she just acted. Her knees turned, she leaned forward and she flew down the hill. She had a single glimpse of Kasimir's shocked face as she flew right past him. But she didn't think about that, or anything but the boy's face—the boy who moments before had seemed like a reckless, rambunctious teenager, but who now she saw was barely more than a child.

She reached the bottom of the dune in seconds. Ten feet away from the boy, she twisted hard on her snowboard, digging in for a sharp stop, causing sand to scatter in a wide fan around the boy's friends, who were struggling up towards him. Josie kicked off her snowboard in a single fluid movement and leapt barefoot across the hot sand.

"Are you all right?" she said to the boy in English. His black eyes were anguished, and he answered in sobbing words she didn't understand.

Then she saw his leg.

Beneath the boy's white pants, now covered with blood, she saw the freakish-looking angle of his shin.

She blinked, feeling as though she was going to faint. Careful not to look back at his leg, she reached her arm around the boy's shoulders. "It'll be all right," she whispered, forcing her voice to offer comfort and reassurance. "It'll be all right."

"It's a compound fracture," Kasimir said behind her. She turned and got one vision of his strangely calm face, before he twisted around and spoke sharply in Berber to the other two boys. They scattered, shouting as they ran for the encampment.

Kasimir knelt in the sand beside her. He looked down at the injury. As Josie cuddled the crying boy, Kasimir spoke to him with incredible gentleness in his voice. The boy answered him with a sob.

Carefully, Kasimir ripped the fabric up to the knee to get a closer look at the break. Tearing off a corner of his own shirt, he pushed it into Josie's hand. "Press this just below the knee to slow down the blood."

His voice was calm. Clearly he was good in a crisis. She was not. She swallowed, feeling wobbly. "I can't—"

"You can."

He had such faith in her. She couldn't let him down. Still

feeling a bit green, she took a deep breath and pressed the cloth to a point above the wound as firmly as she could.

Rising to his feet, Kasimir crossed back across the sand and returned a moment later with his snowboard. Turning it over to the flat side, he dug sand out from beneath the boy and gently nudged the board beneath the injured leg. He ripped more long bits of fabric from his shirt, giving Josie a flash of his hard, taut abs before he bent to use the board as a splint.

The boy's parents arrived at a run, his mother crying, his father looking blank with fear as he reached out to hold his son's hand. Behind them another man, dark-skinned, with an indigo-colored turban, gave quick brusque orders that all of them obeyed, including Kasimir. Five minutes later, they were lifting the boy onto a makeshift stretcher.

Josie's knees shook beneath her as she started to follow. Kasimir stopped her.

"Go back to the tent," he said. "There's nothing more you can do." His lips twitched. "Can't have you fainting on us."

She swallowed, remembering how she'd nearly fainted at the sight of the boy's injury. "But I want to help—"

"You have," he said softly. He glanced behind him. "Ahmed's uncle is a doctor. He will take good care of him until the helicopter arrives." He pushed her gently in the other direction. "He'll be all right. Go back to the tent. And pack."

Josie watched anxiously as the boy was carried to the other side of the encampment. He disappeared into a tent, with Kasimir and the others beside him, and she finally turned away. Dazed, she looked down at her clenched hands and saw they were covered in blood.

Slowly, she walked back to the tent she shared with Kasimir. She went to the basin of water and used rose-scented soap to wash the blood off her hands. Drying her hands on a towel, she sank to the bed.

Go back to the tent. And pack.

She gasped as the meaning of those words sank in. She covered her mouth with her hand.

She'd won. By pure mischance, she'd won their race.

There would be no seduction. Instead, from this night forward, she'd be sleeping alone in a separate tent.

Once, Josie would have been relieved.

But now...

Numbly, she rose from their bed. Grabbing her backpack, she started to gather her clothes. Then she stopped, looking around the tent. Kasimir always dumped everything on the floor, in that careless masculine way, knowing it was someone else's job to follow after him and tidy up. Looking across the luxurious carpets piled thickly across the sand, Josie's eyes could see the entirety of her husband's day: the empty water bucket of solid silver. The hand-crafted sandalwood soap. His crumpled pajama pants. And in a corner, his black leather briefcase, so stuffed with papers that it could no longer be closed, none of which he'd glanced at even once since the day they'd arrived here.

In the distance, she heard a sound like rolling thunder.

Tears rose to her eyes, and she wiped them away fiercely. She didn't want to leave him. This was the place where they whispered secrets to each other in the middle of the night. The bed where, if she woke up in the middle of the night, she'd hear the soft sound of his breathing and go back to sleep, comforted that he was beside her.

No more.

When she was finished packing, she grabbed her mother's tattered copy of *North and South*. For the next hour as she waited, sitting on the bed, Josie tried to concentrate on the love story, though she found herself reading the same paragraph over and over.

Kasimir's footstep was heavy as he pushed aside the heavy cotton flap of the door. She looked up from her book, her heart fluttering, as it always did at the breathtaking masculine beauty of his face, the hard edge of his jawline, dark with five o'clock shadow, and the curved edge of his cheekbones. His blue eyes looked tired.

Setting down the book on the bed, Josie asked anxiously, "Is he going to be all right?"

"Yes." He went to the basin and poured clear, fresh water over his dirty hands. "His uncle put a proper splint on his leg. The helicopter just left to take them all to the hospital in Marrakech."

"Thank heaven," Josie whispered.

Kasimir didn't answer. But as he dried his hands, she saw the shadows beneath his eyes, the tightness of his shoulders.

Without a word, she came up behind him. Closing her eyes, she wrapped her arms around his body, pressing her cheek against his back until she felt his tension slowly relax into her embrace.

A moment later, with a shudder, he finally turned around in her arms to face her.

"You were the first to reach him," he said in a low voice. "Thank you."

Her eyes glistened with tears. "It was nothing."

Kasimir gave her a ghost of a smile. "You were much faster than I thought."

"I told you my father and Bree were gone a lot," she said in a small voice. "My babysitter was a former championship snowboarder from the Lower Forty-Eight."

"You grew up in Anchorage, didn't you?" He gave a low, humorless laugh. "Had a season pass at Alyeska?"

"Since I was four years old." She gave him a trembling smile. "If it's any consolation, I'm faster than Bree, too. She's horrible on the mountain. Strap skis or a snowboard on her feet and she'll plow nose-first into the snow."

"I'll keep that in mind."

"But you and I," she said quickly, "it was a close race…"

"Not even." He bared his teeth in a smile. "You won by a mile."

With an intake of breath, Josie searched his gaze. "Kasimir, you have to know that I never meant to—"

"And I see you've packed. Good." He glanced down at her backpack. "I'll show you to your new tent."

"Fantastic," she said, crestfallen. Against her will, she hungrily searched his handsome face, his deep blue eyes, his sensual lips. She didn't want to be away from him. *She didn't.* "If not for the accident," she said, glancing at him sideways, "the race could have ended very differently…"

"Josie, please," Kasimir growled. "Do not attempt to assuage my masculine pride. That would just add insult to injury." Picking up her backpack, he tossed it over his shoulder. "I'll send over your trunk of new clothes later. You'll likely only be here at the camp for another week or two."

"Just me? Not you?"

He set his jaw. "I'm going to go look for your sister."

"I thought you said it was too soon," Josie said faintly.

He gave her a smile that didn't quite reach his eyes. "I'll leave you and go get her. Both the things you wanted. It's your lucky day."

It was ending. He was leaving her. She thought of the time she'd wasted, longing for him to kiss her and doing nothing. Waiting—always waiting—with a timid heart!

"But you said you couldn't trust me. That if you brought back my sister early, I might demand a hundred million dollars for my land…"

He gave a hard laugh. "You're more trustworthy than anyone in this crazy, savage world. Including me." Grabbing her upper arms, he looked down at her. "Serves me right," he muttered. "I never should have tried to get around my promise."

"Take me with you."

His eyes widened, then he slowly shook his head. "It'll

be better...for your sake...for both of us...it's best that we separate."

"Separate," she echoed, feeling hollow.

"Until the land comes through."

She swallowed. "Until we divorce."

His lips curved into a humorless smile. "You know what, I'm almost glad I lost." He tucked a loose tendril of her brown hair behind her ear, then looked straight into her eyes. "Save yourself, Josie. For your next husband. For a man who can deserve you. Who can love you," he added softly.

Turning away, Kasimir started to walk towards the door.

"I intended to lose the race," she blurted out.

She heard his intake of breath. He slowly turned to face her.

"Why?" he asked in a low voice.

She gulped. She had to be brave. To tell the truth. And do it now. Now, without thinking about the risk or cost. Now.

Josie crossed the tent to him. Standing up on her tiptoes, she put her hands on his shoulders and looked straight into his startled blue eyes. "Because I wanted you to seduce me," she whispered.

And leaning forward, she kissed his lips.

So much for his brilliant intelligence. Kasimir had thought he was so smart, finding a loophole around his promise. Passing her in their race down the dune, he'd felt triumphant, his body tight, knowing he all but had her in his arms.

Then there was a scream, and she'd flown past him. She was such an accomplished snowboarder that she'd had no problem handling the textural differences between snow and sand. And she'd seen the source of the scream, the injured boy, half a second faster than he had. It was enough to make any man feel slow. Stupid and slow.

Which was exactly how Kasimir had felt pacing the tent of the boy's family as his uncle, a doctor trained in Marrakech, worked on the boy's ugly compound fracture with his limited instruments at hand. Kasimir had looked down at the sobbing boy, wishing he could do more than order a helicopter on his satellite phone, wishing they didn't have to wait so long, and most of all, dreading the long, jarring journey the boy would face traveling to the hospital in Marrakech.

After Ahmed was loaded on the helicopter with a stretcher, Kasimir had evaded the tearful thanks of Ahmed's family. Shoulders tight, he returned to the tent where Josie waited— not for his seduction, but for her freedom.

The whole afternoon, from start to finish, had left the acrid sourness of failure in his mouth.

And then—Kasimir had tasted the sweetness of Josie's lips against his.

She'd reached her hands around his shoulders, lifting up on her tiptoes, and he'd just stared down at her in shock, telling himself he was completely misreading the situation. Josie, the inexperienced virgin, wouldn't make the first move.

Why would she kiss him? He was a man who stood for nothing and no one. She was an angel who knew how to fly.

I intended to lose the race. Because I wanted you to seduce me.

He heard a soft sigh from the back of her throat. Saw her close her eyes. And she pressed her soft, trembling lips to his.

He didn't immediately respond. He was too amazed. But when she grew shy, and started to draw away, a growl came from the back of his throat. Closing his eyes, he roughly pulled her back against his body and returned her kiss with force, with all the passion and longing he'd tried so hard not to feel. He let himself feel it—all of it—and desire overwhelmed him as it never had before.

Her lips parted as he deepened the kiss. She returned his embrace awkwardly, hungrily. And it was the best kiss of his life.

Outside the tent, he heard the rising wind flapping and

rattling against the heavy waxed canvas. But he was lost in her. Her lips were so soft, her body so womanly, her soul so pure. As he ran his hands down her back, over her loose cotton shirt, he felt the press of her breasts against his muscled chest. Her brown hair now tumbled down her back in waves, tangling in his fingers.

It could have been hours or even days that he kissed her, standing with her in his arms, holding her body tightly against his own. He flicked her mouth lightly with his tongue, guiding her lips, teaching her to kiss. His tongue brushed against hers, luring her to explore further. With a sigh of pleasure, she leaned towards him, her arms tightening around his shoulders.

Josie. So reckless. So beautiful. She had such strange power. She made him want things he shouldn't want.... Made him feel things he didn't know he could still feel....

Lifting her into his arms, never ending their kiss, he carried her to the four-poster bed he'd shared with her in painful chastity for two nights. As he laid her back against the mattress, he looked down at her beautiful face.

"Tell me you don't want me," he said hoarsely. "Tell me to leave you be."

He held his breath, as if waiting for a verdict of his life or death. She shook her head slightly. His heart twisted.

Then her full, pink lips lifted into a tender smile. Her brown eyes shimmered, glowing with desire, and she reached up for him, pulling him down against her in clear answer.

He felt her body beneath him, and knew he'd never again suffer the agony of sleeping beside her without being able to touch her. Because nothing on earth would stop him from taking her now.

Cupping her face, he kissed her passionately, stretching her back against the bed. His hands moved up and down her body until he finally reached beneath her cotton shirt. He felt her trembling hands stroke his bare chest beneath his own ripped shirt, torn into bandages on the dune. Her satin-soft fingertips ran along his flat belly and bare chest, and he gasped at the amazing sensation. He kissed down her throat, and his fingers were suddenly clumsy as he tried to unbutton her shirt, finally popping off the buttons in his desperation to feel the warmth of her skin against his own.

Yanking her shirt off her body, he threw it to the carpet and was mesmerized by full breasts barely contained within a lacy black bra. He sucked in his breath. Distracted, he didn't notice her tugging on his T-shirt until suddenly it was pulled off over his head. He felt the exploratory touch of her fingertips over his flat nipples and down the light dusting of black hair that pointed like an arrow down his muscled body.

Josie. Was this really going to happen? His heart was in his throat as he looked down at her. Here, now?

Outside, the hot wind howled against the tent as he kissed her deeply, pushing her down beneath him, against the soft pillows. He cupped his hands over her bra, feeling the weight of her breasts beneath his hands. He pushed her legs apart with his knee, grinding himself slowly against her, with only fabric separating them. She trembled as he liberated one large breast completely from the bra, watching the rosy nipple pucker and harden beneath the warmth of his breath before he suckled her.

In a single movement, he unclasped the bra and tossed it aside. Leaning back over her, he felt her shiver as he slowly kissed down her neck. Pressing her full breasts together, he kissed the crevice between them, licking her skin.

He felt her fingers tangle in his dark hair as she gasped, clutching him to her. He kissed down to the soft curve of her belly, feeling her tremble, feeling the damp heat of her skin. He slowly pulled off her linen pants, lingering against her thighs and the secret hollow beneath her knees. He removed his cargo shorts. Wearing only his silk boxers, which at the moment were uncomfortably tight, he slid his hips between her legs. Instinctively, she swayed as he rocked himself against her, back and forth over her lacy black panties. He heard her intake of breath as her hands clutched his shoulders, holding him against her.

His lips lowered to suckle a full, pink nipple. He lightly squeezed her breast, pushing her nipple more deeply into his mouth. He heard her soft muffled gasp as he ran his tongue in a swirling motion, nibbling and sucking, as his hand toyed with the other nipple. And all the while, he was slowly grinding himself against her, with only the thin separation of silk between them.

Her hands suddenly gripped his hair. "Stop."

Kasimir sucked in his breath as he pulled back. His body ached as he held himself in check, looking down at her. It would kill him, but if she wanted him to stop....

Josie reached up, running her hands down his bare chest, to the edge of his silk boxers. She looked up, her cheeks red, her eyes bright. "I want to see you. To touch you."

He exhaled.

"Yes."

With tantalizing slowness, she ran her hands along the edge of the waistband, and then—*and then*—he held his breath as she reached beneath the silk. She stroked the hardness of his shaft, running her fingers along the ridges and tip.

He heard a low hoarse gasp, and realized it was his own. Her eyes were huge as they met his. And then...

She suddenly smiled.

It was a smug, feminine smile, full of infinite mystery and pride—as if she'd realized the depths of power she held over him, as she held him completely in her hands.

She pulled down the silk, revealing his body completely to her gaze. She ran her hand over him, exploring. His breathing became ragged. He closed his eyes. Her slightest touch made him wild. He felt as though he could explode at any moment...

No. His eyes flew open, narrowed. With a growl, he pushed her back against the bed. Pulling at her panties, he tugged them slowly down her legs and tossed them to the carpeted sand. He stroked her calves, her knees, then moved back upward, to her thighs. Gently, he pushed her legs apart.

He felt her tremble at being so exposed. She tried to close her knees.

"What are you doing?" she breathed.

"Surrender to me," he whispered. And he lowered his head.

First, he kissed her inner thighs. Then he moved higher. Holding her against the mattress, he stretched her legs wide. For a moment, he just allowed her to feel the warmth and sensation of his breath. Then, very slowly, he moved his kisses to the core of her pleasure. She abruptly stopped struggling.

He took a long, delicious taste. "Like honey," he murmured.

She gave a soft gasp beneath him. He licked her again, swirling his tongue lightly against her, then widening his tongue fully. He pushed a single thick fingertip an inch into her tight, wet core.

She cried out, writhing beneath him as she gripped the sheets. Licking her, sucking her hard nub, he thrust a second finger inside her gently, and she moved her hips unthinkingly, twisting in an agony of need. He lapped her with his tongue, swirling against her taut center, as he felt her tense up. Her back arched off the bed, higher, higher still, until she exploded with a scream of joy.

And just in time. His whole body was sweaty and aching from holding himself back. As she exploded in her pleasure, he could no longer wait. In a swift mindless movement, he drew back and positioned himself between her legs. Lowering his head, he kissed her mouth, and then thrust himself roughly inside her, sheathing himself deep, deep, deep.

CHAPTER EIGHT

JOSIE GASPED AGAINST his lips as he thrust inside her, and she felt an unexpected fleeting pain.

Still deep inside her, he did not move, allowing her to gently stretch to accommodate him. His mouth was motionless against hers in a suspended kiss as she grew accustomed to the now dulling pain. She barely heard the wind outside, or felt the soft mattress beneath her and the weight of him over her. She was overwhelmed by the huge feel of him inside her.

Then, keeping his body still, he flicked his tongue against hers, tantalizing her with a hot, seductive kiss as she grew accustomed to the thick feel of him, like silk and steel inside her. The pain receded, like a wave drawing back beneath her feet. He pressed his naked body over hers, cupping her face with one hand to kiss her more deeply, and her hand trailed down his shoulder to his back as pleasure began to build anew inside her.

She'd never known the pain would be so great—and yet so suddenly gone. She'd never known pleasure could be so intense, so explosive—and could just as suddenly begin again. Sex was a more intense experience than she'd ever imagined. It left her breathless and weak.

So did he.

Josie's heart raced, pounding frantically in her throat, as she looked up at his handsome, sensual face. She'd been bold and daring enough to tell him the truth, and this was her reward. *This*.

Their hot, naked bodies twisted and moved together, sweaty, hard, sliding. She ran her hands down his chest, feeling his hard muscles and taut hollows. His body felt as amazing as it looked. Pulling him down against her, she kissed his shoulder, tasting and nibbling the salt of his skin.

With a shudder, Kasimir pushed her back against the bed, kissing down her throat. She gasped, tilting her head.

He finally began to move inside her, riding her. He filled her in a way she'd never imagined, deeper with each thrust. Her hands scratched slowly down his back, finally clutching his hard backside. She felt new tension inside her, coiled to spring. She felt the tautness of his muscles, heard the hoarse pant of his breath, and knew he was fighting to keep his body under control.

And *she* was causing that. She was the one driving him wild with desire. Her. Plain, frumpy Josie.

But she wasn't that Josie anymore. He'd changed her. Or she'd changed herself. But either way, she'd become the woman she'd always known she was born to be. Brave. Reckless. Even a little wicked…

His eyes closed. His sensual lips parted in a silent gasp as he pushed inside her, filling her to the hilt, stretching her to the breaking point. He was trying not to hurt her, she realized. He was still holding himself back.

Reaching her arms around his shoulders, she dug her fingernails into his flesh and whispered, "Don't be afraid."

His eyes flew open. He looked down at her with a choked intake of breath.

Giving him a little smile, she ran her hand softly down his hard, muscular body. "Stop holding back."

A growl came from the back of his throat, ending in a hiss. Pushing her back hard against the bed, he pushed more roughly inside her, riding her faster and deeper.

Now it was deepening pleasure. Their intertwined bodies tangled in desperate passion, clutching each other tightly as her hips lifted to meet each explosive thrust. Josie heard the hot wind howling outside and didn't care if a sandstorm flung the tent up into the sky. She was already flying....

The new pleasure continued to soar, rising and surpassing the first. It was deeper and different and sharper than before. Clutching his shoulders, she hung on for dear life as the pleasure grew so big it was almost too much to bear. Finally, it exploded inside her. Sucking in her breath, she tossed back her head and screamed with joy, heedless of who might hear, as she fell, fell, fell, plummeting off the edge of reason.

In that same instant, she heard his low answering roar. He slammed inside her with one final deep thrust, gripping her tightly with a low hoarse shout.

His muscular, sweaty body was heavy as he collapsed on top of her. Rolling next to her on the bed, he clutched her to his heart. A smile traced Josie's lips as she closed her eyes, pressing her cheek against his chest. She felt changed, reborn in his arms. She'd been born to be his wife....

It could have been minutes later, or hours, when Josie's eyes flew open in the darkness. She realized she hadn't just given her virginity to Kasimir tonight.

She'd given him her heart.

So this was how it was to fall in love. In all the books she'd read, all the movies she'd seen, she'd dreamed and wondered how it would be. What it would feel like, when she gave herself to a man completely.

It was like this. Overwhelming. Powerful. Sweet and full of longing. But also...

Terrifying.

Because loving him was an astoundingly simple thing to do. She'd been dazzled by him from the moment they'd met. Infatuated before they were wed. But now...she was in love. Truly and deeply in love for the first time.

Josie swallowed, slowly turning to look at the handsome face of the man sleeping beside her. One side of his face was turned toward the silver moonlight glowing softly through the white canvas. The other side of his face was in shadow, dark and harsh.

And that was Kasimir's soul. This was the man she'd given herself to—body and heart. The man she loved had one side filled with light. This side encouraged, protected, demanded, respected. He was strong and calm in a crisis; he'd rushed to the side of the injured boy.

But Kasimir's other half...was filled with darkness.

There are rumors about me, he'd said. *That I am more than ruthless. That I am half-insane, driven mad by my hunger for revenge.*

But loving him changed everything. She no longer wished to escape him. Or even to be his make-believe wife for a few weeks in a marriage of convenience.

Josie wanted to be his real wife. Always and forever. Complete with children and the white picket fence.

But Prince Kasimir Xendzov was not a white-picket-fence kind of man.

She turned her head, blinking back tears. Such a risk. Such a stupid risk. She loved the good in him—the man he'd once been, the man he could be again.

But the pain of past betrayals had warped his soul, turning him dark and ruthless. Giving him reason to keep the world at a distance. Her heart twisted in her chest.

Could she make him see that forgiving his brother wouldn't be weakness, but strength—freeing him for a new life? Could she show him that the world could be so much more? She yearned to show him his life, his future, had just begun.

Just as hers had...

With a low sigh, she nestled closer to him in bed. His eyes remained closed, but his strong arms instinctively pulled her closer against the warmth of his body.

It felt so protective, so good. Closing her eyes, she pressed her cheek against his chest.

She would find a way. She yawned, safe and sleepy in his arms. Kasimir had changed her life.

For so long, Josie had been afraid. Since she was twelve, Bree had protected her like a mother hen, not letting her take risks, warning her about the evils of the world. Josie had listened. After all, Bree, older by six years, was the smart one. The strong one. Josie was the burden. The helpless, hapless one. The one who, just by being born, had caused her mother to die. What right did Josie have to ask for anything at all? What right to speak her mind, to make a fuss, to live her dreams?

But Kasimir had changed her, completely and irrevocably. He'd forced her to be who she really was inside. And shown her that living boldly was the only way to honor the sacrifice her mother had made, and the life she'd been given.

He'd done that for her. She yearned to do something for him. She wanted to teach him that being vulnerable, that trusting others, could be his greatest strength. Josie snuggled deeper into his arms. She would help him break free from the chains of anger and revenge....

Morning sunlight was bright against the white canvas of the tent when Josie opened her eyes. She sat up abruptly. She was alone amid the tangled sheets of the bed. Much of the tent, too, was empty. She saw his packed suitcase beside her own backpack at the door. Weird. Were they going somewhere?

But where was Kasimir?

Kasimir. Just his name was like a song in her heart. Rising from the bed, she splashed fresh cool water on her face from the basin, then pulled on a clean T-shirt, a cotton skirt and sandals from the wardrobe and went outside.

Her heart pounded as she looked for him. She was going to tell him she loved him. Now. Today. The instant she saw him.

But where was he? All of the servants in the encampment seemed to be rushing around strangely, boxing up, packing. She wondered if they were tidying up from the wind storm the night before. Maybe it had been a big one. Not that Josie had noticed. She'd been too distracted by the sensual storm in their bed. A sweet smile lifted her lips. She started towards one of the women, to ask if she'd seen Kasimir. Then Josie stopped.

He was standing alone on the highest dune. His powerful dark silhouette dazzled her. He was like the sun—her northern star.

With an intake of breath, she climbed the sand dune towards him, as fast as she could go. Looking around, she realized she'd come to love the vastness and beauty of the desert. It didn't feel so lonely anymore, or make her feel small.

As long as she was with Kasimir, the world was a wondrous place.

She stopped. Was she making a mistake to tell him she loved him? Would it ruin everything?

She looked at him again, and her shoulders relaxed. Her momentary fear floated away, evaporating like dark smoke into the blue sky, like a shadow beneath the bright Moroccan sun. She didn't have to be afraid. Not anymore. Kasimir had believed in her.

And now, she believed in herself.

"I'm not afraid," she said aloud. Her legs regained their strength. She started to walk towards his broad-shouldered shadow on the top of the dune, silhouetted against the bright sun.

A warm desert wind blew against her skin, tossing tendrils of her hair in her face as she reached him. She was so happy to see his handsome face that tears filled her eyes. "Kasimir. There's something I need to…"

"I have good news," he interrupted coldly.

She looked at him more closely. His desert garb was gone.

No more tight black T-shirts. No more cargo shorts or jeans, either. Instead, he was back in his dark suit with a tie and vest. He looked exactly like the same dangerous tycoon she'd first met in Honolulu.

In the distance, she heard a loud buzzing noise. Suddenly feeling uncertain, she echoed, "Good news?"

He gave a single sharp nod. "I'm taking you with me. To Russia. So I can get your sister."

"Oh," Josie said faintly. "That is good news."

It was. But why was his handsome face so expressionless, as if they were total strangers? Why did he seem so suddenly distant, as if they hadn't spent last night ripping off each other's clothes? Why did he look at her as if he barely knew her when just hours before he had been gasping with sweaty pleasure, deep inside her?

"Time to go," he said flatly.

Looking at him in his suit, Josie suddenly felt cold in the warm morning air. The joyful, emotional barbarian with the unguarded heart, the one who'd taught her to ride horses, to snowboard sand, to make love—was gone. She bit her lip. "When?"

He glanced behind him, and she saw an approaching helicopter in the wide blue sky. "Right now."

Shivering, she wrapped her arms around her body, feeling chilly in her cotton shirt. They stood only a few feet apart on the sand, but there was suddenly a deep, wide ocean between them that she didn't understand.

His cruel, sensual lips curved. "We're leaving to find your sister. Aren't you happy?"

"I am," she said miserably. Then, reminding herself she was brave and bold, she lifted her gaze. "But why are you acting like this?"

He blinked. "Like what?"

"Like…" She looked straight into his eyes. "Like last night meant nothing."

"It meant something." He took a step towards her, his face hard as a marble statue. "It meant…a few hours of fun."

It was like a stab in the heart. "Fun?"

Kasimir gave her a coldly charming smile, looking every inch the heartless playboy the world believed him to be. "Oh, yes." He tilted his head, looking at her sideways. "Definitely fun."

For an instant, Josie could hardly breathe through the pain. Then she saw a flash of something in his expression, something quickly veiled and hidden. Her eyes widened as she searched his gaze.

"You're deliberately pushing me away," she breathed.

His expression hardened as he set his jaw. "Don't."

"Last night meant something to you. I know it did!"

"It was an amusement, just to pass the time. But that time is over. Let's get this done. Get our divorce. Then we'll never have to see each other again."

She licked her lips as the approaching helicopter grew louder. "But you said…we could still be friends…."

"Friends?" He gave a harsh, ugly laugh. "You really think that would work? You expect me to give up my life and join you in your fairy-tale world, where families love and forgive?" He slowly walked around her, his eyes glittering in the white sun. "Tell me. Are you already picturing me mowing the lawn outside your storybook cottage with the white picket fence?"

"You're using my dreams against me?" she whispered. His sneer ripped through her heart. She blinked back tears. "Why are you being so cruel?"

Kasimir stopped. The helicopter landed on the pad some distance behind him, causing sand to fly in waves. His black hair whipped wildly around his face as he looked down at her. When he finally spoke, his voice had changed.

"Whatever happened between us last night," he said quietly, "cannot last. Someday soon you will learn the truth about me. And you will hate me."

She shook her head fiercely. "I will never—"

"I'm not giving up my revenge." His blue eyes suddenly blazed. Reaching out, he grabbed her shoulders. "Don't you understand? You can't make me give it up, no matter how good or kind you are, or how you look at me. I'm never going to change, so don't even try."

"But you can," she choked out. A single tear spilled over her lashes. "You could be so much more…."

A flash of raw vulnerability filled his stark blue eyes as he stared down at her. "A woman like you would be a fool to care about a man like me," he said in a low voice. "Don't do it, Josie. Don't."

She stared at him with an intake of breath.

"It is growing late." The cold mask reasserted itself on his handsome face. Abruptly releasing her, he turned towards the waiting helicopter. "Time to go."

An ache filled her throat.

"It's too late already," she whispered, but he'd already turned away.

CHAPTER NINE

HAPPINESS COULD BE corrosive as acid, when you knew it wasn't going to last.

Kasimir gripped the phone to his ear as he stared at the snowy Russian forest outside the window of the dark-walled study. Greg Hudson's voice was grating on the other end of the line.

"So—the New Year's Eve ball tonight? I am tired of waiting," the man complained.

"Yes. And once you are paid," Kasimir replied tightly, "you will never contact me again, or speak of our deal to anyone."

"Of course, of course. I just want the money you owe me. Especially since my boss at the Hale Ka'nani found out about your bribe and fired me."

"You are sure Vladimir and Bree are attending the ball?"

"Yes. I've been watching them, as you said. You owe me extra, for freezing my butt off in Russia. I could be sipping piña coladas on a beach right now."

"Eleven o'clock." Kasimir tossed his phone across the desk. With a deep breath, he looked back out the window. It was the first time he'd seen snow in ten years.

And a million miles from where he'd woken up that morning. In the heat of the Sahara, waking in Josie's arms to the soft pink dawn, Kasimir had known perfect happiness for the first time in his adult life. He'd held her, listening to the soft sound of her breath as she slept. For thirty seconds, he'd known peace. He'd known joy. And the feelings were alien and terrifying....

Then he'd known that it would all soon end.

So let it end, he thought grimly. After returning to Marrakech, and a stop for the necessary travel documents, he'd taken Josie to Russia in his private jet, to this small remote dacha—a luxurious cabin in the forest outside St. Petersburg.

He'd been cold to her. He'd done what needed to be done. He was hanging on to his control by a thread. He knew what she wanted. He couldn't give in.

He could *not* let himself care for Josie. He couldn't listen to her alluring whispers about a different future. She made him feel things he did not want to feel. Uncertain. Raw. With a heart full of longing for a world that did not, could not exist.

It was time to face reality.

Tonight. New Year's Eve. He would wait until he could speak to Bree Dalton alone, at the exclusive luxury ball at the Tsarina's palace. He would give her his blackmail ultimatum. Now. Before Josie convinced his heart to turn completely soft.

He exhaled.

And once he'd done it...he would tell Josie the truth about who he was. The kind of man who felt nothing, who got what he wanted at any cost. For once and for all, he would wipe that look of adoration off her face. Because he would not, could not give up his plans for revenge. Or keep Josie from finding out about it. For their time together in the Sahara, he'd been happy, truly happy. But it was all about to end.

So let it end. Now. Before the corrosive happiness of caring for Josie, and knowing she'd soon leave, burned his soul straight to ash.

"Kasimir?" Her sweet voice spoke behind him. "Who were you talking to on the phone?"

He whirled around to face her in the dacha's dark study. The decor was very masculine. But then, he'd borrowed this country house from an old acquaintance, Prince Maksim

Rostov, who was spending the week of New Year's in California with his wife, Grace, and their two young children.

Kasimir cleared his throat. He kept his voice as cold as he could. "No one that concerns you."

Josie's beautiful eyes filled with hurt. "I thought, now we were in Russia, maybe we could talk… ."

"There's nothing to talk about." He told himself he was doing her a favor. This small hurt would be nothing compared to how she'd feel when she discovered he'd kept her prisoner all this time to blackmail her sister.

Let her learn the truth of his dark heart by degrees.

He had to let her go.

He had to push her away.

Now. Before she made him surrender his very soul.

Kasimir straightened the black tie of his tuxedo. "I have to go."

Her brown eyes were deep with unspoken longing. "Go where?"

"Out," he said shortly.

She bit her lip. "In a tuxedo…?"

"Bree and Vladimir will be at the most exclusive New Year's Eve ball in the city. I'm going to go have a little chat." He stopped, then kissed her briefly, not on her lips, but on her forehead. He gave her a smile that didn't meet his eyes. "Your sister will be surprised to hear we're married."

"Take me with you," she said.

He shook his head. "Sorry."

"I need to explain to her why I married you." She swallowed. "She'll be so disappointed in me, that I did it to break my father's trust… ."

"Bree? Disappointed in you?" he said harshly. His eyes blazed. "You gave up everything to save her." Forcing his shoulders to relax, he pulled a colorful, brightly decorated phone out of his pocket. "And you can explain that."

She blinked. "What are you doing with my dead phone?"

"All charged up now. I'll give it to her so she can call you here. Tonight."

Kasimir could see the emotions fighting for domination in her expression. But what she finally said was, "Thanks. That is very—kind…"

Kind. Again. Scowling, he turned away. "I have to go."

"Wait," she choked out.

He stopped at the door. He looked back at her.

Josie's beautiful eyes were huge, her soft cheeks pale. "Just tell me one thing," she whispered. "Do you—do you regret taking me to bed last night?"

His eyes met hers.

"Yes," Kasimir said simply, and as he saw her face crumple, he knew it was true. He regretted that for the rest of his life, he'd be haunted by the memory of a perfect woman he could never deserve. A woman he could never have again. A woman who would despise him forever the instant she heard he'd blackmailed her sister.

"Oh." It was the kind of gasp a person makes when they'd just been punched in the gut. She blinked fast, fighting back tears. He wanted to comfort her. Instead, he said, "I'll be back after midnight. Don't wait up."

"Happy New Year," she whispered behind him, but he kept walking, straight out of the house.

As his chauffeur drove him away from the dacha, heading down the lonely road through the snowy forest, Kasimir looked up at the icy moon in the dark sky. His hands tightened in his lap. He missed her. After ten years alone, without ever letting down his guard to another human soul, he missed Josie. He missed his wife.

But his days with her were numbered. They were ticking by with every minute on the clock. And so this had to be done. Although suddenly, even in his mind, he didn't like to specify what *it* was.

It was betraying her.

The New Year's Eve ball was in full swing when he arrived at the elegant palace outside St. Petersburg. Beautiful,
glamorously dressed women stared at him hard as he stepped
out of the expensive car, and he felt their eyes travel down the
length of his tuxedo as they licked their red lips.

In another world, he would have been only too glad to
take advantage of the pleasurable services clearly on offer.
But not now. Kasimir looked down at the plain gold wedding
band on his finger. There was only one woman his body hungered after now. The one woman who would soon leave him,
no matter how much he cared. Turning away, he backed into
the shadows, avoiding notice as much as he could. Watching. Looking.

"There you are," Greg Hudson said from behind a potted
plant. He nodded towards the dance floor. "Your brother and
Bree," he panted her name, "are over there."

Kasimir's lip curled as he looked from the man's greasy
hair to his totally inappropriate sport jacket, which barely
covered his pot belly. With distaste, he withdrew an envelope from his pocket.

Hudson's eyes lit up, but as he reached for the envelope,
Kasimir grabbed his wrist. "If you even hint to Vladimir
I'm here, I will take back every penny, and the rest out of
your hide."

"I wouldn't—couldn't—" With a gulp, the man backed
away. "So goodbye, then. Um. *Da svedanya.*"

Turning away with narrowed eyes, Kasimir looked out at
the dance floor. He moved slowly through the people, on the
edge of the party. Then he saw his brother.

Seeing Vladimir's face was almost startling. For a split
instant, Kasimir saw him walking ahead in the snow on the
way to school, always ahead of him, whether chopping fire-
wood, chasing newborn calves through the Alaskan forest,
or fishing frozen lakes for hours through a cut-out hole in the

ice. *Wait for me, Volodya,* Kasimir had always cried. *Wait for me.* But his brother had never waited.

Now, Kasimir's jaw set.

In the last ten years, Vladimir had grown more powerful, more distinguished in his appearance and certainly richer. He also now had faint lines at his eyes as he smiled down at the woman in his arms.

Bree Dalton. The older sister that Josie had sacrificed so much, risked so much, to save. And there was Bree, laughing and flirting and apparently having the time of her life in his great-grandmother's peridot necklace and a fancy ball gown.

Watching them with dark thoughts, Kasimir waited in the shadows until Vladimir left Bree alone on the dance floor. And then Kasimir approached her. He talked to her in low, terse tones. And five minutes later, he left Bree on the dance floor, her face shocked and trembling with fear.

Serves her right, Kasimir thought with cold fury as he left the Tsarina's palace. Josie had been so desperate to save her, and Bree had been enjoying herself all this time as Vladimir's mistress. A tight ache filled his throat.

So much for Josie's *sacrifice.*

And still, after everything she'd done for Bree, when Josie had briefly spoken to her sister, she'd still tried to apologize.

Kasimir exhaled as his chauffeur turned the black Rolls-Royce farther from the palace and through the snowy, frozen sprawl of St. Petersburg. Letting the two sisters briefly speak on the phone had been a calculated gamble.

Where are you? Bree had gasped. There was a pause, in which Kasimir overheard Josie's blurted-out apology, begging her sister's forgiveness for her marriage of convenience. Panicked, Bree had cried, *But where are you?*

He'd taken the phone away before Josie could blurt out that she was right here, in St. Petersburg, not in Morocco at all. Now, Kasimir silently looked out at the moonlit night, at passing fields of snow, laced with black trees.

It was just past midnight. A brand-new year. As he traveled out into the countryside, towards the dacha, he should have been feeling triumphant. His brother had no idea he was about to lose his company, his lover, everything.

Bring the signed document to my house in Marrakech within three days, Kasimir had told Bree coldly.

She'd answered, *And if I fail?*

He'd given her a cold smile. *Then you'll never see your sister again. She'll disappear into the Sahara. And be mine. Forever.*

Now, Kasimir clawed back his hair as he stared out the window at the moonlit night, with only the occasional lights of a town to illuminate the Russian land in the darkness.

In seventy-two hours, Bree would meet him in Marrakech and provide him with a contract, unknowingly signed by Vladimir, that would give him complete ownership of Xendzov Mining OAO. He should have been ecstatic.

Instead, he couldn't stop thinking about how Josie had felt, soft and breathless, in his arms all night, as the hot desert wind howled against their tent, and they slept, naked in each other's arms, face-to-face, heart-to-heart. Her reckless, fearless emotion had saturated his body and soul. He couldn't forget the adoration in her eyes last night—and the shocked hurt in them today.

His hands shook at the thought of the conversation he'd soon have with his wife. Looking down, he realized he was twisting the gold ring on his left hand so hard his fingertip had started to turn white. He released the ring, then exhaled, leaning back in the leather seat. The last lights disappeared as they went deeper into the countryside. Dawn was still hours away on the first of January, the darkest of deep Russian winter.

The car finally turned down a quiet country road surrounded by the black, bare trees of a snowy forest. Past the empty guardhouse, the car continued down a road that was bumpy and long. The trees parted and he saw a large Russian country house in pale gray wood, overlooking a dark lake frosted with moonlight.

The limo pulled in front of the house and abruptly stopped. For a moment, he held his breath. The chauffeur opened his door, and Kasimir felt a chilling rush of cold air. Pulling a black overcoat over his tuxedo, he stepped out into the snowy January night.

As he walked towards the front door, the gravel crunched beneath his feet, echoing against the trees. In the pale gleaming lights from the windows, he could see the icicles of his breath.

As the chauffeur drove the car away towards the distant barn that was used as a garage, Kasimir went to the front door and found it was unlocked.

Surprised, he pushed open the door. He walked into the dark, silent foyer. The house was silent. As the grave.

Where were the bodyguards?

"Hello?" he called harshly. No answer. With a sickening feeling, he suddenly remembered the guardhouse had been empty, as well. With no one minding the door, anyone could have walked right in and found Josie sleeping, helpless and alone.

He sucked in his breath. This was a safe area, but he had plenty of enemies. Starting with his own brother. If somehow—somehow—Vladimir had found out he was here…

"Josie!" he cried. He ran up the stairs three steps at a time. He rushed down the hall to their bedroom. If anything had happened, he would never forgive himself for leaving her.

He knocked the door back with a bang against the wall. In the flickers of dying firelight from the old stone fireplace, he saw a shadow move in the bed.

"Kasimir?" Josie's voice was sleepy. She sat up in bed, yawning. "Was that you yelling?"

Relief and joy rushed through him, so great it nearly

brought him to his knees. Without a word, he sat down on the bed and pulled her into his arms. In the moonlight from the window, he saw her beautiful, precious face, her cheeks lined with creases from the pillow, her messy hair tumbling over her shoulders, auburn in the red glow from the fire's dying embers.

"What is it? What's wrong?"

Kasimir didn't answer. For long moments, he just sat on the bed, holding her. Closing his eyes, he inhaled the scent of vanilla and peaches in hair, felt the sweet softness of her body pressed against his own.

"Kasimir?" Her voice was muffled against his chest. He finally pulled back, gripping her shoulders as he looked down at her.

"Where are the bodyguards?" he said hoarsely. "Why are you alone?"

"Oh… That." To his surprise, she shrugged, then gave him a crooked grin. "They got in this big fight, arguing over which of them got to watch some huge sports event on the big screen in the basement and which poor slob would be stuck watching me. So I told them in Russian that I didn't need anyone watching me. I mean—" she gave a little laugh "—I've been sleeping on my own for a long time. My whole life. I mean—" she suddenly blushed, looking at him "—until quite lately." Drawing back, she looked at him. "You aren't mad, are you?" she said anxiously. "I promised them you wouldn't be mad."

"I will fire them all," Kasimir said fervently. Pulling her hard against his body, he pressed his lips to hers in a kiss that was pure and true and that he wished could last forever—but he feared would be their last.

This time, she was the one to pull away. "You don't really mean that," she said chidingly. "You can't fire them. They had to obey me. I'm your wife."

"Of course they had to obey you," he growled.

"Good," she sighed. She pressed her cheek against his

chest, then sat up in sudden alarm. "The phone line got cut off when I tried to talk to Bree. Was she mad? Did you cut the deal with Vladimir? When will I see her?"

Kasimir looked down into her beautiful, trusting face, feeling heartsick. "She's safe and happy and you'll see her in three days." His jaw clenched, and he forced himself to say, "But there's something I need to tell you."

Josie shook her head, narrowing her eyes with a determined set of her chin. "I have something to tell you first."

"No—"

She covered his mouth with her small hand. She looked straight into his eyes. And she said the five words that for ten years, he'd never wanted to hear from any woman.

"I'm in love with you," Josie whispered.

With an intake of breath, he pulled back, his eyes wide. He looked at her face, pink in the warm firelight. "What did you say?" he choked out.

Josie's eyes were luminous as she looked up at him with a trembling smile. Then she said the words again, and it was like the home he'd dreamed of his whole life. "I love you, Kasimir."

"But—you can't." He realized his body was shaking all over. "You don't."

"I do." Her eyes glowed like sunlight and Christmas and everything good he'd ever dreamed of. "I knew it last night, when you held me in your arms. And I had to tell you before I lost my courage. Because even if you're mean to me, even if you push me away, even if you divorce me and I never see you again…" She lifted her gaze to his. "I love you."

Standing up, Kasimir stumbled back from her. Pacing three steps, he stopped, clawing his hair back wildly as he faced her in the moonlight. "You're wrong. Sex can feel like love, especially the first time. When you don't have enough experience to know the difference…"

Pushing aside the quilts, she slowly stood up in her plaid

flannel nightgown. "I know the difference." Her eyes pierced his. "Do you?"

His heart started to pound.

He didn't want to think about how being with Josie was so different from anything he'd ever experienced before. Couldn't. "Don't you understand what kind of man I am?" he said hoarsely. "I'm selfish. Ruthless. I've spent ten years trying to destroy my own brother! How can you love me?"

Coming towards him, she put her hand over his. "Because I do."

A tremble went through him then that he couldn't control. Outside, through the windows, the sky was turning lighter as dawn rose pink and soft. It was New Year's Day.

"You should hate me," he whispered. "I want you to hate me."

Reaching up, Josie cupped his cheek, her palm soft against the rough bristles of his jawline. "You don't have to be afraid."

He stiffened. "Afraid?"

"Of loving me back," she said quietly. She took a deep breath. "You want to love me. I think you already do. But you're afraid I'll hurt you or leave you. What will it take for you to see you have nothing to fear? I've never loved anyone before, but I know one thing. I will love you," she whispered, "for always."

Their eyes locked in the gray shadows of the bedroom. The icy wind rattled the window, and the fire crackled noisily.

"There. I'm done." Tears shone in her eyes as she gave him a trembling smile. "Now what did you want to tell me?"

And just like that, Kasimir suddenly knew.

He couldn't tell Josie the truth. Because he wanted her in his life. No, it was more than just wanting her.

He couldn't bear to let her go.

Kasimir's throat ached. But even if he lied to her now, he wouldn't be able to keep the truth from her for long. In three days, when he took her to Morocco for the exchange, she'd discover what he'd done. That he'd been keeping her prisoner all this time. Even she could not forgive that.

Unless…

Was there any way he could keep her as his wife? Any way he could keep her in his bed, with that innocent, passionate love still shining so brightly in her eyes?

Slowly, Kasimir lifted his hand to stroke the softness of her hair. "What I wanted to tell you is…" He took a deep breath. "I missed you."

Josie sighed in pleasure, closing her eyes, pressing her cheek against his chest in an expression that was protective, almost reverent.

In the warmth and comfort of her arms, Kasimir closed his stinging eyes against his own weakness for the lie. Then, in the wintry Russian dawn, against the cold blank slate of a brand-new year, he lowered his mouth to hers for a forbidden kiss. And then another. Until they were tangled together, and he was lost.

Josie had been feeling hurt, with an aching heart, when he'd left her in his tuxedo, to go to the New Year's Eve ball without her. Then she'd been struck by a thought so sudden and overwhelming that it had made her stand still.

Her husband, for all his wealth and power, was completely alone.

Josie couldn't imagine having no family, except a brother who was an enemy. She knew that Bree, for all her overbearing ways, still loved her fiercely. The two sisters had each other's backs—always. But who had Kasimir's back?

No one.

Who loved him on this wide, lonely earth?

Nobody.

Realizing this, Josie's wounded heart had abruptly stopped aching. The tears had disappeared. He had no one who believed in him—no one he could trust. No wonder he'd devoted his life to the success of a business that had never been his childhood dream, to earning money he didn't really need, and most of all—to destroying his only family. His brother.

No wonder his moral compass was so askew. No wonder, when they'd spent the night together in bed and she'd given him her heart, as well as her body, he hadn't known how to react.

But he'd never been loved as she could love him.

Kasimir expected her to stop caring about him the instant he did something cold or rude. Well, he didn't know the type of woman he was dealing with. Josie had been ignored and dismissed her whole life. She'd never once let that stop her from believing the best of people and giving them everything she could.

She knew Kasimir had darkness inside him. She accepted that it was part of him. But as long as he was honest with her, honorable and true, she didn't care. Everyone had flaws. She did. It wouldn't stop her from loving him, the only way she knew how to love someone.

All the way.

Josie loved him. Come what may.

At that simple decision, peace had come over her. The bodyguards, who'd been arguing over who would be stuck watching the crying woman instead of the two-hundred-inch projector screen in the basement, had been astonished when she'd suddenly stopped pacing and told them in clumsy Russian to go watch the game. She'd gone alone to the kitchen. She'd made herself some Russian tea. After speaking briefly to her sister, who sounded very shocked indeed that Josie had married Kasimir, she'd brushed her teeth, put on her nightgown and gone to bed. Rehearsing what she would tell him, she'd waited for her husband to come home.

She'd fallen asleep, but it didn't matter. She hadn't used a word of her little rehearsed speech anyway. She'd just taken one look at the gray bleak shadows on Kasimir's face, at the tight set of his shoulders, and spoken the truth from her heart.

Now, pulling back from his sudden hungry kiss, Josie looked at him. His eyes seemed haunted, tortured, dark as a midnight sea. But he cared for her. She could see it. Feel it. Reaching up, she cupped his cheek. He put his rough hand over hers, then pressed his lips to her palm in a lingering kiss so passionate that her soul thrilled inside her body.

And looking at him, she felt no more trembling fear. She felt only the absolute knowledge, down to her bones, that her love for him was meant to be.

This time, Kasimir was the one who was shaking, as if he felt her words of love like a physical blow. She tried to imagine what his life had been like for the last ten years, unloved and alone—never knowing what it was to be protected and sheltered by another human soul.

Starting today, and for the rest of his life, he would know. She would shelter him. Protect him.

Beside the bed, she pulled the black overcoat off his unresisting body. She removed his tuxedo jacket and dropped it to the floor. Pushing him to sit on the bed, she knelt and unlaced his black Italian leather shoes, then she reached up for his black tie.

He grabbed her wrist. "What are you doing?"

She exhaled, then leaned up, smiling through her tears.

"Let me show you," she whispered.

His eyes widened. His hand numbly released her.

Pulling off his tie, Josie undid the top button of his white tuxedo shirt, then the waistband of his black trousers. She removed all his clothes, one by one, then pushed him back against the bed. Looking down at him, she yanked her long nightgown up over her head. She kicked off her panties. For a split second, she shivered in the cool winter air as they stared at each other, both naked in the flickering firelight, against the misty gray dawn. Then she pulled the goose-down comforter over them.

Beneath the blanket was their own world. She wrapped her arms around his hard, shivering body, trying to warm them both. She kissed his forehead. Then his cheek. Then...

Suddenly, staying warm was not a problem. She felt hot, burning hot, with his naked skin against her own. She kissed him, clutching him to her, and a growl came from the back of his throat.

Putting his hands on both sides of her face, Kasimir kissed her back fiercely, possessively, almost violently. Rolling her body beneath him, he kissed slowly down her neck, running his hands over her naked skin as if it were silk. As if he wanted to explore every inch of her.

Insane, intoxicating need overwhelmed her. If he couldn't say the three words that she yearned to hear, she needed to feel his love for her.

"Take me," she whispered. "Now."

He sucked in his breath, searching her eyes. Then, gripping her hips, he pulled back, then thrust inside her, filling her so deeply, all the way to the heart.

She gasped, gripping his shoulders. He wrapped his arms around her, pressing his hard body against her own, and she felt the heat of his breath against her skin as he rode her slow and hard and deep. She cried out, clutching him to her. Drawing back, he looked straight into her eyes, holding her gaze as he plunged one last time, deep, so deep, that she shuddered all around him, as he shuddered inside her.

Afterward, tears ran down Josie's cheeks as she felt his strong arms around her, keeping cold winter away. *She loved him so.* And when Kasimir reached for her again a brief time later, to show her his love again and again, she knew that fairy tales were true. They had to be. Because even if he couldn't speak the words, he loved her. His body proved it.

They were in love. Weren't they? That meant everything would be all right. Didn't it? So they'd be together forever.

Wouldn't they?

Two and a half days later, in the rustic, dark-walled study of the country house, Kasimir dialed Bree Dalton's number with shaking hands. When she did not answer, he gritted his teeth and called a number he hadn't called for ten years. A number he knew by heart.

Kasimir had waited till the last possible moment to call. For three days now, he'd racked his brain to think of a way to keep both Josie and his revenge. But Bree expected her sister in exchange for the signed contract. There was no solution. Only a choice.

But such a choice. Kasimir had already sent his bodyguards with the luggage to the nearby private airport, where his jet was ready to take them to Marrakech. But then, five minutes ago, outside in the snow with Josie, watching her sparkling eyes as she made a snowman, he suddenly knew the answer.

He wanted Josie more than anything else. So the solution was screamingly obvious.

He would give up his revenge.

He would take Josie to some place where her sister and Vladimir would never find her.

He took a deep breath as Vladimir answered his phone.

"It's me," he ground out.

"Kasimir," his brother replied in a low voice. "About time."

Vladimir didn't sound surprised to hear from him. Strange. And stranger still that after ten years of silence, it seemed as if no time had passed between them. He sounded exactly the same.

"You might as well know, I tried to blackmail Bree," he said abruptly, "into signing your company over to me."

"She already told me," Vladimir replied. "Your plan to turn us against each other didn't work."

Kasimir stopped. "You already know? So what do you intend to do?"

"I am willing to make the trade."

He sucked in his breath. "You're willing to give up your billion-dollar company? For the sake of a woman who once lied to you?" His jaw hardened. Vladimir must really love Bree. "Too bad. I've changed my mind. I no longer have any intention of divorcing Josie, for any price. You can keep your stupid company. In fact…there's no reason for us ever to talk. Ever again."

"Kasimir, don't be a fool," his brother said tersely. "You can still—"

Kasimir turned his head as he heard Josie coming in from the snowy garden. He hung up, dropping his phone into his pocket.

"Why did you run off like that?" She was laughing, wearing a white hooded coat, halfcovered with snow. "We're not even done. The poor snowman only has one eye." Puppy-like, she tried to shake the snowflakes off her coat. Her eyes sparkled like a million bright winter days, and the sound of her laughter was like music. "Ah," she sighed. "I've missed winter!"

He'd never seen anything, or anyone, so beautiful. As he looked at her, his heart twisted with infinite longing.

And he realized: *he loved her.*

His eyes narrowed, and he knew he wouldn't let anyone take Josie away from him. He'd keep her. At any cost.

"I have something to tell you," he said softly. He pulled off her white hooded coat, covered with snow, off her shoulders and dropped it to the floor. "It's important."

Josie gave him a teasing, slow-rising smile. "Hmm. Knowing you…" She tilted her head, pretending to consider, then lifted an eyebrow. "Does that something involve a bed?"

"Ah. You know me well," he answered with a wicked grin. "But no." Growing more serious, he gently used the pads of his thumbs to wipe away the snowflakes from her creamy skin, and those tangled in her eyelashes. Looking down into her eyes, he saw eternity in those caramel-and-honey-colored depths. And he whispered the words in his heart. "I love you, Josie."

Her lips parted in shock. Tears filled her eyes as a sob escaped her. "You love me?"

He cupped her cheek. "Will you stay with me and be my wife?" He gave her a crooked, cocky smile, even as his hands trembled. "Not just now, but forever?"

"Forever," she breathed. A single tear streamed down her cheek. "Yes," she choked out. She threw her arms around him. "Oh, yes!"

He pulled back from her embrace to look down at her. "But there's just one thing." He looked down at her. "If you stay with me as my wife—you must never see Bree again."

"What?" She wiped her eyes with an awkward laugh. "What are you talking about?"

"I saw your sister with my brother at the ball. Laughing. Kissing. They are together now." He set his jaw. "So you must choose. Them…" He tucked back a long tendril of her hair and said in a low voice, "Or me."

Josie blinked fast. "Maybe if we all just talked together, we could…"

"No," he cut her off.

Josie stared at him, her brown eyes glittering. She swallowed, then whispered, "You can't ask this of me."

"I must." He pulled her into his arms. His hands moved to her back, getting tangled in her lustrous, damp brown hair. He kissed her temple, her cheek, her lips. "Choose me, Josie," he whispered against her skin. "Stay with me."

She trembled in his arms, uncertain. Knowing he'd asked her the deepest sacrifice of her life, he persuaded her in the only way he could. He lowered his mouth to hers, kissing her with his soul on his lips, holding nothing back. He kissed her with every bit of love and longing and passion in his heart, until even Kasimir was dizzy as the world seemed to spin around their embrace.

"Let me show you the world," he whispered. "Every day can be more exciting than the last. Choose me."

Her arms twisted around his shoulders as she sighed against his lips. "I can't…"

He kissed her again. In the distance, he dimly heard noises outside the dacha—the call of the birds, the crack of wood in the bare forest.

With a sob, Josie pulled away. A single tear fell unheeded down her cheek. "I love you both." She drew a deep breath like a shudder, then lifted her gaze and whispered, "But if I must choose, I choose you."

Kasimir's heart almost stopped in his chest.

Josie chose him.

It was a selfish thing he'd asked of her, he knew. Selfish? Unforgivable. And yet this amazing woman had chosen him. Over everything and everyone she'd ever loved. He got a lump in his throat. "Thank you, Josie," he said in a low voice. "I'll honor your sacrifice. For the rest of our lives…."

The outside door banged against the wall. Whirling around, Josie gasped, "Bree!"

As if in slow motion, Kasimir turned his head.

Vladimir and Bree stood in the open doorway.

"Josie." The slender blond woman ran quickly towards her younger sister. "Are you all right?"

"Of course I'm all right," Josie tried to reassure her. "You're the one who's been in trouble." She patted her sister's shoulders as if to be sure she was really there. "But are you okay?" she said anxiously. She scowled at Vladimir. "He didn't—hurt you?"

"Vladimir?" Bree looked astonished. "No. Never."

"What are you doing here?"

"We came to save you."

"Save me?" Looking bewildered, Josie looked at Kasimir with a smile then tilted her head. "Oh. You mean from my marriage." She sighed. "I knew you'd be upset I married Kasimir, but you don't need to worry. It started out as a business arrangement, yes, but now we're in love and..."

Her voice trailed off as she looked at the faces of the others. Vladimir folded his arms, glowering at Kasimir. He stared back at his brother warily.

What's going on?" Josie breathed, looking bewildered.

Kasimir set his jaw. He'd been so close—so close to getting her away forever. But now he had no choice but to tell her *everything*—before the others did. He turned to her, his arms folded.

"There's something I need to tell you," he said tightly. "Something I need to explain."

"Go on," she said uncertainly.

He desperately tried to think of a way to make her understand, to forgive. "It was... I thought it was fate." He tightened his hands into fists at his sides. "When you fell into my lap."

He parted his lips to say more, then stopped.

"Kasimir threatened me on New Year's Eve," Bree stated. "He said if I didn't trick Vladimir into signing over his company, he would make sure I never saw you again!"

Josie gasped.

Her sister scowled. "I had to get the contract signed by midnight tonight, or Kasimir was going to make you disappear into the desert forever. Into his harem, he said!"

Josie's face went pale. "No," she breathed. She turned to him. "It's not true," she whispered. "Tell me it's not true. It's some kind of—misunderstanding between you and my sister. Tell me."

Kasimir's shoulders and jaw were so tense they hurt as he looked down at her. "I was going to explain, the night I came back on New Year's Eve. Having you with me, when Bree was with Vladimir, it just seemed—well, I told myself I'd be a fool not to take advantage of the situation." He paused, then forced himself to continue. "I…I was the one who arranged for you and your sister to get jobs in Hawaii."

"You did!"

He gave a single terse nod. "I hoped to convince you to marry me. And I hoped Vladimir would see Bree."

"You mean you hoped I'd cause a scene," Bree retorted.

"Which you did," Vladimir murmured, giving her a wicked grin. She blushed.

"That's neither here nor there," she said primly.

But Josie's soft brown eyes didn't look away from Kasimir's face. "That's why you took me from Honolulu to Morocco?" The color had drained out of her rosy cheeks, leaving her skin white as Russian snow. "You weren't keeping me safe—you were keeping me hostage? To blackmail my sister?"

Kasimir's heart twisted in his chest. "Josie." He swallowed. "If you'll just let me explain…."

And again, she waited, still with a terrible, desperate hope in her eyes. As if there could be any way Kasimir could explain his actions that didn't make him a selfish monster. He took a deep breath. "I did do a terrible thing. But an hour ago, I called and told them the deal was off. I told Vladimir he could keep his company. All I wanted was you." Urgently, he grabbed her hands in his own and looked down at her. "Doesn't that mean something?" he said softly. "I called off the blackmail. For you."

For a moment, Josie's eyes glowed. For that split second, he thought it was all going to be all right.

Then her expression crumpled. "But you were going to separate me from my sister forever, rather than confess how you tried to blackmail her. You were going to force me to give her up, her friendship, her love, for the rest of my life, rather than tell me how you threatened her—with my *safety!*"

"I was afraid." Words caught in his throat. He felt her hands starting to slip away and he tried to grab them, hold on to them. "I was afraid you wouldn't understand. I couldn't take the risk you wouldn't forgive me...."

She pulled her hands away. "If even an hour ago, you'd confessed everything, I think even then I could have forgiven you," she whispered. "But not for th-this." Her teeth chattered. "You d-demanded that I make that horrible choice. When it was never necessary. Even knowing what it would cost me!"

"I'm sorry," he said in a low voice.

Her eyes widened, then narrowed. "You never loved me," she choked out. "Not if you could do that."

Desperately, he took a step towards her. "It was the only way I could keep you!"

She flinched. Closing her eyes, she exhaled. "I always wondered why a man like you would be interested in a woman like me. Now I know." She opened her eyes, and tears spilled over her lashes. "I was just a possession to you. Someone to be married for the sake of land in Alaska, then traded for your brother's company. Then kept at your whim, as what? Your mistress, your sex slave?"

"My wife!"

"You never thought of...of *me.* How I would feel. You either didn't think about it, or you didn't care."

"It's not true!" With a deep breath, he said, "Yes, I tried to use you to get revenge on my brother. But everything changed, Josie, when I...I fell in love with you."

She stared at him. Turning away with a sob, she pressed her face against her sister's shoulder.

"Please," Kasimir whispered, taking a step towards her. "Doesn't it mean anything that I gave up what I wanted most—the company that should have been mine?"

"You don't have to give it up." Vladimir stepped between

them, his face grave. Reaching into his coat, he pulled out a white page. "Here it is."

For an instant, Kasimir stared blankly at the page. He took it from his brother's hand. Looking down, he sucked in his breath. "It's the contract I gave Bree." He looked up in shock. "It transfers your shares in Xendzov Mining to me. You signed it."

"Let this be the end," Vladimir said. "I was wrong to force you out of our company ten years ago. I was angry, and humiliated, and my pride wanted vengeance. But I was the only one to blame. So take back what I owe you, with interest. Take it all. And let this be the end of our war."

Kasimir's mouth was dry. "You're just giving it to me?" His voice was hoarse. "Just like that?"

"Just like that."

"A lifetime's work. You're throwing it away?"

Vladimir's forehead creased. "I'm trading it. For the happiness of the woman I love. The woman who will soon be my wife." His blue eyes, the same shade as Kasimir's own, were filled with regret as he said softly, "And to make amends to the little brother I always loved, but have sometimes treated very badly."

A lump rose in Kasimir's throat.

"I should have waited for you," Vladimir said in a low voice, "all those days we walked to school in the snow." Glancing behind him, he gave a sudden snort. "And I should have listened when you said Bree Dalton was a wicked creature, not to be trusted…"

"Hey," she protested behind him.

Lifting a dark eyebrow, Vladimir gave her a sensual smile. "You know you're wicked. Don't try to deny it." Then he looked back to Kasimir, his expression serious. "I was wrong to cut you out of my life," he said humbly. "Forgive me, brother."

Kasimir's world was spinning. He gripped the contract

like a life raft. "You can't mean it," he said. "You've put your whole life into Xendzov Mining. How can you just surrender? How can you let me win?"

"For the same reason that, an hour ago, you were willing to let it go." Vladimir gave a crooked smile. "I've won a treasure far greater than any company. The life I always wanted. With the woman I always loved. You reunited us in Hawaii. And I have you to thank for that."

"I was trying to hurt you," he said hoarsely.

His older brother's smile lifted to a grin. "You did me the biggest favor of my life. Now you're taking the mining company off my hands, I'm off to Honolulu. I've just bought the Hale Ka'nani resort for Bree."

"You did what?"

"Oh, Bree," Josie breathed, clutching her sister's arm. "Just like you always dreamed!"

"I dreamed of running a little bed-and-breakfast by the sea." Bree's lips quirked as she looked at Vladimir. "Trust you to buy me a hundred-million-dollar hotel for my birthday!"

"It was way easier than trying to buy you jewelry," he said, and she laughed.

Kasimir's throat hurt as he looked down at the signed contract in his hand. He had the company he'd always wanted. He'd soon have Josie's land in Alaska. He even had his brother's apology.

He'd won.

And yet, he suddenly didn't feel that way. He looked past Vladimir and Bree to the only thing that mattered.

"Can you forgive me, Josie?" he whispered. "Can you?"

She looked up from Bree's shoulder. Her cheeks were streaked with tears, her face pale.

His heart fell to his feet. He tried to smile. "It's in the marriage vows, isn't it? You have to forgive me. For better, for worse. Can't we just agree that you're the better, and I'm the worse—"

Josie held up her hand, cutting him off. He stared at her, feeling sick as he waited for the verdict. She'd never looked so beautiful to him as she did at that moment, when he knew all he deserved was for her to walk out the door.

"I was willing to give up everything." She sounded almost bewildered. She put her hand to her forehead. "*Everything*. How could I have been so stupid?" She looked up, her eyes wide. "I was willing to give up everything for you. My family, my home, my life—everything that makes me *me*. For a romantic dream! For *nothing!*"

Kasimir's heart stopped in his chest. "It's not a dream. Josie—"

"Stop it!" Her sweet, lovely face hardened as her eyes narrowed. "It *was* a dream. I knew you were ruthless. I knew you were selfish. But I didn't know you were a liar and more heartless than I ever imagined!"

"I'm sorry," he whispered. He swallowed. "If you'll just—"

"No!" She cut him off every bit as ruthlessly as he'd once done to her, again and again. He flinched, remembering. She took a deep breath, and her voice turned cold. "As soon as my land in Alaska is transferred to your name, there's only one thing I want from you."

"Anything," he said desperately.

Josie lifted her chin, and for the first time, her brown eyes held a sliver of ice. He saw her soul there, what he'd done to her, in a kaleidoscope of blue and green and shadows, glittering like a frost-covered forest, frozen as midnight. "I want a divorce."

CHAPTER TEN

ALMOST FOUR WEEKS later, Josie watched her sister and Vladimir get married in a twilight beachside ceremony in Hawaii.

Seeing their happiness as they spoke their wedding vows, a lump rose in Josie's throat. The sun was setting over the ocean as they stood barefoot in the sand, the surf rushing over their feet. Bree wore a long white dress, Vladimir a white button-down shirt and khakis, and they both were decked in colorful fresh-flower leis. As the newly married couple kissed to the scattered applause of friends and family surrounding them on the beach, Josie felt a hard twist in her chest. She told herself she was crying because she was so happy Bree had found love at last.

Josie had filed for divorce the day before.

When her lawyer had called yesterday morning to tell her that the land in Alaska now officially belonged to Kasimir, Josie had thanked him, and told him to file papers for their divorce.

She'd had no choice. She'd given Kasimir all her trust and faith, and he'd still selfishly asked her to make a sacrifice that would have destroyed her—a sacrifice that didn't even have to be made, if he'd just been honest enough to confess!

But her heart was breaking. She'd loved him so. She loved him still.

She'd never forget when Kasimir had told her he loved her on that cold winter day in Russia. She'd thought she would die of happiness. Now, Josie looked down, her tears dripping like rain into the bouquet of flowers she held as matron of honor.

Love. Kasimir hadn't known the meaning of the word. He'd never loved her. All the time she'd spent worshipping him, all the sunny optimistic hopes she'd had that she could change him—what a joke. She felt like a fool. Because she was one.

Blinking fast, Josie watched Bree's fluffy white puppy happily entwining herself around the happy couple, before running up and down the beach in pure doggy joy. She'd been like Snowy, she thought. Like Kasimir's slavishly adoring pet, waiting by the door with his slippers in her mouth. Pathetic.

And now he'd gotten what he wanted all along. His brother's company and his apology. Seducing Josie had just been a way for the notoriously ruthless womanizer to pass the time.

Everything changed, Josie. She had the sudden memory of his haunted eyes. *When I...I fell in love with you.*

She squeezed her eyes shut. No. She didn't believe it. Kasimir was just a man who didn't know how to lose, that was all. He'd wanted to keep her, but not enough to pursue her back to Hawaii. He'd let her go, and had never bothered to contact her since. If he'd loved her, he would have tried to fight for her. He hadn't.

Should she still tell him?

Josie shivered. Still standing in the surf on the beach, surrounded by applauding friends and her new husband, Bree looked at her sister with worried eyes.

Straightening her shoulders, Josie forced her lips into a quick, encouraging smile. She couldn't let Bree know. Not yet.

She exhaled as the group started walking back up the beach towards the Hale Ka'nani for the reception.

Bree was working sixteen-hour days as the new owner of the five-star resort and loving every minute of it. Her first act had been to double the salaries of the hotel's housekeepers. The second was to fire the vendors who'd been double-charging their accounts. Employee morale had skyrocketed since the tyrannical reign of their hated ex-boss, Greg Hudson, had ended.

And both sisters' futures were brighter than Josie had ever imagined. Thanks to Vladimir, there were no longer angry men demanding that Josie and her sister repay their dead father's debts. Without a company to run, he had pronounced himself—at thirty-five—to be retired. But Bree confided she thought he missed working. "Not for the money. But for the fun."

Fun? Josie had shaken her head. But who was she to judge what made people happy? Life was wherever your heart was.

Her own life had become unrecognizable. She'd left Honolulu a poor housekeeper, desperate, broke and completely insecure. Now, she'd started spring classes at the University of Hawaii, and instead of living in a dorm, she had her own luxurious beach villa, right next to her sister's at the Hale Ka'nani. She'd finally gotten her driver's license—and she'd bought herself a brand-new, snazzy red two-seater convertible. For which she'd paid cash.

But she was going to have to return the convertible to the dealer. And see if she could exchange it for something that had room for another passenger in the back.

Josie put her hand over her belly in wonder. As the small, intimate wedding reception began in the open-air hotel bar, and Bree and Vladimir cut their wedding cake together beneath the twinkling fairy lights in the night, she still couldn't quite believe it. How could she be pregnant? She blushed. Well, she knew, but she'd never thought it could happen.

Pregnant. With Kasimir's baby.

A soft smile traced her lips. She was starting to get used to the idea. Maybe Kasimir didn't love her. Maybe Josie's heart would never recover. But he'd still given her the most precious gift of all.

A child.

No one knew yet. She was afraid of what Bree would say.

At twenty-two, Josie was young to be a mother. Other women her age were worried about the next frat party or calculus test.

But thanks to Kasimir, there was at least one thing Josie would never need to worry about: money. The day after she left Russia, before he'd even gotten the land in Alaska, he'd placed an amount in her bank account that she still couldn't even quite comprehend, because it had so many zeroes at the end.

"Josie? Is everything okay?"

Looking up, she saw Bree in front of her. Her long blond hair tumbled over her flower lei and white cotton dress as she looked at her sister with concern.

"You look beautiful," Josie whispered. "I'm so happy for you."

"Cut the crap. What's wrong?"

Trust her sister to see right through her. Forcing her lips into a smile, she said, "It's your wedding. We can talk later."

"We'll talk now. Is it Kasimir?" Bree's gaze sharpened. "Has he tried to contact you?"

"Contact me?" Josie gave a low, harsh laugh. "No."

Bree scowled. Then grabbing Josie's hand, she pulled her out of the outdoor bar and into a quiet, dark gazebo in the shadowy garden overlooking the cliff. "Look, you're better off without him," she said urgently. "Plenty of other fish in the sea. You'll find someone really great, who appreciates you—"

Josie flinched. "I know," she quickly said to end the horror of the conversation.

"Then what?"

She paused. "Let's talk about it a different day. After your honeymoon."

"Honeymoon?" Bree grinned. "I'm living in Hawaii, in my dream job, with the man I love! I'll be on honeymoon for the rest of my life!"

"I'm so happy for you," Josie repeated, ignoring the ache in her throat. Resisting the urge to wipe her eyes, she looked down at the wet, soft grass beneath her feet. "After years of taking care of me, you deserve a lifetime of love and joy."

"Hey." Bree lifted her chin gently. "So do you. And I can't be happy until I know what's going on."

Josie blinked back tears, trying to smile. "You've always been a mother hen."

"Always." Her older sister looked into her eyes. "So you might as well tell me what's going on, or I'll be pecking at you all night."

Josie took a deep breath.

"I'm…I'm pregnant," she whispered.

Her sister gasped. "Pregnant? Are you sure?"

She nodded.

Bree took a deep breath, then visibly gained control of herself. "It's Kasimir's." It was a statement, not a question.

"He doesn't know." Josie looked away, blinking back tears. "And I don't know if I should tell him."

"Are you going to keep the baby?"

Josie whirled to face her. "Of course I am!"

"You could consider adoption…"

"I'm not giving up my baby!"

"You're just so young." Bree's hazel eyes were full of emotion. "You have no idea how hard it is. What you're in for."

"I know." Josie swallowed. "You were only six when Mom died, and eighteen when we lost Dad. All these hard years, you've taken care of me…"

"I loved every minute."

Josie looked at her skeptically.

"All right," Bree allowed with a grin, "maybe not every *single* minute." She paused. "I was so scared at times for you."

"Because I was always screwing up," Josie said sadly.

"You?" Her sister's lips parted, then she shook her head fiercely beneath the colored lights of the wooden gazebo. "I was scared I would fail you. Scared I'd never be the respectable, honest, careful mother you deserved, no matter how hard I tried."

Something cracked in Josie's heart.

"That's why you hovered over me?" she whispered. "I thought I was a burden to you, forcing you to give up ten years to look after me."

"I felt like the luckiest big sister in the world to have a sweet kid like you to look after." Bree took a deep breath. "But you don't know what it's like to raise a child. To fear for them every moment." She looked down at the wet hem of her white dress. "To pray that your own stupid mistakes won't hurt the sweet, innocent one you love so, so much."

"You worried you might make a mistake?" Josie said in amazement. Shaking her head, she patted her sister's shoulder. "You gave me a wonderful childhood that I'll never forget." Josie bit her lip, and forced herself to say what she'd been too afraid to say before. "But I'm all grown up now. You don't need to be my mother any more. Just be my sister. My friend." She looked at her. "Just be my baby's aunt."

Bree stared at her. Then, bursting into tears, she pulled Josie into her arms, hugging her tightly.

"You'll be a wonderful mother," she choked out, wiping her eyes. "You're the strongest person I know. You've always been so fearless. You've never been afraid of anything."

"Me?" Josie cried.

Bree gave a laugh, shaking her head as she smiled through her tears. "The stunts you used to pull. Snowboarding in Alaska. While I was hesitating over the safest way, or worrying about the risks, you'd just fly straight past me, head-first. And that's how you love." She looked at Josie. "You're still in love with him, aren't you?"

Josie's lips parted. Then, wordlessly, she nodded.

"Are you going to tell him? About the baby?"

"Should I?"

With a rueful little smile, Bree shook her head. "That's a

choice that only you can make." She paused. "Because you're right, Josie. You're all grown up."

Josie hugged her sister tight, then pulled away, wiping her eyes. "I do love him. But he doesn't love me. I know now that he's never going to come for me. I'll never see him again."

"I don't know about that." There was a strange expression on Bree's face as she looked at a point above her ear.

Frowning, Josie turned around.

And saw Kasimir standing behind her, just outside the dark gazebo, in the warm Hawaiian night.

Kasimir's heart was thudding in his throat.

Josie's big brown eyes looked up at him in shock, as if she thought she was dreaming. She was chewing her pink bottom lip in an adorable way, wearing a simple pink cotton bridesmaid's dress, with her soft brown hair hanging in waves over her bare, tanned shoulders.

So beautiful. So incredibly beautiful. Seeing her face, breathing the same air, almost close enough to touch—Kasimir felt alive again for the first time since she'd left him. Especially when he saw she was still wearing her wedding ring.

Kasimir ran his thumb over his own gold wedding band. He'd never taken it off. It had become a part of him.

And so had she.

When he'd burst into the wedding reception, he'd immediately looked for Josie. Instead, he'd seen his brother standing near the bar. It had taken all of Kasimir's courage to tap him on the shoulder.

Still laughing at a friend's joke, Vladimir had turned around. The smile dropped from his face. "Kasimir," he whispered. "I didn't expect you."

"Then you shouldn't have sent me an invitation."

"No—that's not what I meant. I—"

"It's all right. I know what you meant. And until a few

hours ago, I didn't know I was coming either." Reaching into the pocket of his jacket, Kasimir pulled out the contract. He pushed it into his brother's hand. "I can't take this. I don't want it."

His brother stared down at the signed contract now in his hand. "Why not?" he said faintly.

Kasimir blinked fast. "The truth is, I never really cared about taking over your company."

His brother snorted. "You gave a damned good impression."

Kasimir tilted his head and gave a low chuckle. "All right. Maybe I did want it. But what I wanted even more," he said in a low voice, swallowing against the ache in his throat, "was to have my brother back." He lifted his eyes. "I've missed you. I don't want to run your company. But…" He paused. "A merger… We could run Xendzov Mining and Southern Cross together. As partners."

Vladimir stared at him. "Partners?"

"We'd have the second-largest mining company in the world. With your assets in the northern hemisphere, and mine in the southern…. We could dominate. Win. Together."

Vladimir blinked, his eyes dazed. "You'd give me a second chance? You'd trust me with your company? After the way I betrayed you?"

Kasimir gave him a crooked smile. "Yeah."

"Why?"

"Because we're brothers. But no more big-brother-little-brother stuff. From now on, we're equals." He tilted his head, quirking a dark eyebrow. "What do you say?" Nervously, Kasimir held out his hand. "Will you be my business partner? Will you be my brother again?"

Vladimir stared at him for a long moment. Then he pushed his hand aside roughly.

Kasimir sucked in his breath.

His brother suddenly pulled him against his chest in a bear

hug. His voice was muffled. "I've missed you. What do I say? Hell, yes. To all of it."

When the hug ended, both brothers turned away.

"Sand in my eyes," Kasimir muttered, wiping them with his hand.

"Stupid wind. Lifting sand from the beach." Wiping his own eyes, Vladimir cleared his throat in the windless night, then looked back at him and smiled, with his eyes still red. "From now on, we're equals. Through and through."

Kasimir snorted. "About time you figured that out."

"And by the way, your timing couldn't be better. Thanks for coming to save me. Turns out I'm no good at running a hotel." He gave a sudden grin. "This will save my wife the trouble of firing me."

Kasimir laughed. "Although she might miss you when you start commuting to Russia on a daily basis."

"Hmm." He grew thoughtful. "About that…"

The brothers spoke for a few minutes, and then Kasimir sighed. "I am sorry I missed your wedding."

"So am I." Vladimir punched him on the shoulder. "But having you back is the best wedding present any man could ask for." He lifted an eyebrow with a grin. "Though something tells me you didn't just come here for wedding cake. Or even a business deal."

"You're right." Kasimir took a deep breath. "Where is she, Volodya?"

At the use of his old nickname, Vladimir's eyes glistened. "Sorry," he said gruffly. "Sand again." He gestured towards a nearby cliff. "There. Talking to my wife."

Kasimir had looked past the outdoor bar to a gazebo, strung with colorful lights, on the edge of a cliff. He saw a moving shadow. *Josie*. At last! He'd turned to go, then stopped, facing his brother. He'd said in a low voice, "I'm glad we're friends again."

"Friends?" Vladimir's smile had lifted to a grin. "We're not friends, man. We're *brothers*."

Kasimir was glad and grateful beyond words that after ten years of estrangement, he and Vladimir were truly brothers again. But even that, as important as it was, wasn't the reason he'd flown for almost twenty-four hours straight from St. Petersburg across the North Atlantic to Alaska, and then across the endless Pacific to Hawaii.

Now, Kasimir took a deep breath as he looked down at Josie, facing him beneath the gazebo in the moonswept night. At the bottom of the cliff, he could hear the ocean waves crashing against the shore, but it was nothing compared to the roar of his own heart.

"What—what are you doing here?" Josie stammered. The music of her sweet, warm voice traveled through his body like electricity.

"My brother invited me to the wedding."

"You missed it," she said tartly.

"I know." He'd known he was too late when from the window of his plane, he'd seen the red sunset over Oahu. But the lights of Honolulu had still sparkled like diamonds in the center of the sunset's red fire, against the black water. Like magic. Because he knew Josie was there. "But the real question is," he whispered, "am I too late with you?"

Josie's lips parted.

Looking between her sister and Kasimir, Bree cleared her throat. "Um. I think I hear my husband calling me."

She hurried away from the gazebo, her wedding gown flying behind her. And for that alone, Kasimir could have forgiven her anything.

Turning, Josie started to follow. Kasimir grabbed her arm. "Please don't go."

"Why?" She looked at him. "What could we possibly have to talk about?"

"Vladimir and I worked through things," he said haltingly.

He gave an awkward smile. "In fact, we've decided to combine our companies. Be partners."

Her jaw dropped. "You did?"

"I was in Alaska this morning, at the homestead. I had everything I ever wanted. And I suddenly realized something."

"What?" she whispered.

He looked at her. "I realized there's no point in having everything," he said softly, "if you can't share it with people you love."

Josie looked at him, her eyes wide. Swallowing, she looked away. "I'm happy you and your brother are friends again."

"Not friends." Kasimir grinned, remembering. *"Brothers."*

Josie looked at him, her eyes luminous and deep. "I'm glad," she said softly. Then she looked down. "But that doesn't have anything to do with me. Not anymore."

Kasimir knew his whole life depended on his next words. "He's not the reason I came back to Honolulu, Josie."

She looked up. "He's not?"

He shook his head, then looked down wryly at his dark wrinkled suit, white shirt and blue tie. "Do you know I haven't changed clothes for twenty-four hours?" He loosened his tie, then pulled it off. "When my lawyer said the land in Alaska was finally mine, I left St. Petersburg straight from the office. All I could think was I wanted to go home." His lips twisted. "But all I saw in Alaska was a rickety old cabin, piles of snow and a silent forest. It wasn't home." Looking straight into her eyes, he whispered, "Because it wasn't you."

Josie looked up at him, not even trying to hide the tears spilling over her lashes.

With a trembling hand, he reached out and brushed a tear from her cheek. "You're the home I've been trying to find for my whole life, Josie. You're my home."

"Then why did you let me go so easily?" she whispered.

Kasimir took a deep breath, closing his eyes, allowing the warm air to expand his lungs. "After you left," he said in a

low voice, "I tried to convince myself I'd won. Then I tried
to convince myself that you deserved a better man than me.
Which you do. But this morning, in Alaska, I realized something that changed everything."

"What?" she faltered.

He looked straight into her eyes. "I can be that man." He
took her hand in his own, and when she didn't pull it away
he tightened his grasp, overwhelmed with need. "I can be the
man who will mow the lawn by your white picket fence," he
vowed. "The man who will be by your side forever. Worshipping you. For the rest of your life."

"But how can I believe you?" Josie wiped her eyes. "Our
whole marriage was based on a lie. How can I ever give you
my whole heart again?"

Kasimir stared at her, his heart pounding. He finally shook
his head. "I don't know." He gave a low laugh, running his
hand through his dark, tousled hair. "I wouldn't blame you for
telling me to go to hell. In fact, I sort of figured you would."

"Then why come all this way?"

"Because you had to know what was in my heart," he whispered. "I had to tell you how you changed me. Forever. You
made me want to be the idealistic, loyal person I once was.
The man I was born to be."

Covering her face with her hands, she wept.

Falling on his knees before her, Kasimir wrapped his arms
around her. "I'm so sorry I tried to separate you and your sister, Josie. I was selfish and I was a coward. Losing you was
the one thing I thought I couldn't face."

He felt her stiffen, then slowly, her hand rose to stroke his
hair. It was the single sweetest touch of his life.

Kasimir looked up, his eyes hot with unshed tears. "But
I should have thought of you first. Put *you* first. Now, all I
want is for you to be happy. Whether you choose to be with
me. Or—" he swallowed "—without—"

"Shut up." She put her finger to his lips, and his voice

choked off. She said slowly, "I've learned I can live without you."

Kasimir's heart cracked inside his chest. He'd lost her. She was going to send him away, back into the bleak winter.

"But I've also learned," Josie whispered, "that I don't want to." Her brown eyes were suddenly warm, like the sky after a sudden spring storm. "I tried to stop loving you. But once I love someone, I love for life." Her lips lifted in a trembling smile. "I'm stubborn that way."

"Josie," he breathed, rising to his feet. He cupped her face, searching her gaze. "Does this mean you'll be my wife? This time for real?"

Reaching up, she said through her tears, "Yes. Oh, yes."

"You better make her happy!" Bree yelled. They turned in surprise to see Vladimir and his bride standing amid the flowers beyond the gazebo. Bree's eyes were shining with tears as she sniffed. "You'd better…"

"I will," Kasimir said simply. He turned back to Josie and vowed with all his heart, "I will make you happy. It's all I will do. For the rest of my life."

And he lowered his head to kiss her, not caring that Bree and Vladimir stood three yards away from them, with all the partygoers of the wedding reception behind.

Let them look, he thought. *Let all the world see.*

Taking Josie tenderly in his arms, Kasimir kissed her with all the passion and promise of a lifetime. When he finally pulled away, she pressed her cheek against him with a contented sigh, and they stood together, holding each other in the moonswept night.

He could get used to Hawaii, he thought. In the distance, he heard the loud roar of the surf against the shore. He heard the wind through the palm trees, heard the cry of night birds soaring across the violet sky. And above it all, he heard the pounding of his own beating, living heart—his heart which, now and forever, was hers.

"I wish we could stay here," Josie said softly, for his ears only. She looked back at the other couple. "That we could live nearby, and all our children could someday play together on the beach…"

"About that…" Thinking of the decision he and his brother had just made, to build the world headquarters of their merged companies right here in Honolulu, Kasimir looked down at her with a mischievous grin. "I have a surprise for you."

"A surprise, huh?" Tears glistened in Josie's eyes as she shook her head. A smile like heaven illuminated her beautiful face. "Just wait until you hear the one I have for you."

EPILOGUE

THE DAY JOSIE placed their newborn daughter in her husband's arms was the happiest day of her life, after eight months of joyful days.

All right, so her pregnancy hadn't been exactly easy. She'd been sick her first trimester, and for the last trimester, she'd been placed on hospital bed rest. But even that hadn't been so bad, really. She'd made friends with everyone on her hospital floor, from Kahealani and Grace, the overnight nurses who were always willing to share candy, to Karl, the head janitor who told riveting stories about his time as a navy midshipman with a girl in every port.

The world was full of friends Josie just hadn't met yet, and in those rare times when there was no one around, she always had plenty of books to read. Fun books, now. No more textbooks. She'd made it through spring semester, but now college was indefinitely on hold.

The truth was, Josie didn't really mind. Her real life—her real happiness—was right here. Now. Living with Kasimir in their beach villa, newly redecorated complete with a white picket fence.

Now, Josie smiled up from her hospital bed at Kasimir's awed, terrified, loving face as he held his tiny sleeping daughter for the first time.

"Need any help?"

"No." He gulped. "I think."

Looking at her husband holding their baby, tears welled up in Josie's eyes. They were a family. Kasimir loved working with his brother as partners in their combined company, Xendzov Brothers Corp. But for both princes, the way they did business had irrevocably changed. They still wanted to be successful, but the meaning of success had changed. "I want to make a difference in the world," Kasimir had said to her wistfully, lying beside her in the hospital bed last week. "I want to make the world a better place."

Josie hit him playfully with a pillow. "You do. Every time you bring me a slice of cake."

"No, I mean it." He'd looked at her out of the corner of his eye. "I was thinking...we could put half our profits into some kind of medical foundation for children. Maybe sell the palace in Marrakech for a new hospital in the Sahara." He stopped, looking at her. He said awkwardly, "What do you think?"

"So what's stopping you?" With a mock glare, she tossed his own words back at him. "The only one stopping you is *you.*"

"Really? You wouldn't miss it?"

She snorted. "We don't need more money, or another palace." She thought of little Ahmed breaking his leg on the sand dune, far from medical care. "I love your hospital idea. And the foundation, too."

He looked down at her fiercely. "And I love you." Cupping her face, he whispered, "You're the best, sweetest, most beautiful woman in the world."

Nine months pregnant and feeling ungainly as a whale, having gained fifty extra pounds on banana bread, watermelon and ice cream, Josie had snorted a laugh, even as she looked at him tenderly. "You're so full of it."

"It's true," Kasimir had insisted, and then he kissed her until he made her believe he was an honest man.

Josie smiled. Kasimir always knew what to say. The only time she'd ever seen him completely without words was when she'd told him she was pregnant that night of Vladimir and Bree's wedding. At first, he'd just stared at her until she asked him if he needed to sit down—then, with a loud whoop and a holler, he'd pulled her into his arms.

With the divorce cancelled, he'd still insisted on remarrying her and doing it right, with their family in attendance. He'd actually suggested that they wed immediately, poaching Bree and Vladimir's half-eaten wedding cake, and grabbing the minister yawning at the bar. But rather than steal her sister's thunder, Josie had gotten him to agree to a compromise.

Tearing up the pre-nup, they'd married three days later, at dawn, on the beach. The ceremony had been simple, and as they'd spoken vows to love, cherish and honor each other for the rest of their lives, the brilliant Hawaiian sun had burst through the clouds like a benediction.

Then, of course, this being Hawaii, the clouds had immediately poured rain, forcing the five of them—Josie, Kasimir, Bree, Vladimir and the minister—to take off at a run for the shelter of the resort, with their leis trailing flower petals behind them. And once at the hotel, Josie had discovered the ten-tiered wedding cake her husband had ordered her—enough for a thousand or two people, covered with white buttercream flowers and their intertwined initials.

Her husband's sweet surprise was the most delicious cake of her life. Good thing too. Remembering, she gave a sudden grin. They were still eating wedding cake out of their freezer.

Josie glanced through the window in the door of her private room in the Honolulu hospital. In the hallway, she could see Bree pacing back and forth, a phone to her ear, telling Vladimir the happy news of the birth. Vladimir was still in St. Petersburg, finalizing the company's move to Honolulu. They were a very high-powered couple. Bree was having the time of her life running the Hale Ka'nani resort, which was already up in profits, having become newly popular with tourists from Japan and Australia. Vladimir and Bree did hope to start a family someday, but for now, they were having too much fun working.

Not Josie, though. All she wanted was right here. She looked at Kasimir and their daughter. Right now. A home. A husband. A family.

"Am I doing this right?" Kasimir said anxiously, his shoulders hunched and stiff as he cradled his baby daughter.

She snorted, leaning forward to stroke the baby's cheek with one hand. "You're asking me? It's not like I have more experience."

"I'm a little nervous," he confessed.

"You?" she teased. "Scared of an eight-pound baby?"

"Terrified." He took a deep breath. "I've never been a father before. What if I do something wrong?"

She put her hand on his forearm. "It won't matter." Tears spilled over her lashes as she smiled, loving him so much her heart ached with it. "You're the perfect father for her, because you love her." She looked down at the sleeping newborn in his arms. "And Lois Marie loves you already."

Kasimir's eyes crinkled. "Lulu is the best baby in the world," he agreed, using their baby's nickname. They'd named her after the mother Josie had never known. The mother who, along with her father, she would always remember. Josie would honor them both by being true to her heart. By singing the song inside her.

Holding hands, Kasimir and Josie smiled at their perfect little daughter, marveling at her soft dark hair, at her tiny hands and plump cheeks.

Then a new thought occurred to Josie, and she suddenly looked up in alarm. "What if I'm the one who doesn't know how to be a mother?" she asked.

"You?" Her husband gave a laugh that could properly be described as a guffaw. "Are you out of your mind? You'll be the best mother who ever lived." Cradling their tiny baby, securely nestled in the crook of his arm, he reached out a hand to cup Josie's cheek. "And I promise you," he whispered, "for the rest of my life, even if I make a mistake here or there, I'll love you both with everything I've got. And if I screw up, or if we fight, I'll always be the first to say I'm sorry." He looked at her. "I give you my word."

Reaching up, Josie wrapped her hand around his head, tangling her fingers in his dark hair. "Your word of honor?"

His eyes were dark. "Yes."

She took a deep breath.

"Show me," she whispered.

And as Kasimir lowered his head to hers, proving his words with a long, fervent kiss, Josie felt his vow in her heart like bright sun in winter. And she knew their bold, fearless life as a family, complicated and crazy and oh, so happy, had just begun.

* * * * *